Colin Wilson is one of the most prolific, versatile and popular writers at work today. He was born in Leicester in 1931, and left school at sixteen. After he had spent years working in a wool warehouse, a laboratory, a plastics factory and a coffee bar, his first book *The Outsider* was published in 1956. It received outstanding critical acclaim and was an immediate bestseller.

Since then he has written many books on philosophy, the occult, crime and sexual deviance, plus a host of successful novels which have won him an international reputation. *The Spider World* series is his first venture into science fantasy.

# By the same author

SCIENCE FICTION

*Spider World: The Tower*
*Spider World: The Delta*
*The Mind Parasites*
*The Philosopher's Stone*
*The Space Vampires*

OTHER FICTION

The 'Sorme Trilogy':
*Ritual in the Dark*
*The Man Without a Shadow* (retitled
    *The Sex Diary of Gerard Sorme*)
*The God of the Labyrinth*

*Adrift in Soho*
*The World of Violence*
*Necessary Doubt*
*The Glass Cage*
*The Killer*
*The Black Room*
*The Schoolgirl Murder Case*
*The Janus Murder Case*
*The Personality Surgeon*
*Rasputin – a Novel*

NON-FICTION

The Outsider cycle:
*The Outsider*
*Religion and the Rebel*
*The Age of Defeat*
*The Strength to Dream*
*Origins of the Sexual Impulse*
*Beyond the Outsider*
*Introduction to the New
    Existentialism*

Books on the occult and
    paranormal:
*The Occult*
*Mysteries*
*Poltergeist*
*Psychic Detectives*
*Strange Powers*
*The Geller Phenomenon*
*Steiner: The Man and his Work*
*A Directory of Possibilities* (with
    John Grant)

*An Encyclopedia of Unsolved
    Mysteries* (with Damon Wilson)
*Afterlife*

OTHER NON-FICTION

*An Encyclopedia of Murder* (with Pat
    Pitman)
*An Encyclopedia of Modern Murder*
    (with Donald Seaman)
*A Casebook of Murder*
*Order of Assassins*
*Rasputin and the Fall of the
    Romanovs*
*Bernard Shaw – a Reassessment*
*New Pathways in Psychology*
*The Quest for Wilhelm Reich*
*The War Against Sleep – The
    Philosophy of Gurdjieff*
*A Criminal History of Mankind*
*An Encyclopedia of Scandal* (with
    Donald Seaman)
*The Lord of the Underworld – A
    Study of Jung*
*The Craft of the Novel*
*The Strange Genius of David Lindsay*
*Frankenstein's Castle*
*Access to Inner Worlds*
*Eagle and Earwig* (Essays on Books
    and Writers)
*Poetry and Mysticism*
*A Book of Booze*
*Starseekers*
*Brandy of the Damned* (Essays on
    Music)
*The Bicameral Critic – Selected
    Shorter Writings*
*Anti-Sartre*
*Aleister Crowley – The Man and the
    Myth*
*The Misfits*

AUTOBIOGRAPHY

*Voyage to a Beginning*

COLIN WILSON

# Spider World
# The Magician

Grafton

*An Imprint of* HarperCollins*Publishers*

Grafton
An Imprint of HarperCollins*Publishers*,
77–85 Fulham Palace Road,
Hammersmith, London W6 8JB

Published by Grafton 1993
9 8 7 6 5 4 3 2

First published in Great Britain by
HarperCollins*Publishers* 1992

Copyright © Colin Wilson 1992

The Author asserts the moral right to
be identified as the author of this work

ISBN 0 586 20557 8

Set in Palatino

Printed in Great Britain by
HarperCollinsManufacturing Glasgow

*To Rowan*

# PART ONE
# The Assassins

Shortly before dawn he was awakened by a cold so intense that it reminded him of the desert night. He lay there, the bedclothes pulled around his face, and his breath formed moisture on the blanket as he exhaled. He had chosen this room because it faced east, and he liked to be awakened by the sun. Today there was no sunlight; the dawn came like grey mist, until the room was filled with a cold, even light. No birds sang.

Something about the strange silence disturbed him. He crossed to the window, treading on the soft woollen rugs, and found himself looking out on a white landscape. White rooftops seemed to blend into the pearl-grey sky, and the great square was carpeted in the same featureless whiteness. It had even found its way into the corners of the windowframes, and a few fine flakes had frozen on to the outside of the glass.

Niall had heard about snow and read about it, but this was the first time he had ever seen it. Nothing had prepared him for this cold, beautiful whiteness that seemed to blanket the universe. He was suddenly filled with a magical excitement which, although he was unaware of it, had filled thousands of generations of children at the first sight of the winter snow.

Possessed by a longing to touch this strange substance, he pulled on a sheepskin mantle over his tunic, thrust his feet into shoes lined with rabbit fur, and hurried out of the room. The palace was silent and its corridors empty; Niall was usually the first awake. He mounted the staircase to the top floor, passing the sleeping chamber shared by his cousin Dona and his sisters Runa and Mara, then climbed the narrow stairs that led up to the roof. As soon as he opened the door, a rampart of snow tumbled in and deluged his bare legs. He jumped back with an exclamation; he had not realized snow would be so cold. Then he took off his shoes one by one – the snow had fallen into them – and shook them out; the fur now felt cold and wet to his ankles. Yet the morning air seemed surprisingly warm; this was because there was not the faintest breath of wind.

The space between the parapet and the steep roof was deep in snow; it crunched underfoot as he trod in it. He picked up a double handful and moulded it into a ball; but it froze his fingers, so he threw it away. With the sleeve of his mantle he carefully brushed the snow from the parapet, then stood leaning on it, gazing out over the milky whiteness that extended as far as the distant hills. In the centre of the parkland on the far side of the square, the white tower rose like a finger of ivory, but now the surrounding grass was white, it was no longer the most striking feature in the landscape. This distinction belonged to the river, whose blackness split the cold plain like a current of ink; it made him feel colder merely to look at it.

The city seemed empty; there was not a living thing in sight. Then, as he turned to go indoors, his attention was caught by a movement in the square below. Something black was lying in its north-eastern corner. From this distance it might have been an uprooted bush. Then he looked more closely, and saw the red stains in the snow; at the same time, another faint movement made him aware that he was looking at a badly injured spider.

He hurried back down the stairs, holding the balustrade because the snow on his shoes made the marble treacherous. For a moment he was tempted to return to his room to put on warmer clothes; but his sense of urgency overruled the discomfort. He pulled back the bar that locked the main door, and tramped out into the deep snow, ignoring the cold wetness that ran down inside his shoes. The snow had turned the steps into a smooth ramp, so that he had to tread with extreme care; at one point he fell and plunged in up to the elbows. But as he struggled to his feet and waded unevenly across the square, choosing a route where the snow lay thin, his mind was obsessed by a single problem: how a death spider could have met with serious injury in such a wide open space.

As he approached, the spider saw him, and it made a convulsive attempt to rise; but its jointed legs were not strong enough, and buckled under its weight. The black, hairy body was covered in snow, evidently it had been lying there for some time. Niall found this puzzling; spiders are telepathic, and can send an instant distress call to others of their kind. And since this one lay within a few hundred yards of the headquarters of the ruling directorate, on the far side of the square, its presence should have been sensed the moment it was injured.

When he came close enough to see the far side of its body he saw why it had been unable to rise. Three of its legs had been smashed to a pulp; the bottom joint of one of them, with its black claw, was almost completely detached. A trail of blood smears, partly obliterated by snow, showed that the spider had dragged itself for about fifty feet before it collapsed. It was obviously dying.

'What happened to you?' Niall spoke the words aloud, but knew that his meaning would be carried direct to the spider's brain.

The reply that sounded inside his chest made him

wince; it was a blur of pain, and the directness of the communication made Niall experience its misery and exhaustion, so that he himself felt drained and nauseated. It was impossible to distinguish what the spider was saying, but the 'voice' was one that Niall instantly recognized. It was Skorbo, the captain of the guard. Now Niall understood why its communication was an incomprehensible chaos of feeling. The ability to communicate with human beings was a difficult art – the equivalent of a human being learning to read. In spider terms Skorbo was an illiterate peasant, a creature whose chief value to his masters was a certain brutal strength and the ability to dominate others. Niall had always found him repellent; yet now Skorbo was injured and dying, he felt overwhelmed with pity.

He said: 'I'll go and get help.'

It was impossible to hurry through the snow; each step plunged him in up to the knee, and if he tried to withdraw the foot too quickly, he left his shoe behind. To avoid discouragement, he deliberately averted his eyes from the expanse of snow that stretched in front of him, and treated each step as an individual effort. It was a pleasant surprise to find himself suddenly at the foot of the steps in front of the headquarters building. Two wolf spiders would normally have been on guard outside its great double doors; the cold had evidently driven them inside. Niall beat on the door with his fists, not because it was locked, but because he knew he would risk being attacked if he rushed in without warning. There was a movement inside and the door opened; Niall found himself looking up into the enormous black eyes of a brown wolf spider, whose height was at least two feet greater than his own. The chelicerae (or pincers) were extended, so he could see the folded fangs. A moment later, the spider recognized him, and sank down in a gesture of homage, lowering its belly to the floor.

Niall turned and pointed. 'Quick. Skorbo has been injured. Go and fetch him.' Again, the words conveyed his message direct to the spider's brain. Followed by the second guard, it loped across the square towards Skorbo, its enormous strength unaffected by a mere foot of snow. Niall knew there was no point in trying to follow; his whole body felt drained. Instead, he sank down on a bench outside the door, and watched as the guards gently lifted the injured spider. As they approached, he observed the way the legs dragged in the snow, and knew that Skorbo was dead.

They placed the body on the floor, scattering snow on the black marble. Skorbo was still bleeding; his blood was thicker, more viscous, than human blood, and it spread slowly, like a pool of oil. It was running from the spider's head, which lay sideways on the floor, and now Niall was able to see that there was a hole in the skull, about a foot above the single row of eyes that extended in a band around its head. Unlike human beings, spiders have no internal bone structure; the armoured shell is itself an external skeleton. Skorbo's skull had been shattered by a blow. What puzzled Niall was that there seemed to be fragments of broken armour in the hole, as might have been expected if some tremendous blow had been delivered from above. A large segment seemed to be missing. Blood oozed from the hole as from the socket from which a tooth has been pulled.

The wolf spiders were standing there, too respectful to ask questions. Niall said:

'Please notify Dravig of what has happened. Tell him I shall be at home.'

But as he plodded back through the snow, curiosity

overcame his weariness. What had happened struck him as completely incomprehensible. The hole in the skull made it look as if Skorbo had been attacked. By whom? Another spider? That seemed unlikely. Unlike human beings, spiders seldom fought amongst themselves. Yet it was equally difficult to envisage some accident that might have caused the damage.

The obvious way to find out was to go and look. Niall retraced his steps, and took the diagonal route across the plaza, where the forward rush of the wolf spiders had churned up the snow like some enormous plough. When he came to the place where the injured spider had lain, he realized that Skorbo had lost a great deal of blood; his life had oozed away into the snow as he lay there, his brain too damaged to send the signal that would have brought help. In front of Niall, along the eastern side of the square, there were a number of empty houses in various states of disrepair. The city was full of such houses; spiders often made their homes in the upper storeys. But they preferred houses on either side of the street, so they could weave their webs between them; this is why the houses bordering the square had remained empty.

The trail of blood had been obliterated by falling snow; but by bending until his face was within a few inches of the surface, he was able to make out the darker patches. These, he could now see, led back towards the second house from the corner, a tall building whose rusty balconies suggested that it had once been a hotel. Like the others, its windows had been boarded up, and its door was closed – all houses in this square had been forbidden to human beings. Niall tried the door; it seemed to be locked. Yet when he brushed aside the snow on the doorstep with his shoe, a damp bloodstain told him that this was the house in which Skorbo had met his injury. He rammed the door with his shoulder;

it seemed completely immovable. But a sheet of plywood covering a window proved to be less solid, and caved inward when he pushed it with both hands.

He leaned in with caution. If something – or someone – powerful enough to kill a spider was lurking inside, he was going to take no risks. In fact, he found himself looking into a bare hallway whose wooden floor was covered with plaster and rubble; it smelt of decay and damp. Recognizing that his tension was blocking his perceptions, he deliberately relaxed, exhaling deeply and closing his eyes; then, as he achieved inner stillness, concentrated intently. A point of light glowed inside his skull, and the silence seemed to deepen. In that moment, he knew with absolute certainty that no concealed enemies were lying in wait; the building was deserted. Yet this deeper perception also made him aware of another odour, musky and slightly sweet. It was familiar, yet its significance escaped him.

He pushed the plywood violently; the nails that held it to the windowframe tore loose, and it fell into the building. Niall clambered inside. By now he was regretting that he was not wearing warmer clothes; his hands and feet were frozen. But since he was here, it seemed pointless not to explore. The light from the window gave him a clearer view of the hallway. He observed rat droppings among the dust and plaster on the floor. That indicated clearly that no spiders used the building; they regarded rats as particularly appetizing delicacies, and would wait for hours in the hope of catching one.

As he expected, there were more bloodstains on the floor, and clear signs in the dust and rubble that a wounded spider had dragged itself across the floor. The marks continued across the hallway to an open door beyond a collapsing staircase; this admitted light and a draught of air. Beyond this, a corridor led down to an open space that had once been a garden; there were more bloodstains on the floor. The door at the end, which stood half-open, had obviously been forced; its lock had been smashed, and marks on the outside woodwork, made by a chisel or a crowbar, looked fresh.

Niall peeped cautiously into the weedgrown garden, then looked upward at the wall above the door; it rose, vertical and windowless, to the roof, where the guttering was still intact. This disposed of his theory that the spider had been struck by some heavy object – perhaps a piece of masonry – dropped from above. Yet when he brushed aside the snow on the threshold, he saw signs of blood. This garden clearly held the secret of the spider's death.

To Niall's untrained eye there were no obvious clues. The layer of snow on the ground had covered any footprints. The garden, which extended as far as the rear wall of the next building, was divided from the gardens to the right and left by high walls. A dozen feet from the door stood a young palm tree; beyond this, there was a tangle of weeds and shrubbery, which offered a great deal of concealment. When Niall studied this more closely, he observed a number of freshly broken twigs, which indicated that someone had been there recently. But the hard ground had retained no other indications.

He penetrated the shrubbery as far as the rear wall; here the overgrown grass convinced him that no one else had been here for months. But as he was about to turn back, he noticed something that made him pause. In a corner of the garden wall there lay a heap of palm leaves, some of them spreading out from a common centre. They looked so natural in that setting that he almost failed to notice them. But why should there be palm leaves lying in a corner? Then he looked up and saw that the young palm tree had no leaves. In fact, someone had hacked off its top, leaving a bare trunk.

And within a foot of the top of the truncated palm, there was a length of rope.

Now at last he understood. The tree was about twice the height of a man – precisely the distance from the foot of the tree to the rear door of the building. A further search of the shrubbery revealed the stunted tree to whose base the other end of the rope had been tied. The young palm had been bent backwards like a catapult. When the spider had stepped out of the doorway, hesitating as it faced the dark garden, someone had cut the rope, and the tree had snapped over like an immense spring. Skorbo had evidently been standing slightly to one side, or had started to move at the last moment; the tree had smashed his legs and battered him to the ground . . .

Niall returned to the doorway, and looked down at the bloodstains. They showed clearly that his reconstruction was correct. The blow had caused blood splashes which were some distance from the original stain, and other splashes had struck the wall at an angle so they were elongated, with tadpole-like tails. And a few feet away, half-buried in the snow, there was a triangular fragment of the spider's skull, with brain-fragments still adhering to its underside. But the original blow had shattered the legs, not the skull. This could mean only one thing: that while the spider was stunned, someone had deliberately smashed the top of his skull, with the intention of penetrating the brain and destroying his capacity to send out a distress signal.

Niall shivered. He had no liking for Skorbo, but the sheer savagery of the attack horrified him; he felt as if he had been there to witness it.

His shiver reminded him of how cold he was; his facial muscles had lost all feeling, and his eyelids felt as if they were frozen. He retraced his steps back through the empty building. The front door had been wedged shut with a baulk of timber. He heaved it loose, and went out into the square.

As he plodded back through the snow, walking in the deep footprints he had left earlier, he recalled his excitement on first seeing the snow from his bedroom window. It had made the world look like fairyland. Now it was merely cold and uncomfortable, and somehow too real.


Someone had lit a fire in the great fireplace that faced the main door; the sight of flames leaping up the chimney brought a glow of delight, and made him realize why the men of old had regarded fire as a god. But as he stood before the blazing logs, watching the snow melt from his garments, he was surprised by the pain in his limbs as the blood began to circulate again.

In the chamber adjoining his bedroom, his personal servant Jarita had lit the stove and laid out his breakfast on a low table: cold meats, preserved fruits, honey, sweetened milk and newly baked bread. Before he ate, he changed into dry clothes: a baggy woollen suit, in which he felt comfortable, and slippers lined with down. Then he sat cross-legged on the silken cushions, tore a crust from the hot loaf, and spread it with butter and honey. This was usually the time of day that he enjoyed most, the hour before work began, when he could eat good food, and reflect on the incredible twists of fortune that had brought him from a cave in the desert, and made him the ruler of fifty thousand human beings. It was an important hour of the day, for he was still stunned by the swiftness of the change, and his unconscious mind needed time to absorb it; he still woke up in the middle of the night and imagined that he was in the underground den, surrounded by his family.

But this morning he was unable to relax or to enjoy the food. He could only brood on the problem of why Skorbo had been killed, and who had carried it out. Both questions left him baffled. It was true that the city was full of human beings who loathed the captain of the guard and would be delighted with the news of his death. But none of them possessed the kind of courage or determination to lure him into a trap. They had been the slaves of the spiders for so long that they no longer had any will of their own; they were conditioned into total obedience. And there would have been no point in harbouring thoughts of hatred or revenge, for the spiders could read their minds more easily than Niall could read a book.

The men who had been captured from Kazak's underground city were a different matter. Their minds were still unviolated, and they had a long tradition of hostility to spiders. But now they were no longer slaves they had no motive for killing a spider. Most of them were now overseers and supervisors, and contented with their lot. They were delighted to be living in the open air, instead of in an underground fortress. Besides, even they lacked the kind of cunning and ruthlessness necessary to have set the trap . . .

There was a light tap on the door, and a tall, dark-haired girl looked in. This was Nephtys, the commander of Niall's personal guard; because she knew he hated to be disturbed at breakfast, she spoke with her eyes averted.

'The Lord Dravig is here.'

'Ask him to come in.' He smiled at her, wishing that his servants were not so afraid of him. But they had all been trained to fear and respect those who were above

19

them. Their fear of the spiders was like that of a slave for some ruthless tyrant. So they found it awe-inspiring that Niall should speak on equal terms with the tyrants. The point was reinforced when Dravig entered the room, and Nephtys prostrated herself in front of the spider at the same time that Dravig made a ritual gesture of obeisance before Niall.

Dravig was probably the oldest spider in the land, with the exception of the ancient female spider who presided over the ruling council of the city. He stood more than seven feet tall, but was thin and gaunt, and the hairs on his body were turning grey. Insofar as it was possible for a spider to understand a human being, and for a human being to understand a spider, these two understood one another.

Niall moved away from the table and sat on a cushion on the dais. It would have been impolite to continue his breakfast. For some reason, the spiders were profoundly disturbed by the sight of human beings eating or drinking – perhaps in the same way that a human being would be disturbed at the sight of a spider eating a fly or a rat.

He wasted no time on preliminaries.

'Do you know that Skorbo is dead?'

'Yes.'

'Have you any idea who did it?'

'No.'

During this dialogue, Niall spoke aloud while Dravig communicated telepathically. Niall was also communicating telepathically – spiders were unable to understand human language – but he found it easier to speak his words aloud; it seemed to give his thought an added precision.

'Is the Spider Lord very angry?' Although the ruler was a female, she was known to human beings as the Spider Lord.

'Of course. But she will abide by the agreement.'
Dravig understood the question that Niall had in mind
– this was the advantage of speaking telepathically.
While human beings had been slaves, the death of a
single spider had been punished with appalling ferocity
– sometimes with the torture and execution of a
hundred humans. When the slaves became free, the
Spider Lord had agreed that there should be no more
killing.

Niall said: 'Nevertheless, if the murderers can be
found, they must be punished.'

'That is your decision. We shall abide by the agreement.'

There was a silence between them, but it was the
silence of understanding. Intelligence had bridged the
gap between their two species, so that it was as if both
were human or both were spiders.

Dravig said: 'But I cannot understand how human
beings could kill a spider.'

Niall stood up. 'Come with me and I will show you.'

On the spot where the injured spider had collapsed,
a platoon of slaves was shovelling the snow into hand-
carts and washing away the blood with buckets of warm
water. It would have been regarded as a kind of sacri-
lege to leave the spider's blood staining the ground. As
Niall and Dravig went past, the overseer cracked his
whip and made the slaves stand to attention. Niall averted his gaze; the blank eyes and drooling mouths of the
slaves always made him feel uncomfortable.

The door stood half-open, exactly as Niall had left it.
As they entered the rubble-strewn hallway, the spider
paused, and his chelicerae unfolded; Niall was aware
that something had galvanized him into sudden alert-
ness. But the spider said nothing. After a moment, he
followed Niall down the passageway and out into the
garden.

Niall pointed at the truncated palm tree.

'That was what killed Skorbo.'

Dravig failed to understand. Spiders were completely lacking in mechanical aptitude. Niall had to transmit a mental picture before Dravig could understand how a tree could be used as a murder weapon. Even then, he seemed sceptical. Niall had to point out the rope still tied to the top of the tree, and to the bloodspots on the wall, before the spider was convinced.

Niall also pointed out the shape of the blood splashes, with their tadpole-like tails, indicating that they had flown upwards due to the force of the blow. Dravig said with astonishment:

'The human mind is amazingly subtle.'

Niall pointed to the fragment of bone lying in the snow.

'The blow failed to kill him because it struck him to one side, breaking his legs. While he was still stunned, someone attacked him with some heavy weapon – probably an axe – and shattered his skull. That is why he failed to send out a distress signal.'

Dravig said: 'Whoever is responsible will pay for this.' The force of his anger was so great that it struck Niall like a blow, causing him to step backward. He realized then that he had underestimated the strength of Dravig's feelings. For a human being, the murder of a spider could be regarded with detachment. For Dravig, it was the slaughter of a fellow creature, and it filled him with rage and a desire for revenge.

Dravig was instantly aware of the effect produced by his anger on Niall; he made a mental gesture of abasement and apology, to which Niall replied with a similar gesture indicating that apology was unnecessary. In human language the exchange would have been expressed: 'I am sorry. I did not mean to upset (or shock or startle) you,' 'Please do not apologize, I understand perfectly.' Instead, these meanings were conveyed instantaneously, and with a precision beyond the power of language. It made Niall aware of the crudity and clumsiness of human speech.

Dravig advanced towards the palm tree, and gripped it with his pincers and with his four front legs. Niall looked on with a perplexity that changed to embarrassment; surely Dravig realized that it would take far more than the strength of a single spider to uproot a tree? His embarrassment changed to astonishment as he watched the spider's legs brace and strain, and heard the tearing sound as the roots began to loosen. This was not merely physical strength; it was will-power intensified by rage. The spider staggered for a moment as the earth under its feet heaved upwards; he regained his balance and again braced himself. A moment later, the tree was ripped out of the earth. With a gesture of contempt, Dravig threw it away from him, and it crashed down on to the bushes.

Dravig said nothing, but Niall could sense that the effort had relieved some of his rage and frustration.

Niall stepped forward and looked down into the hole, with its torn roots protruding from loose brown earth. The two main roots had been snapped in two; the strength required must have been tremendous. Yet Dravig showed no sign of effort; he was not even breathing heavily. Niall realized that he had used his immense will-force – the will-force that could knock a human being unconscious – to galvanize his muscles into this unbelievable effort. And, as so often since he had been in contact with the death spiders, Niall caught a glimpse of the great secret forces of the will.

Something caught his eye in the loose earth. He bent down and picked up a grey-coloured object that lay between the roots. It was a disc, about four inches in diameter, and its weight surprised him. Niall had heard of lead, although he had never seen it; now he guessed that this was what he was holding.

When he brushed off the earth, he saw that a simple design had been carved into one of the surfaces; this consisted of four curved lines.

Dravig asked: 'What is it?' Niall held out the disc, and the spider took it in his claw.

Niall said: 'It was in the hole. It must have been there when the tree was planted.'

'Does it mean anything to you?'

'No.'

The spider dropped it; Niall picked it up.

'I'll take it with me. I'd like to find out what it is.'

It was too heavy for the pocket of his mantle, so he placed it beside the doorway.

Dravig was looking among the bushes. Niall pointed to the rope tied round the base of the stunted tree.

'This is the other end of the rope they used. Someone must have cut it as Skorbo came out of the doorway.'

Whatever had been used to cut the rope – either an axe or a knife – had been razor-sharp; there were no frayed ends.

Dravig asked: 'Have you any more observations?'

Niall considered. He allowed himself to remain silent

for a long time, aware that the patience of spiders is far greater than that of human beings. He said finally:

'Whoever did this planned it carefully. In my opinion there must have been at least three of them. And for some reason they hated Skorbo.'

'You believe that Skorbo was the intended victim?'

'I am inclined to think so.' He decided against explaining why Skorbo was disliked; it would have seemed discourtesy towards the dead. And Dravig, who sensed that Niall had more to say, was too tactful to press him.

Niall said: 'They probably entered by the front door. But they did not leave by it. They had propped it closed with a baulk of timber. That means they must have climbed over the wall . . . Ah yes.'

He had pushed himself through the gap between the bushes and the left-hand wall, and now found a low gate in the wall. It was made of iron, and was rusted. Yet when he pushed it, the gate swung upon its hinges without a creak. A glance at these hinges showed that they had been greased.

The gate led into a narrow lane, which ran between two garden walls. It had obviously been constructed to afford entrance into the gardens, and a few yards from the gate, it terminated in the wall of the house. In the other direction, it ran on for about a hundred yards before it was blocked with rubble where a wall had collapsed.

Dravig had found it easier to step over the wall than to squeeze his bulk through the gate; now he stood beside Niall in the snow-covered lane. Any footprints that had been left behind had been obliterated by the more recent snowfall. Both stood there silently; Niall had discovered that being with a spider placed him in a calm and contemplative frame of mind, and that this sharpened his powers of intuition. So far his mind had been full of questions and observations, and this made him abnormally aware of his physical surroundings, as if they were thrusting themselves insistently against his senses. Now, quite suddenly, he relaxed, and it was as if the physical world had receded. The discomfort of his cold hands and feet became irrelevant, as if they belonged to someone else. In this new silence, he experienced a kind of awakening of attention, as if some unusual sound or smell was hovering on the edge of his perceptions. As he stood there, totally relaxed, it became stronger. There was something unpleasant about it, something distinctly menacing.

Dravig also stood motionless, without a hint of impatience; yet Niall's contact with his mind told him that the spider was completely oblivious to this sense of unpleasantness. It had often struck him as curious that, in spite of their telepathic powers, spiders seemed oddly lacking in intuition. Perhaps it was because they had so little to fear.

Niall walked on slowly, his head averted as if listening. Because his eyes were on the ground, he noticed the footprints close to the left-hand wall. There were half a dozen of them, and they were pointing in the opposite direction; whoever made them had wandered to one side of the path for a few steps, then returned to the centre. Because the breeze had been blowing from the north, the footprints had been protected by the wall, and were covered with only a light powdering of the snow that had fallen later. Now Niall paused and examined them closely, kneeling down in the snow. The first thing that struck him was that they had been made by sandals – or shoes – of excellent workmanship. Most of the sandals worn by the workmen of this city were poorly made; thick leather soles held on to the foot by leather thongs or strips of reinforced cloth, which were threaded through holes in the leather. In order to prevent these thongs from becoming worn where they made contact with the ground, holes were countersunk in the sole to minimize the friction. So a footprint made by a workman or a slave was quite distinctive, with its three pairs of holes. On the other hand, the human beings captured from Kazak's underground city wore more elaborate footwear. Having far more time at their disposal, the shoemakers of Dira took pride in their craft, and sewed broad leather straps to the sole with waxed thread. The soles themselves were shaped to correspond exactly to the outline of the human foot. It seemed likely, then, that these footprints in the snow had been made by a man of Dira.

Dravig asked: 'These are the footprints of one of the assassins?'

'Yes.'

'They seem to interest you.'

'I am puzzled. If you look at my own footprints, you will see that they have been made with an even pressure – the heel and the sole are of equal depth. In these, the heel is far deeper than the sole.'

'I see that.' Dravig's tone was polite, but Niall sensed that the spider found his interest incomprehensible. The spider mentality seemed averse to mathematical logic. 'And what do you infer?'

Niall straightened up, shaking his head. 'That he was carrying something heavy.' But he was far from convinced by his own reasoning.

Fifty paces further on, the path was partly blocked with rubble where the left-hand wall had collapsed. On the other side of it there was an overgrown garden; the house to which it belonged had once been large, but had now fallen into ruin. Niall paused and stood looking at the house. Once again he had the sense that something was hovering on the edge of his perceptions, like a movement glimpsed out of the corner of his eye. Stepping carefully, he made his way over the fallen stones and into the garden. Instinct told him to turn left and make his way towards a gap in the shrubbery. It was only when he was there that he noticed that there was less snow on these bushes than on the surrounding ones, and that somebody had probably brushed past them, shaking the snow on to the ground.

A dozen yards from the house, he found his path blocked by an empty swimming pool. Its plastic material had long ago become cracked and coated with black mildew; only in places were there glimpses of its original blue colour. The bottom was covered with rubbish: dead leaves, fallen slates and broken glass. But what immediately attracted Niall's attention was the pile of more recent rubbish on the side nearest the house. In the corner of the pool, at the foot of an aluminium ladder that was still firmly attached to the side, there were dead branches, pieces of rotten timber, and a quantity of fallen leaves mixed with snow.

Dravig was standing silently behind him. Niall asked:

'Do you notice anything?'

'No.' The spider's antennae were directed towards the pool.

'There's almost no snow on that lawn. Somebody has gone to the trouble of gathering all the dead leaves' – he pointed down into the pool – 'and throwing them in there.'

He went round the pool and clambered down the ladder; as he did so he noted that the steps were almost free of snow. Standing at the bottom, he reached out and grabbed the end of a length of decaying timber that looked as if it had once been the frame of a door. As he heaved it free, and a dead bush also came away with it, he saw what he had been half-expecting: a human leg protruding from the wet leaves.

A moment later, Dravig was beside him, clearing

away the dead branches. The corpse that was exposed was naked; it was a man, and his head and limbs were swollen to almost balloon-like proportions. The face had turned black, and looked as if it was made of shiny leather. Niall felt the energies drain from his heart; it reminded him of his father's corpse as it lay across the threshold of their underground home in the desert.

Dravig said with satisfaction: 'Skorbo managed to kill one of them before he died.'

Niall leaned forward cautiously until his nostrils assured him that, in spite of its bloated appearance, the corpse had not yet started to decay. He took hold of the foot, and pulled the body clear of the dead leaves. The eyes were open and the lips drawn back from the teeth; he had obviously died in agony. The knees were bent grotesquely in rigor mortis.

Dravig asked: 'Do you know him?'

'No.' But even if Niall had known the man, the swelling would have made recognition impossible.

Niall turned away; the staring eyes and exposed teeth made him feel sick. He climbed the ladder back to the lawn; suddenly he was glad it was cold. On a hot day the corpse would already have been surrounded by bluebottles. And since bluebottles were the size of small birds, the corpse would soon have been devoured.

Niall stood staring at the lawn. Only a few hours earlier, men had worked in the darkness, gathering armfuls of snow and dead leaves to conceal the corpse; they should have left behind some clue to their identity. But the recent snow had buried all the clues. But why should they take so much trouble to hide the body? Did they mean to return later to give it a decent burial? Niall dismissed that idea. The man's clothes had been removed because they might afford a clue to his identity; the body had probably been concealed for the same reason. But that suggested that the killers were men who belonged to this city. And Niall found such an idea almost unbelievable.

Dravig had been waiting patiently while Niall stood there, lost in thought. As Niall shook his head and sighed, he asked:

'Do you have any idea who might be responsible?'

'None. The whole thing is completely baffling.'

From over the rooftops came the sound of a gong. In the days when men were enslaved, it had been used to announce the evening curfew; anyone found abroad after that time was subject to instant execution. Now it was used in the mornings to announce the beginning of the working day.

Niall said: 'I must go back. There is a meeting of the Council in half an hour.' Its full title was the Council of Free Men, but Niall shortened it in order to avoid the risk of causing offence.

As they walked back through the bushes, Niall observed something that had caught on a twig. It was a fine, thin chain, made of a gold-coloured metal; suspended on it there was a medallion of the same colour. One side was blank; on the other was the symbol that he had already seen once that morning. Niall held it out on the palm of his hand. But Dravig stared at it blankly. The spider mentality, for all its intelligence, found symbols incomprehensible.

Niall said: 'It is the same sign we found on the lead disc under the tree.'

'But what does it mean?'

'I don't know. But I shall try to find out.'

As they returned along the path between the walls, Niall stopped and pointed to the footprints.

'Now I understand why the heel is deeper than the toes. He was walking backwards, helping to carry the body.'

'But why did they not leave the body where it was?'

30

'By removing it, they thought they were leaving no clues behind. If the snow had been heavier, we would never have discovered how Skorbo died.'

Dravig said: 'The snow was their ally.'

'And also their enemy.'

In the damp-smelling hallway, with its dust and rubble, Niall paused again to look around. This time he was able to find the prints of two sets of sandals in the dust. He said:

'There is still one thing I cannot understand. How did they lure Skorbo into the building?'

'I can tell you that.' Niall stared at him in surprise. 'They used the scent of a female spider in season.'

'Of course!' It was the smell that had intrigued Niall when he first stepped into the hallway. When he had returned with Dravig, it had gone. But the spider's more acute senses had detected it.

Dravig said: 'What do you wish me to say to the Death Lord?'

The question took Niall by surprise. After all, he had nothing to do with Skorbo's death. Now, suddenly, he realized that his attitude revealed a lack of maturity and understanding. He was the ruler of all the human beings in this city. Therefore the murder *was* his responsibility, whether he liked it or not.

He said: 'Please tell the Death Lord that I shall do everything in my power to find the criminals. When they are found, they shall be handed over to you for punishment.'

'Thank you.' Their minds made momentary contact; it was the equivalent of a human handshake. Then Dravig turned away and went out into the square. When he and Niall were alone, he omitted the ritual gestures of homage, knowing that Niall found them embarrassing. Dravig would have preferred to make the gestures; like all spiders, he found them natural and satisfying to his sense of order. That he omitted them now was a sign of friendship and respect.

About to follow Dravig into the square, Niall remembered the leaden disc, which he had left outside the door that led into the garden. He went back down the corridor. The disc was gone. Niall could remember the exact spot where he had left it; in fact the indentation was still in the snow, with some faint earth marks.

The slaves were now clearing the snow from the pavement in front of the house. The overseer, a powerfully-built man whose face looked as if it had been carved out of wood, snapped to attention as Niall approached.

Niall asked: 'What is your name?'

'Dion, sir.'

'Have you seen anyone go into that house in the last ten minutes?'

'No, sir.'

Niall was probing his mind as he spoke, and could see he was telling the truth.

'None of the slaves has been in there?'

'No, sir.' This time, Niall sensed his hesitation. It was understandable enough. Watching slaves shovelling snow was scarcely a demanding job; what could be more natural than turning his back and gazing into the distance?

Niall looked thoughtfully at the slaves. It seemed inconceivable that any of these pathetic creatures could have taken the disc. To begin with, it would be too heavy for the pockets of their garments. Slaves *were* notoriously inclined to steal, but they were usually interested in food, or attractive shining objects. Niall scanned the minds of those who were closest to him. It was as he had expected. Slaves seemed to live in a permanent mental fog, a perpetual present without past or future; their minds were little more than a reflection of their environment. By comparison, even the overseer was an intellectual prodigy. Niall always found it depressing to probe the minds of slaves; they took their emptiness so completely for granted that it was contagious, like a disease.

Niall said: 'Listen to me, Dion. Behind this house there is a garden with a gate in the wall. Follow my footprints along the lane. They will lead you to an empty swimming pool, in which you will find the body of a man. Have him carried to my palace. Do you understand?'

'Yes, sir.' If the man was surprised, his face showed no sign of it. Under the spiders, the overseers had been trained to obey like machines.

As he retraced his footsteps through the snow, Niall was lost in thought. The events of the past few hours had left him baffled. Yet he found them irritating and puzzling rather than alarming – a tiresome interruption of more important affairs.

The past six months had been the most absorbing and exciting of his life. Since the spiders had granted men their freedom, life had become a continuous adventure. In the days of slavery, men had not been allowed to use their minds. Children had been raised in strictly supervised nurseries; any who showed signs of unusual intelligence were destroyed. Books had been forbidden; so had any form of mechanical device. Even the servants of the bombardier beetles, who had always enjoyed relative freedom, had been forbidden to construct any kind of machine on pain of death.

In practice, the beetle servants had ignored the prohibition; for generations, their children had secretly learned to read. But the men of the spider city had been allowed no such latitude. Ever since birth, their minds had been systematically violated by their masters; even their most secret thoughts had been open to inspection by the spiders. Most of them had never even dreamed of the possibility of freedom.

The men of Dira were a different matter. Until their capture by the spiders less than a year ago, they had always been free. But their minds had been cramped by generations of confinement in an underground fortress, and by the need for the strictest obedience if they were to avoid the vigilance of spider patrols. In order to guarantee their safety, their rulers – like the late King Kazak – had demanded total submission and loyalty. Even the women of Dira were treated by Kazak as his private harem. So the men of Dira were almost as ill-equipped as the men of the spider city to deal with the experience of self-determination.

It had not taken Niall long to realize that men need to be taught to exercise their freedom. Too much freedom bewildered them and made them lazy. So the men of the spider city continued to go to work daily under the supervision of the female commanders. But these commanders were now – theoretically at least – under the orders of the Council of Free Men. In fact, they continued to work closely with their old masters; they regarded the spiders with a loyalty that had been instilled into them since childhood. As far as they were concerned, Niall was merely an overseer who had been appointed by the spiders. They had no desire for 'freedom'.

Yet humans differed from spiders in one basic respect: their craving for novelty. Niall had soon recognized that this could be used to increase their capacity for freedom. The beetle servants were now manufacturing all kinds of novelties: pressure lamps, clocks, kitchen appliances, mechanical toys, electric torches, children's picture books, even bicycles. When the first examples of these things were seen in the spider city, they created a sensation. Mechanical toys were in such demand that grown men would barter their food and clothing for them. But the men of the spider city possessed few goods that could be used for barter – one man had been known to offer a hundred hours of manual labour in exchange for a pressure lamp. Recognizing their frustration, Niall decided to offer them the most startling novelty so far: money. In exchange for their daily work, men were paid in brass coins, cast in the newly built mint. They could use these coins to purchase food, clothing and 'novelties'.

The results surpassed all Niall's expectations. Within weeks, all the men were working longer hours to accumulate more money to buy the novelties. After dark, the windows of the city glowed with the lights of pressure lamps. Manufacturers of clothing and footwear began to produce 'luxury' goods that could command higher prices. Bakers began to create cakes and tarts and sweetmeats, and the coarse grey bread that had been the staple diet of human beings for as long as they could remember gave way to a fine white bread that was baked daily. The use of dyes spread from the city of the bombardier beetles; soon all the women of the spider city were wearing brightly coloured garments and necklaces of glass beads. As men and women were once again allowed to live together – the spiders had kept them segregated – they ceased to live communally in basements, and began taking over empty buildings. Nearly all the windows in the spider city had been broken; now the beetle servants taught the art of glass manufacture, and men and women spent their free time repairing and decorating their new homes. After nightfall, the spider city had once been dark and silent; now its streets were more crowded in the evening than during the day. And the men and women who walked the streets had a new sense of confidence and responsibility; Niall could see it in their eyes, and it filled him with satisfaction. He had no illusions; he knew that most of them were little better than innocent and greedy children. Nevertheless, it was a beginning. In a few generations – perhaps after Niall's death – they would be capable of shaping their own destiny.

This is why Niall was so excited at the thought of the Council meeting. Every meeting was a landmark. Four of the twenty members were from the city of the bombardier beetles, and during the early meetings, they had dominated the proceedings with their suggestions and advice; now it would take a very perceptive observer to guess which of the members were beetle servants. At the last meeting, one man had suggested that the darker streets should be lighted by large pressure lamps, which should be paid for jointly by all the inhabitants of the street; only Niall realized that the streets of ancient cities had been illuminated by municipal lighting. Another man, a cook who had once prepared a nightly meal for a hundred men, and who now lived with his wife and child, had asked permission to convert an empty room into a dining hall, where men and women could come and buy the meals that he and his wife would cook; only Niall knew that restaurants were almost as old as civilization. And the charioteers, who had once worked exclusively for the commanders, and spent most of their days waiting for their masters, were now suggesting banding together to create a public transport system. It was exciting to realize that all these people – Niall thought of them as *his* people – were embarking on an adventure of self-development, and that one day their story would occupy an important place in the history books.

And now, just as men were beginning to understand the meaning of freedom, this murder threatened to undermine everything they had accomplished. Niall was aware that many of the spiders resented this new situation; they regarded human beings as slaves, whose lives were as unimportant as those of the lowest kind of insect. Now they had been told that these human vermin were under the special protection of Nuada, the Goddess of the Delta, and that the Spider Lord had ordered that they were to be treated as equals under the Law. That was, of course, preposterous. Nothing could make a spider regard a human being as his equal.

But because they were accustomed to obedience, they observed the letter of the Law, and ceased to treat human beings as slaves. They continued to regard them with contempt, but they no longer showed it openly. And because human beings continued to regard the spiders with fear and respect, there was no open friction.

But if these human lice could murder a spider, then the whole situation had become outrageous. It would surely deserve the utmost severity – as in the old days, when rebels had been tortured and executed in batches of a hundred at a time?

Dravig had said that the Spider Lord would stick to the agreement; human life would continue to be respected. But since spiders were telepathic, they were far more aware of one another's feelings than human beings were. If the feeling became too strong, even the despotic old Spider Lord might feel obliged to change her policy . . .

Niall was aroused from these disquieting reflections by the sight of two charioteers who were labouring breathlessly through the deep snow; behind them in the cart sat a big, fleshy man, who was shaking his head with visible impatience. Niall recognized him as an overseer named Broadus, a prominent member of the Council of Free Men. When he saw Niall, the expression of irritation dissolved into an ingratiating smile. He made a bow from a sitting position.

'Good morning, highness. I'm sorry I'm late.'

'Good morning, Broadus.' (Broadus's smile changed into something like a smirk; he loved hearing his name spoken aloud.) 'I'm afraid we're all late. Would you tell the Council I'll be with them in a few minutes?'

'Certainly, highness.' He shot a wrathful glance at the charioteers as he clambered out into the snow.

As Niall started to mount the stairs, Nephtys came

hurrying down to meet him. She said in a whisper:

'The Princess Merlew is waiting to see you.'

'Oh no! I've got a Council meeting.'

'I've told her that.'

'All right. Thank you, Nephtys.'

As he approached his chamber, the door opened, and Merlew came out; she must have been waiting behind it.

'Good morning, Niall.'

'Good morning, princess.' He deliberately used the formal title.

She was looking dazzlingly beautiful in a short dress of red spider-silk, which clung to the curves of her body; her red-gold hair was combed straight down her back.

'You must be cold.' She took his hands in both of hers. 'Oh yes, you're frozen! So is your face.' She had placed her hands on his cheeks; they felt pleasantly warm. He felt his impatience melting away; he had never been able to maintain an attitude of coolness towards Merlew.

'I've got a Council meeting . . .'

'I know. You can keep them waiting. That's your prerogative.'

'Punctuality is the politeness of kings.'

She laughed. 'That's clever! I must remember that.'

He was tempted to tell her that he had found it in an old book, but she interrupted him.

'I've got a present for you.'

He grunted noncommittally; he was pulling off his boots, and the thick woollen socks.

'It's a new servant girl. Her name is Savitri. I've trained her myself.'

He was buckling his sandal, and was glad his face was averted.

'Thank you, but I can't accept her.'

'Why not?'

'This house is run by women – it might cause problems.'

'I'm sure it wouldn't. I'll speak to your mother.'

'I'd rather you didn't. Why don't you give her to my brother?'

'Because Veig . . .' She lowered her voice. 'Because Veig already has enough body servants.' She laid a delicate emphasis on the word 'body'. Veig was notorious for his susceptibility to attractive girls.

'So have I.'

She sighed. 'I wish you weren't so hard to please.' She took from his hands the belt with the ceremonial short-sword, and passed it round his waist. For a moment, her pointed breasts pressed against his chest, and her lips came close. In that moment he realized how easy it would be to relent and say yes. All that restrained him was the knowledge that his womenfolk would regard the new girl as a spy, and resent her accordingly. As Merlew finished buckling his belt he said:

'I have to go.'

'There's something else I have to tell you.'

'Yes?' He hesitated at the door.

She stepped back and lowered her eyes; it was a reaction that always made him suspicious.

'I've heard a rumour . . . The Council intends to ask you to get married.'

'Married!' He was genuinely taken aback.

She said quickly: 'It's nothing to do with me. I only heard it at second hand.' She reached up and made an adjustment to the front of his tunic.

He looked down at her quizzically. 'And what do you think?'

'I quite agree, of course.' She coloured. 'I'm not suggesting you should marry me. There are plenty of nice girls among the commanders.' He made a movement of impatience. 'But you *do* need someone to help you.'

He should have known from past experience that she could exert an almost hypnotic power of attraction. Yet it never failed to take him by surprise. He was aware that she had put on this red dress for his benefit, and that she wore a perfume distilled from gorse flowers because she knew it was his favourite. But she exuded a magic that made these things unimportant; it was urging him to take hold of her bare shoulders and kiss her mouth. He looked away from her with an effort.

'I'm afraid we shan't be discussing marriage this morning.'

She looked up quickly. 'Why not?'

'There's something more important. Have you heard about Skorbo?'

She shook her head.

'He's been murdered.'

'Oh no!' Her surprise was genuine; he was able to see into her mind as she spoke, and he could register her sense of shock. That came as a relief. Merlew had detested Skorbo, and it had crossed Niall's mind that she might be behind the murder.

Merlew was also intelligent enough to understand the implications of the killing, and they worried her. She was Kazak's daughter, and she knew how the spiders would react.

'Who can have done it?'

'I have no idea.'

'Surely not a human? Are you sure it wasn't another spider?'

'No. It was a human all right. But now I have to go.'

This time she made no attempt to detain him. Yet it cost him an effort to leave her. As he hurried along the corridor, he shook his head with amusement. He had caught himself feeling a flash of gratitude to Skorbo's assassins for distracting Merlew.

The Council of Free Men met in the main dining hall of the palace. (In fact, Niall's researches had revealed that the 'palace' had once been the Royal Insurance Building, and that the Council chamber had been its board room.) Now, as he crossed the main hall towards its great double doors, someone waved to him from a curtained recess. From the shabby green tunic, the colour of dying moss, Niall recognized Simeon, the chief physician of the city of the bombardier beetles; since the days of freedom, Simeon had founded a college of medicine. He was also one of the most active members of the Council. At the moment, it was obvious that he was anxious not to be seen. As Niall approached, he disappeared behind the curtain. Niall followed.

Simeon said quickly: 'A word in your ear. The Council has got some plan to marry you off.'

'I know.'

'Who told you?'

'Merlew.'

Simeon grunted sarcastically. 'She's behind it.'

'Who proposed it?'

'Corbin.'

'I should have guessed.' Corbin was also a member of the stadion, the council of the city of the beetles; he and Merlew had always been friendly.

'I thought I'd better warn you anyway.'

'Thanks. Now we'd better go – we're late.'

Simeon said: 'Let me go first and give me two minutes. I don't want them to realize we've been speaking.'

Niall smiled ironically as he watched him go; it seemed absurd that being a ruler of men involved so much plotting and counter-plotting.

There was a knock on the main door; since there were no servants nearby, Niall went and opened it himself. The overseer Dion was standing there; behind him stood half a dozen slaves, carrying the corpse on an improvised stretcher made of planks.

'Where shall we put him, sir?'

'On the table there.'

Dion shook his head. 'I wouldn't advise putting him too near a fire, sir. He'll start to pong.'

'No, of course. Have the table carried out into the courtyard, and put him on it.'

Dion beckoned for more slaves. Niall hurried into the Council chamber.

The members were talking earnestly amongst themselves, and at first failed to notice his entrance. Then all jumped to their feet, and raised both arms to chest level in a ritual salute.

'Please sit down, gentlemen. I'm sorry I'm late.' He drew up his chair at the head of the table. 'We have some important business . . .'

Broadus, whose seat was next to Niall, jumped to his feet with a deferential smile.

'*Very* important business, if I may say so, highness. Perhaps I may . . .'

Niall raised his hand. 'One moment please, Councillor Broadus. Gentlemen, I would like you all to look out of the window.'

All turned and looked outside. The door into the courtyard had opened, and four slaves carried out the table into the snow. There were sharp intakes of breath as the others followed with the corpse, and lifted it on to the tabletop.

Simeon was the first to speak. 'Who is that?' He was so surprised that he forgot to address Niall as 'sire', a formality he always observed at Council meetings.

'I don't know. I was hoping one of you might be able

to tell me. Would you mind stepping outside?'

A door from the chamber led direct into the court-yard. They all followed Niall into the cold air. The face of the dead man was blacker and more swollen than when Niall had last seen it. The Council of Free Men looked at him with distaste, but without revulsion; this was not the first time they had seen the body of a man killed by spider venom.

'Does anyone recognize him?'

Some moved to get a better view; one by one, all shook their heads.

'Simeon, could he be from your city?'

'No. I know every man there. This isn't one of them.'

As they looked at the corpse, Niall watched them carefully, his mind receptive to impressions. It was obvious to him that none of them knew anything about Skorbo's death.

Simeon was peering closely at the feet. He asked Niall: 'Notice anything?'

Niall studied them closely. 'They're unusually hairy.' The man's legs, and the upper portions of his feet, were covered with dark hairs.

'Not that.' Simeon took hold of two of the dead man's toes, and pulled them apart. 'Look. He was born with webbed feet, like a duck. The webs were severed later.'

Mastering his revulsion, Niall looked more closely, and was able to see the flaps of loose skin between the big toe and its companion. He shook his head.

'What does it mean?'

'Just a birth defect – I've seen it once or twice. But it proves that he wasn't born in this city.'

Some of the others looked puzzled. But Niall under-stood his meaning. The spiders bred human beings for physical perfection; those who had the slightest defect were killed at birth.

Niall turned to Dion. 'Cover him over with a sheet.

Then have the body removed to the mortuary.'

He led them back inside again; they were all looking shaken. Simeon said:

'Does anyone know what happened?'

'Yes. He was killed by Skorbo.' There were some angry murmurs. Niall said: 'But it was understandable. He was responsible for Skorbo's death.'

That shocked them, as he had known it would. Someone said incredulously:

'A lone man killed a spider?'

'There were three of them. It was an ingenious booby trap. They cut off the fronds of a young palm, then bent it down like a spring. As Skorbo approached, they cut the rope . . .'

There was no need to elaborate; Niall's words, reinforced by mental images, conveyed his meaning direct to their minds.

Niall took the pendant on its gold chain from his pocket and handed it to Broadus.

'Has anyone seen this before?'

As it was passed around the table there was a shaking of heads.

Simeon asked: 'It belonged to the dead man?' Niall nodded. 'It is of ancient workmanship. No modern jeweller would have the skill to make this chain.'

'Have you any ideas about that symbol on it?'

Simeon said slowly: 'In my younger days I was interested in the old science of alchemy. This reminds me of a symbol of a bird of prey.'

'Yes, of course.' Now he looked more closely, Niall could see the resemblance.

Corbin, a fat young man whose head was covered with tight blond curls said: 'I hear that Skorbo was the most hated spider in the city.' He spoke with a certain complacency.

Niall said reprovingly: 'That may be true. But it

doesn't help us to find out who killed him.'

'I'm certain it wasn't one of our people.' The speaker was one of the captives from Dira; his countrymen occupied one third of the seats on the Council.

Niall said: 'You could be right, Massig. But *someone* in this city must know something about it. I need the help of every one of you. You must all realize how serious it is.'

Corbin asked: 'And what happens if we find them?'

'We must hand them over for punishment.'

Massig asked: 'Couldn't we execute them ourselves? We are a legally constituted authority.'

Niall understood his objection. The spiders would devise the most horrible death that could be imagined.

'That is true. But we must also show that we possess a sense of justice.' He looked round at their faces, and could see that none of them was convinced. 'Listen to me. I used to wonder why the spiders hated men so much. I thought it was because they were monsters. Then I found out the real reason: because they were afraid of us. They regarded *us* as the monsters. They had to enslave us because they believed we threatened their existence. And nothing that has happened since then has made them change their minds. Yet they agreed that there should be peace between the spiders and men. They agreed there should be no more killing. And now it looks as if we have broken our side of the bargain. What if they decide that it is time to break theirs?'

In the silence that followed he could read their thoughts: the fear and confusion and self interest. They all enjoyed being on this Council, playing at being men of authority. Now they remembered what it was like to be slaves, and the thought chilled them.

Hastur, one of the beetle servants, asked:

'Do you think that might happen?'

'Not at the moment.' He could sense their relief. 'But it *could* happen. That is why we must show our good faith.'

Broadus asked: 'What can we do, sire?'

'I want you to go back to your own people and find out what you can. Someone must have seen these men. Perhaps someone spoke to them. They cannot have entered the city unnoticed. If you learn anything, report back to me immediately.' He stood up. 'And now I think it is time to adjourn this meeting.'

All rose and made ritual obeisance. As they filed out of the room in silence, Niall beckoned to Simeon. When they were alone, he closed the door, then sat down at the table.

'Give me your advice.'

Simeon shook his head.

'What can I say? This is a bad business.'

'But who do you think was responsible?'

Simeon frowned.

'It's baffling. We know it can't be one of your people – they wouldn't have the courage or the enterprise. My people detest the spiders. But they've simply no reason to kill Skorbo. It would be an act of stupidity. That only leaves the men of Dira. Plenty of them have reason to kill spiders. Some of them saw their relatives and friends murdered when the spiders overran the city. Some of them saw their children eaten. As far as I can see, they're the only ones with a good reason for killing a spider.'

Niall shook his head.

'I don't think they were responsible.'

'Why not?'

'There's something I didn't mention. Dravig tore the palm tree out of the ground. And in the roots there was a metal disc – I think it was made of lead – with a symbol on it: the same symbol as on the pendant. It seemed to me that it must have been there at least a year.'

'What makes you think it had been there so long?'

'Because the roots had grown around it.'

Simeon stared at him with astonishment.

'You're saying that the tree was *specially planted* to kill Skorbo?'

'Can you think of any other explanation?'

'Isn't it more likely that it was put there later, to bring good luck to their enterprise?'

'It's possible. But I got the impression that it had been there since the tree was planted. And that must have been at least a year ago – before Dira was captured by the spiders.'

Simeon shook his head; he was obviously perturbed.

'If you're right, then they've been planning this for a very long time.'

Niall nodded. 'That was my own thought.'

'Then who the devil *are* they?'

'Have you heard of human beings outside this city – in other parts of the country?'

'No.' Simeon was silent for a long time. 'I suppose there *are* some, of course. I once heard rumours of people to the north – people who are more like animals. But I never believed them.'

'Why not?'

'Because the spiders would have hunted them down.'

Niall had to agree that this sounded reasonable. In the days of slavery, spider balloons had constantly patrolled all areas suspected of concealing human fugitives.

Simeon said: 'Could I see this lead disc?'

'It disappeared.'

'Disappeared?'

'It was too heavy for my pocket, so I left it by the door. When I came back, it had gone.'

'So these men must have been hiding nearby?'

Niall shook his head. 'It was more likely one of the slaves. They were working right outside the building.'

'Did you question the overseer?'

'He saw nothing.'

'But why should a slave want a piece of lead?'

'You know slaves. They'll steal anything.'

'But you didn't have them searched?'

'It hardly seemed worth the trouble.' Yet now he thought about it, he could see that Simeon was right.

Simeon persisted.

'Look, if someone went to the trouble of stealing a heavy piece of lead, he must have had a reason. Even a slave wouldn't have much use for a lump of lead. What if Skorbo's killers were among the slaves?'

Niall shrugged. 'It's possible. But they looked just like an ordinary squad of slaves.'

'Even so, I think we ought to go and check.'

'Yes, I suppose you're right.' Yet he stood up reluctantly, feeling that he was giving way merely to humour Simeon.

Outside, the pale winter sky was cloudless, and the reflected sunlight was painful to the eyes. At least the slaves had trampled a path through the snow, so that walking was easier. The slaves were no longer in the square, but the wheelmarks of the cart that had been used to transport the dead man were clearly visible.

The mortuary was situated in the same building as the newly-founded medical school, three blocks south along the main avenue. As they reached the corner, they could see the slaves shambling in irregular formation beside the cart, not far from their destination. They were hurrying after it when the cart halted; the body – still covered by a trailing sheet – was removed, placed on a plank, and carried into the building. The overseer was about to follow as Niall and Simeon arrived, breathless from their exertion. Niall called him back.

'Dion, I want you to line up all the slaves. Call the others from inside.'

The overseer saluted and shouted an order; a few moments later, the body re-emerged from the building. It was on a single broad plank, and the arms and legs hung down on either side. Niall ordered them to replace it on the cart. Then the slaves were ordered to stand in line along the road. Niall counted them, then asked the overseer:

'How many should there be?'

'Thirty, sir.'

'Then why are there only twenty-nine?'

The overseer blinked with astonishment, and counted them slowly, pointing at each one as he did so. He said:

'Yes, you're right.' He turned to face the squad. 'Attention!' The slaves clicked their heels, and made a half-hearted attempt to look like soldiers. Dion said: 'Do any of you know what happened to the other fellow?'

'I do.' The speaker was a hollow-chested man with a hare lip, who was standing next to the cart. When he showed no sign of offering further information, Dion shouted impatiently:

'Well, where is he, you fool?'

The man raised his hand and silently pointed into the building. The overseer cursed.

'I thought I told you all to come out.' The man gazed back blankly with cow-like indifference.

Niall beckoned to Dion. 'You'd better come with us.'

Simeon said: 'Someone had better watch the rear of the building, in case he tries to escape that way.'

Niall had already been here several times. The ground floor had been converted into a casualty department and maternity ward. It smelt of the chlorinated lime used as a disinfectant. This was a large building, and the man could have gone in one of many directions. As they stood, hesitating, Dion said:

'If necessary I'll get a squad and search the whole place.'

Niall pointed. 'Look, he went up there.' He had noticed a fragment of melting snow on one of the stairs.

They climbed the stairs quietly, so as not to forewarn their quarry. The next floor was in process of being converted into a ward, and they could hear carpenters sawing wood from behind a closed door; it seemed unlikely the man had gone that way. Niall led the way up the next flight. This part of the building was still in its original state, and the floor had not even been swept; it was covered with plaster that had fallen from the walls and ceiling, and with broken glass and fragments of lath. A glance at the floor of the corridor told Niall that no one had been this way recently; but the overseer was already flinging open doors and peering into empty rooms. Niall swore under his breath; the man they were seeking must have heard the noise.

'He may be heading for the roof. Could he get into the next building?'

'Probably.' Simeon opened the nearest door; through the broken window of the empty room, they could see that the building next door was less than six feet away – a distance posing no problem to an agile man.

'We'd better hurry.'

Simeon laid a hand on his arm.

'Careful. There's a spider living in the roof space. It might jump on us and ask questions later.'

His caution was justified; although spiders were now forbidden to attack human beings, the invasion of its personal territory might be regarded as extreme provocation.

'A death spider?'

'No, a pink glue spider.' This was the name given to spiders of the species *oonopidae*, generally regarded as harmless, since they were smaller than the death spiders and had no poisonous sting. But they were many times stronger and swifter than any man, and their tarsal claws were powerful enough to sever an arm.

Niall mounted the stair softly and cautiously and, as he reached the top step, suddenly found himself face to face with the glue spider. It had obviously come to investigate the noise. For a moment, both were equally startled; its immediate reaction was to immobilize him with a concentrated burst of will-power. Niall felt exactly as if his whole body had been frozen in a block of ice, so that he was unable to move a muscle. Six months earlier, he would have found such an experience terrifying; now he had become so accustomed to spiders that it hardly caused his heartbeat to accelerate. His passivity and lack of fear convinced the spider that he was harmless, and it released him almost immediately.

Niall had never seen a glue spider at close quarters, and he was struck by the beauty of its colouring; its body, legs and head were all of the same flesh pink colour, like the cheeks of a healthy country girl. But, unlike the wolf spiders or death spiders, whose chelicerae resembled tufts of beard, the face of the glue spider entirely lacked the slightest touch of humanity. The great dome of a head, not unlike that of a bald-headed man, surmounted the smooth pink chelicerae with their unfolded fangs; the six eyes were in two rows, with four above and two below, and the end eyes of the upper row were turned outward; since they were also pink, they looked like glass globes rather than eyes. The creature seemed as alien as a Martian.

Yet perhaps because it seemed so totally non-human, perhaps because of its warm colouring, Niall felt that he had nothing to fear. He addressed the spider telepathically, also speaking the words aloud.

'We are looking for a man. Have you seen him?'

The spider seemed startled. It shifted uncomfortably on its feet but made no reply. The bulb-like eyes – on a level with Niall's own, since the spider was less than six feet high – seemed blank. Niall repeated the question – this time trying to transmit the image of a man – but there was still no reply. He stepped forward cautiously; the spider stepped back and then moved aside. Niall beckoned to Simeon and Dion to follow him.

He attempted to place himself in the mind of the fugitive. If he had arrived at the top of the stairs, and found that he could go no further, what would he do? This floor, like the others, consisted of a corridor with rooms on either side. The rooms on the right side over-looked the narrow side street, and through the nearest open door, Niall could see the web of the glue spider stretching across the street to the house opposite. The fugitive had almost certainly noticed this before he entered the building, so it was unlikely that he had gone to the right.

And if a man knew there was a spider in one of the rooms on the right, he would move to the left, probably on tiptoe. Niall looked carefully at the dust and rubble on the floor, mixed with the wings and carapaces of dead flying creatures, and saw what he was looking for. The marks would have been unnoticeable to anyone who was not looking for them, mere disturbances of the plaster and debris. The man had, as Niall suspected, been walking on tiptoe, and the slight signs were repeated at regular intervals of about eighteen inches – a man on tiptoe takes smaller steps than a man walking normally. In front of the first door on the left, there was a clear footmark where the man had paused to open the door. Niall did the same, and found himself looking into an empty room with unbroken windows. There was no place of concealment, and this was clearly why the man had continued on tiptoe to the next door. It was unnecessary to open this, for the marks continued on along the corridor, sometimes becoming invisible where there was no dust or rubble, but also resuming further on. Outside the third door the traces ceased; there was no sign of disturbance further along the corridor. Niall raised his hand to halt the others; his heart was beating violently. Cautiously, he turned the handle and pushed open the door. To his disappointment, the room was empty. But its cracked window had been raised. He hurried across the room and peered out. An ornamental ledge ran under the window along the whole length of the building; it was only six inches wide, but would present no problems for an agile – or desperate – man. What puzzled Niall was that there was no accessible window in the building across the alleyway, only a blank wall; to achieve access to such a window, the fugitive would have to move twelve feet along the ledge in the direction of the main avenue. And the window opposite this spot was closed and unbroken. The alternative, it seemed, was to go in the opposite direction, and around the corner at the rear of the building. And looking down at the ground four storeys below, Niall had to admit that only desperation could have induced him to make such an attempt.

Simeon said: 'What about the next room?'

Niall shook his head. 'The footprints stopped outside this one. Wait . . .' He stooped and examined the floor. His nerves tensed as he realized that the signs showed that the man had gone back across the room – back towards the corner, where there was another door. It looked like an inbuilt closet or cupboard. He looked towards it, and the others understood his meaning. Niall tiptoed towards it, and noticed that it had been left open a crack; the man inside had evidently been unable to close it completely. But while he was still several feet away, the door burst open, and a man darted out and ran to the open door of the room. He was so quick that they were all taken by surprise. Niall was the first to recover; he gave a cry and ran in pursuit. The man was already halfway down the corridor, but his run was heavy and awkward, and Niall had always been fleet of foot. Within a few strides, Niall had gained on him, and seized the shoulder of his slave tunic. The man swerved and stumbled, crashing to the wall. For a moment, Niall gazed into his eyes. They were large eyes, and seemed very dark and piercing. But as Niall prepared to grapple, he experienced a sensation that made him drop to his knees. It was exactly as if someone had struck him violently in the face, and at the same time gripped his windpipe to cut off his breathing. For a moment everything became dark, although he had the confused impression that time had gone into slow motion, and that his arms and legs were also moving in slow motion, like those of a swimmer. It was like being half-awake and half-asleep.

When his vision cleared, he saw that the man was now lying on the floor, held down by the front legs of the glue spider. His face and hands were covered in some shiny substance, and as Niall watched, the spider squirted more from its chelicerae. It was some kind of transparent glue, and as it struck the man's face, he suddenly ceased to struggle, collapsing as if dead.

Niall dragged himself to his feet, helped by Simeon. He was feeling oddly sick and dizzy. He looked at the spider, and transmitted a message of thanks. The spider released its victim. But as soon as it did so, the man twisted sideways and jumped to his feet – it was evident that he had been shamming. His hand darted into his bosom, and emerged with a knife in a sheath. As he pulled off the sheath and dropped it to the floor, his eyes met Niall's in a smile of triumph. There was something animal-like in the way the lips revealed his yellow teeth. He raised the knife, and Niall shrank back, expecting to be attacked. Instead, to his astonishment, the man slashed at his own forearm, making a superficial cut. Then, as the spider again seized him from behind, he sagged to his knees and collapsed on to the floor. This time it was obvious that he was not shamming.

Simeon knelt beside him and twisted his face sideways by grabbing his hair. The man's eyes were closed, and the glue on his face was already hardening into a mask. Simeon took his wrist and felt his pulse.

'He's dead. Don't touch that!' this last was shouted at Niall as he bent forward to look at the knife. But Niall had no intention of trying to pick it up. What interested him was the symbol burned into the wooden handle of the knife – the same symbol he had already seen on the leaden disc.

The spider was retreating along the corridor. Then it reached up, and its tarsal claws gripped the edge of a hole in the ceiling. A moment later, it had pulled itself upward and heaved its body through the trapdoor. Its abdomen seemed too large, and stuck for a moment; then it disappeared.

Simeon asked: 'Are you all right?'

'Yes.' But Niall staggered as he said so, and almost lost his balance.

'What did he do?'

'I don't know.' He was feeling sick again, and had no desire to answer questions. He turned to the overseer. 'Please go to the headquarters of the Spider Lord, and ask Dravig to come here.' When the man looked alarmed, Niall turned to Simeon, whose face seemed oddly distorted, as if seen through water. 'Would you mind going too? They'd pay more attention to you.'

Before they were out of sight, Niall sat on the floor,

his back propped against the wall. Waves of heat were rising to his forehead, and he could feel himself breaking out into perspiration. After a few moments, the nausea retreated again. He was breathing heavily, through his mouth, and his body felt drained of strength. But after resting for five minutes, a feeling of normality began to return. He opened his eyes, and looked at the dead man, whose face was turned upwards towards the ceiling. It was easy to see how he had succeeded in masquerading as a slave; he had a beak-like nose, large ears and a receding chin – only the abnormally pale face distinguished him from other slaves. But Niall recalled the strange glance of those dark eyes, and realized that he had been dealing with a man of intelligence. He had also been dealing with a man of formidable resolve; his instantaneous suicide proved that.

And he had, he now realized, been dealing with an alien, a man who was neither a native of this country, nor of Dira. The proof was that the man had somehow learned the spiders' trick of striking direct at his willpower. Yet there was an obvious difference. When the pink glue spider had paralysed him at the top of the stairs, it had somehow paralysed his nervous system, so that he was fully conscious, yet unable to move a muscle. This man had used some direct, brutal psychic force, like a blow with a blunt instrument. It had left him feeling sick and weak, while the momentary paralysis of the spider had had no after effect. The difference was obviously that the spider intended only to stop him from moving; the man had intended to hurt him.

As he stared at the mask-like face of the corpse, he experienced a strange sensation that sent cold waves through his scalp; for a moment, he was convinced that the man was still alive. It took him some moments to understand what had happened. His sense of bafflement had led him to make an attempt to probe the mind of the corpse. It was a purely automatic reflex, for he knew the man was dead. The result should have been totally negative, like stirring a dead body with his foot. Yet he had encountered an eerie sense of warmth and vitality. There was some sense in which the body was still alive and yet unconscious, like a plant or vegetable. Niall allowed his mind to become blank, and tried again. This time, he experienced a reflex of disgust which made him instantly withdraw, as if he had touched something unpleasant and slimy. There was something about the lingering life-field of the dead man that repelled him like an unpleasant smell. It was something as distinct as a smell, and therefore inexpressible in words. He had occasionally encountered it in the desert, in the minds of predators – for example, in the nightmare creature called a saga insect, which had held a cricket in its claws and then crunched its way down its body as if eating a stick of celery. And he could still remember the revulsion he experienced on accidentally catching a glimpse into the soul of some demonic, bat-like creature in the Delta; it had seemed to be entirely malevolent, as if consumed by the desire to kill.

The sound of footsteps brought him back to the present. It was Simeon, followed by Dravig. Niall started to rise to his feet, then thought better of it as the waves of nausea rose to his head. He sank down again, his back against the wall.

'Hello, Dravig. I'm sorry to bring you here.'

'Are you hurt?' Niall was flattered by the genuine concern in the spider's query.

'No, I'll be all right.'

Dravig looked at the corpse. 'Who is this man?'

'One of Skorbo's assassins.'

'You have done well. Where is the third?'

'I don't know. But now we know why they removed

all the clothes of the dead man. He must have been dressed in a slave uniform, and they didn't want us to know he was hiding among slaves. I think it might be worth searching the slave quarter.'

'I will give the order. How did this man die?'

'He killed himself with that knife. Be careful.' The spider had picked it up in his tarsal claw, and raised it towards his face. 'It's poisoned.'

'Yes. It is the venom of the green rock scorpion, perhaps the deadliest poison on earth.' The spider's sense of smell was far more acute than that of a human being. 'It is fatal even for spiders.'

'Then you should warn the searchers to be careful. The other may be armed with one too.'

The spider signified affirmation; the mental gesture was independent of words, like a nod. He asked: 'Do you need help?'

'No thank you. Simeon will help me.'

'Then I must return to make my report.' He drew himself up, as if standing to attention, and said formally: 'In the name of the Spider Lord I thank you for hunting down this assassin.' Niall understood enough of the spider mentality to know what he was trying to convey: that he accepted that the human beings of this city were in no way responsible for Skorbo's death.

Niall inclined his head. 'Thank you.'

When Dravig had gone, Simeon picked up the knife, and carefully replaced it in its sheath. 'I'll get this analysed. The poison must be deadly.' He had been unable to hear Dravig's side of the conversation.

'It is the venom of the green rock scorpion.'

'Great goddess!' Simeon almost dropped the knife. 'If I'd known that I'd have picked it up with gloves.' He took a large handkerchief from his pocket, and carefully wrapped the sheath, tying the corners in a knot.

Niall pushed himself cautiously to his feet, and was

relieved to find that he no longer felt dizzy; but the feeling of tiredness remained. Simeon looked at his face with concern.

'You're very pale. Did he hit you in the stomach?'

Niall shook his head. 'He struck at me with his will-force, like a spider.'

Simeon stared incredulously. 'Are you sure of that?'

'Quite certain.'

'He didn't touch you physically?'

'No.'

Simeon absorbed this in silence. He looked down at the body, shaking his head.

'Then who the devil could he be?'

He dropped on his knees beside the body, and searched the pockets. They yielded only a soiled handkerchief of coarse linen, and a wooden spoon and fork – slaves carried their own eating utensils.

Niall said: 'Look round his neck.'

There was, as he expected, a fine gold chain with a pendant. Simeon removed it and held it out to Niall.

'Do you want it?'

'No. I already have one.'

But this was not the real reason he refused to take it. He felt a curious intuitive revulsion, a feeling that the pendant was somehow unclean.

Before he was halfway down the avenue, Niall realized it had been a mistake to walk. Every muscle in his body ached, and his feet felt as if they were made of lead. In spite of the sunlight, the cold air made him shiver. He brushed the snow from a low wall, and sat down.

A few hundred yards away, in the centre of the square, the white tower sparkled in the sunlight; its purity made even the surrounding snow look grey. As he stared at it, framed against the pale blue sky, Niall felt again the sensation he had experienced the first time he saw it: the curious spark of pure joy. He and his family had been prisoners of the spiders, and they had looked down on this city from a hilltop to the south. Some intuition had told him that the white tower represented freedom and hope. Now, as he looked at it, the surge of delight caused the exhaustion to vanish, and he realized that his mind had been increasing the fatigue by paying attention to it.

The tower stood in the midst of a square space of green lawn, now invisible under the snow. Even in the days of slavery, the spiders had allowed their human captives to trim the grass and keep it free from weeds. They had detested the tower, as a symbol of past human supremacy; they had even attempted to destroy it. Yet they had respected it as a mystery beyond their understanding.

In fact, the tower was virtually indestructible. What looked like semi-translucent white crystal was, in fact, an atomic force-field, made to look solid by causing it to reflect the light; it rejected solid matter in exactly the same way that the pole of a magnet rejects the like-pole of another magnet. In the course of about a million years, the force-field would drain away, and the tower would collapse. In the meantime, it would continue to serve as a time capsule, a giant electronic brain whose memory cells stored the accumulated knowledge of the men who had once been the sole masters of the earth.

Now he had regained his breath, Niall stood up and walked on towards the tower. The men and women who passed him hardly gave him a second glance; in his long cloak, with the fur-lined hood, he was indistinguishable from most of them. It was a relief not to have to return their salutations. During his early days as the ruler of this city, they had prostrated themselves on the ground and remained in that position until he had gone past. He had tried issuing a proclamation that he wanted to be ignored, but it had made no difference; the idea of ignoring their king shocked them profoundly. So Niall had issued a second proclamation, declaring that he preferred to be saluted with a bow. This time the citizens had obeyed him, but sometimes they bowed so deeply that they fell over, and Niall felt obliged to go and help them up. On the whole, he greatly preferred to be ignored.

The snow that covered the lawn around the tower was free from footprints. Although there was no law forbidding citizens to walk on the grass, no one ever did so, even to take a short cut; the tower seemed to inspire feelings approaching religious awe.

The white tower was thirty feet in diameter at its base, and about two hundred feet high. Yet as he looked up, it seemed to stretch as high as the clouds. This was an optical illusion, due to some quality in its milky surface, which seemed to shimmer like the air above a hot road; Niall had once compared it to liquid moonlight. As he approached within a few inches, he experienced the familiar tingling sensation throughout his body, the sensation a water diviner experiences as he stands above an underground stream. He felt as if he was being pulled forward by a magnet. The sensation became stronger as he made his way round to the north side of the tower, where he knew its vibrations were precisely attuned to those of his own body. There the pull became irresistible, and he moved forward. As his body encountered the surface, there was a sensation like walking into water. He experienced a momentary dizziness, a loss of orientation, as if he was on the point of fainting or falling asleep, and everything became dark. Then it grew light again, and he stepped inside the tower.

Yet what faced him now was not the circular room he had anticipated, but a breathtaking panorama of snow-clad mountain peaks, ice-covered ridges and misty blue valleys, stretching out in all directions for what seemed hundreds of miles. Clouds rested like feathery pillows in some of the glaciated valleys, but the clouds above his head looked as jagged and broken as the granite ridges and slopes far below. He was standing on a mountain top on hard-packed snow, and the air was so clear that it seemed to sparkle. Less than six feet in front of him there was a sheer drop into a valley that must have been at least a mile deep; to his right, a sloping ridge like a snow-covered rocky spine ran down to another peak far below.

Niall was startled, but not deceived. He knew that the scene spread out before him was an illusion. The first time he had entered the white tower, he had found himself standing on a sandy beach, facing a line of steep cliffs; that had also been a panoramic hologram, a film projected into three-dimensional space to produce an illusion of solid reality. Even the cold wind that now blew against his face was an illusion created by electronic technology; a stream of charged particles bombarded his nerve-ends, creating an illusion of moving air. Yet everything looked so completely real that it was impossible to detect the deception.

He rubbed his feet on the hard snow; it felt exactly like the snow he had left behind outside. But as soon as he closed his eyes he was aware that he was standing on a smooth wooden floor. He took three steps forward, so he was standing on the edge of the sheer drop. Intellectually, he knew he was still standing on the hard floor. Yet when he tried to force himself to take an additional step into the void, his feet refused to obey him, and he experienced a rush of fear that almost took his breath away. He could see the worn granite face of the great slope opposite, with its snow-filled crevasses and razor-like edges, in the most precise detail. Yet as soon as he closed his eyes it all vanished – even the cold wind – and he knew that he was on a solid floor.

He walked two steps forward, then opened his eyes. He was suspended in mid-air, looking down at the striated rock face a mile below, and on the cloud-filled valley floor. It was like floating on a magic carpet. He went on walking, now intellectually confident, while his emotions continued to sound frantic alarm bells and to flood his bloodstream with adrenalin. A few steps further, and they gradually became calm, leaving him suddenly relaxed and triumphant.

At that point the mountain landscape disappeared with the abruptness of a bursting bubble, and he found himself in the familiar room, with its curved white walls and luminous white ceiling. In its centre there was a marble-coloured column, above three feet in diameter, stretching from floor to ceiling; it had the same texture as the outer walls of the tower, but seemed even more unstable, as if made of a kind of grey liquid smoke, which flowed as if it were alive. When Niall stepped forward into the surface, it admitted him, and he found himself surrounded by a white odourless fog. As if his body had suddenly become weightless, he was floating upward; it was such a pleasant sensation that he would have liked it to last for hours. But a few moments later he stopped with a slight jerk. A single step forward, and he was standing on a flat roof, with a pale blue sky overhead, and the panorama of the spider city stretched around him – the view with which he had become so familiar from the roof of his palace.

This was not, in fact, a flat roof, but a room consisting of a force-field in the shape of a glass dome. But a glass pane is visible because it has accumulated a layer of dust; the force-field, being uncontaminated by dust, was virtually invisible.

This room was comfortably furnished; tubular metal furniture was covered with a black, leather-like material that was warm and yielding to the touch; the thick black carpet was as soft as spring grass. The only unusual item was the tall black box that stood against the southern wall, with its sloping panel of opaque glass and row of control knobs. This was the Steegmaster, the creation of Torwald Steeg, which was responsible for this tower and almost everything in it.

Standing beside the Steegmaster, staring out over the square, stood a man in a grey suit. The tall figure was slim and upright; only the white hair betrayed that he was old.

He asked: 'Did you recognize it?'

'It was the Himalayas, wasn't it?'

'Your geography is improving. You were standing on the summit of Mount Everest, looking south towards Nepal. The summit in the distance was Kanchenjunga.'

It was a game they played every time Niall came to the white tower. Yesterday it had been the South Pole;

two days before that, the crater of Mount Etna in full eruption. Niall had guessed wrong both times.

He went and joined the old man by the window, and was surprised to see that the square was no longer empty. In the few minutes since he had entered the tower, a large contingent of men had formed ranks outside the headquarters of the Spider Lord; there must have been at least a hundred of them. As he watched they were joined by another squad who marched out of a side street. At an order from one of the black-clad commanders, all stood to attention. A moment later, the double doors of the headquarters building opened, and death spiders and wolf spiders began to emerge. They were marching in a single file, and Niall recognized the spider at the head of the column as Dravig. They crossed the western side of the square, and moved north towards the river; the slave quarter lay on its further bank. As the spiders continued to pour out of the building, Niall found it hard to believe that it could have held so many. By the time the doors closed, there must have been at least three hundred spiders on the march. The men, with two commanders at their head, marched behind them.

Niall asked his companion: 'Do you know what is happening?'

'I assume this is connected with the death of the spider?'

'Do you know who killed him?'

The old man shook his head.

'You overestimate the powers of the Steegmaster. Its purpose is merely to gather and correlate information.'

It was true that Niall had only the vaguest idea of the capacities or limitations of the Steegmaster; wishful thinking inclined him to regard it as an all-knowing intelligence.

'But you knew about the death of the spider?'

'Naturally, since it took place only a hundred yards away.'

'But you've no idea who might have killed him?'

'I would like to help you. But I lack the information to assess the probabilities.'

'I thought the Steegmaster could read minds.'

The old man said patiently: 'Not minds. Thoughts. That is an entirely different matter. A thought-reading machine can decipher the information stored in the memory circuits of the brain, but it operates best when the person is asleep. It is almost impossible to read the thoughts of someone who is awake because the mental processes are too complex, and most of them operate on a subconscious level. The Steegmaster has no power to read feelings and intuitions, which operate on frequencies far beyond its range. To work efficiently, the Steegmaster requires specific information.'

Niall took from his pocket the pendant on its gold chain. He held it out on his palm, with the symbol uppermost.

'How about this? Can you tell me anything about it?'

The old man studied it for a moment.

'I would say that it is a magical sigil.'

'Sigil?' Niall had never heard the word.

'A type of symbol used in magic or alchemy.'

'But what does it mean?'

The old man smiled at him. 'Let us see if we can find out.'

As he finished speaking, he vanished. And since he had been forewarned by the smile, Niall accepted the disappearance without surprise. Throughout their conversation, he had been aware that he was actually speaking to the computer that stood between them. Like the mountain range that had confronted him on entering the tower, the old man was a computer-created hologram; this was why Niall sometimes addressed him by the name of his creator, the twenty-third-century scientist Torwald Steeg. Niall was also aware of his purpose in disappearing, rather than leaving the room in the normal manner. Steeg's aim was to teach him a new set of reflexes and reactions; it was an attempt to make him trust his reason rather than his senses.

Now reason told him the old man would be found in the library. He stepped again into the column in the centre of the room. As the mist surrounded him, he again experienced the sensation of weightlessness; his body seemed to be a feather drifting gently into a gulf. When the slight jerk told him that the descent had ceased, he stepped out of the column.

Of all the rooms in the tower, the library was Niall's favourite; he loved to breathe its smell of dust, old parchment and leather-bound books. To refer to it as an illusion would have struck him as a kind of blasphemy. The library, was, admittedly, a creation of the Steegmaster; but a creation of such complexity was in some way more real than mere physical reality. After all, what was reality but a force-field of subatomic energies?

The library was a vast hexagonal room, about fifty yards wide, and so high that its domed ceiling was almost invisible. The walls were lined with bookshelves, and with wrought-iron galleries that encircled the room; Niall had once counted them and discovered that there were precisely a hundred. Between these galleries ran black iron stairways whose steps, like the galleries themselves, were fretworked with a design based on a motif of leaves and petals. On either side of the library, an old-fashioned cage-like lift ran up to the topmost gallery.

These shelves, according to the gold plate above the door, contained copies of every book in the world, a total of 30,819,731 volumes. Every book had been photographed page by page and stored in the memory of the computer – a project that had taken an army of scholars more than fifty years. The undertaking had been inspired by the notion of the twentieth-century writer H. G. Wells, who had advocated the creation of an encyclopedia encompassing the whole range of human knowledge. This library was even more ambitious than Wells's 'world brain'; it contained, quite simply, every idea that man had ever committed to print.

The design of the room had been based upon a combination of the Reading Room of the British Museum, the Bibliothèque Nationale, and the Vatican Library. The centre of the library was occupied by a large circular desk, staffed by librarians; from this, like spokes in a wheel, radiated blue leather-covered tables illuminated by reading lamps. Niall had never discovered the identities of the people who sat at these tables and trod softly around the galleries; he liked to believe that they were real men and women of the twenty-third century, whose identities had been captured and preserved by the miraculous technology of Torwald Steeg.

The old man was standing at the central desk, talking to one of the librarians; now he turned and beckoned to Niall, pointing to the nearest lift. Niall joined him as he was pulling aside the creaking concertina of a door, and followed him into the wood-panelled interior, whose rear wall bore the notice: 'Maximum load three persons.' The old man touched a button; nothing happened. He opened and closed the concertina door again; this time, the lift began to rise slowly, with a soft, whining sound. Niall had no idea how all this was accomplished, and no desire to know; he preferred to bask in the illusion that he had been transported back into an earlier century.

They stepped out at the twenty-eighth level – each level had its number cast in the ironwork of the front of the balcony. These galleries made Niall nervous, since the fretwork made it possible to see through the floor and the sides of the balcony, which were scarcely three feet high. He knew it was impossible to fall, yet would have felt more comfortable if the floor and wall had been solid.

As he followed Steeg along the gallery, Niall observed that many of the titles of the books were in Latin: *Turba Philosophorum*, *Speculum Alchamiae*, *De Occulta Philosophia*, *Aureum Vellus*; others were in Greek or Arabic. They halted before a shelf whose metal-engraved label read: Hermetica, KU to LO.

'What's hermetica?'

'Magical studies, named after the legendary founder of magic, Hermes Trismegistos – Thrice Great Hermes.' He reached up to the shelf and removed, with some effort, a large volume bound in black leather; Niall had time to read its title: *Encyclopedia of Hermetic and Alchemical Sigils*, before it was placed on one of the tables that stood in each angle of the hexagonal gallery. The book's edges were uncut, and the handmade paper was thick and unglazed.

The old man clearly knew what he was looking for; he quickly located a page towards the end of the volume.

'I think this is what you are looking for.'

The symbol on which he had placed his finger was unmistakably the same as the one on the pendant, in spite of some slight variations in shape.

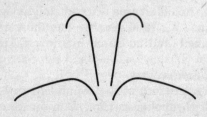

Niall bent forward eagerly, then looked up, his face wrinkled in disappointment.

'What language is that?'

'German.'

'And what does "rache" mean?'

'Revenge. The text says that this is a sigil dating from the thirteenth century, representing revenge. The lower part represents the wings of a bird of prey. The upper part represents the horns of *der teufel*, the devil. The bird of prey is winging towards its prey, carrying a terrible vengeance on its back.'

As Niall stared at it, he felt a crawling sensation in the nerves of his scalp, as if someone had poured cold water over his head; it was like a premonition of danger. He examined the sigil intently, as if he could force it to give up its secret.

'Does it say whether this was a famous symbol?'

'It doesn't, but the answer is almost certainly no. A symbol like this would be known only to students of hermeticism.'

'Then how do you suppose Skorbo's killers knew about it?'

'That is something I cannot answer.' He replaced the book on the shelf. 'Perhaps they *were* students of magic.'

As he followed him back towards the lift, Niall experienced a deep sense of frustration. It seemed absurd to be surrounded by so much knowledge, and yet to be baffled by a simple question.

'Why should anyone want to study magic?'

'Because it is far older than natural science.'

'Yes, but . . . but surely it's just a kind of superstition?'

'That is what most people believed in the nineteenth and twentieth centuries. But in the twenty-first century, many anthropologists came to a different conclusion.

71

They studied primitive tribes and concluded that some of them were able to perform certain feats of magic – rainmaking, for example.'

Niall shook his head. 'Do you believe that?'

The old man smiled apologetically. 'I do not believe or disbelieve. I am merely a machine. But Torwald Steeg was a rationalist, and he refused to believe it.'

As they stepped into the lift, Niall asked:

'And how is magic supposed to work?'

'All primitive peoples say the same thing – that magic is performed with the help of spirits.'

'But spirits don't exist, do they?'

The old man smiled. 'Torwald Steeg certainly did not think so.'

The sensation of descending brought a return of the feeling of nausea; waves of heat seemed to be rising from his stomach. Niall pulled a folding seat out of the wall and sat down.

'Are you feeling ill?'

'Just tired.' Niall closed his eyes and leaned his head back against the wall. 'One of Skorbo's killers struck me with his will-force, like a spider.'

'Although he was, in fact, a human being?'

Niall controlled his impatience. 'Of course.'

'I see.' It was at times like this that it was obvious that the old man was a machine; he had no power to register astonishment. 'In that case, I have a suggestion that might help.'

The lift rattled to a halt. As they stepped out, the old man politely held the door for a middle-aged woman in a tweed skirt; she gave them a tight smile as she stepped past them. In response to the silence around them, Niall automatically lowered his voice.

'Suggestion?'

The old man waited until they were outside before he spoke.

'If your mind has been in contact with the mind of the killer, then he has left us a clue to his identity.'

'How?'

'Every event is bound to leave a trace – that is one of the basic principles of science. And it applies to mental as well as physical events.'

Niall shook his head in bewilderment.

'But how could you *see* a mental trace . . . ?'

'It can be done – with the aid of the peace machine.'

Again Niall's scalp tingled, but this time with pleasurable excitement. It was the sensation he experienced every time he approached the tower, the excitement a child feels when he hears the words 'Once upon a time . . .'

His expression must have betrayed his feelings. The old man said:

'Do not be too hopeful. The art of self-reflection is difficult and dangerous. But you will have to learn sooner or later. Come.'

This time the old man led the way into the column. A few seconds later, they stepped into the hall of the peace machine.

This room was another of the Steegmaster's magical creations. Like the library, it was far too large to be accommodated in the tower. It was a broad gallery, about a hundred feet long, whose walls were covered with a rich brocade of blue and gold. At regular intervals there were pedestals with busts and statues. But the city Niall could see through its round-arched windows was not the spider city; to begin with, it was bathed in a sunlight so dazzling that waves of heat shimmered over its houses. The square outside contained a market, whose stalls were covered with bright-coloured canopies, and the people who crowded between them were also dressed in bright garments; many of them carried swords. The city was surrounded by turreted walls, and beyond these there were green hills with terraces and vineyards.

But Niall was now so familiar with this panorama of fifteenth-century Florence that he paid it little attention. His eyes were fixed on the machine of blue-coloured metal that stood in the centre of the gallery. This consisted of a bed or couch above which was suspended a blue metal canopy whose lower face was covered with frosted glass. Even to look at it made Niall feel serene and relaxed. This was the peace machine, invented in the mid-twenty-first century by Oswald Chater and Min Takahashi, and capable of inducing a state of consciously controlled relaxation equivalent to dreamless sleep.

But as he was about to climb on to the couch, the old man raised his hand.

'Wait. Before you do that it is important for you to understand the principles of controlled self-reflection. Please sit down.' He pointed to a bench that ran between the busts of Aristotle and Voltaire. 'To enter the state without preparation could be highly dangerous.

'You know that the first thought-reading machine was invented in the early 2090s by a team at the University of Albuquerque, led by W. S. K. Sawyer. It was Sawyer who discovered that habit-memories have a molecular structure similar to that of DNA, and that an electric current can cause them to discharge. When you try to remember something without success, this is because you are too tired to cause the memory molecule to discharge.

'One day, an assistant of Sawyer's named Carl Meiklejohn was amplifying the memory circuits of an albino rat, and feeding them through to his own temporal cortex by means of electrodes implanted in his scalp. Suddenly, he discovered that the rat had formed a strong attachment to a pretty lab assistant named Annette Larsen. Now it so happened that Meiklejohn himself was in love with Annette, but had been too shy to show his feelings. So he naturally enjoyed studying the rat's feelings towards her. In fact, he enjoyed it so much that he began to make a habit of staying behind in the laboratory so he could play the memory circuits over and over again. One evening, when he was very tired, he fell into a half-sleep as he was playing the memory circuits. And in this state, he seemed to receive a strong impression that the girl was just as interested in him as he was in her. When he returned to his normal waking state, he was inclined to believe that he had been dreaming. But he had also noticed something else while he was half-asleep: that the girl had a circular patch of brown skin on her neck between her shoulder blades. The following day, he walked up behind her when she was peering down a microscope, and saw that she had a patch of brown skin precisely where he had seen it the night before. This so impressed him that he asked the girl to go out to dinner with him. She accepted, and that night they became engaged.

'Now Meiklejohn thought a great deal about this experience. He asked the girl if she had ever allowed the rat to walk over her shoulders and the back of her neck; she said of course not. In fact, she had seldom taken it out of its cage. So how could the rat's memory contain the knowledge of the patch of brown skin? Now Meiklejohn reached an important conclusion. He recalled that the rat's memory had also told him that Annette was interested in him, and that this had proved to be true. So was it possible that the rat's memory contained far more than mere physical impressions of the girl: that because it was attached to her, it had somehow *read her mind*. And Meiklejohn, in turn, had read the rat's mind when he was half-asleep, and therefore in a state of deep relaxation.

'These conclusions were, of course, revolutionary. For it meant that a rat's memory is capable of recording impressions of remarkable complexity – impressions too complex for the rat itself to understand. And that, moreover, Meiklejohn in his waking state was unable to grasp these complex impressions. He had to be totally relaxed and on the edge of sleep.

'Now Meiklejohn realized that he had made a discovery of tremendous importance, and that it would probably win him the Nobel Prize. So he decided to keep his discovery a secret until he had conducted some further experiments. And this proved to be a mistake. One morning, he was found wandering around the university building wearing nothing but his shirt, and in a state of psychotic anxiety. Attendants from a local mental hospital had to put him in a strait-jacket. Under heavy sedation he eventually recovered, and told them what had happened. He had made recordings from the memory circuits of a stray dog. And the dog had belonged to an alcoholic who had treated it with extreme cruelty before he went insane. In a state of deep relaxation – Meiklejohn had been using the peace machine – he had played back the dog's memory circuits, and had been so shocked that he had an instant nervous breakdown.

'The story has a happy ending. Meiklejohn married Annette Larsen, and made a complete recovery; he also received the Nobel Prize. And he went on to invent a device for recording and amplifying memories which he called the psychoscope – a kind of telescope for looking into the mind. It became known to the general public as the internalizer. And the psychoscope led him to an even more important discovery: that he was able to study his own memories, and observe all kinds of complex impressions that he was not even aware of having received. For example, he discovered that Annette was pregnant at a time when neither of them had even thought of the possibility.

'Cheap forms of the internalizer became immensely popular towards the end of the twenty-first century – people love to play with their own minds. But it caused so many nervous breakdowns, and so many cases of violent crime, that governments finally banned its sale, and made private possession of internalizers illegal.'

Niall said: 'But how could it tell me anything about Skorbo's killer? I only saw him alive for about half a minute.'

'Your minds came into contact. That is enough. But before you try exploring these memory impressions, I would advise you to experiment with a few simple pictures.'

Niall found it hard to conceal his excitement. What he had just heard seemed to open up almost unimaginable vistas of possibility. There was nothing to prevent him from exploring his own past like a picture gallery, from reliving the brightest moments of his childhood, or the excitement of his first visit to the underground city of Dira. His heart was beating almost painfully as he stood up and went to the peace machine.

'Where is this internalizer?'

'There is one already built into the peace machine.'

Niall climbed on to the bed, and lay down under the frosted glass; the yielding velvet surface was as soft as eiderdown. A light came on behind the frosted glass, and there was a faint humming sound. The relaxation that instantly pervaded his body was so deep that he felt as though he was expelling the aches and fatigues of a lifetime. He had not even realized that he felt so tired, or that the encounter with Skorbo's killer had so drained his energies. Wave after wave of delight flowed from the soles of his feet up to his head, then seemed to retreat back again like the tide flowing back down a beach. In spite of his efforts to remain conscious, one of these waves picked him up and carried him into oblivion.

As soon as he opened his eyes, he remembered where he was. He sat up hastily.

'How long have I been asleep?'

'About two hours.'

The thought filled him with guilt.

'I must get back to the palace.'

'Why? You are the ruler. You can do what you like.'

This, of course, was true. Moreover, the Council meeting was over for the day. He allowed himself to relax again, adjusting the pillow under his head. Now he noticed the device that was lying beside him on the couch; it was made of half a dozen curved strips of metal, in the shape of a cap. A wire ran from it to a socket in the side of the couch.

'Place that on your head and adjust it until it is comfortable.'

On the inside of each metal strip there were a number of felt pads; when Niall touched one of these with his fingertip he discovered that it was damp. He adjusted the cap on his head, with the front strip across his forehead, the rear one at the back of his skull. There was a faint electrical tingling where the pads touched his bare skin.

Behind the frosted glass screen, the light came on again; this time he was already relaxed, so it merely induced a warm glow of pleasure.

'Now, close your eyes and try to make your mind a blank.'

Niall tried to imagine total darkness, and was surprised at his success. It was as if he was suspended in endless space. Then, with a suddenness that startled him, he heard his mother's voice.

'It has to be grated and pounded, then cooked for at least two hours. Otherwise it is a deadly poison.'

He was so surprised that he opened his eyes to make sure that she was not in the room. Even with his eyes open he could hear her voice saying:

'My grandmother used it to make a kind of wine.'

The voice of his grandfather, Jomar, said:

'She is right. It can also be ground into flour for making bread.'

The old man asked; 'What can you hear?'

'It's my mother talking to my grandfather.'

And even as Niall answered, the conversation continued. Suddenly, Niall could recall exactly when it had taken place. He was about seven years old, and the family had only just moved into the burrow, the lair of the tiger beetle on the edge of the desert. Before that, they had lived in a cave at the foot of the great inland plateau; but it had been hot, uncomfortable and unsafe. By comparison, the burrow was cool and secure. When they first moved in, it had smelt of the acrid smoke of the burnt creosote bushes that had been used to drive out the tiger beetles. Now, as Niall listened to his mother and grandfather discussing how to cook the roots of the cassava plant, he could also smell the burnt creosote wood. There was another smell which he found more difficult to place; then it came back: the poultice made from the crushed root of the devil plant, which had been used to dress the wound in his grandfather's thigh – a wound made by the mandibles of a dying tiger beetle.

As Niall lay there, he experienced many conflicting emotions and sensations. A part of him had become a seven-year-old boy, with all the feelings and thoughts of a seven-year-old. Yet he was also aware of his older self lying there on the couch of the peace machine, conscious of the presence of the child inside him. It seemed incredible that his memory had preserved this section of his childhood with such precision and exactitude, with every single word spoken by his mother and grandfather, and later by his cousin Hrolf, and Hrolf's mother Ingeld. And this recognition of the reality of his own past induced a feeling of elation, of sheer joy in being alive, together with a certainty that all the problems of human life are trivial, and that human beings only take them seriously because they are stupid and short-sighted. All these insights were so powerful that they seemed self-evident, as if he had known them all his life.

The old man's voice interrupted his thoughts.

'Can you see where you are?'

'No.'

'Very well. I want you to keep your eyes tightly closed, but *imagine* opening them.'

At first it was difficult to follow this instruction. When he tried to imagine opening his eyes, he felt his eyelids twitch, and caught a glimpse of the glass panel above him. Then he tried placing his hands over his eyes, so that it was impossible to open them, and envisaged lying on his bed of rushes in the burrow, with his mother only a few feet away. Quite suddenly, the cave was there, and he could see the face of his grandfather, illuminated by the single oil lamp. It seemed incredible that his father's father, who had been dead for more than three years, should be sitting there in all his living reality, talking to Niall's mother Siris, who sat with her back towards him. With a sudden total depth of conviction, Niall reflected that time is an illusion.

The old man said: 'Have you succeeded?'

'Yes.'

'Very well. Now I want you to try something rather

more difficult. I want you to *change* this scene completely.'

Niall said: 'How?' The idea seemed absurd. He was there, in the cave, listening to his mother and grandfather, and waiting for his father and his uncle Thorg to return from a hunting trip.

'Imagine some other scene, and try to *see* it.'

Niall tried to envisage the outside of the burrow, with its grey-looking shrubs and creosote bushes, and the tree-like euphorbia cactus; but it made no difference. Then, suddenly, everything became dark. A moment later, his mother was saying:

'It has to be grated and pounded, then cooked for at least two hours. Otherwise it is a deadly poison.'

His grandfather's voice replied:

'It can also be ground into flour for making bread . . .'

The old man asked: 'What is happening?'

'It's gone back to the beginning.'

'Good. Now try again.'

Niall tried concentrating. This made the voices fade; but when he stopped concentrating, they came back again. In some strange sense, his efforts seemed to be counterproductive.

The old man said: 'Try imagining something that gave you great pleasure.'

Niall tried to conjure up the first time he had seen Princess Merlew. She had been standing beside her father, King Kazak, in the throne room of the underground city, and her red-gold hair had been held in place by a circlet of gold. He could still remember the way his heart had lurched when she smiled at him, showing the white, even teeth that were unstained by the juice of berries. He could feel the softness of her skin as they clasped forearms in greeting . . .

Then, with a suddenness that startled him, he was holding her in his arms, and she was saying: 'I've come

82

to take you back with me.' Her mouth was warm against his ear, and he could feel the curves of her body through the red spider-silk of the dress. His own voice replied: 'You know I can't do that.' At that moment, Niall recalled that they were no longer in the underground city, but in the city of the bombardier beetles, and that he was waiting for an audience with the Master. And now Merlew was checking the door, to make sure the latch was secure, before she lay down on the couch, and drew him down beside her. His whole body was responding to the softness of her mouth as she pressed against him. His surge of desire was so powerful that he opened his eyes, embarrassed by the presence of the old man. Like a light being extinguished, the scene disappeared. But this time he was aware of what he had done to make it disappear. He had switched his attention elsewhere, like turning his head to look at something else.

The old man had also disappeared. Niall felt relieved, and at the same time amused with his own stupidity. The old man was a machine, yet his reflexes continued to treat him as a living reality. And all this training was designed to teach him to control his reflexes.

He readjusted the metal bands, pressing the contacts against his forehead, then closed his eyes and made his mind a blank. Once again he was surprised by the total darkness that supervened, as if he was suspended in empty space. This time he turned his thoughts to his cousin Dona, whom he had seen for the first time in Kazak's underground city. He was trying to conjure up the living quarters of the house where she lived with her mother Sefna. Instead, he found himself sitting beside her on a bench in the garden of the nursery in the spider city. The sunlight was warm, and there was a hissing sound as a fountain threw a spray of water into the air. A few feet away, his brother Veig was sitting on the lawn with Runa and Mara, telling them a story. And he and Dona were looking into one another's eyes, while cautiously allowing their fingers to touch . . .

As he now looked at her – and she seemed as real as a living person – he found himself wishing that Merlew had some of Dona's gentleness and kindness, and that Dona had a little of Merlew's jaunty vitality and seductiveness. Because the image of Merlew had so recently been present to his senses, he found it easy to conjure up her presence, as if he was still holding her in his arms. For a moment, Dona receded and gave way to Merlew. By a mental effort, he caused Merlew to recede, so that he was once again sitting beside Dona. It was as if he were in two places at once, and as if the two women were both trying to occupy his consciousness. Yet his consciousness was not a room in which Dona and Merlew jostled for space; it was a unified awareness in which both women were equally present. With a sudden flash of insight, he realized that this awareness was *his* awareness, and that it depended entirely upon his own power to sustain it. With a spontaneous and instantaneous mental gesture, he blended Merlew and Dona, so they ceased to be two persons. Merlew took on the gentleness of Dona, while Dona suddenly glowed with a new seductiveness.

This result astonished him. He had become so accustomed to the vagaries of the imagination, to his mind's inability to sustain a mental image for more than a few moments, that he found it hard to believe what had happened. It was true that this new Dona-Merlew was not as real as either of the two women; he was aware that if he reached out and tried to hold her hand, she would dissolve back into her constituents. Yet he could look at her, could study the amazing way that Merlew's pale skin blended in to Dona's golden-brown complexion, and the way that Merlew's blue eyes and Dona's brown eyes united in an intermediate shade of green. Even their clothes had blended, and the new Dona-Merlew was wearing a nursemaid's blue tunic made of a clinging spider-silk that emphasized the curves of her body. But what surprised Niall most of all was that the new girl, although less real than either Dona or Merlew, was undoubtedly a separate individual, a human being with her own unique reality. It seemed impossible to believe that she was merely a fantasy, a creation of his own mind.

The old man's voice said: 'You may find it simpler to use this.' When he opened his eyes, no one was there, but on the pillow, a few inches from his face, there was a small black box, about three inches square, whose upper face contained four rows of black numbered buttons. By now, Niall knew enough of electronics to guess that it was a control unit. And since the voice issued no further instructions, he cautiously pushed the first button. This was clearly the on/off switch. The curious sense of excitement and vitality disappeared immediately, and the world around him seemed to become solid and normal. It was a sensation not unlike waking up. When he pressed it again, he experienced a slight distortion of his senses that made him screw up his eyes; this passed, and he felt once again the electrical tingling that produced such an odd sense of expectancy and interest. The effect was not unlike that of the thought mirror with which the old man had presented him on his first visit to the tower; but the thought mirror amplified the powers of concentration, as if looking at the world through a magnifying glass, while this device seemed to induce a sense of relaxation and delight, as if the sun had emerged from behind a cloud.

This feeling disappeared as soon as he pressed the second button. This time the distortion of his senses made him feel sick and giddy; when it vanished, his body felt heavy and languorous, and he was overwhelmed by a dreamy sensation that made the world seem unreal; it was like being awake and asleep at the same time. He pressed the button again, but this only had the effect of increasing the dream-like sensation until his senses blurred, and he felt as if he were hopelessly drunk. But as soon as he pressed the on/off switch, his senses cleared. It was an immense relief to be restored to everyday reality, and for the first time in his life, Niall realized that the sense of normality deserves to be regarded as a luxury.

The pleasure of exploration soon induced him to press the 'on' switch. Then he pressed the button labelled '3'. Nothing happened. He switched off and tried again. Still nothing happened. He knew that he merely had to speak aloud, and the voice of the Steegmaster would explain what was wrong. But he preferred to work it out for himself. He stared at the device in his hand, and wrinkled his nose. The first button switched it on and off. Without that, the second button would not work. Perhaps the second button had to be pressed before the third would work? He tried it, touching the second button quickly and lightly – he had already worked out that the intensity of the effect depended on how long he held it down – and then pressed the third button. The darkness that supervened told him that his guess was correct. A moment later, he was startled by the sound of birdsong, and a noise of running water. At the same time, he could smell the indefinable yet distinct odour of wet grass and leaves. But since he was still in darkness, he had no idea where he was. Then, suddenly, he was in motion, and could hear the sound of wheels on the hard road, and of the feet of charioteers. He lay flat, and tried to imagine that he was opening his eyes. This time it worked immediately, and he found himself sitting between his mother and his brother in a cart pulled by four runners. They were passing through a stretch of woodland, and the branches overarched the road and formed a green tunnel. Between the branches overhead, the sky was a deep blue, but he could see stormclouds hanging over the distant hills; as they passed between two steep banks, he could reach out and touch the wet grass. They had just landed in the country of the spiders, and were being taken to the city of the white tower. On the sea voyage from North Khaybad, Niall had saved the life of a wolf spider who had been swept overboard; this is why they were being treated as guests instead of prisoners. And now, for the first time since his birth in the desert, Niall was looking at rain-soaked woodland and hearing the song of the thrush and the blackbird. It had been one of the most memorable sensations of his life, and now, as he experienced it again, he was bathed in a sense of delight and nostalgia. Although it had been less than a year ago, it seemed to be in another lifetime, like a memory of childhood.

A moment later, this memory was suddenly replaced by another with which it seemed interconnected. This time he was marching along a moonlit road with a group of men who were dressed like slaves. In fact, they were young men from the city of the beetles, and they were setting out on a venture whose dangers were far greater than they realized: to try to gain access to the old fortress and its arsenal of weapons and explosives. Ulic, Milo, Yorg, Mostig, Crispin, Marcus, Hastur, Renfred, Kosmin, Cyprian were all drunk with the spirit of adventure; only Doggins, their leader, was aware of the danger. Within a few hours, three of them would be dead, including Cyprian, who was now marching next to Niall . . . But in the meantime, Niall breathed in the cold sweetness of the night air, and absorbed the enchantment of the silvery mist; some strange inner glow of optimism told him that tonight would change the whole direction of his life . . .

Now, at last, Niall felt he was beginning to understand some of the complexities of the internalizer. One memory had evoked another because they had some basic factor in common; and what they had in common was not simply that both experiences involved the countryside, but that both involved the same curious sense of delight and freedom.

He pressed the fourth button. Again there was darkness, but a darkness in which he could hear the sighing of the wind, and smell the sharp, salty odour of the sea. Without even having to restore the sense of sight, he knew that he was standing on top of the high mountain pass that divided the desert from the coastal plain of North Khaybad, and that he was smelling the sea for the first time. His heart swelled with a tremendous exultation. A moment later he was looking down on the green plain with its trees and bushes, and at the blue expanse of the sea that lay beyond. Then the vision blurred and darkened, and he was lying by a campfire, smelling the woodsmoke and the cold night air, and listening to sailors harmonizing the chorus of a sea shanty. He knew he was back in North Khaybad, on his way to recover the body of his father, and that their party was encamped in the midst of the same green plain he had seen from the high mountain pass.

At this point a strange thing happened. As he lay there on the couch, listening to the singing and the crackling of the fire, he felt himself drifting into sleep. It was then that he realized that his 'earlier self' must have fallen asleep at about this point, and that he had been witnessing that drift into the twilight world between sleep and waking. And now he was fascinated to observe the blurred images that wandered like slow clouds before his inner vision, and the alien voices that uttered meaningless yet strangely significant phrases – one of them said: 'His greenness will be more obstinate when he finds his tail.' Then the voices seemed to turn into water which seeped into the cracks of his unconscious mind and ran into some underground lake of darkness. The effect was so strange that it made him feel sick and dizzy, as if everything had become unreal. He groped for the 'off' button of the control unit, and felt a flood of relief as the normal world returned like daylight after a nightmare.

His curiosity about the control unit still strong, he touched the final button of the bottom row, which was labelled '20'. The result was as unexpected as it was unpleasant. He was suddenly gripped by a convulsion of sorrow and misery that struck with the unexpectedness of a summer storm or a violent blow. He was standing in the entrance to the burrow, looking down at a hideously swollen corpse which he could just recognize as that of his father. The face was black and the open eyes were bulging. The arm, wearing a copper bracelet, was flung up as if to protect the face from the fangs of an angry spider.

The old man's voice said: 'I think that perhaps you should switch off the machine.'

He was standing again by the couch. Niall's energies had been so drained by the shock that it cost him an effort of will to press the 'off' button. He said:

'Why did it do that?' Even his lips felt numb.

'The electrical pulses of the internalizer cause memory circuits to discharge. You selected a frequency connected with traumatic memories.'

'But what *good* is it?' He knew the question was irrational, but the shock was turning to anger.

'Far more than you think.' The old man's voice was so calm and reasonable that his anger evaporated. 'I would advise you to repeat the experience.'

'Why?' Niall's faith in the Steegmaster was implicit, but the idea appalled him.

'Because it will make the pain disappear. Try it.'

Bracing himself as if for a blow, Niall switched on the unit, then pressed the button labelled '20'. Again he was assailed by waves of misery as he looked at his father's distorted face; this time he even noticed the puncture marks on the underside of the arm where the spider had injected the poison. Yet he was also aware that the misery was being experienced by the Niall who was standing in the entrance to the burrow, and that he himself was feeling it at second hand.

'Again.' The old man's voice actually sounded sympathetic.

As he pressed the button, and the memory returned to the beginning, he was even more clearly aware of the gap between his present and his past self. When that past self had experienced a sense of numbness, it had been a defence against an overwhelming surge of emotion; now the emotion had lost some of its power, Niall ceased to experience the numbness. Instead, he experienced rage and pity, and a sense of the futility of his father's death.

'Again.'

This time, even the rage and pity had lost their force.

'Again.'

This time he felt only pity.

'Again.'

The pity became a sense of sadness mingled with futile regrets.

'Again.'

Now he could see that even regret and sadness were pointless; it had happened, and there was nothing he could do about it.

'Again.'

Niall shook his head.

'There's no need to do it again.'

He felt curiously calm and peaceful; he was also experiencing an odd sensation, as if he was growing physically older second by second. He asked:

'How did the machine do that?'

'It didn't. Your own mind did it. Any negative emotion can be erased by reliving it.'

To his surprise, he found himself yawning. The sense of shock had given way to a pleasant feeling of relaxation. But his brain felt tired, with the kind of fatigue he had experienced after making too much use of the thought mirror. He closed his eyes for a moment, tempted to fall asleep, then remembered why he was there, and forced himself back into wakefulness.

'You said I could learn about Skorbo's killers.'

'You wish to make the attempt now?'

'Yes, if it's possible.'

'It is possible, but perhaps not entirely advisable. You need more practice with the internalizer. I would suggest at least another day.'

Niall shook his head. 'There's not time. One of them may still be in the city, and he could be gone by tomorrow.'

'It is your choice. You understand the dangers.'

He asked with misgiving: 'Dangers?'

'You have already encountered the worst of them. Negative emotions.'

'The worst?' He could not keep a note of relief out of his voice.

'You should not underestimate negative emotion.' There was a hint of reproof in his tone.

'Of course. But if you don't object . . .'

'It is not for me to object or approve.'

Again Niall had to remind himself that Steeg was a computer, not a human being.

91

'Then tell me what I have to do.'

'First of all, concentrate upon this man. Try to envisage him clearly. It may help you to hold the pendant in your hand. Then, when you are ready, press number two, which induces the alpha state, then number nine, which amplifies short-term memory – the experiences of the past few hours. You may then begin to receive impressions. If this fails, try deepening the alpha state.'

Niall took the pendant from his pocket, and held it in his right hand. But this seemed pointless; after all, he could not see it while he was holding it. Instead, he placed the chain round his neck, so the pendant rested on his chest. Then he touched the second button. The dreamy sensation returned, accompanied by a feeling that was like falling backwards. Now he closed his eyes, and envisaged the face of the dead man, with its large eyes, beak-like nose and weak chin. For a moment it was real; then it became blurred. Even in the hour since he had seen it, the memory had faded, overlaid by other impressions. The more he tried to visualize it precisely, the less clear it became. He opened his eyes and touched the ninth button. The result was startling. He was again standing in the rubble-strewn corridor, smelling its distinctive odour of damp plaster and dust, and looking into the strange, dark eyes. He braced himself, knowing what was about to happen. There was the sensation of being struck violently in the face, while at the same time, his breathing was cut off as if someone had gripped his windpipe. His senses blurred, and everything seemed to go into slow motion. Yet because he was also observing it all from a distance, he also continued to stare into the face of his attacker, and to observe its expression of uncertainty and anxiety. He even experienced a flash of sympathy: this man was alone in a hostile city, surrounded by enemies. His safety depended on not being recognized, and now he had been recognized, he had ceased to be the hunter, and become the quarry . . .

Over the man's shoulder, Niall saw the glue spider lowering itself silently out of its hole in the ceiling. The man heard it as its feet touched the floor, and started to turn. Before he could do so, he was struck by the will-power of the spider and immobilized; moments later, he was being held down on the floor by the spider's front legs, and a fine spray of glue was being squirted into his face. At the same time, Niall's vision cleared, and he became aware that Simeon was bending over him and helping him to his feet.

He knew what would happen next, and the thought sickened him. Even as he was pressing the 'off' button, the man was leaping to his feet and reaching for the knife hidden inside his garment; then, like a light being extinguished, he vanished.

The old man said: 'You learned what you wanted to know?'

'No.'

'What happened?'

'The man was about to commit suicide, and I didn't want to see it.'

'I see.'

The calm, level voice made him feel ashamed of himself. In the silence that followed, he said:

'I'll try again.'

'One moment.' Niall paused, his finger on the control. 'Every time you do this, you use up mental energy. The more tired you become, the less you are likely to discover – the tired mind is unobservant.'

Niall knew he was right; his brain was feeling heavy and dull.

'I'll try just once more.'

'Very well. But a word of advice. The longer you hold down the second control, the deeper the alpha state.

This will increase your sensitivity. But it will also make you more vulnerable. I would suggest that you keep your finger on the off control.'

'Thanks. I will.'

He closed his eyes and made his mind a blank, deliberately inducing relaxation. Then he pressed the 'on' switch and touched the second button. The dreamy sense of unreality was a little like sinking into a sea of some soft, silky material that caressed his senses. He was aware of hovering in the borderland between sleeping and waking, where the slightest relaxation of attention would allow him to drift into sleep. A huge wooden cart with massive timber beams trundled across the threshold of his mind, while a female voice stated clearly: 'All elephants are misfits in the world of fleas.' An effort of will propelled him back towards consciousness, and he depressed the ninth button, on which his finger was already resting. He was immediately back in the corridor, running after the man in slave uniform. As he seized the shoulder of his tunic, the man stumbled and crashed sideways against the wall. The scene had the clarity of a dream, and was in such vivid detail that it seemed to be taking place in a kind of slow motion. The man was turning his head, and Niall was looking into the large eyes, and experiencing his sense of panic and desperation; it was so acute that Niall felt sorry for him. Then came the sensation of a violent blow, and the choking sense of suffocation. But this time, Niall saw the 'blow' coming: the concentration of the will, the focusing of a beam of aggression, the deliberate assault on the control centre of his nervous system. Then, as their minds came into contact, his own identity seemed to blend into that of his assailant, as if they had become the same person. For a few seconds, the man's whole life was spread out for his inspection. What he saw shocked and repelled him.

Once again, he experienced the unpleasant sensation, like a disagreeable smell, and this time was aware that it sprang from a certain ruthlessness and brutality. The sheer complexity of what he was seeing was bewildering, although its salient features were clear enough; it was a little like looking down on the earth from outer space. He needed time to study and take it in.

But already the man was springing to his feet and reaching into his bosom; his hand was emerging with the knife as Niall touched the 'off' control.

'Well?'

Niall said: 'He was a trained killer.'

'Was Skorbo the intended victim, or was he chosen at random?'

Niall had to search his memory. It was like trying to remember a dream.

'The intended victim.'

'Where do they come from?'

'Somewhere . . . underground.'

'Dira?'

'No, not Dira. Some . . . other place.'

'Do you know where?'

Niall closed his eyes and tried to focus the memory, but it was no good.

'No. It all happened too quickly.'

'That can be remedied, of course. What else did you find out?'

'Hatred . . . I could sense hatred. This man was a kind of trained butcher or executioner. And there was something else I didn't understand . . . He wasn't entirely human.'

'In what sense?'

'I don't know. It was just something I felt.'

There was a silence. Niall said:

'It seems incredible . . . that there could be another underground city. Surely you'd know about it?'

The old man shook his head.

'I am afraid our information-gathering system is not infallible.'

'But a whole city . . .'

'There *is* a curious legend that dates back to the twentieth century, a legend of space travellers from a distant galaxy who landed on earth when they were at the end of their resources. Solar radiation was deadly to them, so they built colonies underground, and created a complex civilization when mankind was still living in caves. But the hardships of living underground gradually caused their numbers to decrease. Many of those who were left began to suffer from a kind of insanity, so they turned into monsters.'

'Monsters?'

'They ceased to behave rationally. Some of them began to eat human beings. The stories declare that these people were the origin of legends about vampires, ghouls, troglodytes, and other sinister creatures from underground.'

'But is that *true*?'

The old man chuckled. 'Torwald Steeg would have said that it was obvious nonsense. But he would also have acknowledged that it is impossible to know how much truth there is in a legend.'

'Then how *can* we find out about this underground city?'

'At the moment, your main hope lies in the internalizer. Your minds were only in contact for a moment, yet you may have learned far more than you realize.'

Niall reached for the control unit, then hesitated. 'You say I should wait until tomorrow?'

'That is your decision. If you are tired, the results will be poor.'

Niall's head ached and he felt exhausted; yet his curiosity was stronger than his fatigue.

'I think I'll try just once more . . .'

He lay down, closed his eyes, and touched the 'on' button. The headache dissolved away, and he experienced an overwhelming temptation to fall asleep. He resisted this and touched the second button. It was even more difficult to resist the waves of dreamy relaxation that tried to wash away his consciousness. Before this could happen, he touched the ninth button.

Once again he was in the rubble-strewn corridor with its smell of damp plaster. But this time the experience was so vivid that it was hard to believe that it was unreal. As in a dream, the walls looked quite solid, and the floor under his feet was obviously hard. His underlying tiredness seemed to sharpen his perceptions, with the effect of slow motion. Even as he was pursuing the man along the corridor, he could see the glue spider looking out of its hole in the ceiling, and this observation made him aware that his perceptions were not confined to his memory of the event. As if in a real life situation, he could direct his attention to anything he chose. As he reached out to grab the man's shoulder, he noticed a few links of the gold chain showing from under the slave garment. Then the man stumbled and turned – Niall felt that he now knew his face as well as that of his own father or mother; he also noticed the badly shaven chin and the oddly feral quality of his teeth. When the blow came, it seemed to be like a kick deliberately aimed at his solar plexus. He was interested to observe that the man was using a kind of emotional negative energy; it was as if he had looked at Niall with hatred, and the hatred had somehow turned into a physical force, like a clenched fist. And this, Niall now realized, was because it had been directed at his own emotional centre.

As their minds came into contact he was again aware of his distaste, a desire to turn away his face, as if from an unpleasant smell. But this time he resisted the impulse, determined to try to understand as much as possible of the killer's life and background. Again there was a vertiginous sensation of seeing too many things, so many that his mind had no chance to retain them.

It was at this point that the whole quality of the experience underwent a change. So far, he had been aware that he was studying a kind of recording, a memory trace that had been fixed in time. Now, suddenly, he had the curious sensation of being in contact with a living mind. This was obviously absurd, since the man was dead. Yet the experience was unmistakable. The difference between studying a memory-recording and probing a living mind was as plain and distinct as the difference between touching the cold flesh of a corpse and the warm flesh of a living person.

His mind recoiled in fear and alarm. In that moment he became aware that both he and Skorbo's killer were standing in a narrow stone chamber, in complete darkness. There was an impression of cold. A few feet in front of them, a man was seated in a stone chair that was not unlike the throne on which King Kazak had received visitors in Dira. In spite of the darkness, the man in the chair was completely visible, as if to some sense other than sight. He was dressed in a long, black garment like a monk's robe, and his face was concealed inside its cowl. Yet in spite of being able to see in the dark, Niall was unable to see the face inside the hood; only the whites of the eyes were dimly visible, and they seemed to stare with an unblinking intensity that was unnerving.

Dark shoes with curled tips peeped out from under the robe. The only other part of the man that was visible were the hands that rested on the arms of the chair. Niall observed that these seemed to be scaly, like the skin of a lizard or a snake, although the flesh was the colour of normal human flesh. The fingers were connected together with a web of almost transparent flesh.

In the moment Niall suddenly found himself in his presence, this man was apparently questioning Skorbo's killer, who was standing before him with bowed head, in an attitude of respect. But as Niall stared with astonishment at the man in the stone chair, Skorbo's killer seemed to sense Niall's presence; a moment later, the seated man also became aware of him. Niall had the impression that the eyes had narrowed, and as they turned on him, it cost him an effort not to take a step backwards; there was an almost physical force in the stare. His bodiless state seemed to amplify his sensitivity, so that he was abnormally conscious of the personality behind the eyes. Oddly enough, there was no sense of evil or malice; only of ruthless fanaticism that was akin to blindness. He sensed that this was a being who would regard anyone who opposed or disagreed with him as an enemy who deserved to be exterminated.

The man raised his right hand from the arm of the chair and pointed at Niall with a finger that seemed to have a claw instead of a nail; it might have been a gesture of admonishment. As he did so, Niall experienced an agonizing sensation in his chest. It felt as though some small crab-like creature had leapt on to his chest and clung there, gripping with sharp little claws that seemed to extend in a circle, like those of certain bugs or lice. The pain made him gasp; yet as his fingers tried to tear it away, he could see there was nothing there.

A moment later, he was back on the couch in the white tower, and the sun was streaming in through the window. His feeling of relief gave way to horror as he realized that the invisible entity was still tearing at his chest, as if intent on eating its way into his heart. The internalizer had been switched off, the room looked solid and normal. Yet he was still aware of the gaze of the narrow brown eyes, and of the intense pain in his chest. As his hands clawed at the neck of his tunic, they snapped the fine gold chain that held the pendant round his neck; it flew across the room and landed on the floor. At that moment, the pain stopped, and he ceased to be aware of the brown eyes.

'What happened?'

Niall shook his head; once again, he felt drained and exhausted. But this time it was not the tiredness that follows a shock, but an aching sense of fatigue, as if he had just been subjected to some enormous strain that had brought him to the verge of physical breakdown.

He pointed at the pendant, which was lying against the wall.

'That thing nearly killed me.'

The old man picked it up.

'That is impossible. It is merely a piece of metal.'

Niall felt too exhausted to argue. He said:

'It's some kind of transmitter.'

The old man shook his head.

'My analysis indicates that it is an alloy of copper and zinc, with a trace of gold. It is quite solid, and therefore contains no transmitter.'

'I don't give a damn what your analysis says.' Niall was aware that his tiredness was causing his voice to choke with frustration. He forced himself to be calm, and allowed his head to sink back on the pillow. The peace machine immediately began to vibrate – he realized this was an automatic response to his tension – and he experienced an instant sense of relief. 'Please switch that thing off.' The vibrations ceased. 'I don't want to go to sleep. I want to find out what happens.'

'Yes, of course. I understand.' The mechanically

soothing voice caused a wave of irritation, and he had to remind himself that it would be pointless to lose his temper with a machine. 'Please describe what happened.'

Niall drew a deep breath. 'I found myself standing in a dark room with Skorbo's killer. There was an old man sitting on a kind of throne – a man in a long black robe. And when he realized I was there, he attacked me with his mind.'

'At which point, I realized you were having a nightmare, and switched off the machine.'

'It was not a nightmare!' Niall found it hard to keep his voice down. 'I'm certain he was real.'

'Very well, he was real.' The flat, reasonable voice was infuriating. 'And what of Skorbo's assassin?'

'He was real too. He was the first one to notice me.'

'Then he was not dead after all?'

'Yes, he's dead.' His own voice sounded dull and flat.

'How is that possible? You said he was alive.'

'I said he was real. Perhaps he was some kind of a ghost.'

'The Steegmaster does not make allowance for the existence of ghosts, except in the psychological sense. Torwald Steeg believed that ghosts are a primitive superstition.'

Niall spoke with his eyes closed. 'I don't care what Steeg believed. I'm telling you what happened.' The peace machine switched on again; as the waves of relaxation flowed through him, Niall was tempted to allow it to soothe away his tiredness and frustration. But something in him revolted at this surrender to mere physical comfort. He said: 'Turn that thing off. We've got to get to the bottom of this.'

'Of course.' The vibrations ceased. 'But please consider what I am saying. Your description bears all the hallmarks of a nightmare. You insist that it was real. But you forget that the psychoscope has the power to make dreams appear to be realities.'

It sounded highly plausible. Niall realized suddenly that the old man could be right after all.

'But why should a nightmare make me feel so exhausted?'

'This is why I warned you against using the psychoscope when you are overtired. Tiredness creates negative emotions, and the psychoscope amplifies them.'

'But would it make me feel as if something had drained all the life out of me?'

'Not normally. But that is something that can easily be tested.'

'How?'

'By measuring your life-field.' He passed out of Niall's line of sight, behind the peace machine, and emerged a moment later holding two retractable wires – coiled so they were like long springs – which terminated in bell-shaped cups. He held out one of these to Niall. 'Please place this against your inner thigh.' Niall raised his tunic and pressed the cup against his flesh, where it immediately attached itself. 'Please moisten your lower lip.' He pressed the second cup against Niall's lip; Niall felt his flesh sucked inward as it gripped.

'What does it do?'

'Measures the electrical field associated with your vitality.' He disappeared behind the machine; there was a humming sound, which lasted only a few seconds.

Niall said: 'Well?'

'That is strange.' He detached the two cups. 'Your lambda reading is down to 8.5.'

'And what should it be?'

'A normal reading is between 10.5 and 11.'

'So it could have been real?' He experienced a sinking

of the heart; it had been pleasant to believe that the man with the webbed fingers had merely been a dream.

'Not necessarily. You forget that your energies were drained by the man who attacked you. And the psychoscope uses up a great deal of vital energy.'

'Don't you have some machine for putting it back again?'

'Of course.' Niall looked at him with surprise; his comment had been intended as a joke. 'The peace machine has an inbuilt Bentz apparatus for inducing an artificial life-field. That should at least restore your electrical potential.'

Niall's weariness was turning into a headache, accompanied by a feeling of nausea.

'Can it stop me feeling sick?'

'I think so.'

A bright blue light came on behind the frosted glass panel, accompanied by a whining sound that soon passed beyond the range of audibility. The light hurt his eyes, and he closed them tight. Then, as the sound faded, his headache faded with it. At the same time he began to experience a curious inner glow of optimism. He felt an absurd desire to chuckle, and a sensation that made him feel slightly breathless, as if someone had sprayed ice-cold water in his face. He gasped and drew a deep breath as the weariness turned into a pleasure that was close to pain. There was a brimming sensation of vitality, one curious consequence of which was a tickling sensation at the back of his throat; a moment later, this exploded into a sneeze. The blue light immediately vanished, and the serenity gave way to a feeling of normality that was like waking up. He groped in his pocket for his handkerchief; as he blew his nose, there was a flash of pain in the back of his skull.

The old man stood silently, looking at the dial. The silence lasted so long that Niall asked: 'Is something wrong?'

'Something is causing your life-field to leak.'

He felt a twinge of alarm. 'What does that mean?'

'It means that we are dealing with some unknown factor that I cannot explain.'

Niall watched with curiosity as he picked up the pendant on its broken chain, carried it to the other end of the room, and dropped it into a cylindrical object that might have been a waste paper basket made of copper-wire mesh.

'What are you doing?'

'Taking a simple precaution. The rupture of your biophysical membrane suggests that you have been in contact with some hostile entity. If this pendant is its transmitter, then an electromagnetic field will render it harmless.'

'So you think it wasn't a nightmare after all?'

'I cannot judge. Your earlier encounter may have done more damage than you think.'

Even as he was speaking, Niall could feel the euphoria induced by the Bentz apparatus leaking away, like air escaping from a punctured balloon.

'Can the damage be repaired?'

'Certainly. It will heal itself in due course, like a cut or graze. But the process can be accelerated by the Bentz apparatus.'

As he spoke the blue glow radiated from behind the frosted glass, and the electrical hum rose in pitch until it passed beyond the range of the human ear. This time the glow was less intense; it might have been the pale blue of a winter sky. The sensations that accompanied it were correspondingly less intense; but the headache dissolved slowly, as if blown away by a faint breeze.

As the vitality seeped back into him, like water into

parched earth, Niall suddenly knew, beyond any possibility of doubt, that the man in the black robe was a reality, and that his own life was now in danger.

It was already dark when he emerged from the tower, and the temperature had dropped below freezing. In the cold black sky the stars looked like fragments of white ice; a faint glow on the western horizon announced the rising of the moon. The snow had frozen, so that with every footstep he had to crunch through the hard surface. In the great avenue, lights glowed behind windows, and the sound of music drifted on the bitter wind. He had always found it pleasant to observe lighted windows, particularly in upper storeys; in the days of slavery, human beings had been confined to basements, and lights had to be extinguished soon after dusk. But now he experienced only a sense of foreboding; it was as if the human beings in the lighted rooms were too vulnerable.

One thing was clear: the killers had time on their side. The tree that had struck Skorbo to the ground had been planted at least a year ago, the symbol of revenge hidden beneath its roots. If necessary they could afford to wait another year to claim their next victim . . . Yet the tree had failed to kill Skorbo, and one of the executioners had died as he tried to redeem the failure; that proved they were not infallible.

In the entrance hall of the palace, the log fire still blazed in its huge grate. His brother Veig was standing in front of it, one arm round a girl as he whispered in her ear. The sound of the closing door made them break apart, and she ran away towards the kitchen – Niall recognized her as the prettiest of the kitchen maids, a girl called Nyra. He felt a twinge of envy – not for his brother's amorous escapades, but for the simplicity of his life.

Veig said cheerfully: 'Had a hard day, brother?'

'A long one.' Niall stretched out his hands towards the blaze.

'Why don't you take a day off. You *are* the king, you know.'

Niall accepted the bantering tone without resentment; he understood the difficulties of his brother's position. Veig had always been fond of his younger brother, as well as highly protective. Now, suddenly, he was merely the king's elder brother, with nothing much to do but hang around the city and flirt with pretty girls. A less amiable man might have been envious and resentful; Veig was far too good-natured for that. But he still felt the need to assert his independence.

Nephtys leaned over the stone balustrade above them.

'Are you ready to eat, my lord?'

'Yes, I am.' It had reminded him that he had not eaten since breakfast, and was famished. He asked Veig: 'Have you eaten?'

'Yes, but I'll join you in a glass of wine.'

It had been many months since the brothers had shared a meal together. Niall had been too busy with his duties, while Veig seemed determined to make up for the years during which he had been starved of female company. Even now, as they mounted the stairs behind Nephtys, his eyes studied the shapely legs under the short tunic.

In Niall's chamber, burning wood crackled in the stove, and the air was full of its smell. Jarita, the maid-servant, was already setting out food on the low table.

Nephtys pointed to a long bundle wrapped in sacking, which leaned against the wall inside the door.

'A man brought that for you.'

'Do you know his name?'

'Yes. The overseer, Dion.'

Niall laid the bundle on the floor, and unwrapped the sacking. It was an axe, with a haft about four feet long. The shining blade was stained with dried blood. Etched into the blade was the sign with which he was already familiar: the symbol of revenge.

'Did he say where it had been found?'

'He said in the garden, among the undergrowth.'

Veig picked it up and swung it through the air.

'It's beautifully balanced. And as sharp as a razor.'

'Be careful. It's the axe that killed Skorbo.'

'I guessed that.' Veig tested the blade with his thumb, then snatched his hand away. 'My god, it's sharp!' A drop of blood ran down his thumb.

'Go and wash it, quickly!' Niall was remembering the poisoned knife that had killed Skorbo's assassin in a matter of seconds. To his horror, Veig licked the cut and said casually: 'It'll be all right.' It was only when, a minute or so later, Veig was still obviously unaffected that he allowed himself to relax.

Niall rewrapped the axe in its sacking, and handed it to Nephtys. 'Here, take it away.'

Veig threw himself down on a heap of cushions, and poured two glasses of the pale golden mead; it had been freshly made, and was still sparkling with rising bubbles. He drank down half the glass in one draught, then lay back with a smile of contentment.

'Well, whoever killed Skorbo did a good job.'

Niall shook his head warningly, glancing towards Jarita, who had just entered the room with a dish of roast skylarks. Veig grinned broadly and raised his eyebrows. With his curly black hair and bright blue eyes, he exerted a charm that made it impossible to be annoyed with him. When Jarita had left, he asked:

'Don't you trust her?'

'Of course, but I don't want to shock her. You forget that most of the people in this city still think of the spiders as their masters.'

'That may be so.' Veig picked up a roast skylark and dipped it in the savoury sauce. 'But they still hated Skorbo.'

'Why? Most of them didn't even know him.'

Veig chewed and swallowed before he replied, wiping the gravy from his beard with the back of his hand. 'But they knew all about him.'

Niall was intrigued by his tone. '*What* did they know about him?'

'He had a reputation as a brute. He enjoyed killing human beings. They say he even enjoyed killing children – not just to eat them, but for the fun of making them scream. And of course, they say he's never stopped.' Veig returned to gnawing the bird.

'Never stopped what?'

'Killing and eating human beings.'

Niall stared at him incredulously. 'Are you serious?'

'Didn't you know?' Veig shook his head in mild surprise. 'I thought everybody knew.'

Niall put down the bird he was eating.

'Where did you hear that?'

'I think Sidonia told me.' Sidonia was the captain of the Spider Lord's household guard; Veig was known to spend much of his time in her company.

'But *what* did she tell you?'

'Oh, that Skorbo and a bunch of his cronies didn't like the idea of giving up human flesh. Besides, they'd got quite a few left over from the days of slavery. They thought it'd be a pity to let all that meat go to waste, so they went on eating it.'

Niall heaved a sigh of relief.

'I thought you meant they were *still* eating people.'

'So they are. Nyra told me that one of her brothers disappeared a few weeks ago.'

'Nyra? That girl from the kitchen? Then why didn't she report it to me?'

Veig resumed his bird. 'I think most people assumed you knew about it.'

Niall felt stunned.

'They really thought I'd allow *that* to go on?'

'Well . . . I suppose they thought there was nothing you could do about it.'

Niall had to make an effort to keep his voice under control. He said:

'When the Spider Lord agreed to end slavery, she also agreed that there should be no more killing of human beings. The terms of the treaty were that men and spiders should be free and equal. Now you tell me the spiders have never kept their side of the bargain . . .' He took a drink of mead to steady his voice.

Veig said mildly: 'Don't blame me.'

'I'm not blaming you.' Niall felt as if the ground had collapsed under his feet. 'But are you certain the Spider Lord knew about this?'

'Oh no, I didn't say that. I'm pretty sure she didn't. What Sidonia told me was that Skorbo and a few of his mates resented the idea of not eating human flesh. So they went on eating the people in their larder. And when they'd finished those, I suppose they decided to restock the larder.'

Niall picked up the handbell on the table and rang it. Jarita hurried into the room.

'Go down to the kitchen and ask Nyra to come up here.'

'Yes, lord.'

When they were alone, Niall chewed moodily at a piece of bread crust; his appetite had all but vanished.

Veig was eating with undiminished gusto. Niall said:

'I can't understand why you didn't tell me the moment you learned about it.'

Veig looked embarrassed.

'As a matter of fact, I didn't come back to the palace for a couple of days.'

'Then why didn't you tell me as soon as you came back?'

'You weren't here then. You were inspecting the harbour installations. You always seem to be so busy that I didn't like to disturb you.' He picked up a napkin and dabbed at his bleeding thumb. 'You always work so hard that you make me feel like a layabout.'

Niall felt a glow of affection for his brother; but it was still outweighed by his sense of foreboding.

'There's nothing to stop you working.'

'At what?' Veig spread out his hands. 'I'm no good on committees and councils. What else is there for me to do except lounge around and eat too much?' It was true that Veig had put on a great deal of weight recently. 'But I'll tell you one thing.' He spoke with sudden seriousness. 'I've often wished I was back in the desert and setting out for a good day's hunting.'

Niall grunted. 'There aren't any girls in the desert.'

'Oh, you can have too much of anything . . .' He was about to say more when they were interrupted by Jarita's return; she was followed by Nyra. The kitchen maid was a shapely girl in her early teens, with soft brown eyes and a startlingly perfect profile. The beauty of the girls in the spider city never ceased to amaze Niall, even though he knew it was the result of selective breeding.

She stood in front of them, her eyes downcast, her hands clasped over her apron. Her long brown hair had been plaited, and coiled around her head – one of the rules for girls working in the kitchen.

Niall said: 'Veig tells me that one of your brothers has disappeared?' She nodded, evidently too nervous to speak. Niall tuned in to her thoughts, and realized that she was almost paralysed with self-consciousness. It shocked him to realize that she regarded him as an almost godlike being, and that she was afraid he had sent for her to dismiss her for flirting with Veig. He said gently:

'Tell me what happened.'

She cleared her throat. 'He went out after dark and didn't come back.'

'Where do you live?'

'In the street of the leather beaters.'

'Is it very dark?' She nodded. 'And where did he go?'

'Across the street to see a friend. He'd left his horse there.'

'His horse?'

'A wooden toy. He just ran across to get it.'

'Did you go out and look for him?' She shook her head. 'Why not?'

'We don't go out after dark.'

'Why not?'

'It's not really allowed . . .'

'But that was in the days of slavery! Now you can go anywhere.'

She nodded, her eyes still on the ground, her cheeks bright red with embarrassment. Suddenly Niall understood. This girl's family found it difficult to adjust to their new freedom. It was almost impossible to break the habit of a lifetime. This was why they had failed to report the child's disappearance. He had been out after dark, and that was against the law; therefore they had been punished.

'Have you heard of any more disappearances?'

'Only one. A girl in the next street.'

'Did anyone see or hear anything?'

'No.'

That was to be expected. A spider dropped silently out of the dark, paralysing its victim with will-force, and whisked him back into the air in a matter of seconds; there was almost nothing to see or hear.

'All right. Thank you, Nyra. I'll see if there's anything I can do.' She was still so tongue-tied and self-conscious that he had to add 'You may go' before she curtseyed and hurried out of the room. Veig stared after her with admiration. Niall had shared the feeling when she came in; now it had evaporated. Looking into her mind had made him aware of her essence, which was that of a normal teenager of average intelligence. Veig, who lacked his brother's telepathic powers, was entranced by her remarkable beauty, and therefore possessed by a desire to explore it and discover whether her mind was equally fascinating. Niall knew in advance that he would be disappointed – and yet that there was no possible way in which he could share the insight with his brother. This realization saddened him and made him thoughtful.

Veig said: 'What are you going to do?' He was pouring another glass of mead.

'I shall have to speak to the Spider Lord.'

'Is that a good idea?' The thought of voluntarily seeking a confrontation with the Spider Lord appalled him.

'Why not?'

'It might only make things worse . . .'

'That's why Skorbo was able to go on killing human beings – because no one dared to say anything about it. If someone had told me sooner, Nyra's brother might still be alive.'

'I suppose you're right.' He was obviously unconvinced.

There was a light tap on the door, and Nephtys came in.

'The doctor would like to speak to you, my lord.'

Veig asked: 'Doctor?'

'That's what they call Simeon. There was no such thing as a doctor in this city before he came. Ah, come in, Simeon. Would you like a glass of wine?'

'Thanks. I need one.' Simeon looked and sounded tired. Nephtys took his cloak, while Jarita helped him to take off his boots, which were covered with snow. He sank down with a groan of relief on to the cushions, and accepted the glass of mead that Veig offered him. He drank with obvious appreciation, then sighed deeply.

Niall asked; 'Where have you come from?'

'The slave quarter.' He was already helping himself to one of the birds.

'Did they find the other assassin?'

'Oh yes, they found him.' Simeon spoke through a full mouth.

'Where is he now?'

'Dead.'

'How? Did he kill himself, like the other one?' Still chewing, Simeon shook his head. 'Did a spider kill him?'

'No.' Simeon swallowed. 'The spider had him pinned down so he couldn't move a muscle. The first thing I did was take his knife away. Only then did the spider release him. I asked him questions, but he didn't reply – he pretended not to understand. So I told the spider to hurt him a little – I didn't like doing it but I wanted to learn where he came from. The spider squeezed him a little and he screamed. But he still wouldn't talk. I'll say this for him, he was a brave man.'

Niall winced at the picture Simeon conjured up. When Simeon spoke of squeezing he was not referring to physical pressure. A fully grown death spider could squeeze a man by sheer will-force, like a nut in a nutcracker, until he felt his bones cracking under the pressure. Niall had experienced it in his first encounter with the Death Lord, and the thought still made him shudder.

'What happened then?'

'They decided to take him back to the headquarters of the Spider Lord. I followed on in a chariot. But halfway across the bridge, they sent for me to come and examine him. He was dead.'

Veig said: 'Probably died of fright.'

'No. It looked like a heart attack – blue lips and a dead white face.'

Niall asked: 'Where is he now?'

'In the mortuary.'

'I'd like to see him.'

Simeon and Veig both stared at him with amazement.

'What for?' Simeon obviously suspected him of harbouring some morbid obsession about corpses.

'There's something I'd like to find out.'

Veig asked: 'Is it a secret?'

'No.' He turned to Simeon, who had resumed eating. 'Was this man wearing a pendant around his neck?'

'Yes.'

'Did you remove it?'

'No. Why should I? It was the same as this one.' He gestured towards his chest.

Niall experienced a chill that was like a cold wind.

'You're wearing it round your neck?'

'Yes. Why not?'

Niall kept his voice calm and casual.

'Could I see it please?' He held out his hand. Simeon was obviously puzzled; nevertheless he reached under his tunic, lifted the gold chain over his head, and handed the pendant to Niall. As Niall held it in the palm of his hand, he felt for a moment that it was alive, like some small insect; he dropped it hastily. A moment later, when he picked it up again, the sense of life had vanished; it was merely a piece of metal alloy. Moved by some natural instinct, he dropped it into his glass of mead. The other two were watching him with astonishment.

Simeon asked: 'What was all that about?'

Niall hesitated, realizing that it would sound absurd; for a moment he even thought of prevaricating, then decided against it. He gestured at the glass.

'I think that's what killed him.'

Simeon shook his head in bewilderment.

'Why?'

Niall said: 'Why do you suppose they were all wearing these things around their necks? As some kind of decoration? That would be stupid. If one of them was caught, it would mean that the other two could be identified more easily. No, it's some kind of communicator.'

Both of them stared at the pendant, which was now coated with bubbles. Simeon asked:

'What makes you think so?'

'I took the other one into the white tower.'

Simeon nodded. 'Aha, I see!'

Niall allowed the misapprehension to stand; it saved explanation.

Veig said: 'But why did you put it in there?'

'Because wine is alive. The vibrations might confuse it.'

Simeon said: 'But a communicator can't kill.'

Niall said: 'I think this kind can.'

Veig was still unsatisfied. 'But *why* do you think so?'

For a moment Niall considered telling them about his experience in the tower, then dismissed the idea; it would take too long, and place too great a demand on their credulity. The internalizer had to be experienced

116

to be understood. Instead he said:

'It's just a guess. That's why I'd like to see the body.' He asked Simeon: 'Will you come with me?'

'Of course. But do you mind if I finish eating first? He won't get up and walk away.'

'I'm sorry.' Niall had forgotten that Simeon was tired. 'Please don't hurry.'

Aware that he had sounded brusque, Simeon said: 'You haven't finished eating either.'

'No, of course.' Niall forced himself to eat a piece of buttered bread; but his appetite had gone.

As Veig and Simeon emptied the carafe of mead, he pretended to listen to their conversation. But as his thoughts revolved around the pendant, and the man with the pointed head, he found himself wishing that he could talk to Dravig; it was so much easier to communicate with an intelligent spider than with a human being. The image of the man in the black robe was so vivid that he seemed to be able to see the bushy eyebrows, the pointed ears, the webbed fingers, and had to shake his head to disperse the illusion. A moment later he was staring at the rising bubbles in the glass, and experiencing a curious passivity that was akin to hypnosis.

There was a thunderous knocking that shocked him into attention; he started as if from sleep. A moment later he realized with astonishment that it had only been the sound of Nephtys tapping at the door.

She said: 'The Lord Dravig is here, my lord.'

'Good. Ask him to come in.'

Veig and Simeon clambered to their feet as Dravig entered the room; they were sufficiently conditioned to feel uncomfortable remaining seated in the presence of a spider. Niall acknowledged the gesture of obeisance with an inclination of his head.

'I am glad to see you.'

Dravig said: 'I felt that you wanted to see me – that is why I came.'

The other two resumed their seats. Aware that spiders had a distaste for the sight of human beings engaged in eating, Niall said: 'Let us go into the other room.' He asked Nephtys: 'Please tell Jarita to bring more wine for my guests.'

The bedroom was illuminated by the clear light of the moon, which shone through the window, and by the red glow from the stove. Niall said:

'Simeon has told me about the man's death. Do you know how it happened?'

'No. But I suspect he was killed.'

'So do I.' For several moments neither of them spoke; since their minds were open to one another, there was no element of discomfort in the silence. Then Niall said:

'Do you know this man?'

He accompanied the words with a mental image of the man in the black robe; it was exactly as if he had shown Dravig a photograph.

'No. Who is he?'

'The man who sent the killers.'

Dravig said: 'Then your own life is in danger.' He had made this statement out of his total grasp of the situation, and again Niall experienced the satisfaction of direct communication. He said:

'I know.'

'You must take special precautions. I will send guards to stand outside your palace.'

'Thank you.' Niall disliked the idea, but he knew it was common sense. Anyone could walk into the palace at any time. Until today he had felt totally secure. But the man who had been responsible for the death of two assassins was himself an obvious target for assassination.

Dravig said: 'I will go and attend to it now.'

'Wait. There is something else I have to talk to you about. Did you know that Skorbo was still killing and eating human beings?'

'No!' The force of Dravig's surprise made it evident that he was speaking the truth.

'My brother tells me that many people knew about it, including Sidonia, the commander of the Death Lord's guard.'

'Then why did she not speak? She shall be punished.'

'No. She is not to blame. Like the others, she assumed the Death Lord knew about it.'

'That is absurd!' Dravig was close to anger. 'The Death Lord gave you her word, and her word is sacred.'

'I know that. But the human beings of this city do not yet understand it. They must be given time to learn.'

Dravig had already sensed the next thought that Niall was about to express.

'Was Skorbo the only one?'

'No. I gather there were a number of others – Skorbo's close associates.'

'I know who they must be. Skorbo had his own special friends – all came from the same region of Astigia, where the Black God of the Mountain is worshipped. I was told they were infidels, but I never believed it until now. They must be punished.'

'Is that wise?' The spider expressed incomprehension. 'It might cause resentment to punish spiders for killing human beings.'

'It must be so. They have not only disobeyed the will of the Death Lord, but the will of the goddess. That is an offence punishable by death.'

Niall was silent; he had no particular desire or reason to defend Skorbo's murderous associates.

Dravig sensed that the conversation was at an end.

'With your permission I will leave you.'

'Wait. I'm coming with you.'

Nephtys was still keeping guard at the door; Niall told her to summon his charioteers.

'Are we ready to go?' Simeon rose to his feet.

Niall turned to Dravig. 'I would like you to accompany us to the hospital.' With the equivalent of a human nod, the spider transmitted his aquiescence.

Simeon said: 'I think your brother had better come too. I'd like to do something about that thumb.'

'Is it still bleeding?' He saw that the handkerchief around Veig's thumb was soaked in blood. When Veig removed it, blood welled out of the clean cut. 'Why isn't it clotting?'

Simeon said: 'My guess is that there was an anti-coagulant on the blade. I've got a poultice that should cure it.'

Outside, it was a cold and brilliant night; the moon was almost directly overhead. As they stood waiting for the charioteers, Niall looked across the square to the house where Skorbo had been attacked. To his surprise, it was no longer there; instead there was merely a gap. Dravig followed the direction of his gaze.

'It has been demolished. We regard a house where a murder has taken place as unholy ground.'

Niall asked: 'Did the workmen find the leaden seal?'

'I have not been told of it. But I will make enquiries.'

Simeon, who had been able to hear Niall's part of the conversation, asked:

'Do you think the seal is a transmitter?'

'It's possible. What did you do with the pendant?'

'It's here.' Simeon patted his pocket.

'Be careful. It could be dangerous.'

The charioteers, muffled in furs, finally arrived. Niall climbed in, followed by Veig and Simeon.

'Take us to the hospital.'

Dravig followed the chariot, walking with long

unhurried strides; even when the charioteers were running, it cost him no effort to keep up with them.

Niall looked at his brother, who was sitting between them, and then down at his bandaged hand – Jarita had provided a long strip of cloth.

'How do you feel?'

Veig grinned cheerfully. 'Fine.' He held up his hand; the bandage was already stained with blood. 'It won't stop bleeding, but otherwise there's nothing wrong.'

But as the chariot bounded and jarred on the frozen snow, Niall observed his brother's face with concern; it seemed unnaturally pale, with a pallor that was more than an effect of the moonlight.

The front door of the hospital building was closed, but opened when Niall pushed against it. Simeon led them down the dimly lighted corridor, which smelt of chlorinated lime and medication. A woman in slave uniform looked out of a doorway, but blenched and hastily retreated when she saw the spider. The door of the maternity ward stood open, and they could hear the heavy breathing of a woman in labour. Simeon turned left at the end of the corridor, and halted in front of a plain wooden door. He shook his head in annoyance.

'I told them to leave someone on guard.' He pushed open the door, then halted. 'Great goddess!'

Niall, who was directly behind him, found it difficult to see what had caused the exclamation. The small oblong room, with its white-painted walls, was lit by a single rush lamp which burned in a corner alcove; white gowns hung on the walls. Two benches stood in the centre of the room, and a third against the rear wall. On this bench lay a corpse, its feet towards the door. It was only when Niall looked more closely that he saw what had startled Simeon. The corpse had no head. A moment later, Simeon was kneeling beside another corpse that lay between the benches.

Veig peered over Niall's shoulder. 'Who's that?'

'The caretaker, Jude. Give me a knife.'

Even in the poor light, Niall could see that the dead man's face was swollen and suffused with blood, and that the lips were drawn back from the teeth in a grimace of agony.

Simeon was sawing with a knife in the region of the man's throat. He shook his head.

'It's no good. The cord's tied so tight I'd have to cut his throat to get it off. He's dead anyway.'

Dravig had followed them into the room, although his enormous bulk almost filled it. He stood looking down at the headless corpse.

'This is the man who died this afternoon.'

Niall said: 'I know.' He was looking at the cut on the forearm made by the poisoned knife.

Simeon said: 'They've taken the other body.'

Niall asked: 'Are you sure it arrived?'

'Certain. I watched them carry it in before I came to see you.'

Veig voiced the thought that was in Niall's mind.

'Perhaps he wasn't dead after all.'

Simeon said: 'He was dead all right. I'd stake my life on that.'

Niall lit a second rush light from the one in the corner, and held it near the floor.

'Look. Someone carried the head out of the door.' There were splashes of dried blood on the wooden floor.

Simeon said: 'Which means there were at least three of them.'

Veig asked: 'Why three?'

'A man carrying a severed head holds it by the hair, and he holds it away from himself to avoid the blood. That's what happened here. So there must have been three – two to carry the body, one to carry the head.'

'But why should they want the head?'

Niall was in the corridor, bent close to the floor. The trail of blood ran diagonally across it to another door. When he opened this he found himself looking into a small yard enclosed by a high wall; it was clearly illuminated by the moon, which was directly overhead. Against this wall lay a pile of chopped logs, and the snow between the door and the logs had been trampled by many feet. But the trail of blood ran across the yard, and out of a rusty iron gate, which stood slightly ajar. The snow in this part of the yard was still deep and untrampled. It showed clearly the single line of footprints that accompanied the trail of blood.

Niall pointed. 'Only one man.'

Simeon shook his head. 'That's unbelievable. Unless a dead man can walk.'

Veig said: 'Or unless he was still alive.'

Simeon said: 'He certainly looked dead.' But his tone of voice indicated that he was beginning to experience doubts.

Outside the gate, the blood trail ceased. The snow here had been trampled, and was too hard to show footprints.

Niall said: 'He must have realized he was leaving a trail.'

Veig said: 'But how could he stop it bleeding?'

Simeon grunted. 'Turn it upside down and tuck it under his arm.'

The moonlit street was empty, although lights burned in some of the buildings. Veig had dropped on to his knees and was studying the snow; Niall knew him well enough to know that his hunting instinct had been aroused. But after several minutes, he stood up, shaking his head. He pointed down the street.

'I'd guess he went that way. But only because I think

he wouldn't risk going back to the main avenue.'

Dravig asked: 'Shall I summon the guard?'

Since the others were unable to hear the question, Niall repeated it aloud. Simeon shook his head.

'If he knew he was being followed, he'd hide in the nearest empty building, and we might never find him.'

Veig was already walking along the street, away from the main avenue, his eyes on the ground; Niall recognized in the bent shoulders the total concentration of the hunter. He was attempting to allow his intuition, like an animal's sense of smell, to guide him back to the trail. And as he watched his brother, Niall suddenly became as fascinated by Veig's efforts as by their immediate objective; he recognized the peculiar 'inwardness' that he himself knew so well, the inner contraction of the faculties that seemed to awaken some hidden power.

Veig halted at the next intersection, a narrow street that was hardly more than an alleyway. The moonlight caused the houses on the left to throw a sharp black shadow. The snow here was untrampled; the only visible tracks were those of a wolf spider. Yet Veig stood there, his head turning to right and left like a tracker dog that has picked up the scent. Then he disappeared into the shadow of the building.

'Bring a lamp here.'

Niall carried his own lamp, which was shaded by a glass chimney, to the spot where Veig was standing. Veig took it from him and knelt. He gave an exclamation of satisfaction.

'This is it.'

He had, in fact, discovered a line of footprints that ran along the left-hand pavement. Niall was about to ask how he could be so sure, then changed his mind. Veig, at least, seemed to have no doubts. He handed the lamp back to Niall, and hurried forward, his body bent almost double.

A hundred yards further on, the alleyway joined the other main avenue that ran from east to west across the square. Common sense suggested that their quarry had not turned east into the square, where his position would be completely exposed, and the same reasoning suggested that he would avoid turning west into the avenue. The alternative was to cross the avenue into the narrow street which ran down towards the river. Here again the snow had been trampled, so no individual print could be distinguished. As they passed close to the rear of the house in which Skorbo had been attacked, Niall was struck by the thought that their quarry could have taken refuge in any one of a dozen empty buildings. Yet Veig continued to hurry forward without hesitation, so that by the time he reached the embankment he was almost running.

Niall was the first to see the fugitive. He was walking along the road, about fifty yards to their right, towards one of the smaller bridges that crossed the river to the slave quarter. There could be no doubt about his identity; the object he was carrying under his arm looked like a cabbage. Afraid to shout, in case he betrayed their presence, Niall flung up an arm and pointed. The man was walking slowly, in a curiously stiff, doll-like manner, as if both legs were giving him pain. A moment later, Niall felt the blast of will-force that emanated from Dravig; it was so powerful that it made him wince. He expected to see the man fall to the ground as if pole-axed. Yet, incredibly, he continued to walk, in the same stiff-legged manner, towards the centre of the bridge. Dravig was also incredulous; it was the first time in his life that a human being had failed to respond to a mental command. As they watched, the man halted and climbed on to the parapet of the bridge. Again, Dravig hurled a thunderbolt of will-force that should have knocked him backward; it had no visible effect. A moment later the man jumped; the wind carried the sound of the splash away from them.

Dravig hesitated no longer; a few strides carried him to the embankment and over its low wall. A few seconds later Niall reached the spot, expecting to see the man struggling in the water, or in the grip of the spider's forelegs. Instead he saw Dravig standing in the middle of the river – which was about six feet deep at this point – looking bewilderedly to right and left.

They hurried down the steps that led from the embankment to the flagstoned path beside the river. The slow-flowing water was flat and calm, reflecting the moonlight; the only ripples were caused by Dravig himself.

Veig said: 'He must be swimming underwater.' But as they stared intently at the smooth surface, it became clear that this was unlikely; no one could hold his breath that long.

Dravig began to wade slowly downstream, and they followed, walking under the black shadow of the bridge. As Dravig emerged from the shadow he halted, and suddenly plunged under the water. A moment later he reappeared, holding the body of a man in his forelegs. In two strides he had regained the bank. Since the body was upside down, and remained motionless, it seemed clear that the man was either dead or unconscious. Then, as he landed with a thud on the flagstones, it became obvious that he was dead. The blank eyes gazed directly ahead and the mouth gaped open like that of a fish; the right arm was still bent against his side, as if holding the head; but the head itself had escaped.

Simeon knelt beside him and touched one of his eyelids, then pinched the flesh of the cheek. When he looked up, his face was very pale.

'This man has been dead for hours.'

'How can that be?' Veig's voice sounded incredulous, almost angry.

Simeon took hold of the left arm and tried to bend it.

'Look. Rigor mortis. That doesn't set in for at least four hours after death.'

'But we all saw him walking. Dead men can't walk.'

'Can you think of any other explanation?'

Niall also touched the cheek; it was like cold rubber. There was something repulsive about the face; it was flabby, with a receding double chin and a thick, sensual mouth; the nose was like a pig's snout. Controlling his aversion, Niall tore open the tunic, exposing the white, hairless chest. He pointed to the pendant, which lay against the base of the throat.

'That's what killed him.'

Simeon asked: 'How can you be so sure?'

'Look.' Niall pointed to the circular red spot above the heart; it was about an inch in diameter and might have been a burn mark. Then he took hold of the pendant and extended it on its chain; it covered the red mark precisely. 'That's why he died of a heart attack.'

Simeon's hand went up to his own chest.

'Great goddess; I've been wearing one of those things all afternoon . . .'

Niall said: 'But he had no reason to kill you. On the contrary, it would have given him away.'

Veig said: 'But who is "he"?'

'I don't know his name. But he's some kind of magician. Only a magician could make the dead walk . . .' Niall's voice trailed off as he spoke the last words; it was as if he felt that even speaking them aloud was dangerous.

Simeon removed the pendant from round the man's neck, and handed it to Niall.

'Now at least he'll stay dead.'

As soon as Niall's head touched the pillow, he fell into a deep and dreamless sleep. Yet when he woke, two hours later, it was as if struggling out of a nightmare. He immediately experienced a strong conviction that there was someone else in the room. He raised his head and listened; there was no sound but the wind, which howled against the corner of the building. He reached out cautiously to the lamp that burned in an alcove above the bed, and turned up the wick. The yellow flame revealed that the room was empty. Yet when he stilled his senses, retreating to the silent place inside himself, he still experienced the feeling that he was being watched.

He sat up in bed and took the lamp from the wall. Then, walking silently on bare feet, he went into the next room. Yet even as he tiptoed across the floor, he felt that these precautions were absurd. It was as if the watcher was looking down on him from above, or from some direction beyond the reach of his senses.

The glass containing the mead stood on the table. Now it contained two pendants, one taken from Simeon, the other from the corpse by the river. As soon as he saw them, Niall knew he had made a mistake to put them together. Now each one reinforced the power of the other, creating a living force-field that was aware of everything that moved within its radius.

He reached out his hand towards the glass, then snatched it away; it was like trying to reach out to a striking snake. In fact, the pendants with their intertwined chains seemed to be two snakes with their coils intertwined; he felt they were daring him to reach out and touch them.

For a moment Niall considered taking them to the white tower, where they could be rendered harmless by the electromagnetic field of the Steegmaster. The thought of the freezing wind deterred him. Then he was struck by another possibility. In the basement below the hall, there were a number of stone jars made of some black, granite-like substance; they were so heavy that no one had ever attempted to move them. No one seemed to know what they had been used for. But one day the children had discovered that they possessed a peculiar property: pins, needles and small iron ornaments stuck to them so firmly they were difficult to remove. Simeon told him they had been carved from an ore named magnetite.

With an effort that cost all his power of self-discipline, Niall reached out and picked up the glass. It was hard to dismiss the idea that the two pendants were alive and about to rear up and crawl over the sides. A few seconds later, his hand began to tingle with a sensation like pins and needles. Carrying the lamp in his other hand, he went out into the corridor and down the stairs. In the hall, the air was warm, and red embers still burned in the grate. But as he crossed to the door that led to the basement, the pins and needles turned into a numbing sensation, so that he felt he had to grip the glass more tightly to avoid dropping it.

At that moment he became aware that the force-field of the glass was being reinforced from elsewhere; somewhere out in the city, an even more powerful field was joining its energy to theirs. At the same time, he seemed to be surrounded by a dull grey light that made everything unreal. The flame of the lamp was no longer necessary; the light seemed to illuminate the room like the first grey mist of dawn. The sound of his own footsteps seemed very far away. As he pushed open the door into the basement, he realized he was sweating, and that his teeth were chattering. He was seized by an overwhelming desire to put down the glass and run away; the presence that had been watching him now seemed so strong that he expected it to materialize. He was aware that the watcher was exerting all his force to make him lose control. If all this had happened a year ago, it would have succeeded. But contact with the spiders had taught Niall something of the use of his own will-power, and of the hidden force in the depths of his being. Now, as he braced himself to resist, the danger of panic receded, as if the watcher recognized that his self-control refused to be undermined.

He hurried on down the stairs to the basement. This was a great stone-flagged room that had once been a wine cellar; a few months ago it had been full of rusty wine racks and broken bottles. Now it was used as a storeroom for food; it smelt of preserved smoked meat and spices. Along the rear wall stood six black stone jars, each about three feet tall, and carved out of a veined stone whose surface showed brown streaks of rust. Niall placed the glass and the lamp on the ground, then used both hands to lift the cone-shaped plug in the neck of the nearest jar; it was so heavy that it made him gasp. He placed this on the floor, then, gritting his teeth, raised the glass and inverted its neck over the jar. The pendants fell into its depths with a faint metallic clink.

The grey light immediately vanished, and he experienced a curious inner-shift of focus. At the same time, the numb sensation left his hand and forearm – not slowly, like a limb to which circulation had been restored, but instantaneously, as if the numbness was some kind of delusion. The tension that had made his teeth chatter dissolved away, to be replaced by a relief that was so powerful that it seemed to drain him of strength. As he walked back upstairs, his legs ached as if he had walked to the point of exhaustion, and he had to hold on to the marble banister to support himself. By the time he was back in his room, waves of fatigue were making him walk like a drunken man. But as he threw himself into bed, he noticed that the sensation of being watched had disappeared; even the howling of the wind seemed friendly. As soon as he closed his eyes, he fell into a heavy sleep.

He woke up with a start, to find Jarita standing by the bed; sunlight slanted through the window.

'What time is it?'

'Two hours after dawn.'

'You shouldn't have let me sleep so late.' He threw back the bedclothes.

'I looked in twice but you were sleeping deeply. And you have no Council meeting this morning.'

'Thank you, Jarita.'

He was hoping she would go, but she continued to stand by the bed. She wanted, he realized, to help him bathe and dress. This was one of the problems of getting up late. The underground cave in which Niall had spent his childhood and youth had been extremely cramped; nevertheless, the men and women went to considerable lengths to preserve their modesty. Here in the spider city, the female servants expected to help their masters to dress and undress; they enjoyed anointing his body with scented oils, and even climbing into the bath with him and administering a massage in the warm water. Veig openly revelled in all this attention, surrounding himself with attractive slaves. Niall also enjoyed being pampered, but he found that he preferred to be alone when he dressed; it seemed oddly pointless to allow someone else to help him put his clothes on. This is why he liked to rise with the dawn. Now he realized that Jarita would regard it as a rejection if he declined her services. So he stood there passively, and allowed her to remove the knee-length tunic that he wore in bed, then fetch a bowl of warm water and sponge down his body. She did this with such obvious pride and pleasure that he found himself feeling guilty about his impatience.

There was a knock at the door, and Nephtys looked in. Niall could tell she was surprised to find Jarita there, and that Jarita herself was pleased to be found kneeling at his feet.

'What is it?' His embarrassment made him speak abruptly.

'The doctor is here, my lord.'

'Tell him I'll be there in a moment.'

Simeon was already seated at table, drinking herb tea, when Niall came in; Niall made a gesture to prevent him from rising.

'What brings you here so early?'

'Your brother. His cut has been bleeding all night – the comfrey poultice didn't work. I've had to put in a couple of stitches.'

'But it was only a small cut.'

'That's what's so odd. There must have been a strong anti-coagulant on the blade of that axe. But even that shouldn't stop it from healing after twelve hours. Could I see the axe?'

Nephtys, who overheard the request, left the room, and returned a moment later, carrying the bundle wrapped in sacking.

'For heaven's sake be careful. It's very sharp.'

'I can see that.' Simeon studied the blade at close quarters, but made no attempt to touch it. 'No wonder it killed Skorbo. How do they make a blade as sharp as that? And such superb metal . . .'

'They obviously have a high level of culture.'

Simeon looked at him from under his bushy eye-brows.

'And do you have any idea of who "they" are?'

'Only what I can guess. Have you?'

'I noticed one rather strange thing – the skin of those dead men. It was too pale. I've only once seen skin as pale as that – it was an old man who went mad and locked himself in his room for twenty years.'

Niall said: 'As if they lived underground.'

'That's right.' Simeon glanced at him sharply. 'So you *do* know something about it?'

Niall shrugged. 'The Steegmaster told me of a legend of a race of men who came to earth from the stars, and who lived underground because the sunlight was deadly to them.'

'Did he say where they lived?'

'No. He thought it was just a story.'

Simeon shook his head. 'I'd swear that those men had lived underground, or been kept in a dungeon.'

Jarita brought in another pot of herb tea; it was made from the leaves of a plant called delium, and diffused a delicate and delicious odour. The tea had a faintly astringent quality that seemed to sharpen the senses. As Jarita poured, she said:

'My lord, forgive me for interrupting, but the Lord Dravig is waiting to see you.'

'But why is he waiting? Ask him to come in.'

'I told him you were eating breakfast, and he said he would wait.'

Simeon looked uncomfortable. 'I'd better go.'

'There would be no point. Dravig prefers to wait. Spiders have infinite patience. He would only feel embarrassed if we allowed him to interrupt our meal.'

Simeon looked at him curiously. 'You seem to understand spiders very well.'

'No. I understand a little. But I think it would be impossible for a human being to understand all the subtleties of the spider mind. In some ways they know far more than human beings.'

Simeon spread honey on a piece of hot crust.

'Do you suppose Dravig might know where these people come from?'

'I doubt it. He told me he had no idea of their identity.'

'Yet it seems incredible that no one should know who they are or where they live.'

Niall asked: 'What do you know of the land to the north of this city?'

'Not much. It's said to be extremely dangerous. But, as you know, the servants of the beetles were only recently granted freedom to go where they liked. And very few of them have been far from the city.'

'What kind of dangers?'

'I've heard of a beetle that has a shell so tough that no weapon can penetrate it, and jaws that can bite through a steel spear. But I must admit I've never met anyone who's seen one.'

'Not even the bombardier beetles?'

'Oh no. They hate travel. They say that some of them have never even ventured outside the city.' He emptied his cup and replaced it on the table. 'I'd better go. Tell Veig to come and see me if he has any more problems.'

He and Niall clasped forearms; the old man's forearm was stringy and muscular. At the door, Simeon paused with one hand on the latch.

'There *is* one more thing I meant to ask you. Why do you think that creature chopped off the head, then took it away?'

Niall smiled. 'For the same reason he took his own head away.'

Simeon frowned. 'His own head? But that was on his shoulders.'

'Quite.'

'Yes, but *why* did he want the head?'

Niall said: 'He didn't want it. He only wanted to get rid of it, so we couldn't find it. And if we hadn't caught him, both heads would now be at the bottom of the river.'

'But what could we learn from a head?'

'A head contains a brain. And a brain contains information.'

'Not when it's dead it doesn't.'

'You could be wrong. This man is a magician. He knows many secrets that we do not know. The only thing he does not know is how much *we* know. That is why he wanted to get rid of the heads.'

Simeon looked at him curiously. 'You seem to know a great deal.'

He was interrupted by Nephtys, who appeared in the open doorway.

'My lord, the Lord Dravig . . .'

'Yes, I know.' Niall stood up. 'Tell him I'm coming now.' He bowed in acknowledgement as Simeon withdrew. Jarita said:

'Your cloak, my lord.'

As he stood there, allowing her to fasten the soft grey cloak about his neck, he noticed that her hands lingered slightly longer than necessary – and that Nephtys was also aware of it. And since he could see into the minds of both women, he knew that Nephtys had been meant to notice. It disturbed him to realize that he was an object of a subtle rivalry between these two women, and that by allowing Jarita to dress him, he had intensified the rivalry. So, while Jarita was still smoothing the cloak, he followed Simeon out of the room.

Dravig was standing close to the fire, obviously enjoying its heat; as Niall appeared on the stairs he made the ritual gesture of obeisance. There was no greeting exchanged between them – because they were telepathic, spiders found such human formalities incomprehensible. But since Niall was obliged to speak first he asked:

'What brings you here so early?'

'The Death Lord requests your presence in her headquarters.' (The image transmitted was, in fact, of a web.)

'Of course.' He hoped that Dravig had not noticed his uncontrollable reaction of dismay. Although he was, in theory, the lord of the Spider Lord, unpleasant impressions of previous encounters lingered in his memory. As he crossed to the alcove in which he had left his outdoor cloak and fur boots, he asked casually: 'Do you know what it's about?'

'She wishes you to be present at the trial of Skorbo's fellow criminals.'

This time Niall made no attempt to conceal his consternation.

'As a witness against them?'

'That is unnecessary. They have already confessed.'

'Then why does she want me there?'

'To witness that she always keeps her word.'

'When does the trial take place?'

'It will begin as soon as you appear.'

'Oh dear, I'm sorry.' But even as he pulled on his boots, he knew that Dravig found his apology incomprehensible. Spider language had no equivalent of 'waiting'. It would have been as inapplicable to a spider as to a tree.

The sunlight made the air pleasantly warm, although the north wind still had an edge of coldness; the snow

137

was already beginning to thaw. The square was full of people, for today was a holiday – a concept introduced from the city of the bombardier beetles, where men worked for six days and rested on the seventh. As soon as Niall was recognized, people cleared a way for him, then fell on their knees in the snow, bowing their heads. The fact that Niall was followed by Dravig, who walked a few steps behind him – as was required by protocol – obviously increased their respect. Once again Niall found himself wishing that he could stroll among his own people without being recognized.

As soon as he entered the headquarters of the Spider Lord, Niall became aware of a brooding tension. It was, in fact, an altogether curious sensation, as if walking into a kind of cold jelly. This feeling was undoubtedly shared by every spider in the building: a recognition that something of great seriousness was about to take place. In the days when human beings had been lords of the earth, the same atmosphere had probably pervaded murder trials and public executions.

Niall found himself stifled by a sense of oppression. In the dark hallway, he turned to Dravig.

'What would happen if I begged the Death Lord to spare their lives?'

Dravig answered without hesitation:

'That would be inadvisable.'

'You mean she would refuse?'

'No. She would agree. But for the prisoners themselves it would be a shameful humiliation.'

Niall was astonished. 'Why?'

'Because they would owe their lives to the intercession of one they regard as an enemy. They would prefer to die.'

Dravig now preceded him up the stairs. And, as he followed, Niall tried to understand this latest baffling paradox of the arachnoid mentality: that a spider should prefer death to the generosity of an 'enemy'. Then, as he again became aware of the suffocating tension in the air, he suddenly understood. Unlike human beings, spiders were in constant telepathic contact. There would be no way in which a spider could forget or ignore the contempt of his fellows. And that contempt would cause him to see himself as an entirely contempt-ible creature, unworthy of life . . .

The building was in almost complete darkness; every window was covered by a thick layer of dust-laden cobwebs which had accumulated over the centuries. Some long-dead Spider Lord had probably chosen this building as his headquarters because the great main staircase was built of black marble, and the walls were covered with a substance like black volcanic glass. Spid-ers had an instinctive preference for darkness – no doubt because it was necessary for the concealment of their webs.

On the fourth floor, Dravig halted in front of a wide door covered with black leather and decorated with brass studs. The two wolf spiders who stood on guard on either side were so still that they might have been statues. The same was true of the dark-haired girl who stood to attention in front of the door; she was dressed in a black uniform, although her white arms had been left bare; Niall recognized her as Sidonia, the captain of the Spider Lord's household guard. She looked at him without recognition – the slightest wavering of her gaze would have been regarded as a severe breach of disci-pline – then turned her back on them and threw open the door.

In the spacious hall beyond, there was enough light to reveal that the walls and ceiling were entirely covered with dusty cobwebs. At the far end of the room, the cobwebs stretched from floor to ceiling, and were so thick that they resembled layers of netting or a tangle of creepers. From the midst of this jungle, Niall had a sensation of being surveyed by invisible eyes. As he came to a halt, the voice of the Spider Lord sounded inside his chest.

'Welcome, chosen of the goddess.'

Niall replied:

'I am honoured to be in your presence, O lord of the earth.'

As his eyes became accustomed to the darkness, Niall became aware of other spiders standing by the walls; they were so still, and blended so well into the background, that they were virtually invisible.

And then, quite suddenly, it was unnecessary for him to try to penetrate the darkness; every spider in the room became clearly visible. For a moment he thought that a beam of sunlight had penetrated the dusty windows. Then, with a shock, he understood what had happened. The Spider Lord had integrated him into the web of awareness within the room. He had been granted the supreme honour of becoming a part of the general consciousness that united all spiders.

It was, in a sense, the most remarkable experience of his life. Like all human beings, Niall had spent his whole life seeing things from his individual standpoint, like a man sitting alone in a small room; even when closest to others he felt aware of his solitariness. He had taken it for granted that this was what it meant to be alive. Now, suddenly, he was no longer alone; he was a part of a network of other beings, as aware of their existence as he was of his own. The bewildering thing was that his sense of identity had vanished; he had *become* the spiders who surrounded him, while his own identity had somehow become divided amongst them. Yet when he looked inside himself, wondering at this loss of individuality, he realized with surprise that his identity was still there, as it always had been.

It was his sense of being himself, of being Niall, that had disappeared. And now he understood that this had always been an illusion, that he had never been Niall. Niall was merely a set of misconceptions.

All this, he realized, was an act of supreme courtesy on the part of the Spider Lord, an attempt to make amends for centuries of mistrust between spiders and human beings. And since spiders have a natural aversion to human beings, just as most human beings have a natural aversion to spiders, this gesture of integration into spider consciousness was also an act of extraordinary generosity. The generosity was all the more astounding since Niall could now understand why spiders found humans so distasteful; with their cramped little egos, their obsessive self-preoccupation, they must all seem to be suffering from a kind of insanity. Now he could also see why spiders had felt no guilt about treating human beings as slaves; with their blindness and narrowness, men were only one degree less stupid than sheep.

Yet although his new awareness allowed him to blend into the consciousness of the spiders, so that he himself became a kind of honorary spider, he was also aware that the spiders each possessed his own individual consciousness, so that the contents of their minds were hidden from him, just as his were hidden from them. He could betray his thoughts to them, by allowing them to 'overflow', but if he chose to minimize his thought energy, then there was no way in which they could invade the privacy of his mind.

Now, as he stood in silence before the web of the Spider Lord, he understood the proverb quoted by Dravig as the essence of spider wisdom: 'Silence allows Time to hear its own voice.' Because they were directly aware of one another's existence, spiders felt perfectly at home in silence; this was why they could remain silent and motionless for days or weeks at a time. This, he also realized, was why spiders lived so long: the silence allowed them time to renew themselves. While he had been trapped in his own identity, Niall had felt awkward and self-conscious to be standing alone in the middle of the room; now he felt that he could easily stand there for a year without fatigue.

As his attention shifted from the strangeness of his new awareness to the room around him, Niall became conscious of the situation in which he found himself. The web that covered the end of the room like a dark tunnel now seemed transparent, and he recognized for the first time that it was the equivalent of a royal throne, in which the Spider Lord sat surrounded by her courtiers, the ruling council of the spider city; each of these councillors – all were female – had her precise place. The only other occupants of the room, besides himself and Dravig, were six male spiders, who were ranged on either side of the room; these, he now realized, were the prisoners on trial.

As soon as his attention was fixed on them, he was aware that five of the six were nonentities, the spider equivalent of footsoldiers. The leading spirit was the sixth, a captain of the guard who had been Skorbo's closest friend. This spider was smaller and more compact than the others, although his powerful legs and pincers revealed enormous physical strength. Niall was surprised to realize that this spider, like the others, was nameless – for names would have been pointless when spiders had instant telepathic recognition. If one of them wished to refer to a spider who was absent, he could convey a mental image of the spider's essential identity. Names such as Skorbo and Dravig had been bestowed on prominent spiders by human beings.

And now that his attention was focused on the sixth spider, Niall also recognized that a name would have been an absurdity. This spider had come from a distant province across the sea, and he had been born in a privileged position, a member of a family whose natural dominance ensured them a certain pre-eminence. Here, in the spider city, his natural dominance aroused resentment, while his small stature led to him being regarded with a certain lack of respect. And since spiders attached immense importance to being respected this had engendered a certain rebelliousness.

Skorbo, by comparison, had been coarse and stupid; but he also possessed a high degree of natural dominance, so the two had formed a kind of alliance. Skorbo had never understood his companion's rebelliousness, for he himself was a born soldier who regarded obedience as a law of nature; but he admired this 'aristocrat' among spiders.

As members of the imperial guard these two had never given cause for complaint; but when they were off duty, they took pleasure in hunting and tormenting human beings. They were not interested in those who were merely fat and succulent, but only in those who possessed a certain strength and enterprise, some degree of leadership quality. These they observed with infinite patience, studying their movements, waiting until the opportunity came to plunge down on them from the sky and seize the victim in all eight legs. This generated an almost feverish intensity of pleasure. The victim's vocal chords were paralysed so that he could not cry out, but his limbs were left unaffected, for the essence of the pleasure lay in his struggles. To feel a terrified captive squirming frantically produced a delight that in human beings is associated only with sex. Then he would be taken to a lighted room, and allowed to try and escape. One man had even succeeded in leaping out of an upper window, hoping to kill himself; but Skorbo had been crouching in his web, and had caught him before he struck the pavement. (Spiders were able to increase or decrease their speed of descent at will.) The victim had then been tormented for hours until he had died of terror and exhaustion. His body had been eaten while still warm.

All this Niall knew instantaneously on looking at the guard captain, for it had already been confessed, and was therefore in the minds of his companions. He could also understand why, when the Spider Lord had announced the peace treaty between spiders and human beings, Skorbo and his companion had been so shocked and outraged. They were being deprived of a pleasure that had become the keenest and sweetest sensation in life, something that meant more to them than food and drink. Yet Skorbo was willing to accept the new state of affairs; since it was the will of the goddess, he could see no alternative. It was his companion who rebelled at the idea. Although he too was willing to respect the will of the goddess, the notion of treating human beings as equals filled him with fury and contempt. Humans were vermin, obviously intended by Nature to be the prey of spiders. If the goddess had allowed them to go on killing human beings for centuries, it was surely unlikely that she would suddenly change her mind? No, this new prohibition was obviously the decision of the old Spider Lord, who was impotent and senile. It deserved to be flouted.

In any case, there was no hurry about deciding what to do. Their private larder was well stocked with human flesh. A death spider could inject his prey with a poison that would paralyse the central nervous system without causing death; if precisely the right quantity was injected, the victim might live for six months without being able to move a finger or an eyelid. So Skorbo and his companion continued to dine on human flesh for many months after the peace treaty without feeling that they were breaking the law. Then five NCOs of the imperial guard discovered a forgotten communal larder containing a dozen or so paralysed human carcases, as well as some cows and pigs. These were transferred to Skorbo's larder, and the NCOs joined in the nightly feasts. One night, an NCO brought back the body of a slave who had collapsed during an epileptic attack, and they all agreed that the fresh meat tasted so delicious that it would be absurd to forgo the pleasure of eating the occasional slave – besides, no one really regarded slaves as human. But then, human beings from across the river often wandered around the slave quarter at night, and it was quite impossible to know which was which. And so, step by step, without any intention of breaking the law, Skorbo and his companions had drifted back into the habit of eating live flesh . . .

All these facts were communicated to Niall's mind within a few moments of the Spider Lord's greeting; it was unnecessary for them to be communicated serially, one by one, for they existed simultaneously in the mind of the Spider Lord and of every other spider in this room. But he was also aware that the most important part of the interrogation was still to come – a part that, although purely formal, was still essential to the process of justice.

First of all there was a lengthy silence – the silence spiders believed should precede all affairs of importance. As Niall relaxed in this silence, he experienced an almost electrical sensation of delight. The last time he had experienced this sensation was when he and Veig, and their cousin Hrolf, were exploring the country of the ants, and had encountered a shallow stream that meandered in its rocky bed. For the first time in his life, Niall had immersed himself in water, and then had sat there, staring at the rippling surface, with this same sensation of peaceful ecstasy.

The Spider Lord finally spoke, addressing the prisoners:

'You are aware that you have broken the law, and flouted the will of the goddess. What do you have to say for yourselves?'

The accused made no reply. The five NCOs were obviously too ashamed to speak; the captain simply maintained silence.

The Spider Lord said:

'Is there any reason why I should not pass the sentence of death?'

After another silence, the captain replied:

'I would regard the death sentence as an injustice.'

'Why?'

'Because the fault was unintentional. We began by eating humans who had already been destroyed.' (The spider thought-language made no distinction between 'paralysed' and 'destroyed'.)

'We realize that. But you then went on to break the law by killing those who had not yet been destroyed.'

'It is true that I broke your law. But it was not the law of my own country, the land of Koresh.'

At this point, Dravig intervened.

'You are in this country, not in Koresh, and are therefore obliged to obey our laws. Are you trying to deny this?'

Dravig's voice had a note of anger. The captain's reply sounded cool and unemotional.

'I do not deny it. But I submit that this particular law is unfair.'

'Why?' The Spider Lord's voice also betrayed a note of anger.

'I am a stranger in your land. You have no right to ask me to treat human beings as equals. I do not regard them as equals. Moreover, I do not believe you regard them as equals.'

Niall was suddenly struck by an astonishing insight. Spider justice differed from human justice in one basic respect. A spider could not be sentenced to death against his will. If he was to be executed, it had to be with his own total consent. The reason was obvious. If a spider was executed against his will, every other spider in the city would be aware of his misery and agony. Therefore it was necessary for a spider to be convinced of his own guilt, and to consent to his own execution. The captain, apparently, was determined not to die. This, Niall now realized, was why Dravig and the Spider Lord were becoming angry.

But when the Spider Lord replied, it was with remarkable restraint.

'All that is irrelevant. *I* gave my word that there should be peace between spiders and human beings. You have caused that promise to be broken. Therefore you deserve to die.'

This argument was obviously irrefutable; in effect, the captain had now been driven into a corner. Surely he would at last concede the justice of the sentence?

'I agree that I have been the cause of your promise being broken. But I argue that there are extenuating circumstances.'

The Spider Lord addressed the other five prisoners.

'Do you agree that you deserve to die?'

All five made a gesture that signified assent.

The Spider Lord asked: 'Well?'

'I see no reason why my life should be sacrificed to the will of cowards.'

The Spider Lord suddenly lost patience.

'That is enough! I am tired of your equivocations! You have deserved death a thousand times. Bow your head!'

This last sentence – it could also have been translated 'Subordinate your will', or 'Prepare to die' – was spoken in a tone of such menace that the room suddenly seemed to darken. The five NCOs obeyed immediately and abjectly, as if bowing their heads to the executioner's axe. But the captain, although he knew himself to be in an impossible situation, continued to radiate defiance. The Spider Lord and Dravig struck at once with a force that made Niall cringe; a human being would have been squashed like a fly. The captain collapsed to the ground, and lay there, his legs drawn around him in a tight knot; at the same time, his will also collapsed into a defensive posture, surrounding him with a shield of invisible force. The combined strength of Dravig and the Death Lord struck this shield with a force that should have smashed it and crushed the spider underneath it. In fact, it rebounded on to the other five spiders, killing them instantly. There was a crunching sound, and the air was suddenly full of the peculiar pungent odour of spider blood.

Niall felt them die. It was a strange sensation, as if time had suddenly gone into slow motion. His brain was flooded with information – so much information that it was impossible to absorb it, or even grasp its nature. Nevertheless, he knew intuitively what was happening: that in the moment of instantaneous extinction, the spiders were re-living their own lives. The experience was curiously exciting, and completely devoid of the terror he had expected to be associated with death. Then, what seemed to be several minutes later, there was only darkness and a sensation of emptiness.

The captain was still lying there, surrounded by his defensive shield; it was obvious that he had no intention of dropping his guard. All his will was concentrated upon a single purpose: to save his own life. In the pause that followed, the Spider Lord regarded him with angry contempt; he found it unbelievable that any spider should prefer ignominy and disgrace to an honourable death. Then he summoned the others to join with him in the work of destruction. This meant that he and his ruling council would cease to act as individuals, but would unite their efforts in a common purpose. This stratagem – known to the beetle servants as multiple-reinforcement interaction – could be compared to the decision of a group who had been trying to batter down a door by individual efforts to unite their strength behind a battering ram.

The captain sensed what was about to happen, and his fear was so powerful that it overwhelmed the bitter stench of blood. Yet even his terror had an element of calculation. Since its vibrations were being carried simultaneously to every spider in the city, they had all become witnesses of this attempt to destroy him. He was like a man screaming at the top of his lungs in order to mitigate the severity of a beating. But as the multiple reinforcement mechanism began to operate, the terror became muted as it gave way to a grim determination to survive. Niall watched with sickened fascination as the captain exerted all his own will-power in an attempt to preserve his life for a few moments longer. He could understand that terror of sudden extinction – as could every spider in the city. The inter-linked will-power of the spiders was like some giant nutcracker; it seemed impossible that any living creature could withstand such force. Even the corpses of the other spiders were caught in the mesh of power, so they began to crack and crumble, while their blood ran over the floor like water squeezed from a sponge. The captain's mind was also cracking under the pressure, and Niall experienced again the sense of being overwhelmed with information – that curious flood of images that seemed to accompany the conviction of approaching death. The most vivid of these was of a square, grey building surrounded by rich vegetation, including red and yellow tropical flowers. But the inside smelt like a butcher's shop, and from the beams that supported the ceiling, a number of human bodies cocooned in spider-silk swung like pendulums in the breeze.

It was as the blood began to run around his own feet that Niall suddenly understood why this united willforce had not yet destroyed the captain's resistance. It was because he, Niall, was present in the room, thereby inhibiting the Spider Lord from exerting the power that could overwhelm resistance through brute force. Such an explosion of power might well have cracked the walls of the room in which they were standing; it would certainly have squeezed the life out of Niall at the same time as it destroyed the captain. There was only one way in which Niall could cease to be an obstruction: by uniting his own will with that of the Spider Lord, so that his will became a part of the web of power. Yet even as this thought occurred to him, he was aware that it was out of the question. He was a human being, not a spider. The captain might be a sadistic coward who enjoyed torturing Niall's fellow humans; but Niall had no personal quarrel with him. If he took part in this execution, he would be somehow forfeiting his own humanity.

The struggle seemed to continue for a long time; in fact, it may have been minutes, or even seconds. At a certain point, it became clear that the captain had won his fight for life. Without Niall's participation, he could not be destroyed. At that moment, the Spider Lord suddenly released his grip; Dravig and the others did so at the same time. The result was that the captain spun across the room like a projectile, narrowly missing Niall's legs, and crashed into the wall. The force of the impact was enough to deprive him of his senses. But instead of taking advantage of his helplessness, the Spider Lord merely regarded him with contempt.

Several minutes passed as the prostrate spider stirred; then, as if knowing the danger was past, he struggled slowly to his feet.

When the Spider Lord spoke, her voice was cold and detached.

'You will leave this city immediately and never return. But you will not be allowed to return by sea to your own land. No ship will carry a traitor who prefers dishonour to death. Now go.'

The spider dragged himself towards the door, every movement revealing a deadly fatigue. In this state, a child could have killed him. The voice of the Spider Lord followed him.

'You are now an outlaw, and all creatures are licensed to kill you. You must find your way back to your own land as best you can.'

The door swung open; Sidonia was standing on the other side. When the exhausted spider had crawled past her, she closed it again.

The Spider Lord now addressed Niall.

'You have chosen to spare his life. That was your own decision, and I accept it. But the debt is now discharged.'

The implication was that, since Niall had spared the captain's life, he should not complain if more human beings were killed. Niall signified his understanding by making a deep bow. The gesture was intended as a kind of apology, and the Spider Lord understood it as such. Then, followed by Dravig, Niall made his way to the door, walking cautiously to avoid slipping in the blood. Activated by some command that was beyond the range of Niall's perceptions, Sidonia opened the door again, then closed it behind them. It was a relief to be in the clean air. The stench of dead spiders had brought Niall close to the verge of being violently sick.

Sidonia was standing to attention, her face as blank

as a doll's; the shoulder-length blonde hair and the pink cheeks reinforced this impression. But behind the immobility, Niall could sense her nervousness as he stood looking at her.

'Sidonia, I want to talk to you.'

Her colour deepened as he spoke; otherwise she gave no sign of having heard. He said:

'I'd like you to come with me.'

As she followed him down the stairs he could sense her puzzlement; she could imagine no reason why he should want to talk to her, unless he found her attractive, and harboured the same desires as his brother. Dravig was also puzzled, but was too polite to attempt to read Niall's thoughts.

Outside, the sunlight seemed dazzling. On the northern side of the square, he could see the captain moving down the main avenue towards the bridge that led to the slave quarter. Although his movements still betrayed fatigue, he was travelling swiftly, apparently determined to leave the city before someone took advantage of the licence to kill.

Niall sat down on the sun-warmed balustrade, and gestured for Sidonia to take a seat beside him. She sat down awkwardly, as if it made her uncomfortable to cease to stand to attention. Dravig waited impassively; spiders had an odd ability to freeze, as if turned into statues.

Niall asked: 'How well do you know this city?'

'Very well, I think.' She spoke in the clipped voice of one accustomed to giving commands.

'Do you know of a square, grey building, surrounded by green bushes and red and yellow flowers?' He reinforced the question with a telepathic image.

She looked down at the pavement, biting her lip, then shook her head. 'No, lord.'

Niall could see she was telling the truth; yet he could

152

also sense an element of doubt. Something about the image aroused a sense of familiarity.

'Are you quite sure?'

She flushed, thinking that he was doubting her word. Because she was so accustomed to spiders probing her mind, she had no idea that her privacy was being invaded.

'Yes, lord.'

'But have you any idea where it *might* be?'

She frowned. 'There are many flowers in that part of the city.' She raised her hand and pointed to the east, along the avenue that ran past Niall's palace.

'How far?'

'Perhaps two or three miles.'

Niall turned to Dravig.

'Do you know that part of the city?'

'No. My business has never taken me there. It is quite deserted.'

'Why is it deserted?'

'Because it is not suitable for human habitation.'

'I would like to go there. Will you come with me?'

The spider made a gesture of acquiescence. Niall turned back to Sidonia.

'I would also like you to accompany me. Please come to the palace at two o'clock this afternoon.'

The sun now shone from a clear blue sky; the only unmelted snow lay in the shadows of trees and buildings, and the air was full of the rippling sound of water as it ran along the gutters and down the drains. The heat on their backs was so great that Niall and Simeon removed their cloaks and carried them over their arms; only Sidonia preferred the discomfort of the sun to the indignity of being improperly dressed. Dravig, as usual, seemed indifferent to the temperature.

Around his neck, Niall was wearing the thought mirror that had been presented to him on his first visit to the white tower. This was a device for coordinating mental vibrations from the brain, the heart and the solar plexus, producing a concentration that intensified the perceptions. Since becoming ruler, Niall had lost the habit of using it; he found that it heightened the powers of the will at the expense of intuition. Today he was wearing it for a special purpose. On that first visit to the tower, he had used the thought mirror to enable him to memorize the map of the city. It had imprinted the map so powerfully on his memory circuits that now, with its aid, he was able to study it in detail merely by half-closing his eyes. The map showed the eastern part of the city extending to the lower slopes of the circle of hills that enclosed the spider city. But a large area was marked with the words 'Industrial Estate', a description that Niall found baffling, and upon which neither Simeon nor Dravig was able to throw any light. He was aware that industry meant the production and manufacture of goods, and his history lessons in the white tower had included the story of the Industrial Revolution; but in the part of the city they were now approaching, he could see no sign of soot-blackened factories or tall chimneys. The buildings seemed, if anything, to be lower than in the central part of the city.

The sandstone-coloured road along which they were walking looked as new as if it had been built yesterday. In the second half of the twenty-first century, tarmac and concrete had given way to a compound of stone dust and plastic that hardened into a substance not unlike marble, but twice as durable. This is why the road, and the pavements on either side of it, showed no sign of wear. The houses, shops and office buildings in this part of the city had also been built of new compounds, so that they were in a far better state of repair than those in the centre. The total effect was neat and orderly, but oddly dreary.

A mile further on, commercial buildings gave way to small identical dwelling houses built of red brick, each standing in its own small garden. These had once been saved from monotony only by the elaborate patterns surrounding windows and doorways; now the gardens had turned into tangles of overgrown vegetation that sometimes covered the roofs; in one case, a tree had grown up through the centre of the house, so its trunk had pushed its way through the slates, and its branches overshadowed the roof. Niall experienced an intense curiosity to explore one of these houses, to see whether their former inhabitants had left behind evidence about their daily lives; but he knew that only a few more hours of daylight remained.

After another mile or so, the scenery again changed dramatically. The first sign of this was a profusion of bright colour, which began half a mile ahead, where the red brick houses left off. According to the map, this was the beginning of the industrial estate; but the buildings looked as if they had been designed for a carnival or recreation park. They were built of brightly-coloured bricks, many of them triangular or circular, and none of them was more than two storeys high; the favourite colour of the roofing tiles was a mottled shade of emerald green. Like the red brick houses, these were overgrown with vegetation; but this vegetation had a tropical luxuriance. The main plant was a kind of thick creeper, whose broad, glossy leaves were marbled with green and yellow, while the flowers were trumpet-shaped cups of scarlet. A smaller plant also had bright green leaves, round and glossy, and bright blue flowers. Palm trees, such as Niall had seen in the Delta, pushed their way above this mass of vegetation. The total effect was one of strange extravagance, as if it had been designed by a joker.

As they came closer, it became clear that the scent of the plants was as delightful as their appearance, a blend of honeysuckle, lilac, roses, gorse and hyacinth, all overlaid by a rich odour resembling new mown hay. The last time Niall had encountered such a complexity of sweet scents was in the Delta, and the recollection made him nervous. But when Sidonia strolled among the bushes and creepers, burying her face in the flowers with obvious pleasure, Niall also succumbed to the temptation, and found the odours delicious. He asked Sidonia:

'Have you been here before?'

'Yes.' He thought she cast a nervous glance at Dravig.

'And is it always like this?'

She hesitated. 'I think so.'

'Then why doesn't everyone come here? It's beautiful.'

'Because . . .' She was taking a deep breath of one of the scarlet trumpets: 'Because it is not good to have too much pleasure.'

As he looked at her with astonishment, she blushed. But her reaction brought understanding. She was a soldier who took pride in discipline and self-control. These scents aroused a disturbing desire to surrender. And such an attitude would have been regarded with displeasure by the spiders.

Simeon was also studying the plants, but with the detached eye of a herbalist. Niall asked:

'Why do they grow like this in midwinter? Does the sunshine make them think that it's spring?'

Simeon made a gesture of bewilderment.

'I don't know. I've never come across anything like it before.'

'Not even in the Delta?'

'That's different. Most of the plants in the Delta contained some kind of trap.'

'And you're sure these don't?'

'Oh no.' It was Sidonia who spoke; her voice had a dreamy tone, and she was caressing the scarlet trumpet as though it were a pet animal. 'This is not a trap.'

Niall removed the thought mirror from round his neck – it focused his attention too sharply – and saw immediately that she was right. There was something curiously innocent and joyful about this profusion of odours. His intuition told him there was nothing to fear.

'Have you ever seen plants that bloom in midwinter?'

'Not like this.' Simeon was studying one of the thick, glossy leaves. 'You notice the leaves are evergreen.' He felt the petal of an orange flower that might have been an unknown variety of rose. Niall did the same, and observed that it was thick and fleshy. 'And this flower could probably remain intact in a gale.'

Niall asked Dravig: 'Do you know anything about them?'

'My people have no interest in flowers.' The reply

carried an overtone of amusement; Niall had observed before that Dravig possessed a dry sense of humour.

Simeon said: 'Surely it can't be a coincidence that they planted these flowers among these buildings?'

The same thought had struck Niall at the same moment. At close quarters, the buildings looked as if they had been constructed for a child's playground; their bright colours and elaborate patterns produced that same curious upsurge of delight.

'Perhaps this was the nursery of the industrial estate.'

'Industrial estate? Is this an industrial estate?'

'According to the map.'

Simeon nodded slowly. 'That explains it. They used to build them like this in the old days. The workers got depressed if their surroundings were boring and dull. But as soon as they made the surroundings attractive, everyone worked harder. My grandfather read about it in books on history.'

'But that doesn't explain flowers that bloom in winter.'

'No.' Simeon took a deep breath of a great golden flower like a giant snapdragon. 'I agree that's odd.'

Sidonia said: 'Perhaps they brought these plants from the Delta.'

Niall said: 'The Delta didn't exist in those days.'

'No?' It was obvious that she knew no history.

A light breeze rustled the bushes, mingling the scents so that they became almost overpoweringly sweet; they produced a shimmering, swooning sensation that made him want to lie down on the damp grass and close his eyes. With an effort, he replaced the thought mirror round his neck. The dreamy sensation vanished instantly, to be replaced by a hard sense of clarity that seemed almost brutal in comparison. The feeling of joyousness also vanished, swept away by the sense of concentrated will-power, a desire to hurl himself into practical activity.

'It's getting late. We ought to move on.'

Simeon turned his back on the flowers with a sigh. But Sidonia pulled back her shoulders, thrust out her breasts, and followed him with a firm, purposeful stride.

Simeon's account of the industrial estate was obviously correct. All the buildings had the same deliberate gaiety, which at times approached vulgarity. Niall could imagine it as it was when originally built; with its smooth lawns, and coloured buildings surrounded by bright flowers, it must have looked like an annexe of fairyland. Simeon pointed out one curious structure, built entirely of green stone, that looked like some unknown species of cactus pushing its way out of the rich soil.

Niall shook his head. 'But surely they got bored with it after a day or so? Everyone gets used to the same surroundings sooner or later.'

Simeon shrugged. 'My grandfather didn't say anything about that.'

By half-closing his eyes, Niall was able to study the map he had memorized in the white tower. It amazed him that, with the aid of the thought mirror, his mind could re-create every detail with the precision and clarity of a photograph; it was an awesome glimpse into the unknown powers of memory. The map indicated that the industrial estate was roughly circular, and more than two miles in diameter. There was a large lake, still attractive although now overgrown with reeds and algae, an industrial museum, and an administration block that resembled the pipes of some vast organ. Yet it was obvious to Niall that none of these buildings bore the slightest resemblance to the square grey structure

159

they were seeking. A grey building would have been out of place in this explosion of colour. But after passing the administration block, which stood in the centre of the complex, the nature of the buildings began to change. Presumably the lessees were unable to afford the more elaborate premises, or the designers of the estate had run out of money; at all events, the buildings became increasingly functional, and many were built of plain red brick. Then, towards the eastern edge of the estate, Niall saw something that made his heart contract: the top part of a grey building that rose behind the trees. He pointed.

'That looks like it.'

Simeon surveyed it dubiously.

'It looks like an electricity generating station. There's one exactly like it on the other side of the city.'

In fact, as they changed their angle of approach, they could see that the grey building stood beside a water tower. For a moment Niall was convinced that he had made a mistake. Then, as they emerged from a side path, he was able to see the lower half of the building, and the banks of rich vegetation that surrounded it, with their red and yellow flowers. At that moment, he knew with intuitive certainty that they had discovered Skorbo's secret larder. A curious wave of cold energy, like a shiver, emanating from Dravig, told him that the spider was also aware of it.

They were approaching the building from the rear, and they found themselves facing a blank wall, with no sign of doors or windows. It would clearly be necessary to find their way round to the front. This proved to be less simple than it looked; a prickly hedge, which seemed to form the eastern boundary of the estate, blended into the mass of bushes and small trees that surrounded the building. On closer inspection, this hedge proved to be a tangle of needle-like spikes, and it stretched up more than four feet above their heads – too tall even for Dravig to step over. It was Sidonia who solved the problem by drawing her shortsword, and stepping boldly into the bushes; with each heavy blow, severed branches and creepers fell at her feet. Within a few minutes she had hacked her way through to the wall, and exposed an overgrown concrete path, about four feet wide; this had prevented the vegetation from approaching too close to the wall, and they were able to force their way round to the front of the building.

What faced them was a grey façade with half a dozen broken windows and a massive steel door, whose blue-tinged metal was still unrusted; a handle at one end indicated that this was of the type that slid open on rollers. Niall braced himself and heaved; the door slid open about four feet, then jammed. Sidonia, still holding her sword, took a cautious step inside. As she did so, Simeon shouted a warning, and something hurled itself out of the darkness. Sidonia was thrown violently on to her back, her head striking the concrete floor. The force of the blow probably saved her life; the spider that stood over her was poised to strike at her throat, and would undoubtedly have done so if she had moved. Because she lay still, the fangs remained poised for long enough for Dravig – who had just squeezed his way round the corner of the building – to transmit a mental command. The spider froze in astonishment. But when Dravig ordered it to move back, it ignored the command and remained in a threatening posture. Niall was incredulous. It was the first time he had ever seen a spider defy the order of a superior.

Now he looked more closely, he was not even certain that the creature was a spider. The legs seemed to be encased in a kind of shell, like those of a scorpion. The huge black body, which was also encased in a jointed shell, like a wood louse, was circular, completely lacking the waistline that separates the cephalothorax from the abdomen in most spiders. It was also lacking anything resembling a head; the eyes and the fangs seemed to be set in the body. The big body and powerful legs gave an impression of immense physical strength; it was obvious that the mandibles could sever the girl's head with a single pincer movement.

Dravig was also astonished; as the special adviser of the Spider Lord, he had become accustomed to instant obedience. Now it seemed unbelievable that this uncouth monster, who looked more like a black beetle than a spider, should be ignoring him. Perhaps the creature was mentally subnormal, or had simply failed to recognize him? Once again he snapped a mental command. Still the stranger continued to stare back, its feelers trembling slightly, as if from tension, its eyes glinting red as they caught the light. Dravig's impatience turned to anger, and exploded in a burst of will-force that made Niall wince; the spider cringed and retreated a step backwards. Like Dravig, Niall expected it now to give way and submit to Dravig's superior dominance. Instead, its sullen defiance turned to anger, and it lashed out with a burst of will-force that was like a heavy blow. Dravig, who was unprepared, reacted exactly as if he had been struck by a physical force; his two back legs started to buckle, and the grey hairs on his body quivered as if a wind had blown over them. Dravig responded with outrage, drawing himself up like a patrician who has been insulted by a commoner. But the other spider was unimpressed; it was obviously a stranger to this city. It took a step forward and braced itself over Sidonia's body, its tarsal claws raised to the fighting position. Niall observed nervously that Sidonia was beginning to stir; then she opened her eyes and stared up at the hairy belly poised above her. Fortunately, the challenger was paying too much attention to Dravig to notice her.

Then the two spiders were locked in a combat of wills. This was no longer a question of blows, but of strength pitted against strength. It was the first time Niall had witnessed such a combat, and he was fascinated to observe what happened. It was as if each spider was surrounded by an energy field, like the lines of force surrounding a magnet. These two energy fields met head on, producing exactly the same effect as the like-poles of two magnets approaching one another and creating repulsion. Where they met, it was as if the lines of force darkened in colour, so they became visible. In fact, these force-fields were invisible to Simeon, who could only see two spiders facing one another at a distance of about twelve feet, each one braced as if walking into a powerful gale, or as if pushing at one another like two wrestlers. Niall could see the force between them because he was on the same telepathic wavelength as Dravig.

He could also see that Dravig was out of condition for this kind of combat. He was older, and it had been many years since he had been called upon to assert his authority through force. And although his will-power had the controlled thrust of a rapier, he lacked the sheer brute force of his adversary, whose aggressive energies had the same strength as his squat body. Moreover, Dravig's conviction was undermined by a feeling that this combat was an undignified absurdity. And although it seemed that the two were locked in equal combat, neither giving nor losing the slightest advantage, Niall was aware that Dravig was losing strength sooner than his opponent. What would happen if Dravig was finally forced to give way? Niall could almost see it as if it were happening at the moment.

The only way in which Dravig could save his own life would be to make a ritual gesture of surrender, the equivalent of an animal turning tail. And this was inconceivable. Even now, as his energies remained locked in precise counterpoise, Dravig's stance expressed a furious loathing of his opponent, a desire to see him punished and utterly abased. This meant that, when Dravig was finally forced to give way, he would inevitably be killed. And to a spider, death would have been a matter of indifference after surrendering to one he regarded as an inferior.

Suddenly it struck Niall as absurd to be standing there while Dravig was engaged in a life and death struggle; it was an affront to his own courage. His state of inner tension – and his desire to see the stranger defeated – was such that he could also have faced death with indifference. Then his tension made him aware of the thought mirror against his chest; it produced a burning sensation, exactly as if it had been a flame. At the moment, its concave side was turned inward, reflecting his thought-energies back inside himself and intensifying his powers of concentration. Now he reached inside his shirt, turning it the other way, and directing the force of his concentration at Dravig's adversary.

The spider was startled by this additional attack, and immediately gave ground. A moment later, it registered with amazement that its adversary was a human being. With a strength that Niall found incredible, and without losing an inch of ground, it braced itself to meet this new challenge, and began to fight back on two fronts. Niall immediately felt as if some invisible force was pushing him backwards, and for a moment he felt absurdly lightweight and inadequate. Then he again concentrated his will, and used all the force of the mirror to press home his attack. The mirror became so hot that it burned his flesh, and he found himself wishing that he had taken the precaution of suspending it outside his tunic. He ignored the pain, and summoned all his force to resist the power that was trying to force him backwards and then crush him to the ground.

Several minutes passed. They were deadlocked. Niall's intervention had made it impossible for the stranger to win; with all its brute strength, the spider was not sufficiently strong to press home the attack on two fronts. Yet it seemed capable of holding its opponents at bay indefinitely, and Niall found himself wondering how long he could maintain this intensity of concentration. His sense of urgency had steeled him to a level of effort that he would normally have found impossible to maintain for more than a few minutes. But attempting to batter down the will of this squat, powerful stranger was like trying to push down a brick wall by sheer physical force. He was aware that his own strength was beginning to flag.

Then, with startling suddenness, all resistance vanished. As Niall stumbled and fell to his knees, he experienced an agonizing shock that seemed to tear his intestines like a white hot flame. He looked down, expecting to see blood gushing through his tunic, and was relieved to see that everything looked normal. The stranger was staggering backwards, as if struck by a powerful blow. It took Niall a moment to realize what had happened: that Sidonia had driven her sword into its belly and ripped it sideways. Now he saw her withdraw it, and then roll aside like an acrobat as the pincers tried to decapitate her. The pain in his stomach had been the result of telepathic contact.

Unlike Niall, Dravig had continued to exert his willforce; it was this that had caused the spider to stagger backwards, and which now smashed it to the ground like some immense club. As it lay there, dazed and defeated, blood gushed from its stomach over the concrete floor. Dravig contemplated it with cold hostility for a moment, then, holding it paralysed with his will, he stepped forward and drove his poison fangs into its head. He remained in that position for several seconds, his legs braced, as the poison was injected. Niall was startled and shocked by the ferocity of the attack; he had somehow expected Dravig to show mercy. Then, as Dravig withdrew his fangs and stood back, Niall caught a glimpse into his mind, and realized that he felt no fellow feeling towards the creature he had just killed. It was simply a dangerous wild animal that had just threatened his life; now he had destroyed it with the same lack of compunction that it would have shown towards him.

The poison must have been powerful; the spider gave a convulsive jerk that turned it over on to its back, then became perfectly still, its legs bunched crookedly underneath it. Simeon went over and examined it with interest; Sidonia wrinkled her nose with haughty distaste. But when Dravig said 'Thank you' – it was addressed to both of them – she blushed like a schoolgirl. And Niall realized with astonishment that she would have sacrificed her life for Dravig without a second thought. To save her the embarrassment of thinking he had noticed her blush, Niall turned to Simeon.

'Is it a spider?'

'Not strictly speaking. It's called a bull spider – my father used to call them druggets. I think it's a member of the bug family.'

'Have you ever seen one before?'

'Oh yes. The beetles kept two of them as work animals. They're incredibly stupid but immensely strong. Also incredibly loyal. Skorbo had probably ordered him to let no one in. And he'd be prepared to attack the Spider Lord herself rather than disobey.'

Sidonia said: 'There's a colony of them in the old mine over there.' She gestured vaguely towards the east.

Since the dead bull spider was occupying most of the doorway, Niall and Simeon had to drag it aside – like all spiders, it was surprisingly light for its size – before they could enter. Then they pushed back the steel door to its limit – the groove in which the castors moved was filled with compacted rust and grit. The first thing they saw was a mutilated corpse lying in a pool of blood. It was a woman, and her head and left arm had been eaten away. Her clothing, still covered in spider web, lay nearby; it had been neatly sliced off by the bull-spider's mandibles. They had evidently interrupted it in the course of eating its dinner.

Niall looked up. In the dim light that pierced the dusty windows he could see a dozen or so human-shaped cocoons suspended from the beams that supported the ceiling. They swayed gently in the breeze, exactly as he had seen them in his glimpse into the captain's mind. In fact, he was startled to realize how closely this shed corresponded to that momentary glimpse, as if all its essential features had been conveyed instantaneously. There was only one slight difference. The slaughterhouse of his vision had stunk of blood; this place only had a damp and musty odour. And this, he realized, was due to the difference between the senses of a man and the far keener senses of a spider.

Niall asked Simeon: 'Do you think any of them are alive?'

'She *was* alive.' Simeon indicated the woman's corpse. 'Otherwise her blood wouldn't have flowed like that.'

Niall turned to Dravig. 'Do you think any of them could be saved?'

Dravig's mental gesture was the equivalent of a shrug.

The warehouse was virtually a bare concrete shed, empty except for a number of packing cases stored in its farthest corner. The suspended bodies hung six feet or so above their heads. Each was covered with a semi-transparent gauzy mesh of surprising delicacy, far thinner than normal strands of spider web. As Niall's eyes became accustomed to the poor light, he was able to distinguish the features underneath the gauze that covered the faces – in one case, even to observing that the eyes were open.

Simeon pointed. 'That looks like a child.'

The body hanging closest to the far wall was only about three feet tall; through the thin web that covered his face like a hood, Niall could see dark curly hair. Simeon voiced the thought that was in Niall's mind.

'Could that be the brother of your kitchen maid, what's her name?'

'Nyra. It could be.' He asked Dravig: 'Is it possible to cut him down?'

The spider braced himself against the wall and reached up with the legs containing the tarsal claws, steadying the body with one of them while the other snipped the thread that held it suspended. He caught it neatly with his pedipalps as it fell.

As Niall took the body from him, the sticky web clung to his fingers and his tunic. He carried the child into the sunlight, and lowered him carefully to the floor. The gauze covering the face was like a film of sticky rubber, and resisted all attempts to tear it. Niall borrowed Sidonia's shortsword, which had an edge like a razor and, pulling up the mesh so it was clear of the face, carefully sliced his way through the clinging threads. The face that was exposed was that of a boy of about seven. The face was deathly pale, and there was no sign of breathing. But as Simeon was cutting away the mesh that covered the arm, Dravig extended his pedipalps above the chest and said: 'He is alive.' A moment later, Simeon placed his thumb on the child's wrist and pronounced that he could feel a faint pulse.

Niall placed his hand on the cold forehead. 'Is there any way of reviving him?'

Simeon shook his head. 'I don't know. If it's a poison that paralyses the central nervous system, the damage may be irreversible. That one's probably dead already.' He pointed to a face that was as emaciated as a skull.

Niall asked Dravig: '*Is* he dead?'

Dravig stretched upwards, raising his pedipalps towards the swaying body.

'No. He is alive. They are all alive, although the woman at the far end is close to death.'

Sidonia startled them with a cry. 'That one moved his eyes!'

She was standing underneath a body that hung from the centre of the beam, where the light from the doorway was strong. The body was small – it might have been that of an overgrown child or teenager. Behind the gauze that covered the face, the eyes were closed. Niall stared intently, but could detect no sign of breathing.

'Are you sure?'

'Quite sure. His eyelids moved.'

Niall addressed the face that swayed above his head.

'If you can hear me, try to open your eyelids.'

Nothing happened. He repeated it, slower and louder. This time, after a long delay, there was a faint but unmistakable movement of the eyelids. Sidonia said:

'You see. He is alive.'

Dravig said: 'It is not a he. It is a woman.'

From the other side of the shed, Simeon gave an exclamation of excitement. He was looking at the packing cases that stood in the far corner.

'What is it?'

'This stuff is labelled hospital equipment. Lend me that sword, would you? I want to try and get the lid off.'

As Niall looked down at the child who lay on the concrete, a flash of pain in the back of his skull warned him that he had been wearing the thought mirror for too long; he removed it and dropped it into his pocket. The relief was so intense that he felt dizzy; he had forgotten that the thought mirror consumed so much energy. Momentary darkness clouded his vision, filling his head with a buzzing noise, and he felt himself swaying. To avoid falling, he crouched down on his heels, balancing himself with both hands on the floor.

A few moments later the blackness began to pass away, and the child's face became visible. And then, quite suddenly, he was overwhelmed by a feeling of intense cold. It felt exactly as if he had been plunged into the depths of some icy lake, where the light found it impossible to penetrate. At the same time, he experienced a return of the nausea of the previous day, the peculiar exhaustion that had succeeded the attack by Skorbo's assassin. There was an odd sensation that something unpleasant had happened. Niall started around in bewilderment, and was relieved to see that everything looked so normal. Simeon and Sidonia were trying to open one of the packing cases, with Dravig looking on; it was obvious that they had noticed nothing. Through the open door, the bushes were glowing in the late afternoon sunlight – oddly enough, they seemed to be wavering, as if seen through a heat-haze. Yet he was gripped by an icy cold so intense that he had to clench his teeth to prevent them from chattering. He was also aware of a sense of vulnerability, as if a layer of skin had been stripped away, leaving all nerve-ends exposed.

The sunlight outside looked infinitely alluring, yet his weariness was so deep that he found it impossible to drag himself to his feet. It was a temptation to lie down on the floor and close his eyes. Yet he felt that if he gave way to the temptation, he would freeze to death. It cost him a convulsive effort of will to allow himself to sink into a sitting position, then to turn over on to his hands and knees and force himself to stand up. As he did so, he again felt his senses leaving him; but he mastered the nausea, and forced himself to take the half dozen steps that carried him out into the sunlight.

It was like plunging into a warm bath. The warmth seemed as startling and inexplicable as the cold of a few moments before. He breathed a deep sigh of relief, at the same time placing both hands on the nearest bush to prevent himself from swaying. As the warmth soaked into his body, he tried to understand what was happening. This glowing sensation was not simply the heat of the sun; it was a vital energy that made his heart beat faster and filled his blood with a pleasurable excitement. And the cold inside the building was not physical cold; it had the effect of draining his vitality; it was a sensation like bad news.

As the freezing sensation gradually melted away, his senses readjusted to the soothing warmth. The shimmering energy that surrounded him felt exactly as though warm air was rising through vents in the ground. It was associated with a pleasant tingling in the nerves, as if tiny bubbles were bursting all over his skin. With his eyes closed, he could sense that some form of energy was rising from the ground, and was somehow being converted into a spray by the plants and bushes. This was why he felt as if he was standing in a shower of spray from a fountain.

Yet why was the polarity reversed inside the building, so that it drained his vitality instead of increasing it?

Now that his energies felt recharged, this question filled him with curiosity. Deliberately bracing himself, he stepped forward across the threshold of the warehouse. It was, as he expected, like plunging into icy water. Yet there was an important difference. Cold water would have produced a freezing sensation in his feet and legs. This cold seemed to attack his face and shoulders, like an icy wind blowing down from above. As he took another slow step forward, it struck the crown of his head, causing the skin to contract so his hair felt as if it was standing on end. Then, as he forced himself to take another step, it was concentrated on his scalp and the skin of his neck and shoulders. And since he was now standing directly under the central beam, with its suspended bodies, it seemed reasonable to assume that the cold was associated with the bodies. This was confirmed when he took another step, and the freezing sensation moved to the back of his head and the upper part of his spine. It cost an effort of self-discipline to turn and walk back under the bodies; it felt as if he was naked and standing in a shower of icy rain.

Yet why should unconscious bodies produce this sensation? The question so intrigued him that he mastered the desire to go out into the sunlight, and forced himself to stand there, trying to understand what was happening. Was it possible that these devitalized bodies were somehow stealing his own vital energies? But if that was the explanation, why had the others not noticed it? For a moment he considered hanging the thought mirror round his neck, but was deterred by the thought of the agony it would produce in his present state of fatigue. Instead, he closed his eyes and twisted his face into a grimace of intense concentration. The relief was immediate; it was as if he had interposed a barrier between himself and the suspended bodies. Even so, the cold was beginning to make his shoulder muscles ache.

It was at this point that he realized that his efforts had attracted Dravig's attention. The spider was staring at him so intently that it produced a prickling sensation in the roots of his hair. He had time to register this as unusual – Dravig would normally have regarded it as a form of rudeness – when there was an explosion of light inside his skull, and a sensation as if the breath had been snatched from his lungs. For a moment he felt as though he was drowning, and was overwhelmed with panic. Then the breathlessness passed, and as his senses cleared, he realized he was being held up by Sidonia and Simeon. He straightened his legs and forced himself into an upright position, realizing that his legs had buckled underneath him. At the same time he noticed that the cold had vanished, and that the air in the building felt pleasantly warm. His voice sounded thick as he asked:

'What happened?'

Dravig said: 'Did you not realize that you were being attacked?'

Niall shook his head. 'No. I just felt cold.' He still felt as if he had just climbed out of an icy river.

'You were cold because you were being attacked. Your energies were being drained.' Responding to the question in Niall's mind, Dravig indicated the body that swayed above Niall's head. It was the girl whose eyelids had moved. Niall stared up at her, trying to distinguish the features beneath the gauze that covered them.

'But she is unconscious.'

'Yes. She is unconscious. You were being attacked *through* her. You have a dangerous enemy.'

As he spoke, Niall was overwhelmed with a sense of his own stupidity. Suddenly, everything was obvious,

173

and he found it difficult to understand how he could have failed to see it. Because he had assumed that the unconscious bodies were draining his energy, he had looked no further for an explanation.

He asked: 'What did you do?'

'I tried to attack your enemy through your mind. But it was too late. He had already withdrawn.'

Simeon said: 'Come on. Let's get you into the sunlight.'

Niall needed no persuading; he still felt frozen to the bone. As he walked outside, with Simeon's hand on his elbow, his legs felt numb and stiff. The feeling of the sunlight on his face brought a sense of relief; yet he was aware that something had changed. The air was no longer full of shimmering heat-waves; this was merely the normal sunlight of a winter afternoon. The bushes still glowed with the same magical brightness; but when he reached out and touched them, there was no longer a sensation like standing in a shower of fine spray.

He asked Dravig: 'Is it possible to reach this girl and cut her down?'

'Of course.' He returned into the building, and a few moments later, emerged with the web-encased body gripped in his pedipalps and front legs. He laid her on the ground at Niall's feet.

'Your sword please.' Sidonia handed it to him. Niall pulled the web clear of the face, and carefully cut it open; as it parted, it made a faint tearing sound like rubber. Niall sliced down as far as the waist. As he had expected, she was wearing a slave's tunic. Simeon watched with curiosity as he reached down inside the neckline. Niall found what he was looking for between the small flat breasts; the tightness of the web had prevented it from falling out. Niall snapped the chain, and held out the pendant on the palm of his hand.

Simeon shook his head incredulously. 'Another one of those.' He took the girl's chin in his hand and turned her face towards him. 'She doesn't look like the others.'

It was true. Her hair was short, like that of a boy, but the features had the delicacy of a girl, with a finely shaped nose. The face might have been made of wax, and the lips were so bloodless that they looked white.

Simeon tore aside the gauze of web, freeing her arm, and placed his thumb on her wrist.

'There's a pulse all right.' He stared with curiosity at the pale face. 'But I'd like to know how she got here.'

'Like the others. Walking around at night. She's lucky she wasn't eaten.'

Simeon said: 'I wonder if she's the reason they killed Skorbo.'

The same idea had occurred to Niall.

'It's possible.'

'In that case, she's dangerous.'

'Dangerous?' For a moment he was puzzled; the unconscious girl looked anything but dangerous.

'He may be willing to kill to get her back.'

He shrugged. 'That's a risk we'll have to take.' But he was aware that he sounded more confident than he felt. He turned to Sidonia. 'Would you mind staying here to guard her until we return?'

'Of course, lord. But would it not be simpler for me to carry her?'

'Carry her?' The idea had not even occurred to him.

'She looks as light as a child.'

Her words reminded him of the child who was still lying on the concrete floor. Now the sun was sinking below the treetops, the air was becoming chilly.

'No, Dravig can carry her. But do you think you could carry him?'

'Of course.' She picked up the child as easily as if he had been a doll, cradling his head on her shoulder.

As they walked back towards the setting sun, Niall's body ached with weariness. A chill wind sprang up from the north, and he pulled up the hood of his cloak and drew its folds more closely around him. The events of the day had left him profoundly tired, and fatigue had numbed his senses, so he walked mechanically, oblivious of his surroundings. Yet underneath the exhaustion there was a sense of deep satisfaction, which revived every time he looked at the child in Sidonia's arms, or at the girl who was now being carried by Dravig. And now, in retrospect, he could begin to understand what had happened in Skorbo's larder. As he had removed the thought mirror from his neck, he had experienced momentary loss of consciousness. His enemy had seized the opportunity to insinuate himself into his mind like an invisible leech. Yet this had proved to be a serious miscalculation, since he had alerted them to his presence. The result was that this girl – whose identity would otherwise have gone unsuspected – was now their hostage. The enemy might be unpredictable and dangerous, but he was obviously not infallible . . .

Niall had become so absorbed in his thoughts that it came as a surprise to realize that they were already entering the main square. The sun was sinking below the western rooftops; only the top half of the white tower reflected its golden light. Most of the snow had vanished from the square; it remained only on the grass that surrounded the white tower.

As they halted at the bottom of the steps, he saw the two wolf spiders who kept guard on either side of the door.

'What are they doing here?'

Dravig said: 'The Death Lord ordered them to keep guard. He was afraid that some of Skorbo's friends might bear you malice.'

'Please thank her for her consideration.' A few hours

earlier, the thought of guards outside the palace would have struck him as ridiculous; now they brought a sense of security.

As he entered the main hallway, Nephtys was descending the stair; her smile of welcome turned to astonishment as Dravig entered, with the girl resting in his pedipalps. Sidonia followed, with the child in her arms.

He asked her: 'Is the kitchen maid Nyra still here?'

'Yes, my lord.'

'Ask her to come here.'

Dravig laid the girl on the matting in front of the fire; Sidonia set down the child beside her. A moment later, Nyra came in, looking apprehensive. Niall pointed to the child.

'Is this your brother?'

As she looked at the still form her face became deathly pale; for a moment Niall thought she was going to faint. He said quickly: 'He is alive.'

She gave a cry and dropped on her knees beside the child. When she saw that he was breathing, she seized him and covered his face in kisses. Then, to Niall's embarrassment, she rushed over to him, seized both his hands, and pressed them to her lips. He freed one of them and placed it gently on her hair.

'There. The next task is to revive him.' He turned to Simeon. 'What do you advise?'

'Give him a warm bath, and massage his arms and legs.' Niall could sense that he was less than optimistic; but Nyra was too excited to notice.

Nephtys was looking down with curiosity at the girl, whose breast was also rising and falling gently.

Niall said: 'She was also destined for Skorbo's dinner.' His words made her shrink, but he was too tired to care. 'I want you to prepare the room next to mine, and place her in a warm bed. The door is to remain locked and bolted all the time.' The sight of her pale face reminded him of the pendant. He excused himself and went down into the basement; it was in darkness, but the light through the open door enabled him to grope his way to the urn in the corner. As he removed the pendant from his pocket, his fingertips told him that it had ceased to be inert; it seemed to squirm like a living beetle. He removed the heavy lid with both hands and dropped the pendant into its depths. As he replaced the lid he experienced a curious sense of lightness.

An hour later, he was stretched out on the cushions in his chamber, eating a dish of river prawns that had just been cooked by Jarita. Simeon was helping Nyra to bath the child. The sound of excited voices told him that Nyra's parents had arrived; they had been summoned to the palace. He tried to generate the energy to go and see what was happening, then decided to drink a glass of mead instead. Ten minutes later, as Jarita was laying the table for supper, Nephtys came into the room, smiling with pleasure. 'He's just opened his eyes . . .' She became silent as Jarita shook her head and pointed. Niall was lying on his back, sleeping deeply.

PART TWO
# The Living Dead

That night was made memorable by another curious experience.

He woke up in a darkness that was as warm and suffocating as a blanket. For a moment he imagined he was back in the burrow; then the collapse of the ashes in the stove made him aware that he was in his own room. He lay there with all his senses alert, wondering if he had been awakened by some noise. When his sixth sense assured him that he was alone, he threw back the blankets and turned on his back in the velvet darkness, wondering why he found it so difficult to breathe. His heart was pounding, and his body covered in perspiration.

Inevitably, his mind returned to the warehouse with its hanging bodies, and he visualized them so clearly that he even seemed to be able to see them suspended above him in the dark. Even by daylight the scene had been unpleasant enough; now, in the middle of the night, he found himself imagining how the victim felt as a spider landed on him, immobilizing him with its will-power, then sinking its fangs into the flesh and injecting the venom that would bring total paralysis. He could envisage how the victims felt as they were carried, fully conscious, to the warehouse, wrapped in a cocoon of sticky spider-silk, then suspended upside down, in the full knowledge that they were to be eaten alive. The thought was so horrifying that he writhed as if in pain.

In fact, he knew that it was stupid to be tormented by these imaginings, and that in the daylight they would vanish like a nightmare. Yet even this thought became a kind of torment, for he was aware that the horror was real. Eventually, by using his will-power to relax his muscles and slow down his heartbeat, he succeeded in restoring a sense of peace and equilibrium. As the grey light of dawn began to seep into the room, he felt himself drifting back into sleep.

The dream that followed had a curious air of reality. He was standing outside the palace, and the air was full of falling snow; flakes of snow were melting on his cheeks. He was trying to push open the door, but it seemed to be locked. Then he heard footsteps from inside, and someone drew back the bolt. The door opened, and his father was standing there. His mother, who was leaning over the balustrade at the top of the stairs, called: 'Who is it?', and his father answered: 'It's only Niall. He's been looking for the magician.' For some reason, this answer struck Niall as incongruous. How could his father know about the magician, since he had died before Niall came to the spider city? The realization that his father was dead made Niall suddenly aware that he must be dreaming. He looked carefully at his father, to see if there was any obvious indication of his unreality; in fact, he looked as real and solid as usual. The beard and moustache were streaked with the grey hairs that had developed in the final year of his life, and he was wearing the shabby garment of the caterpillar skin that he had worn on the journey to Dira. The hall in which they were standing also looked completely normal, and when Niall put out a finger to touch the flecked green marble of the wall, it felt cool and solid, exactly as he had expected it to feel. Then he looked down at the floor, which should have been made of the same substance, and experienced a sense of triumph when he saw that it was made of triangular slabs of a stone that looked like granite. This was undeniable proof that he was dreaming. But in that case, where was he? The obvious answer was: lying asleep in bed. Yet when he moved his shoulders to see if he could feel the bed, it seemed obvious that he was standing in the hall. It then struck him that if his body was lying asleep upstairs, the simplest way to find out would be to go and look.

He took a step towards the stairs, then decided that, since he was dreaming, he might as well fly. He raised his arms in the air and rose gently from the ground and up over the balustrade where his mother was standing. Floating on up the second flight of stairs, he alighted on the floor outside his chamber. Inside, he found Jarita laying the table for breakfast; she was so preoccupied that she did not even notice him. He opened his bedroom door and went inside; just as he expected, he was lying in bed, fast asleep, with his left arm lying on the coverlet and his right hand under the pillow. He went and stood by the bed, looking down on his body with a kind of pleased astonishment, wondering what would happen if he leaned over and shook himself by the shoulder: would his other self wake up and speak to him? Then suddenly he knew what would happen: he would wake up and find himself in bed. But he had no desire to wake up yet; the situation was far too interesting. Therefore he stepped back quietly and tiptoed out of the room. Jarita was still so absorbed that she failed to notice him, and he was tempted to give her a pinch; he decided against it in case she screamed and woke him up. He tiptoed out into the corridor.

Now he recollected that he had ordered the unconscious girl to be placed in the next room. He pushed open the door and entered. Simeon was in the room, standing by the bed, which was underneath the window, and cutting the spider-silk from the girl's body with a huge pair of scissors whose blades must have been over a foot long. As the snapping steel reached her feet, Simeon pulled open the silk with a jerk. The girl was not wearing shoes, and Niall observed that there were marks around her ankles, as if they had been tied. He asked Simeon: 'What are those?' and Simeon shook his head and said: 'Damned if I know.' The phrase was quite uncharacteristic of Simeon, reminding Niall that this was a dream.

And now, to Niall's surprise, Simeon began cutting off the slave uniform, starting at the top near the neck. The big shears sliced through the coarse grey cloth until they reached the bottom of the garment, which fell apart, revealing that she was naked underneath. The first thing that struck Niall was that her body was unusually pale, and that faint blue veins showed in the skin of her thighs, which were delicately curved. But he was puzzled by fragments of some brown substance that was sticking to the small, flat breasts; there were also traces of it on her belly and thighs. Niall reached out and peeled off one of the larger pieces; it was dry, like a fragment of leaf mould.

He looked down at the sleeping face. 'I wonder what she's called?'

'Charis.'

'How do you know?'

Simeon made the curious reply: 'It's written on her heart.'

A sound from the street drew Niall's attention, and he looked out of the window. In the square below, a gang of workmen, led by the overseer Dion, were pulling a large cart, on which there was a wooden packing case; he recognized it as being one of those from the corner of the warehouse. He turned to Simeon. 'One of your cases has arrived.' Simeon looked out of the window and said with enthusiasm: 'Good! Let's go and unpack it.' Niall asked: 'What are you expecting to find?' 'What does it matter? It's sure to be interesting.' He pulled the bedclothes up over the naked girl, and hurried to the door. As they stepped into the corridor, Niall turned the key in the door and dropped it into his pocket. Simeon looked surprised. 'Why lock the door? She won't escape.' Niall lowered his voice. 'I don't trust Jarita any more than I trust Skorbo.' At that moment he glanced towards his own chamber and saw that Jarita was, in fact, looking through the partly open door. His certainty that she must have overheard made him feel guilty and apologetic. Then, to his surprise, she wrinkled her nose at him and stuck out her tongue. He was so startled that he woke up.

The sun was shining through the half-closed curtains; from its position on the wall he guessed that it was about seven o'clock. From outside he could hear the sound of birds. It was then that he realized that he was lying with his left arm on the coverlet of the bed, and his right hand under the pillow, just as he had seen himself in his dream. The realization startled him; he usually slept on his left side or his right. Was it possible that the strange dream contained some element of reality?

He yawned and stretched, then climbed out of bed. He winced when he accidentally touched the red spot in the middle of his chest – the bruise caused by the thought mirror during his encounter with the bull spider; the skin was peeling from it, as if it had been subjected to intense sunburn. It made him aware that a certain feeling of weariness still lingered in his muscles. He slipped into the sheepskin mantle that he used as a dressing gown and went out into the corridor, closing the door quietly behind him in case he woke Jarita, who slept in the next room. On the other side of his chamber was the room to which the girl had been taken. As he reached out to the handle, he noticed that the brass key in the keyhole was the same key he had seen in his dream.

But the room itself was different. It contained more furniture, and the bed was against the right-hand wall, not under the window. He half-expected to find Simeon there, and felt oddly relieved to find it empty. Even now, his tiredness created a faintly dreamlike sensation, so that for an absurd moment he found himself wondering if he was still asleep.

The girl was lying on the bed; she had been covered with a blanket that left only her face visible. When Niall pulled this back, he saw that she was still encased in a cocoon of spider-silk. Her breathing was scarcely visible, and when he touched her forehead the flesh felt cold. As he looked down at her, he experienced again the sensation of his dream – a feeling of being on the verge of some interesting discovery. Like an empty house, her sleeping mind seemed to invite him to investigate its secrets. Yet even as he placed his hand on her cold forehead, he experienced an oddly uncomfortable sensation as if he was being observed.

He crossed to the window, which was closed – in the dream, it had been open. It cost some effort to open it – the brass screw that controlled the sliding opener was thick with dust, and the hinges were rusty. But even before he forced it open, he was aware that the dream had been incorrect in another particular: the view from this window was not of the square, but of an empty building next door.

When he pushed open the casement to its limit, a small portion of the square in front of the palace became visible. He breathed deeply, enjoying a fresh breeze. As he did so, he heard voices in the square and the sound of laughter. Suddenly, he knew with absolute certainty what he was going to see next. A moment later, four men came into view, dragging a baggage cart by the shafts. Then, as the cart itself became visible, he saw that it contained one of the large packing cases from the warehouse. Another four men were pushing from behind, and the overseer Dion was walking beside it. For a moment, the dreamlike sensation intensified, and he shook his head to get rid of it, pulling the sheepskin closer round his throat.

The door behind him opened; Jarita stood there in her night clothes – a knee-length tunic of thin cotton-like material. She looked embarrassed to find him there.

'Is my lord ready for his bath?' She spoke with eyes on the ground, but Niall observed that she had stolen a glance towards the bed. He was glad that the girl was covered with the blanket.

'Yes, in a moment.' He spoke curtly, vaguely annoyed that she had interrupted him. She withdrew in silence.

The square was now empty; at this time of the morning, there were few people about. Jarita's interruption had somehow destroyed the curious sense of anticipation. After another glance at the unconscious girl, he realized that the desire to probe her mind had evaporated. As he closed the door behind him, he turned the key in the lock and dropped it into his pocket.

Niall's bathroom was less elaborate than the equivalent room in Kazak's palace, in which the circular bath was tiled with white porcelain, and was the size of a small swimming pool. This bath was a square stone tub, about six feet wide, sunk into the floor; a furnace underneath kept it perpetually warm. Neither was the water in this tub scented; to the bafflement of his womenfolk, Niall preferred plain water.

As he descended slowly into the water – which was a little too hot for comfort – Jarita came in with bath towels. She placed them on a wooden bench, then stood waiting. He knew she was hoping to be asked to join him in the water, but he wanted to be alone.

'Shall I bring the oil of roses, my lord?'

'No thank you.'

When the door had closed behind her, he sat down in the warm water – it came up to his shoulders – and leaned back against the wall of the tub. Then, in the relaxation that followed, he set out to recall his dream. Unlike most dreams, this one had not faded, and he was able to go over it step by step, from the moment he had found himself standing outside the palace in the falling snow. The sensation of floating up the stairs had been quite clear; so had the curious experience of standing and looking down at his own body as it lay asleep. This struck him as oddly significant, yet he was unable to understand why. He also recollected the size of the pair of scissors that Simeon had used to cut off the girl's clothes; they were so large that they seemed almost comic. But when he recalled standing at the window, and watching the baggage cart go past, he remembered that there had been no snow on the ground. That seemed to prove that it was nothing more than a dream. In which case, what was the significance of its strange symbolism? What were the brown, leaf-like fragments on the girl's body? Why had Simeon said that her name was written on her heart? (He tried hard to recollect her name, but was unable to do so.) And why had he told Simeon that he would not trust Jarita any more than Skorbo? This seemed typical of the stupid, irrational statements made in dreams. Yet although the whole thing had the absurdity of a dream, he still felt that it concealed some deeper meaning.

Niall stifled a yawn. This weariness troubled him; it seemed absurd to feel so sleepy when he had been awake for less than half an hour. In an attempt to shake it off, he gripped his nostrils between thumb and forefinger, and plunged his head below the surface of the water. There was a roaring sensation as the water entered his ears. Yet this was accompanied by an instantaneous feeling of relief, as if something inside his brain was expanding. When he came up gasping for air, the sense of relief continued, although he noticed that the weariness began to return as he leaned his head back against the wall of the tub and closed his eyes. He gripped his nostrils again and plunged his head under water. Once again, he experienced the sensation of relief, as if a window had opened inside his head and a cool breeze was blowing in. He allowed his body to slip down inside the bath until he was lying on the bottom; the depth of water above his head produced an oddly comforting sensation. This time he held his breath until his lungs were bursting.

When his head broke the surface, he was startled to realize that someone was standing beside the bath; he had to rub the water out of his eyes before he recognized Jarita.

'I'm sorry, my lord. I knocked twice.'

'What is it?' He was beginning to feel resentful about these interruptions.

'The doctor is here. He wants to know if he can look at the axe.'

'The axe? What does he want it for? Oh, never mind. Give it to him. And ask him to stay and have some breakfast.'

It was only after she had gone that Niall realized that the feeling of weariness had vanished completely.

When he entered the room, five minutes later, Simeon was seated at the table, with the axe lying in front of him. Its head was resting on a white cloth, and Simeon was carefully scraping the edge of the blade with a knife. He was so absorbed that he failed to hear Niall entering the room, and only glanced up at the sound of the closing door.

'What are you doing?'

'Taking scrapings from the blade.' He indicated a few traces of a brownish-black substance on the white cloth. 'I'm going to try to find out if it's been poisoned.'

'Is my brother no better?'

'Worse. He has a fever.'

Niall's heart contracted with anxiety.

'Is it serious?'

'I don't think so. That's what puzzles me. If the axe had been poisoned, I'd expect him to be dead by now.'

Jarita came in from the kitchen, carrying a plate containing a pile of pancakes. As they seated themselves at table, Niall asked:

'How will you test it?' He was aware that Simeon's laboratory in the hospital was primitive.

'To begin with, dissolve these scrapings in a salt solution, then examine them on a microscope slide.'

'Microscope? You have a microscope?'

Simeon chuckled as he poured honey on a pancake.

'I've more than that. Those packing cases contained some marvellous stuff. Hypodermics, scalpels, even a spectroscopic analyser. You ought to come and see.'

Niall said: 'The brown stain on the blade is Skorbo's blood. Could that explain Veig's fever?'

'I doubt it. Why should it? Spider blood's not poisonous.'

'What if there was spider venom on the axe blade?'

Simeon nodded. 'I thought of that too. A very small quantity of spider venom might explain the symptoms. If so, he'll be all right in a day or so, as he builds up resistance.'

They were interrupted by a timid knock on the door. Jarita opened it. Niall recognized the slight, blonde girl who stood there as Crestia, Veig's maidservant.

'My master is coming to see his brother.'

Simeon snorted. 'That's stupid. He's not well enough.'

The girl was obviously unhappy. 'That is what I told him . . .'

'Well go back at once and tell him I forbid it.'

'Too late.' Veig stood in the doorway. 'I thought I'd come and join you for breakfast.'

If it had been later in the day, Niall would have assumed he was drunk. Veig was swaying slightly, and he spoke slowly and hesitantly, choosing his words with care. Niall signalled to Jarita.

'Set another place for my brother.' He crossed the room and took Veig's arm. 'Come and sit down.'

'Thank you.' Veig disengaged his arm. 'There's nothing wrong with me – just a slight fever.' He sank down on the cushions and leaned his back against the wall. 'I won't have anything to eat. Just some fruit juice or milk.'

Niall could see why Simeon looked concerned. Veig's forehead was covered in perspiration, and his face was pale. There were dark rings under his eyes – so dark that they looked like bruises – and the bandage around his right hand was soaked in blood.

Jarita placed a large goblet of papaya juice on the table. Veig picked it up in both hands, drank thirstily until he had almost drained it, then began to cough. Finally, he leaned his head back against the wall, his eyes closed; a drop of juice ran down into his beard. Niall watched him with concealed anxiety. When Veig's breathing became heavy and regular, Niall gently probed his mind – assuming, correctly, that in his present state of affliction, his brother would be unaware of the intrusion. What he observed troubled him. Although he seemed to be awake, Veig was actually half-asleep; his consciousness was being invaded by confused images from the world of dreams. The worst of these was a black, shapeless being, more like an octopus than a man, that was trying to engulf him. Now Niall understood why Veig had come to join them; he was afraid to be alone.

He also realized that the best way to allay his brother's fear was to behave normally. He therefore called to Jarita, asking her to bring the herb tea and the hard-boiled quails' eggs. Then he continued his conversation with Simeon.

'Do you know what happened to the little boy we brought back?'

'He regained consciousness last night. But he is still too weak to move.'

'How did they wake him?'

Jarita, who was bending over the table, said: 'They gave him a warm bath and massaged his body with oil of roses.'

Niall asked Simeon: 'Do you think that might work for the others?'

'It's possible. But I doubt it. Children are more resilient than adults.'

Veig opened his eyes

'I hear you brought a girl back with you.'

His voice was still heavy and slurred, yet he seemed more alert.

Niall nodded. 'She's in the next room.'

'Who is she?'

Niall waited until he was sure Jarita was out of hearing before he replied.

'We think she is an accomplice of the men who killed Skorbo.'

Simeon said: 'Although I can't imagine why they wanted to bring a girl with them.'

Veig said: 'Perhaps she was some kind of housekeeper. They must have had a hide-out somewhere.'

Niall asked: 'Would you like to see her?'

Veig grinned. 'Is she pretty?'

Niall also grinned, glad to hear his brother sounding more like his normal self. 'Very.'

'In that case, yes.'

Niall pushed his plate away. Veig said:

'Finish your breakfast – there's no hurry.'

'I'd finished anyway.'

Simeon asked Veig: 'Are you feeling better?'

'I think so. This thing comes and goes.' But as he rose, he swayed, and had to clutch at the wall for support.

The maidservant Crestia was waiting outside the door. She looked anxiously at Veig but, to Niall's relief, made no move towards him. Niall knew his brother well enough to know that he would resent any attempt at help.

He unlocked the door and let them in. As he stepped inside, Niall was again reminded of the dream. The memory was so clear that he hung back, waiting to see what Simeon would do next.

In fact, Simeon pulled back the blanket and lifted the girl's wrist.

'Nothing wrong with her pulse.'

Simeon raised the girl's eyelids with his thumb, then opened her mouth. 'My God!'

'What is it?' Niall looked into her mouth and saw what had startled Simeon. The tip of the girl's tongue was split, so that it resembled the tongue of a snake.

Simeon touched it gently with his fingertip. 'Poor girl. That looks to me as if it's been deliberately cut.'

Niall could see why he thought so; a V-shaped segment of the tongue was missing.

'Why should anyone do that?'

Simeon said grimly: 'Perhaps she talked too much.'

'Would that prevent her from talking?'

'It would make it difficult. When you speak, notice

how often you press your tongue against your teeth.'
He drew the blanket down to her feet, then tugged at
the spider web that still encased the lower half of her
body.

'Let's have this off.'

He reached into the side pocket of his tunic and took
out a pair of scissors. Niall was almost relieved to see
that they were not the grotesquely large pair of his
dream, but only slightly larger than normal; it seemed
to confirm that the dream had been merely a freak of
his sleeping consciousness. When he had sliced the web
down to her feet, Simeon pulled it free and threw it on
the floor. It was so light that it scarcely made a sound.
Niall was now able to observe that her feet were bare,
and that around both ankles there were faint red marks.

'Now this, I think.' Simeon began to cut the slave
tunic, starting from the neck. The scissors were obviously very sharp and as the fabric parted, Niall was
able to see that, just as in the dream, the girl was naked
underneath. A moment later, his heart contracted and
the blood rushed to his cheeks. On the white flesh of
the belly and thighs, there were a number of brown
fragments that might have been damp autumn leaves.

He reached out and peeled one from her thigh.

'What do you think this is?'

Simeon took it from him and peered at it.

'I'd say it's a piece of seaweed.'

'Seaweed? Why should she be wearing seaweed?'

Simeon shrugged. 'I'm damned if I know.' As he
spoke, Niall experienced a curious sensation of two
overlapping realities.

He pointed to the red marks around the ankles.

'What do you suppose they are?'

Simeon studied them carefully.

'Looks as though she's been tied up. But it must
have been for a long time, or the marks would have

disappeared.' He peered at the space between her big toe and its neighbour; Niall could see they were connected by a thin web of flesh. 'And she hasn't had the operation to separate the toes.'

Remembering the words spoken in the dream, Niall asked:

'I wonder what she's called?'

But Simeon merely shook his head, looking blank.

Staring at the still face, Niall was tempted to probe her mind. But he decided to leave it until he was alone.

'What do you think we should do with her?'

'I'd advise you to leave her until we know more about spider poison. It may simply work itself out of her system.'

A muffled sound, like a groan, came from Veig. He had been standing close to the door since they came into the room, leaning against the wall; Niall had been so absorbed in the girl that he had paid him little attention. Now he was shocked to see that Veig's face was glistening with perspiration, and had become so pale that Niall wondered for a moment if he was about to lose consciousness. When he probed his brother's mind, he seemed to plunge into a roaring confusion in which Veig's heartbeats sounded like hammer blows. In this chaos, the borderline between reality and a nightmarish unreality had become almost indistinguishable.

Niall placed his hand on Veig's shoulder.

'Are you all right?'

Veig stared at him, but seemed hardly to recognize him. Then he looked across the room, and his eyes focused on the naked girl; a puzzled look crossed his face, as if she was an acquaintance whose name he had forgotten. A drop of sweat ran, unnoticed, down the side of his nose, and lost itself in his moustache. He began walking unsteadily towards the bed, his steps as heavy as if he were climbing a mountain. Niall and Simeon exchanged glances; Niall shook his head slightly, to indicate that he felt that Veig should be left alone. The girl lay there, naked, one arm hanging loosely by the side of the bed. It seemed to Niall that her breathing had deepened and become faster. Veig had halted two paces from the bed and was staring down at her; he was breathing through his mouth, and seemed to be in some kind of trance. Then he lunged forward, placing one outstretched hand on her forehead, one on her solar plexus. Simeon also started forward; but it was unnecessary. As Veig reached the bed, his knees buckled. His hands clawed at the air in an oddly confused way; then he collapsed on top of the girl. He landed so heavily that Niall was afraid he might suffocate her. Simeon obviously felt the same misgiving; he took Veig under both armpits and tried to lift him. Veig was too heavy; but he slid off the bed and rolled on the floor, coming to rest with his face upturned to the ceiling.

Niall glanced at the girl. This time there could be no doubt. She was breathing more deeply, and there were faint spots of colour in her cheeks.

Simeon shook his head.

'He shouldn't have left his bed. He's in a fever.' He opened the door; Niall was glad to see that Crestia was standing outside. Simeon said:

'Get some servants, and have him carried back to his chamber.'

Niall stooped beside his brother, and placed his hand on his forehead. It felt surprisingly cool. A moment later, Veig opened his eyes, and struggled into a sitting position. When Simeon tried to restrain him, he shook off his hand impatiently.

'Let me alone. I'm all right.'

Simeon said: 'You fainted.'

'No I didn't. I just tripped and fell.' His voice was surprisingly insistent, almost angry.

Simeon said soothingly: 'All right. You tripped and fell.'

A moment later, Crestia came into the room, followed by two muscular servants from the kitchen. As Veig began struggling to his feet, she tried to help him; he pushed her away angrily.

'I'm all right. Let me alone.'

The girl looked appealingly at Simeon. 'The doctor says you should go back to bed.'

Niall touched his brother's arm.

'Please do as she says.'

The appeal had its effect. Veig nodded and walked towards the door, followed by Crestia. But as he went out, Niall noticed that he cast a glance back towards the bed.

Niall asked: 'Do you think he'll be all right?'

'I think so. He's suffering from some kind of recurring delirium. But it doesn't seem too serious. I hope that girl can persuade him to stay in bed.'

Niall turned to Jarita, who was lingering in the doorway.

'Find my mother, and ask her to go to my brother. Tell her that he must be made to rest.'

As he pulled the blanket back over the girl, he noticed that her breathing was so faint as to be almost unobservable, and that her cheeks were again without colour.

Simeon said: 'I'm going to the hospital. Are you coming?'

He hesitated, wondering if he should stay with Veig. Then he realized there was nothing he could do.

'Very well.'

As they started along the corridor, Nephtys came to meet them.

'Councillor Broadus wishes to speak to you, my lord. He's waiting below.'

'I'm coming now.'

Simeon said in an undertone: 'That man's a terrible bore. Don't let him waste too much of your time.'

Broadus was standing in front of the fire in the hall, warming his hands; beside him stood a small, bald-headed man whom Niall recognized as a Council member from Dira. As Niall approached them, both made a ritual gesture of obeisance. Broadus was beaming; he was evidently well pleased with himself.

'Highness, I have made a discovery of the first importance.'

'About Skorbo's killers?'

'Yes, highness. I have found out where they were hiding.'

'Excellent! Where?'

'In a house in the slave quarter.'

Niall looked at the bald-headed man, who was shuffling uncomfortably; he remembered him as one of the less articulate Council members.

'And your colleague?'

Broadus said offhandedly:

'Ah yes, Fergus . . . You remember Councillor Fergus?'

'Of course.' The bald-headed man bowed awkwardly. 'And what part did you play in this discovery, councillor?'

'I . . . sp-spent the evening in the slave quarter, asking about strangers.' The little man had a slight speech impediment, and even his bald head blushed as he spoke. 'S-someone remembered three men and a woman who lived in a house near the river. The door was locked, but I managed to force the lock. The place was empty . . .'

Niall nodded. 'It would be.'

'But there were signs that several people had been living there. And they were not slaves.'

'How could you tell?'

'They had too many clothes. Most slaves only possess one garment.'

The little man was obviously intelligent as well as competent. At this point Broadus – who had become distinctly restive while his colleague was speaking – interrupted.

'They must have planned it all very carefully. They chose a house near the river because they know slaves are afraid of rats. I've been to look at it, and I'm certain these people were not slaves.'

'Good work. I shall commend you both at the next Council meeting.' The little man looked embarrassed, but Broadus glowed with satisfaction.

'Would you like us to escort you there, my lord?'

'Not now, thank you. There's something else I have to do first. But there *is* something I'd like you to do for me. Go to the headquarters of the Spider Lord and ask to see Sidonia, the captain of the guard. Tell her to send guards to prevent anyone from entering the house before I arrive.'

'Of course, sire.' Broadus performed his most graceful bow.

Simeon waited until the door had closed behind them then said:

'You can see what happened there, can't you? The little chap did all the work, and Broadus wants to take all the credit.'

'I don't care who takes the credit. This could be the breakthrough we've been hoping for.'

It was another sunny day, although the north wind had a cutting edge. The sky was a cold blue, and piled high with fleecy white clouds that looked as if they were made of cotton wool. The few patches of melting snow that remained were on the grass surrounding the white tower, and these were stained with mud. Oddly enough, the top of the white tower, which was slightly curved, was still covered with a thick layer of snow, some of it projecting over the edge, like the guttering on a roof. As they watched, a large slab of it came sliding off, and crashed to the ground.

From the corner of the main avenue, they saw Sidonia emerge from the headquarters of the Spider Lord, and approach Broadus and Fergus, who were waiting on the pavement, under the gaze of two wolf spiders. Simeon said:

'Do you really think guards are necessary?' He grinned. 'Or was that just to get rid of Broadus?'

'No. I'm not taking any risks. I think it would be a mistake to underestimate our opponent. He always seems to be two steps ahead of us.'

'You seem to have done fairly well so far.'

Niall nodded.

'Yes, luck has been on our side. But it won't continue unless we can find out who this man is and what he wants to achieve.'

Simeon asked seriously: 'You're sure he is a man?'

Niall was startled by the question.

'What else could he be?'

'You called him a magician.'

'Isn't that a man?'

Simeon shook his head.

'My grandmother – goddess rest her soul – used to say that there are three orders of supernatural being. There are the gods who made the earth. Then there are nature spirits, who care for nothing but trees and lakes and mountains. Then there are the magicians, who are halfway between gods and men. Your magician sounds like that.'

Niall felt no surprise to hear Simeon speak of gods and nature spirits. He had become accustomed to the fact that even the servants of the bombardier beetles took such beliefs for granted. In fact, Niall himself had shared them until the Steegmaster had taken his education in hand.

'All the same, I don't believe he's a supernatural being.'

'Then what is he?'

'A man. A spiteful and ruthless man, but a man nevertheless.'

Simeon gave him a sidelong glance. 'You sound as if you know all about him.'

Niall said: 'I think I have even seen him.'

Simeon stared at him with amazement.

'You've *what*?'

Niall hastened to explain: 'It was only in a dream.'

'And what did he look like?'

'He had a forked beard' – Niall tried to indicate its shape under his chin – 'and his face was hidden in a black hood.'

Simeon nodded, his face serious. 'That sounds like a magician all right. My grandmother used to say they're twice as clever as a human being and twice as vindictive. She used to say she'd rather tease a swamp cobra.'

As he spoke, Niall experienced a peculiar sensation, as if a cloud had covered the sun. They walked the remaining distance to the hospital in silence, each pre-occupied with his own thoughts.

Two four-wheel carts stood at the side entrance, one empty, the other containing three bodies wrapped in their cocoons of spider web. Niall observed that pedestrians averted their eyes and hurried past, as if afraid of being contaminated by the sight. It reminded him that, in this city, most of the human beings still preferred not to know the secrets of their former masters. Overhead, on a web that stretched across the street, a brown- and black-striped hunting spider looked down curiously, probably wondering why good meat was being allowed to go to waste. A massively-built workman came out of the yard, slung a body over his shoulders like a sack of potatoes, and carried it inside.

The unconscious bodies had been laid out on trestle tables in a large room next to the women's ward. A tall young man with shoulder-length dark hair was cutting open a cocoon of web with an enormous pair of scissors. When he saw them, Niall experienced a tingling of the scalp; these were altogether more like the scissors of his dream.

Simeon said: 'I don't think you've met Phelim – my nephew and assistant.'

Niall and Phelim shook hands. The young man's face was not handsome, but with his deep-set eyes and irregular nose, was full of character. He had a powerful grip and an open, friendly smile. Niall was glad that he made no attempt to bow.

Simeon asked: 'Anything to report?'

'Only this.' He approached the body of a man wearing slave uniform, and tugged at a chain that hung round his neck. 'Any idea what this is?' He dangled a pendant between his thumb and forefinger.

Niall and Simeon exchanged glances. Simeon asked: 'Have you found any more of them?'

Phelim shook his head. 'No. What is it?'

Simeon was tugging the remainder of the cocoon off the man's feet, then the sandals. He pulled open the toes; Niall could see the scar tissue where the web between the toes had been severed.

Niall said: 'It's a communicating device.'

Phelim looked blank. 'Are you joking?' A moment later he gave a slight start, and dropped the pendant.

'Why did you do that?'

'Oh, nothing.' He touched the pendant gingerly with his fingertip. 'I thought I got a tingling feeling . . .'

Niall picked it up; it felt completely inert.

Phelim turned to his uncle and asked with mild exasperation: 'What on earth's happening here?'

Simeon explained to Niall: 'He only arrived a couple of hours ago. I haven't had a chance to tell him.' He took the scissors from Phelim and used them to cut off the slave tunic. The naked body was that of a man of about thirty. His breathing was faint but distinctly perceptible. The face bore a family resemblance to the others Niall had seen: a beak-like nose, a lined forehead, an oddly large and sensuous mouth, and a receding chin which, in spite of its lack of prominence, somehow conveyed no impression of weakness. The body looked hard and muscular, but the flesh was very pale. The black hairs that covered the chest and legs gave him an animal-like appearance.

Simeon reached out to the hairy midriff and removed a tiny brown fragment that looked like a piece of dried leaf.

Phelim asked; 'What is it?'

Simeon handed it to him. 'What do you think?'

Phelim sniffed it. 'Seaweed? Has he been swimming?'

Simeon said: 'That's what we'd both like to know.'

Niall was staring at the immobile face, and at the yellow teeth that were just visible through the partly-open lips. He placed one hand on the lined forehead, and experienced an odd sense of repulsion as he felt the cold flesh. Then, ignoring the others, he allowed his mind to become a blank, and to blend with the consciousness of the sleeper. There was the oddly familiar sensation that he knew from past experience: of losing his own identity and becoming someone else. But since this man was unconscious, the 'someone else' was a kind of blankness, like hovering in empty space. Niall had to reach out and hold on to the edge of the table to steady himself. After a few moments, his mind seemed to become accustomed to the blankness, as the eyes become accustomed to darkness. There were faint flashes in the darkness, like distant lightning; Niall assumed these to be some kind of electrical activity in the man's brain. Then, to his surprise, there was a crash like a distant roll of thunder. A moment later, the darkness began to give way to a pale blue light, which seemed to vibrate when there was another crash of thunder. A strange landscape became dimly visible, as if seen from a great height. Niall almost ceased breathing, suddenly gripped by the certainty that he was about to learn something important.

Then two things happened. He experienced a sickening sensation that reminded him of a bad smell – the same smell he had experienced when probing the mind of Skorbo's assassin – and at the same time he felt his consciousness hurled outward, as if by an explosion, and ejected violently and suddenly from the brain of the stranger; it was as if some powerful force had gripped him and thrown him through the air. There was a sharp pain in his eyeballs, as if they were being forced out of his head, and the nausea struck his solar plexus like the blow of a fist. Simeon and Phelim, who had been watching him in silence, saw him gasp and stagger backwards. Phelim caught him as his knees buckled.

When he opened his eyes he was lying on one of the trestle tables, and Phelim was taking his pulse. He heard Simeon say: 'He's dead.'

'No I'm not.'

Simeon said: '*He* is.' He pointed at the body of the man. Niall forced himself upright, fighting off the nausea that spread upward from his stomach, and lurched off the table, supported by Phelim's hand on his arm. He could see at a glance that Simeon was right. The dead eyes stared glassily at the ceiling. The jaw had sagged open, and the hairy chest had ceased to rise and fall.

Niall groaned and struck himself on the forehead with his fist. 'What an idiot I am!' He tore the chain from round the man's neck and hurled it across the room.

Phelim shook his head in bewilderment. 'Would someone tell me what's happening?'

Niall said bitterly: 'I killed him out of pure stupidity, that's what.'

Simeon laid a hand on his shoulder. 'It wasn't your fault.'

'Oh yes it was. I should have removed the pendant first.'

'But it wasn't even touching him. It was on the table.'

'That makes no difference.' He looked down at the dead face, with its yellow teeth. 'He can kill from a distance.'

Phelim asked: 'Who can?'

'The man who sent him. The magician.'

Phelim looked at Niall in blank astonishment. 'A real magician?'

Simeon said quickly: 'I'll explain it all later.'

'But . . .'

'We've other things to do now.'

Phelim was obviously troubled.

'I'd still like to know what killed him.'

'If you want my guess, a heart attack.' He reached out and closed the staring eyes.

'But I thought . . .'

Simeon silenced him with a gesture. 'Before we do anything else, let's get the rest of these webs off. I want to see if there are any more pendants.'

Ten minutes later, the spider-silk had been removed from the remaining bodies. There were fourteen in all, and their garments made it obvious that all came from the spider city. Their faces made it even plainer; all had the striking but somehow vapid good looks of human beings who have been deliberately bred for beauty and stupidity. Three of them were workmen, four adult women, and seven youths and girls – some hardly more than children. Phelim pointed out that each of them had fang marks on the neck or shoulders: evidence that they had been attacked from above.

Niall watched all this in a state of angry self-reproach; he was still cursing himself for his stupidity. When the last of the webs lay on the floor, Phelim said:

'No more pendants.'

Simeon voiced what Niall was thinking.

'That means the girl is the last one alive. We must guard her carefully.'

'Or better still, find some way of waking her up.'

Phelim said: 'How about the viper serum?'

Simeon considered it. 'Yes, I suppose it might work. It's worth trying, anyway.'

Niall asked: 'But what does it do?'

'It's an antidote to the poison of the horned marsh viper. I made it by injecting a horse with the venom until it built up a resistance – it cured my wife in the Great Delta. The poison of the marsh viper has roughly the same effect as spider venom – a small quantity causes paralysis, a large quantity causes death.'

'But what if it killed her?'

'Why should it? The poison in a serum is already neutralized. In any case, we could try it on one of these sleeping beauties first.' He turned to Phelim. 'Help me find one with a good, strong pulse.'

Phelim lifted the wrist of the girl closest to him.

'How about this?'

Simeon took her other wrist, and nodded. Then he opened her eyelid, and very delicately touched her eyeball with his fingertip. Niall thought the girl's other eyelid twitched.

From a wooden medical chest Simeon took an instrument that Niall recognized as a hypodermic syringe. He had never seen one, but his history lesson in the white tower had made him familiar with their use. Simeon guessed what he was thinking.

'I'd never seen one either.' He held it out for Niall's inspection. 'Beautiful, aren't they? One of these would have saved the life of my father. Now we've got six dozen.'

A voice said: 'Twelve dozen.' A boy of about fourteen had come into the room. His dark hair was close-cropped; otherwise he bore a striking resemblance to Phelim.

'You've found more? Good.' Simeon placed a hand on the boy's shoulder. 'This is my nephew Boyd, the mechanical genius of the family.'

Boyd said: 'And guess what I've found? An electric generator. Isn't that tremendous?'

Phelim snorted. 'It would be if we had any use for electricity.'

'Any use?' Boyd's tone was outraged. 'What do you mean, any use?'

Phelim said: 'Well, you tell me what we can use it for.'

'Well, lighting this place, to begin with. That's what

it's for. It's an emergency generator. Don't you know anything?' It was obvious that the brothers maintained an attitude of mutual criticism.

Simeon said: 'Never mind him. I think it's wonderful. What have you got there?'

Boyd was holding a curved metal band of a pale gold colour.

'I'm not sure. It's either a bipartite encephaloscope or a Gullstrand apparatus. I thought you might know.'

Phelim took it from his brother.

'It looks like an ordinary headband to me.'

This was true; it reminded Niall of the kind of band Merlew wore to keep her hair in place. Yet there was something about its pale gold colour and graceful form that fascinated him.

Simeon said: 'Why don't you go and look it up in the big medical encyclopedia? Have you finished unpacking?'

'Of course not. There's a whole crate yet.'

'Well go and finish it. We'll come up in a moment.'

Boyd turned to Niall. 'Do you want to come?' It was the first time he had acknowledged Niall's existence.

Simeon said: 'No, he'll come up with us. Go and unpack the other crate.'

Boyd exchanged a glance with Niall and pulled a wry face. As he ran off down the corridor, Phelim said resignedly: 'My younger brother is brilliant, but he's a terrible pest.'

In fact, Niall had taken an instant liking to the boy, whose eyes radiated intelligence.

Simeon had already turned back to the girl, and was studying her forearm.

'Give me the viper serum.'

Phelim handed him a small glass bottle containing a yellow fluid. But as Simeon filled the syringe, Niall experienced an odd sense of misgiving.

'Wouldn't it be safer to try a small quantity first?'

Simeon shrugged. 'It shouldn't do any harm. But perhaps you're right – I don't want to waste the serum.' He squeezed some of it back into the bottle by pressing the plunger.

Niall looked down at the girl's sleeping face. She was a pretty, dark-haired teenager with an olive skin and full lips. There was something very attractive about its serenity. Almost without being aware of it, his consciousness passed beyond her sleeping face and into her brain. It was like plunging into a sea of oblivion, total absence of being. Through this nothingness, Niall continued to be aware of his own body, standing there and looking down at her. Yet he was no longer inside his body. Nor did he possess any identity. He was like a new born baby, gazing blankly out on the world.

Yet this consciousness of nothingness was dimly illuminated by flashes of somethingness, like a faint dawn on the horizon. This was the girl's sleeping consciousness, dimly aware of her body and of the room she was lying in. This vague, almost non-existent consciousness became momentarily more aware as Simeon drove the needle into her arm and pressed the plunger.

Simeon said: 'Do you realize this is the first time in a thousand years that one of these things has been used?'

His voice produced a slight shock that brought Niall back into his body. It was pleasant to re-enter his own identity and to become aware that he was Niall, and not a fragment of nothingness.

The three of them stood there in silence, looking down at the girl's face, and at the rising and falling of her breasts. After about a minute her breathing became faster, and spots of colour appeared in her cheeks.

Phelim said: 'It's working.'

Simeon shook his head. 'Don't speak too soon.'

As he said this, Niall once again probed the girl's mind. As soon as he did so, he realized that something was wrong. There was an acute sense of discomfort, a feeling of suffocation, and a scalding sensation in his veins. The waves of delirium made him feel so unbalanced that he hastily withdrew.

The girl was now breathing fast, as though in a fever, and Simeon was beginning to look concerned. Phelim reached out and raised her eyelid. Niall could see that the eye was moving around rapidly, showing the white of the eyeball; the effect was unpleasant, as though she were a frightened animal. Simeon, who was holding her wrist, shook his head.

'You were right. Thank heavens I didn't give her a larger dose.'

'What happened?'

'I don't know. The two neurotoxins may have opposed one another.'

Phelim took another bottle from the medicine chest.

'How about belladonna?'

Simeon shook his head emphatically.

'Fatal. Atropine stimulates the heart and her pulse is already a hundred and thirty. Hyoscin might work. But I don't want to take any more risks.' He dropped the wrist. 'I think she'll be all right.'

But Niall, who was aware of the feverish tumult in the girl's brain, was less confident. Even to share her consciousness at second hand produced a burning sensation of thirst and an irrational longing to plunge into cold water.

Simeon said: 'There's nothing more we can do for now. Let's go and see how Boyd's getting on.'

It was a relief to follow him out of the room. It was not until Niall was halfway along the corridor that the burning sensation disappeared.

The large room at the top of the stairs had been

recently vacated by the carpenters, and smelt of freshly sawn wood and varnish. The five packing cases from the warehouse now stood against the wall; the floor and two large trestle tables were covered with an assortment of objects, from rolls of bandages and cotton wool to strange items of medical equipment that reminded Niall of things seen in the control room of the white tower.

Boyd was enthusiastically levering the lid off a packing case with a crowbar. He pointed to a large satinwood box on the floor. 'That's an electron microscope. Do you know how many times it can magnify?' Phelim shook his head. 'Half a million!' He pointed to a gleaming chromium-plated device on the table. 'That's a comparison microscope.' He touched a button at its base, and a small but powerful light came on, illuminating the slide-holder. Phelim was astonished.

'What made it light up?'

Boyd said scornfully: 'A battery, of course. By the twenty-second century they'd invented batteries that could store a thousand volts. How about this?' He picked up a black tube from the table and pushed a button; a powerful beam of light shone on the opposite wall. Boyd pointed it at Phelim's face, and twisted the base; the light became so blinding that Phelim covered his eyes with his hands. 'Isn't that marvellous? An emergency operating-theatre light . . . And look at this.' He opened a polythene box and took out a flat device with a handle at the centre of its base. It was about a foot square, and seemed to be made of cloudy glass.

'What is it?'

'A portable x-ray.' He turned to Niall. 'Put your hand on the table.'

Niall did as he was told. Boyd held the clouded glass above it, then squeezed a switch. A pale green light illuminated the glass. Niall gazed with astonishment as his flesh disappeared, and he found himself looking at the hand of a skeleton. Boyd chortled with delight, and held the device up against Phelim's face; Phelim's head immediately turned into a grinning skull with empty eye sockets. As Phelim started to move away, Boyd said: 'Hold still a minute.' Using both hands he pushed a slide on the handle. Phelim's head became slowly clothed with flesh – not normal flesh, but a kind of semi-transparent jelly in which all the veins and arteries were clearly visible. Inside the skull, it was possible to see the outline of Phelim's brain. 'There, you see, uncle, you were wrong – Phelim *has* got a brain.' He ducked a playful blow from Phelim.

Niall picked up a gleaming metal tube from the tabletop; it was a foot long and two inches in diameter. It reminded him of the expanding metal rod he had found in the land of Dira. Like the metal rod, it was startlingly heavy for its size. One end was covered with a frosted glass screen, and the control button on its side rested in a graduated slot. When Niall pushed the button upward, the glass was illuminated with a green glow.

He asked Boyd: 'What's this?'

'I'm not sure.' It obviously pained him to admit ignorance. 'Some kind of torch?'

Niall shone it on the palm of his hand. To his surprise, the green light produced a pleasant, cool sensation not unlike a breeze. As he pushed the button upwards in its slot the light intensified, and his hand became increasingly cold. Before the button had reached the halfway mark, his hand felt frozen, as if immersed in icy water. Even when he turned the light away, the flesh remained achingly cold, so that it was difficult to move his fingers. He whistled with pain.

'That's freezing!'

Boyd said: 'Ah, now I know what it is. It's a cold

light. They were invented to replace refrigerators.'

Phelim was studying a large sheet of paper. 'Yes, it's here on the inventory – Rykov Dethermalizer or cold light. What's an otoscope?'

Boyd said: 'A thing for looking in your ear.'

'What's an electrodiagnostic analyser?'

'I don't know.'

'Well, there should be one in here somewhere. And a Gullstrand apparatus, whatever that is . . .'

Niall was no longer paying attention. As the freezing sensation gradually disappeared from his hand, he was struck by an interesting idea. While the others were bent over the packing case, he slipped out of the room and tiptoed downstairs.

The girl was now in a fever; her cheeks were flushed, and she was breathing in short gasps. Niall placed the cold light gently against her damp forehead, and pushed the switch. As he did so, his consciousness blended with hers, and he felt her shock wave of relief as the sudden coolness invaded her brain. Within thirty seconds, the flood of emergency signals that had overloaded her nervous system had diminished to a trickle, and her breathing was calmer. Yet as he continued to hold the cold light against her forehead, Niall was aware that he was treating only the symptoms, not the cause of the problem. Her nervous system was in shock as a result of the reaction between the spider venom and the snake serum. And after six weeks of hanging upside down in Skorbo's larder, her vitality was too depleted to cope with the crisis. Even as her heartbeat slowed down, Niall was aware that she lacked the strength to fight off this new invasion of poison that Simeon had introduced into her bloodstream. Trapped in the confused electrical storm of her consciousness, Niall felt completely helpless.

Yet when he was once again looking down at her

flushed face, he experienced a surge of anger at this pointless waste of her life. It seemed absurd that there was no way in which he could transfer some of his own excess vitality into her body. On a sudden impulse he switched off the cold light and placed one hand on her forehead and the other on her solar plexus. In doing so, he was consciously imitating the posture he had seen his brother adopt earlier that morning. He recognized immediately that it established a sense of contact between their physical organisms. As his consciousness blended with hers, he instinctively synchronized their vibrations, so she could absorb the energy he was trying to give her. A warm sensation flowed down his arms and through his fingertips. And since the sense of contact was still inadequate, he bent over and pressed his mouth against hers. Her lips were dry, so he moistened them with his tongue. And now contact was fully established, her body responded to the flow of vital energy as parched ground responds to water. It was a curious sensation – allowing his vitality to be sucked into the vortex of her need. It felt as if their sexes had been reversed, and that he had become the female, she the male. Then, just as the strain of the position was beginning to turn into physical discomfort, he felt the power inside her respond to the power that was flowing out of his own body; like waterlogged soil she had taken as much of his vitality as she could absorb. A moment later, he felt her lips move, and knew she was returning to consciousness. As he straightened up, he experienced a sudden dizziness that made him sway on his feet and grip the edge of the table. The darkness passed, and he saw that her eyes were open. He smiled at her, but she stared back blankly, without recognition. Then she sighed deeply and closed her eyes as the weakened spider venom once more plunged her nervous system into a state of paralysis.

When the others came into the room a few minutes later, she was breathing normally and peacefully. Simeon noticed the change immediately.

'Hello, she's looking much better.' He took her wrist. 'Yes, her pulse is back to normal.'

Niall said: 'I think your serum must have worked after all.'

Simeon gave him a suspicious glance from under his bushy eyebrows, but said nothing.

His charioteers were waiting for him when he came out of the hospital. He was grateful to them for their foresight; the events of the past half-hour had filled him with a dreamy but not unpleasant tiredness. He told them to take him to the slave quarter, then, with a sigh of gratitude, relaxed into the cushions, wishing the journey ahead was longer.

In spite of the tiredness, he was in a curious state of inner excitement. The world around him seemed marvellously fresh and real. This, he realized, was because he had made a voyage outside his own body and into the mind of the unconscious girl; now his own identity seemed new and strange, like a suit of new clothes.

This excursion into the mind of a stranger had also made him aware once again of the odd mental vacuity of these citizens of the spider city. The spiders had gone to a great deal of trouble to breed all the imagination out of their human servants. Yet what had intrigued him about the girl was that, in spite of her lack of imagination, she was obviously happy – like the crowds of people who were now enjoying the sunlight in the main square, or strolling down the tree-lined avenue that led to the river, mingling freely with wolf spiders and a few bombardier beetles. She had never been outside the spider city, yet she was contented with her lot in life. And was he, in spite of his imagination, so much better off? He had freed his fellow humans from their slavery, and he was the ruler of this spider city. Yet in spite of this, he continued to experience an obscure feeling of discontentment, almost of anticlimax.

Oddly enough, these thoughts caused him no distress. On the contrary, as the cart crossed the bridge that led to the slave quarter, he experienced a curious feeling of satisfaction, as if he was at last getting to grips with the problem. If he was not to surrender to the mindless contentment of the spider servants, then he had to learn to develop his own deeper sense of purpose. And what had just happened seemed to offer him a clue: to leave his own body behind, to be able to float freely in the open space that exists around all human beings . . .

The charioteers paused on the far side of the bridge. 'Which way, highness?'

Broadus had not given precise instructions, but he had said that the house faced the river. Niall said: 'Turn right here.'

Half a mile to the east, the explosion of a vast underground ammunition store had destroyed a large area of the slave quarter, and the river flowed into the crater, forming a lake. Bloated bodies still occasionally floated to its surface, to be fought over by the razor-bill gulls who had now come to nest around its edges. These gulls, whose wing-span was more than two feet, occasionally attacked children, and had stolen at least one baby from a pram that had been left outside a front door; for this reason – and also because they were afraid of the rats, who were as big as small dogs – the slaves had moved away from the houses adjoining the lake. This suggested to Niall that men who wished to remain unnoticed might choose the roughly triangular area bounded by the lake to the east and the river to the south.

Most of the houses along this riverfront area were damaged; some had lost their roofs, most had broken windows. If the ammunition store had not been so deep and so well-protected, the explosion would have destroyed half the city. Now, as they approached the lake, and a few curious gulls squawked and soared above them, Niall observed that one of the birds was behaving in an unusual manner. It was swooping upward, turning a backward somersault, then losing control and fluttering frantically towards the ground before it readjusted itself and soared again on outspread wings. When it carried out this strange manoeuvre a third time, the other gulls took fright and flew off towards the lake, leaving their companion to swoop upward and repeat the same clumsy and incongruous somersault, squawking with alarm. This time it failed to regain control and crashed into a chimney, then rolled, bumping, down the side of a roof. Niall observed the spot where it had disappeared from sight.

'Turn left at the next street.'

A few white feathers showed where the gull had hit the pavement; the bird itself was now in the mandibles of a wolf spider, which was standing guard outside a house a few yards down the road. Niall had guessed he would find it there; the gull's behaviour could only be explained in terms of a bored wolf spider indulging its sense of humour. (Wolf spiders were hunters who enjoyed swift movement, and lacked the immense patience of other species.) It was now so absorbed in its prospective meal that it failed to notice their approach, and started nervously as they moved into its field of vision. When it recognized Niall – telepathically rather than visually – it dropped its prey and made a clumsy gesture of obeisance; the bird squawked and fluttered feebly. Niall pretended not to notice the spider's embarrassment, and hurried past it through the open front door.

He noticed immediately the tidiness of the hallway. Although large slabs of plaster were missing from the

218

walls, and the floorboards were worn and uneven, the floor itself looked as if it had been scrubbed. For a house in the slave quarter, this was unusual; slaves were notoriously untidy, and even slave women were sluttish housewives. The next thing he observed was the smell – a smell that for a moment eluded him, because he had encountered it late in life. Then he remembered: it was the iodine-like smell of seaweed, and it seemed to blend naturally with the cry of the gulls above the rooftops.

He tried the nearest door, which should have led into the front room; it was locked or jammed. But the next door stood slightly ajar. He found himself in a large room whose floor space was almost entirely occupied by furniture – four beds, several chairs, and a chest of drawers. Otherwise, it was a bare, uncomfortable-looking room, like most other bedrooms in the slave quarter. It differed only in one respect; the beds had been tidily made up, and the floor space between them looked as if it had been scrubbed. Like the hallway, it had a distinctive sea smell.

He found himself unable to suppress a feeling of disappointment. The room seemed to contain no personal belongings, nothing to offer a clue to those who had lived in it. At this point, he recalled a remark of the bald-headed little councillor, Fergus: that these people could not have been slaves because they possessed too many clothes. He picked his way between the beds – there was barely space to walk – towards the chest of drawers in the corner. Halfway across the room, he halted and listened intently: a faint creaking of floor-boards had sounded from the room above. A few moments later, soft footsteps descended the stairs. Niall groped in his pocket, cursing himself for not bringing the expanding metal rod or some other weapon. For a moment he considered lying between the beds, then realized that, in the silence of the house, the creak of the floorboards was bound to give him away. A moment later, alarm turned to relief as the huge body of a spider blocked the doorway.

'Dravig! What are you doing here?'

Dravig was able to sense his relief. 'I apologize for alarming you. I was with the Death Lord when your message arrived. She ordered me to see what you had discovered.'

'This is the hide-out of Skorbo's killers.' Niall looked around the bare room. 'Did you find anything upstairs?'

'Nothing. The rooms are unused.'

'Then for some reason, they all lived in this room. Probably because they didn't want to draw attention to themselves. Look at the windows.' Dravig did so, but obviously failed to comprehend. 'They're thick with dust, yet the room itself is spotlessly clean. Clean windows might have given them away – slaves never clean windows.'

He crossed to the chest of drawers, and pulled open the top one. Inside, as he had half-expected, were slave garments, neatly folded. He pulled these out in armfuls and tossed them on to the nearest bed. The drawer contained nothing else. The second drawer also contained slave garments, and several pairs of sandals; Niall was intrigued to observe that, unlike the sandals usually worn by slaves, these were of excellent workmanship. They might have been made by the workmen of Dira.

Under these, at the back of the drawer, lay five small objects, wrapped individually in cloth. When Niall touched one of them, he observed that the material was damp. Inside the cloth was a layer of brown seaweed, like the fragments Niall had already seen on the flesh of the unconscious girl. When this was removed, he found himself looking at an object made of smooth green stone. It was about two inches high, and his first impression was that it was a carving of a frog or toad. It was a small, squat creature with bulbous eyes, a flat face and a large slack mouth. As a desert dweller, Niall had seen very few frogs or toads; but this one struck him as too humanoid for either. To begin with, the tiny feet on which it supported itself looked more like human hands, although they had webbing between the fingers. The fat little belly had a navel, and the chest had two diminutive nipples. What struck Niall as most intriguing was that both the bulging eyes had darker patches of green that might have been pupils. These seemed to be a natural part of the stone; it must have taken the sculptor a long time to find a stone with two such dark patches in exactly the right place.

He held it out to Dravig.

'What do you think this is?'

Dravig reached out both feelers, then quickly withdrew them.

'Do not touch it. Put it back.'

'Why?' Niall stared at him in surprise.

'Can you not feel it?'

Niall withdrew into the still centre of his mind, and opened all his senses. Now, suddenly, he understood what Dravig meant. There was something strange about the object in his hand, a kind of force or energy that was not unlike the force of a living creature. And as he looked at the toad-like face, it now seemed oddly malevolent – although a better word might have been predatory, like a hunter lying in wait and watching the approach of its victim. Niall had observed it many times among the carnivorous plants of the Great Delta. Even so, the emanation from the stone was mild, almost undetectable; Dravig must have possessed remarkable sensitivity to observe this without even touching it.

Niall rewrapped it and replaced it in the drawer.

Then, one by one, he removed the others and unwrapped them. Each, he observed, had been placed with its face towards the back of the drawer. Each was subtly different from the others, although there was a strong basic resemblance. Some had more humanoid faces than others, and one had an open mouth inside which teeth were visible. But these teeth were like no others that Niall had ever seen. They were not triangular and pointed, like the teeth of a fish, nor flat like those of a herbivore, but a combination of the two, with oddly irregular points. One figure had a curious protuberance, not unlike a short trunk, and one had closed eyes, although the face seemed to have the same vaguely menacing watchfulness as the others.

Dravig watched all this with an air of doubt that amounted to disapproval. Niall was aware that he seemed to feel that all this curiosity was unnecessary, almost indecent – much as humans might feel about ransacking someone's personal possessions. Once again he was struck by the alienness of the spider mind, its strange lack of curiosity. Spiders were intelligent and observant; yet they seemed to have very little of the natural inquisitiveness of human beings.

He asked Dravig: 'Why do you suppose they keep their lucky charms wrapped in seaweed?'

Dravig replied: 'They are not lucky charms. They are their personal gods.'

Now, suddenly, Niall understood. Spiders had a highly developed sense of the unknown forces of nature, and a boundless awe for the great goddess. This was why Niall himself was now treated as a kind of god; the spiders regarded him as an emissary of the goddess. Dravig was perturbed because Niall was failing to display respect for sacred things. Yet his disapproval was muted since Niall himself shared their sacred nature.

Niall carefully rewrapped the last of the images, and replaced it in the drawer.

'I'd still like to know why they wrap them in seaweed. I thought they lived underground.'

He was trying to open the bottom drawer, but it yielded only with difficulty; its wood seemed to be swollen and damp. The drawer proved to contain a flat wooden box, about eighteen inches long and a foot wide. Niall had often come across such boxes in the kitchens of deserted houses, during the hours of rambling exploration; they usually contained cutlery, although on one occasion he had found one full of small bottles containing herbs and condiments. He placed this one on top of the chest of drawers and pushed up its catch. To Niall's surprise, it proved to contain nothing but a mass of brown seaweed and a quantity of liquid, presumably sea water. The iodine-smell of the weed filled the room. He lifted a corner of the weed and looked underneath; there was nothing. But he noted that the inside of the box had been treated with some grey substance that looked slimy, but was, in fact, quite hard to the touch; it was evidently intended as waterproofing. The weed itself had a slippery, leathery consistency, and as he raised it, he noted that it was not, as he had first thought, a mass of separate leaves, but a single sheet of weed. When he lifted it in the air, holding it in both hands, it became clear that it was a roughly rectangular mat which had been folded in two. One side of the mat was smooth and leathery; the other side consisted of sucker-shaped buds, each one about half an inch across. At the edge of the mat there were a number of trailing stems or tendrils; these made it clear that this was a single piece of natural weed which had been removed in its entirety.

He held it out towards Dravig, its water dripping on to the floor.

'What do you make of that? What do you suppose they did with a piece of seaweed?' Dravig made a mental gesture that was like a head-shake.

Niall replaced it in the box and closed down the lid. When he rubbed his wet hands down his tunic, he noticed that a few fragments of brown weed stuck to the cloth.

The rest of the room yielded no further clues. A cupboard in the corner proved to be empty except for two grubby slave tunics. Niall tossed these on to the bed with the others, then looked through the pockets. As he had expected, these were empty. Finally, he left the room and explored the rest of the ground floor. When the locked door of the front room failed to yield to a determined push, he turned the handle, and rammed it with his shoulder. The door burst open. But the room, as he had expected, contained only dusty furniture, and had evidently not been used for a long time, possibly centuries. All the windows were broken, and shards of glass still lay on the floor.

Since this was a small house, the only other room on the ground floor was the kitchen. This proved to be spotlessly clean, and the few cups and dishes had been washed and left to drain. A dish towel hung from a rack above the sink, and two dish cloths had been spread out to dry from the edge of the draining board. Saucepans and other utensils were upside down on a shelf. The stove contained burnt wood ash. A waste bin underneath the sink was half full of decaying remains of vegetables, and some rabbit bones.

The kitchen drawers contained knives, forks and other implements, some of them rusty and evidently dating back to the days when humans ruled the earth. The cupboard underneath was locked, and an attempt to force it open with a rusty pair of scissors only broke the blade of the scissors. But by removing the drawers,

Niall was able to look down into the cupboard; in the middle of the top shelf lay a key. He tried it in the lock; the cupboard door opened. His first impression was that it was empty. Yet in that case, why hide the key? Kneeling on the floor, he peered sideways into the bottom shelf, and gave a grunt of satisfaction. In the far corner there was a small wooden box, which had been placed so far back that he was able to reach it only with his fingertips. It proved to be a few inches square, and made of a black, polished wood. What puzzled him was that it appeared to have no lid; there were no hinges and no sign of a catch. It took him several minutes of careful study to realize that it had a sliding lid, so carefully crafted that its groove was virtually invisible. When he placed his hand firmly on the lid and pushed, it slid open. Inside, there was a brown glass bottle, and a curious device whose purpose eluded him. It was made of the quill of a bird, and one end was sharpened to a point; the other was covered with a small bulb made of a rubber-like substance. Niall uncorked the bottle and sniffed it; the liquid inside had a medical smell. He dipped the quill into it and squeezed the bulb; a yellow liquid was drawn up into the tube. But he still found it impossible to guess why the end was pointed. After squeezing the liquid back into the bottle, he replaced them in the box, and dropped it into the pocket of his tunic. Simeon would certainly find it interesting.

He concluded by looking at the upstairs rooms. But these, as Dravig had said, were empty and showed no sign of occupation; except for Dravig's footprints, the dust on the floors was undisturbed.

Back in the bedroom, Dravig was waiting with that infinite patience Niall found so admirable – he had apparently not even changed his position since Niall left the room. Niall sat down heavily on one of the beds and surveyed the room. Dravig could sense his frustration. He asked with carefully controlled courtesy – so as not to imply that Niall had been wasting his time: 'What message shall I take to the Death Lord?'

Niall sighed. 'You mean what have I learned? Not much, I'm afraid.' Dravig's mind transmitted a wordless sympathy; in fact, the direct communication between them meant that his sympathy was plainer than words. Niall said: 'All I can tell you is this. There were five of them here, but not all at the same time, since there are only four beds. It was a carefully planned expedition.' He pointed to garments on the bed. 'Some of those slave tunics were manufactured for the journey. If you look at them closely, you'll see that they're made of a finer material than these' – he pointed to the soiled slave tunics – 'which are the real thing. As soon as they could obtain real slave garments, they put their travelling clothes in a drawer. Someone might have noticed the difference. And they were anxious not to draw attention to themselves. That's why they left the windows uncleaned, and why they haven't attempted to board up the front windows. Instead, they kept the inner door locked, in case someone climbed in through the broken window.'

Dravig had been listening with deep attention. 'Your powers of observation are remarkable. How did you come to develop them?'

'All hunters have to develop them, or their catch would be poor. But in this case observation is less important than reason. You notice, for example, that these people were obsessively tidy – these floorboards have been scrubbed until they're almost white. That reveals immediately that they were not slaves. And anyone who came into this room would realize it. So why did they not avoid that risk and leave the place as untidy as most slave dwellings? Because they have been trained to be tidy. To live in an untidy room would be worse than discovery.'

Dravig said: 'But they also had a woman who had nothing else to do. Slave women stay at home all day.'

Niall shook his head. 'You forget that she had already been captured by Skorbo. Only men lived in this room the past few weeks, yet they have continued to keep it tidy.' He pointed to the soiled slave tunics. 'These were probably left in the cupboard, waiting to be washed, on the morning they set out to assassinate Skorbo.'

He was struck suddenly by another thought. 'On that morning, there were only three of them left. Two were hanging up in Skorbo's larder. Is that why Skorbo was chosen as the victim – because they knew that he was responsible for the disappearance of the other two? That would explain something that has been puzzling me. The tree that killed Skorbo must have been planted at least a year ago, probably more. And at that time, they had no reason to kill Skorbo – he was simply the captain of the Death Lord's personal bodyguard.'

'Then who was the chosen victim?'

'You.'

'I?' It was the first time that Niall had seen Dravig taken aback.

Niall laughed. 'I am only guessing. But who else? The Death Lord never leaves his headquarters. Next to him, you are the most distinguished spider in the city.'

'But why should they want to kill me?'

'Why should they want to kill anyone? I believe these people are driven – or rather, that their leader is driven – by a consuming hatred of the spiders and their servants.'

'But what could they hope to achieve?'

Niall realized, with wry amusement, that Dravig was beginning to credit him with some almost supernatural insight.

'We can only guess. If they hate your people, then presumably their ultimate desire is to destroy them, and to take their place as the rulers of the earth.' Here Niall was drawing upon his own memory of lifelong hatred of the spiders. But if Dravig guessed this, he was far too tactful to allow it to show. He only said mildly: 'It is difficult to see how that could be accomplished.'

Niall shrugged. 'Whatever their plans, my guess is that Skorbo spoiled them. So they sent for reinforcements and decided to make Skorbo their first victim. And at that point, everything began to go wrong. Skorbo killed one of them, and they had to conceal the body. They removed his clothes so we wouldn't guess he was pretending to be a slave. But by then, Skorbo had dragged himself out into the square, and raised the alarm. They couldn't escape through the fresh snow without leaving a trail. So they tried to blend with the squad of slaves outside. Even at that point they might still have escaped – in fact, one of them *did* manage to slip away without being noticed. Fortunately, Simeon guessed what had happened, and we caught the other one at the hospital.'

Dravig said: 'And now they are all dead.'

'Not all. There is still the girl.'

'Ah yes. I still cannot understand what part the girl played in their plans.'

Niall shook his head. 'Neither can I. And she cannot tell us yet.'

'We must guard her carefully.'

'I shall.' Niall looked around the room. 'I think we should also leave a guard on this place, in case some of them should return.'

'You think there may be more of them in the city?'

'Not now, perhaps. But when their master knows he has failed, I think he will try again.' He was suddenly struck by a sense of the preposterousness of the situ-

228

ation. 'But, in the name of the goddess, where are they *coming from*?'

'Our patrols have been instructed to search the area for fifty miles around the city. There are no reports of intruders.'

'I wasn't thinking about intruders. Where is *their* city?'

'There are no reports of large concentrations of human beings in the lands ruled by the Death Lord.'

Dravig's impassivity, and the oddly impersonal manner in which he delivered information, produced in Niall a mixture of frustration and amusement.

'How far do these lands extend?'

'I cannot give you precise figures. My people lack an interest in such matters. I would advise you to speak to the commander of the aerial survey force.'

Niall was intrigued. The spiders never volunteered information about their political or military organization, so that even after six months of working with them, he knew little more than at the beginning.

'What is his name?'

'Your people call him Asmak.'

'Where can he be found?'

'At the headquarters of the Death Lord. Shall I send for him?'

'No. I'm going back now. There is no more to be learned here.'

Dravig made ritual obeisance.

'In that case I shall return to deliver my report.'

Niall waited until he was sure Dravig was out of the building, then took from the drawer one of the stone figures, still wrapped in its cloth – Dravig, he knew, would advise him against it. This he placed in the pocket of his tunic. He then replaced the clothing on top of the other figures, and closed the drawer. Finally, he took the flat wooden box containing the seaweed, wrapping it first in one of the slave garments, to prevent the water from dripping.

The wolf spider was still standing on guard – now, under observation from the charioteers, as rigid as a statue; a few scattered feathers drifting in the gutter were all that remained of the seagull.

Niall said: 'I would like you to keep guard inside the house with the door closed. I will send another guard to relieve you shortly.' It was not clear whether the spider understood; its two main eyes, and the four subsidiary eyes beneath, stared rigidly and unwaveringly into space. But by the time the chariot turned the corner at the end of the street, it had vanished into the house, and the front door was closed.

As they crossed the main square, Niall ordered the charioteers to halt beside the green lawn that surrounded the white tower. He then dismissed them, telling them to go and eat; his insight into their minds told him that they were ravenously hungry.

As soon as he approached the tower, he knew there was something wrong. It normally exerted upon him a peculiar feeling of attraction, like the pull of a magnet. Now this familiar sensation was absent, as if his body had been encased in some insulating substance. And in fact, when he reached out to touch the wall, there was no longer the sensation of plunging his hand into water; it was merely touching a solid surface.

This baffled him. He walked round to the north side, where the vibrations were usually stronger. It made no difference; the milky, almost translucent wall, remained solid; it even looked solid, instead of appearing to shimmer, like some crystallized smoke.

Could it be the box he was carrying? He set this down on the marble platform that surrounded the base of the tower; but even as he did so, he knew it made no difference. Next he removed from his pocket the stone figurine. As soon as his fingers touched it, he experienced a return of the sensation he had felt on first handling it, a mild vibration not unlike that of a living creature – perhaps one of the carnivorous plants of the Great Delta. And as soon as he placed it on the ground, he felt a return of the familiar tingling sensation induced by the force-field of the tower. Even so, it seemed somehow duller, less powerful than usual. It was not until he placed the figurine on the grass that he experienced again that curious sense of vibrancy, as if the atoms of his own body were somehow resonating at the same rate as those of the tower.

He picked up the box, still wrapped in the damp slave garment; this made no difference. Then he stepped forward into the curious electrical embrace of the wall, which was like water tingling with living energy. A moment later, he walked out into the inner room of the tower, with its luminous curved walls.

It was the first time in many months that this had happened. He normally found himself in some strange and often frightening landscape. On one occasion it had been the yellow, sulphurous mists of Venus; on another, the boiling maelstrom of water at the foot of the Victoria Falls; once he had even found himself sharing a sunlit pond with other animalculae. But the Steegmaster, who had inaugurated this guessing game, clearly felt that now was no time for distractions.

Niall said aloud: 'What's happening?'

As he spoke the words, the old man was standing in front of him, exactly as if he had been there all the time. He offered only the briefest nod of greeting.

'The walls of the tower were designed to exclude potentially hostile entities.'

'I do not understand.'

'The creature you tried to bring into the tower was potentially destructive.'

'But it wasn't a creature. It was a piece of stone.'

The old man stared at him from under the bushy eyebrows.

'Are you certain of that?'

'Quite certain. It was a kind of odd little statuette.'

'Where did it come from?'

'A room in the slave quarter. It was the hide-out of Skorbo's killers.'

The old man shook his head.

'I suspect you have been deceived. Describe the circumstances in which you found it.'

Since this was precisely why he had come, Niall described the events of the past hour in some detail. The old man listened without expression – Niall suspected that it was part of his present policy to accustom Niall to the fact that he was merely a machine – then said:

'I must see this artifact.'

To Niall's astonishment, he walked into the wall and vanished. Niall stepped after him, and found himself standing in the sunlight – it was always a slightly vertiginous sensation to walk through a solid wall and step into nothingness. The old man was already bending over the cloth-wrapped figurine on the grass. A few passers-by in the square apparently took him for someone like themselves, for no one paid any attention to him.

Niall found it impossible to resist asking:

'Have you ever been out here before?'

The old man shook his head. 'There has never been any occasion for it.'

He unwrapped the cloth from the figurine, and held it on the palm of his hand.

Niall said: 'Well?'

'I admit that I cannot understand why it has produced this anomalous reaction. It is clearly a piece of silicate mineral related to nephrite.'

He turned and once again vanished through the wall of the tower. Niall followed him in. The old man was still studying the figurine – Niall observed that it was the one with closed eyelids – in the palm of his hand. He shook his head.

'I must confess that this problem is beyond the capacity of my information circuits.'

Niall could not repress an ironic smile.

'You mean it contradicts Steeg's conception of the universe?'

'Precisely.'

'Doesn't that suggest that your information circuits need to be extended?'

'That inference seems reasonable.' Niall reflected that the advantage of a machine is that it is not ashamed to admit that it might have been wrong.

'What do you propose to do?'

'First of all, to neutralize it.'

He placed it on the floor, then stepped back. What happened next made Niall jump. A beam of intense blue light stabbed down obliquely from above, illuminating the figurine. There was no obvious source of light; it appeared to emanate from the plain white surface of the ceiling. In its glow, the figurine appeared to be faintly luminous. The air around them became suddenly chilly.

Niall asked: 'What's that?'

'A cold beam.'

'I thought they were green.'

'They normally are. But this one induces a temperature of absolute zero, reducing all the molecules to immobility. If there is any vestige of life, it will be placed in suspended animation.'

'Wouldn't that destroy it?'

'Not if the freezing process occurs rapidly enough. In the great ice ages, fish were sometimes frozen instantaneously in rivers, and were able to swim away when the ice melted.'

The temperature had plunged swiftly; Niall's breath now turned to vapour as he exhaled. But as he shivered and pulled his cloak around his neck, the blue beam vanished, and the room seemed to become instantly warmer. Water vapour immediately froze around the figurine, turning it white. Niall winced as the old man bent and picked it up, aware that his own flesh would have been seared as if by a white hot iron. After contemplating it steadily for several seconds – Niall was aware that he was performing some kind of analysis – the old man once again stepped into the wall. A few moments later he reappeared, but this time without the figurine. In answer to Niall's look of interrogation he said:

'The cold has neutralized its force. But caution suggests that it would be better left outside.'

'Have you any idea of the nature of the force?'

'None, except that it is biological.'

'What makes you so sure?'

'Because it was neutralized by the cold.'

'But you admit that Steeg didn't understand it?'

'I admit that he made no allowance for it in creating my information circuits.'

'Doesn't that suggest that he may have been mistaken about the existence of magic?'

'Magic signifies supernatural interference in natural processes. Steeg regarded that as a primitive superstition.'

Niall said patiently: 'Look. A group of murderers came to this city, carrying pendants inscribed with magical symbols of revenge. They also brought stone figures that appear to be alive. Surely Steeg himself would have agreed that this was something beyond his understanding?'

'Steeg knew that the universe is full of things beyond his comprehension. But he would have denied that these things can contradict the basic laws of logic and reason.'

'Perhaps they don't. Perhaps they simply obey a different kind of logic.'

'What are you suggesting?'

'Well, you have hundreds of books on magic, don't

235

you? Some of them *must* contain clues about what's going on. Couldn't you find out?'

'You are asking me to make a comprehensive search of more than three thousand volumes.'

'*Could* it be done?'

'Of course. But it would take a long time.'

Niall's heart sank. 'How long?'

'Perhaps half an hour.'

Niall burst out laughing.

'That's all right. I can wait that long. I'll go to the dining room. Would you give me a call when you're ready?'

The dining room was on the same floor as the 'Florentine' gallery. It was a small room, containing no more than a dozen tables, although since Niall had been eating there regularly, these had been enlivened with attractive table cloths, and the food was served on decorated china plates instead of plastic dishes. There was no fresh food available, but the food synthesizer was of such a high standard that its products were greatly superior to the food cooked by Niall's own kitchen staff. Even after six months he was still astonished by its variety.

The synthesizer was an oblong metal box, about three feet long, which was attached to the wall beside the window. The menu that was displayed above it offered a list of food and drink amounting to more than a hundred items, beginning with hamburgers (with or without onions) and ending with Burgundy, Bordeaux and American Chardonnay. Over the past six months Niall had sampled everything on it, from pâté de foie gras and tournedos Rossini to peach melba and crêpes suzettes; he had finally concluded that his taste was too unsophisticated for most of these culinary marvels, and that he preferred a two-course meal of fish and chips and pecan pie with pistachio ice cream. This is what he now proceeded to order from the synthesizer, unaware that in so doing he was merely confirming the verdict of dozens of generations of teenagers. He also ordered a glass of sparkling apple juice, whose taste he greatly preferred to that of wine.

As he ate he looked out of the open window at the bustling market scene, which looked exactly as it must have looked in the days of Lorenzo de'Medici. Niall had come to recognize many of the stallholders and their typical cries, as well as many of the servants and housewives who made regular visits to the market. The man who ran the butcher's stall on the corner had a hoarse shout that could be heard above all the other sounds of the city, including the bellowing of cattle and the bleating of sheep. Like most of the males in the square, he took a keen interest in the red-haired peasant woman who ran the vegetable stall that was directly opposite Niall's window. This woman, who was in her mid-thirties, was taller than the average man, and had a magnificent ringing laugh and a jaunty way of throwing back her head and placing her hands on her hips. She made Niall think of a noisier and coarser Princess Merlew. Most of the men enjoyed laughing and joking with her, and although Niall was unable to understand the language, he guessed from the ribald laughter that many of the jokes must have been indecent.

She was also the object of admiration of a wealthy young man who stopped at her stall at least once a day – he wore a purple doublet, a hat that reminded Niall of an inverted flower bowl, and rode a chestnut mare. This young man was regarded with dislike and derision by the male stallholders, particularly the butcher; but Niall sensed that their hostility was based on envy, and on a certain fear that the redhead would one day surrender her virtue to the lovesick gallant. Niall entertained the same suspicion; one day towards evening, when most of the stallholders had packed up and left, he had seen the young man present her with a bouquet of flowers, and – after glancing around to see that no one was watching – the woman had accepted them and hidden them under her stall. But when he leaned forward and whispered something in her ear, she had shaken her head vigorously. And the butcher, who had come out from behind his stall at that moment, had scowled angrily, and as the young man rode away, he spat on the ground.

Now, as Niall gazed out of the window, he witnessed an interesting scene between the red-haired woman and a boatman who had moored his craft by the first flight of steps that ran up from the river to the market square. The boatman was carrying a large fish – it must have been more than a foot long – and was obviously trying to persuade her to buy it. She shook her head, as if objecting that he was asking too much. He leaned forward and said something; she looked thoughtful, then finally nodded her head and handed over money and a basket of a green vegetable not unlike cabbage. The man went behind the stall and placed the fish in a box. Then, as he was turning away, he took the woman's arm and pulled her towards him. Niall could not see what happened next – the man's body was between them – but the woman's reaction was to give him a box on the ear that made him stagger. The woman on the next stall began to laugh loudly – she had a most unpleasant cackle – and this seemed to enrage the man, who tried to take back his fish. The woman grabbed the box and held it out of his reach. Within a few seconds there was a noisy quarrel involving at least half a dozen men and two women, as well as a half-starved mongrel, which barked furiously and tried to bite the fisherman's leg. The man quickly got the worst of it – he had clearly expected to be allowed certain liberties in exchange for selling the fish cheaply – and he slunk off to his boat, leaving the basket of vegetables behind. And the stallholders, obviously sorry that the diversion was over, went reluctantly back to work. The overexcited dog went on barking until a man gave it a kick that lifted it off the ground; it vanished towards the river with a pathetic yelp.

Niall had been watching all this with such total absorption that he jumped in alarm when the old man's voice spoke in his ear.

'I am sorry I have taken so long. The task was more complicated than I expected.'

'It doesn't matter. I've been watching that woman down there.' He was struck by a sudden suspicion. 'Or did you arrange it all to keep me amused?'

'No. Today is market day. If you had been here yesterday the square would have been empty.' He pulled up a chair and sat down on the other side of the table. Since he was unreal, this pantomime was unnecessary; yet, as he had often explained to Niall, the crowning achievement of the Steegmaster was the extraordinary detail of its realism.

Niall spooned up his deliquescent ice cream. 'Did those people down there really exist?'

The old man looked at him with mild reproof.

'Since the camera was not invented in 1490, that is obviously an impossibility.'

Niall looked down at the red-haired woman, who was now showing off her fish to the woman on the next stall.

'So if I was a magician, and I could travel back to 1490, these people wouldn't be there?'

The old man sighed. 'What you call time travel is a verbal misunderstanding. Time is merely another name for process. In theory, process can be reversed, but to restore the universe to its state of five minutes ago would take an infinite amount of energy. Therefore to travel into the past would be quite impossible.'

Niall asked: 'And is that also true of the future?'

'Not quite. Anyone can predict the future. I can tell you the exact time the sun will rise tomorrow. I can even tell you what the weather will be like. Yet I am not a magician.'

Niall said: 'I dreamed of the future last night, and when I woke up, it happened exactly as I dreamed it. Does that mean I *am* a magician?'

The old man shrugged. 'I am not programmed to answer that question.' Then, oblivious to Niall's grimace of frustration, he went on: 'Do you wish to hear what I learned about the nature of magic?'

Niall sighed. 'Very well.'

'I admit that I was mistaken to believe that it was merely an irrational superstition.' Niall looked up with renewed interest. 'It appears to be an oddly consistent system of belief, whose foundations cannot be clearly distinguished from those of religion.'

Niall frowned; he always found abstract jargon difficult to absorb. 'I see.'

'As far as I can see, it appears to be based upon a number of propositions. The best known of these is attributed to the legendary founder of magic, Hermes Trismegistos, and it states: "As above, so below." This appears to mean that every man is a miniature version of the whole universe.'

Niall tried to look as if he understood.

The old man went on:

'But according to magical philosophy, the universe does not consist of dead matter – in fact, there is no such thing as dead matter. Everything in the universe is alive.'

Niall said: 'Like that stone figure I tried to bring into the tower?'

'Possibly.' The tone was noncommittal. 'The magical view is that all matter exists outside space and time, in a multi-dimensional universe. We only see one small aspect of a being that reaches back through many invisible planes of existence. It follows, of course, that human beings also exist on many planes of existence, although they are not aware of it. According to the Cabalists, there are ten planes of existence, the highest being God and the lowest earth. In human beings, these planes of existence are planes of consciousness. Am I going too fast for you?'

'No.' This last comment had aroused Niall's attention. 'So there are ten planes of consciousness?'

'According to the Cabala.'

'Are you saying that if you could get up to a higher plane, you'd be a magician?'

'That appears to be the position.'

Niall shook his head and sighed.

'I don't follow that. If I can rise to a higher level of consciousness, surely the only person it affects is me? It's like getting drunk. When I've had a few glasses of mead, everyone seems much nicer. But they haven't really changed – it's just me.'

'A perceptive comment. But according to magical philosophy, the best way to change the world is to change your own consciousness. One alchemist wrote: "Magic is the art of causing changes in consciousness at will." According to the same writer, luck is an example of the use of magic. When you feel lucky, you usually *are* lucky. You somehow make lucky things happen to you. And people who feel unlucky seem to make unlucky things happen to them. According to another alchemist, this is the real meaning of "As above, so below." Everyone knows that the mind can be affected by the external world – that a dull day can make you feel dull. But the magician is someone who

241

knows that the mind can also affect the external world. When you are full of courage and optimism, you somehow make good things happen to you.'

Niall shook his head in wonderment. 'And that's magic?'

'According to the books I have consulted.'

Niall said thoughtfully: 'This magician doesn't seem to have been very lucky.'

'I beg your pardon?'

'This man who sent Skorbo's killers. First two of his servants get carried off by Skorbo. And when they've killed Skorbo they all get caught. That doesn't sound very lucky, does it?'

The old man's face remained inscrutable, an indication that he failed to grasp what Niall was talking about.

'No doubt you are correct.'

Niall said thoughtfully: 'So it sounds as if it's my luck against his.'

This time the old man made no comment. After a long silence he said: 'Do you wish me to continue to summarize the nature of magic?'

Niall shook his head. 'Not now, thank you. But I'd like to ask your opinion about that dream. Do you know about the girl we found hanging upside down in Skorbo's larder?'

'Yes.' The Steegmaster's ability to read thoughts meant that it was able to perceive every important event that occurred in the city.

'I dreamed about her last night. I dreamt that Simeon came and cut off her tunic with a big pair of scissors, and I saw that she had bits of brown stuff, like dead leaves, stuck to her skin. Well, when I woke up, Simeon did cut off her tunic with a pair of scissors, and she did have bits of brown stuff stuck to her skin. How can you explain that?'

'And were they dead leaves?'

'No. They were this stuff.' He bent down and picked up the flat box from under his chair. 'Seaweed.'

The old man took a damp brown frond between his thumb and forefinger, and stared at it intently. Niall knew enough of the operations of the Steegmaster to know that it was being chemically analysed.

'This is not seaweed.'

'It's not?' Niall was astonished. 'It smells like it.'

'Sea water contains a precise percentage of magnesium, sulphur and calcium, as well as fifty-eight other elements. This contains far too much of all three, as well as a high percentage of phosphorus. That indicates that it comes from a freshwater lake with a high mineral content. It could be the crater of an extinct volcano.'

'Could it be an underground lake?'

'Impossible. Even weed requires light to grow. As you can see, this weed was not originally brown but green.' He placed his finger on a small area of weed that was, in fact, a pale green. 'It has oxidized to this brown colour.'

Niall stared at the brown mat of weed, whose smell filled the room.

'And that means sunlight?'

'Of course. Plants live by photosynthesis – absorbing carbon dioxide to produce sugar.'

'Have you any idea where it might have come from?'

'I cannot be specific. There are a dozen extinct volcanoes within fifty miles.' Niall recalled from his sleep-learning sessions that the approach of the comet Opik had produced many volcanic eruptions.

'And are there many lakes with that kind of high mineral content?'

'Certainly not in this region.'

'Could it be identified?'

'Unfortunately I know of no such lake. But you must

remember that most of my geological information dates back several centuries.'

Niall lifted the mat of weed, and held it up by its corners.

'Why do you suppose the magician's servants brought this with them?'

A silence of ten seconds indicated that the Steegmaster was surveying many alternatives.

'Possibly it has some religious significance.'

'Religious?' This idea bewildered him.

'Or it may have been used in some kind of magical ritual.'

'What kind of ritual?'

'That is impossible to say. There was a tribe of Indians in Ecuador who wore a garment made of leaves from a sacred tree for their magical ceremonies. You observe that this mat is a human artifact.'

This also came as a surprise. Niall spread out the weed on the tabletop. Now he examined it closely, he could see that the old man was correct. A number of pieces of weed had been woven together so skilfully that it was virtually impossible to see the joins. He held it out at arm's length. Yet it was obviously a mat, not some kind of a garment. He sighed with exasperation as he refolded it and replaced it in the box.

'They must have had *some* reason for bringing it. But what could it have been?'

'I can offer no other suggestions.'

Niall looked out of the window at the sunlit market scene, which was now busier than ever.

'And if time travel is impossible, how did I dream of the future. Can your books on magic explain that?'

'Magical philosophy states that the mind exists outside space and time. Only the body is subject to these limitations. So when the body is asleep, the mind may be able to pass beyond space and time.'

Niall asked with excitement: 'Do you think that's true?'

The old man smiled gently. 'How could I?' Niall shrugged impatiently. 'I have no means of judging whether such a theory is true or not. I exist merely in space and time. You are alive, which means that you are not entirely limited by space and time. You must judge for yourself.'

Niall felt a twinge of remorse. 'I'm sorry.' He stood up. 'And thank you for your help.' Apologizing made him feel calmer, less frustrated.

'It is always available.' His courtesy made Niall feel even more ashamed of his impatience.

The position of the sun in the sky showed that it was about two hours after midday. As he moved from behind the table, Niall became aware of the box in his pocket. He had totally forgotten about it.

'Have you any idea what this is?'

The old man took the pointed quill and held it in the palm of his hand.

'Yes. This is a primitive form of hypodermic syringe, of the kind invented in the seventeenth century.' He uncorked the bottle and sniffed its contents. After a pause he said: 'And this is human blood serum containing traces of spider venom.'

Niall snapped his fingers.

'Of course! I should have guessed! A serum against the poison of the death spiders. Do you think it will work?'

The old man shook his head.

'There is only one way to find out – by experiment.'

'Thank you.' Niall was already halfway to the door when the old man stopped him.

'You have forgotten your lakeweed. Where are you going in such a hurry?'

'To the hospital. It's full of people who've been paralysed by spider venom.'

'In that case, they will still be there when you arrive, will they not? Remember that impatience is the worst of human failings.'

But Niall was already out of the room.

As he approached the hospital, Niall saw that the main doorway was blocked by a small crowd. The hall beyond was also full of people, and a babe in arms was crying lustily. Niall made his way round to the rear entrance, and was relieved to find it deserted. The first person he saw when he stepped inside was Phelim.

'What's happening?'

'Word got around, and they've all come looking for relatives.'

At the far end of the corridor, three nurses were forming a human barrier to hold back the crowd, and a powerfully-built woman, whom Niall recognized as the matron, was admonishing everyone to make less noise. The door of the room in which the unconscious bodies were laid out stood open. As they approached, a woman rushed out, her hands over her face, wailing noisily. Behind her, Simeon was shaking his head with angry disgust.

'Damn fool! She wants to take her husband back home. I told her he'd be better here.' He noticed Niall, and made an obvious effort to regain his equanimity. 'Hello, my boy. You can see what chaos we're in.'

Half a dozen people were wandering around among the prostrate bodies, peering anxiously into unconscious faces. One of them, a dark-haired girl in a simple yellow dress, seemed vaguely familiar.

Boyd came into the room, carrying an oblong metal container, with a large and badly worn book balanced on top of it. He was obviously pleased with himself.

'Look what I've found.'

Phelim said resignedly: 'Go on. What is it?'

'An ECT apparatus.'

Simeon said: 'A what?'

'Electro-convulsive therapy. Look, here's a piece about it.' He opened the book and handed it to Simeon, who fumbled in his pocket and took out a pair of gold-rimmed spectacles, which he balanced on his nose. Boyd watched his face anxiously as he read.

'Worth trying, don't you think?'

Simeon said nothing for several seconds, then shook his head.

'No. It's for curing depressives. And it recommends administering a light general anaesthetic before use. These poor devils are already anaesthetized.'

'But it might wake them up.'

'Too risky.' The experiment with the snake serum had obviously made him cautious. 'Thanks anyway.'

Boyd shrugged disconsolately. As he left the room Simeon called after him: 'Keep trying.'

Niall said: 'I think I may have the answer.'

'To what?'

'Waking them up.' He produced the box from his pocket, and slid back the lid.

'What on earth's that?'

'I found it in the hide-out.'

Simeon stared at it through his spectacles, then held the brown bottle up to the light.

'What do you suppose it is?'

'I think it's antidote to spider venom.'

Simeon's face brightened. He took up the quill and squeezed the bulb.

'You could be right. This is obviously a crude hypodermic needle.' Two spots of red on his cheekbones were the only indication of his excitement. He turned to Phelim. 'What do you think? Should we risk it?'

Phelim said cautiously: 'That's your decision. I'm only the assistant.'

Niall understood his doubts. If the 'antidote' killed the patient, it would be hard to know what to tell the relatives.

Simeon turned to Niall.

'What do you think?'

'I think it's probably safe. The Steegmaster said it contained only small traces of spider venom.'

A girl's voice said: 'Please try it on my brother.'

It was the dark-haired girl in the yellow dress; she had come up behind them as they were speaking. She was now the last of the visitors left in the room.

'What is your name?'

'Quinella. I am from Dira.'

'Ah yes. Where is your brother?'

'Here.' She led them across the room. 'You know him. His name is Eirek.'

'Eirek! Of course!' Eirek had been one of the crowd of children with whom Niall had played in Kazak's underground city. But now he looked down at the thin, pale face he was scarcely able to recognize him.

Niall's eyes met Simeon's. He asked the girl: 'Do you understand the risk? This serum is untried. It could do him harm.'

Simeon added: 'It could even kill him.'

She said: 'But I feel he will die if he remains like this.'

Niall understood her fear. Many of the children of Dira had died on their march across the desert; even now, Eirek's ribs showed clearly through his skin.

Simeon shrugged. 'Very well.' He turned to Phelim. 'Hand me a new syringe.' He dipped the needle into the brown bottle, and drew up some of the pale yellow fluid into it. Then he carefully selected a spot on the underside of Eirek's forearm, slapping the flesh to make the vein stand out. Then he drove home the point and pressed the plunger. After only a moment he withdrew the needle.

'I don't want to risk using too much.'

The girl smiled palely. 'Thank you.' Her eyes had not left her brother's face. Simeon said gently:

'It could take hours, or even longer. Why don't you go home? We'll look after him.'

She shook her head. 'Please let me stay.'

He sighed. 'All right. You'd better find yourself a chair.'

Phelim muttered: 'Here's more of them.'

There was a sound of voices in the corridor. The matron appeared in the doorway. 'Can I let some more in?' Simeon nodded, and half a dozen subdued-looking men and women shuffled into the room. A moment later, as Simeon was taking Eirek's pulse, they were all startled by a loud shriek; it came from a middle-aged woman with dyed golden hair.

'My husband! My dear husband!' She flung herself down on one of the bodies and began to kiss the face. The trestle table on which it was lying almost collapsed. Simeon said sternly:

'Madam, unless you control yourself, you must leave immediately.'

She appeared not to hear him.

'Is he alive?'

'Yes. But please lower your voice.'

The woman began patting the man's cheeks with both hands – the pats were so hard they amounted to slaps.

'Noldi! Wake up! It's me.'

Simeon glanced at the matron, who took the woman firmly by the arm. She immediately burst into loud cries and shook herself free.

Niall had seen the problem before: in the spider city,

there were many middle-aged women who had become domineering and prone to uncontrolled outbursts of emotion. In the days of slavery, men and women had been kept segregated. The men, under the direct domination of the spiders, were little more than workhorses. Women, on the other hand, had little direct contact with the spiders; they were under the supervision of female commanders, and were generally well-treated. Compared to men, they saw themselves as a kind of aristocracy. Older ones – like this woman – were usually promoted to matrons in charge of women's hostels, and became accustomed to authority. But without a husband and children, they often became self-centred, and prone to violent outbursts of emotion, like the one they were now witnessing.

Eventually the woman was persuaded to sit down, and a nurse was despatched to fetch her a cup of herb tea. Meanwhile, the other visitors had finished their survey of the paralysed victims. Most of them were obviously disappointed. Only one sad-looking woman continued to stand by the body of a child, tears running down her cheeks. Niall asked:

'Do you know her?'

'She is my daughter. But I think she is dead.'

The girl was a slight, thin child, about twelve years old; fragments of cobweb were sticking to her blonde hair.

'No. She is still alive.'

He confirmed this by probing her mind. To his surprise, the child seemed to be fully conscious. For a moment he suspected her of shamming, then realized that, although aware of all the sounds from the surrounding room, she was unable to move a muscle.

The girl in the yellow dress gave a sudden cry.

'He's waking up!'

In fact, Eirek's eyelids were fluttering in a manner

that suggested a nervous twitch rather than someone waking from sleep. A moment later they closed again. Then the rib cage expanded in a deep breath, and he shook his head violently, as if someone had slapped his face. A moment later the eyes opened, and stared around with a startled expression.

The girl said: 'Eirek. Do you know me?'

He smiled faintly and nodded. 'Quinny.'

Simeon said: 'That's remarkable. It took less than five minutes. No, please . . .' These last words were addressed to Quinella, who had seized his hand and was pressing it to her lips. Simeon pointed to Niall. 'He's the one you should thank – he brought the antidote.'

There was a loud cry from the middle-aged woman, who had joined the group round the table. Now she flung herself at Simeon's feet.

'Please give it to my husband! I beg you in the name of the great goddess . . .'

Simeon blushed with embarrassment as the woman tried to embrace his legs.

'Please get up, madam. I'll do my best for everyone.'

'Promise me first. Promise me you'll give him some.'

Simeon took a deep breath; for a moment Niall thought he was going to lose his temper. Then he said:

'Very well, madam. But please get up and promise to behave yourself.'

'I swear!' A calculating expression came into her eyes. 'But you'll give it to him now, won't you?'

'Very well.'

The woman's husband was a handsome, powerfully built man, obviously at least ten years her junior. Because the spiders had always paid so much attention to the physical wellbeing of their human subjects – breeding them like prize cattle – this city was full of magnificently handsome men with the physique of

Greek gods and women with superb figures. For Niall, it was a perpetually disillusioning experience to glimpse their minds and realize that they were utterly without the power of reflection.

Simeon drove the needle into the man's forearm, withdrawing it almost immediately. The woman asked: 'Are you sure that's enough?'

Simeon said gruffly: 'This is all we have, and it has to serve for a dozen people.'

Niall's eyes encountered those of the mother of the twelve-year-old girl; he could see that she was too shy or too timid to speak. He placed his hand on Simeon's arm.

'Give some to the little girl. It shouldn't take much.' The mother gave him a warm smile of gratitude.

Simeon slapped the child's thin forearm to bring up the vein, then drove in the needle. As he did so, Niall once again probed her mind, and again was puzzled to realize that she was as wide awake as he was. The likeliest explanation, he concluded, was that because she was so small, the spider had injected a carefully graduated dose of venom, precisely enough to paralyse the nervous system without killing her. This was confirmed when, a few seconds later, the girl's eyelids fluttered and she opened her eyes. She smiled at her mother, then immediately turned to look at Niall, although he had been standing beyond her line of vision. Niall reached out and took her hand.

'What is your name?'

'Wenda.'

'How long have you been awake?'

'All the time.'

Simeon was obviously baffled by her reply.

'What does she mean?'

Niall asked her: 'Ever since the spider jumped on you?' She nodded. Simeon said:

'Great goddess!'

Niall was puzzled by her composure.

'Wasn't it horrible?'

She shook her head. 'No, it was a kind of . . . sleepy feeling.'

Niall began to understand. His grandfather had once described how he had been seized by a death spider, and how, instead of feeling terrified, he had experienced a curious dreamy sensation, as if he was in no danger. Now it seemed plain that, as they pounced, the spiders somehow anaesthetized the mind against fear. On reflection, this seemed logical. A victim in the grip of terror would die sooner than a victim who experienced an illusory sense of security.

The middle-aged woman grabbed Simeon's arm.

'Look! He's waking up.'

Her husband was shaking his head and staring around him in a bewildered manner.

'How long have I been asleep?'

It was obvious that he had no idea of what had happened to him.

The matron appeared in the doorway. 'Is it all right to let some more of them in?'

Simeon snapped impatiently: 'No it isn't. Keep them out for at least half an hour.' He was taking the man's pulse.

'Do you feel strong enough to walk?'

'Of course.' He jumped off the table.

'Good. Take him home, madam.'

The woman seized her husband by the arm, and hurried him out without pausing to say thank you.

The child was now in her mother's arms. Niall asked the woman:

'When did she disappear?'

'Exactly six weeks and two days ago.'

Niall asked the child:

'And you were awake all that time?' She nodded. 'And you weren't afraid?'

She shook her head firmly. Simeon muttered: 'Incredible!'

The child said: 'But I didn't like the nasty man.'

'What nasty man?'

'The man with the funny lips.'

Niall and Simeon exchanged glances; the phrase evoked Skorbo's assassins, with their strangely sensual lips. Niall took the child's hand, gazed into her eyes and probed her mind. What he saw there startled him. He asked her: .

'You saw this man with the spiders?' She nodded. 'And they didn't attack him?'

'No. They were friends.'

Niall could see that further questioning would be pointless; she had told him all she knew, and her mind was succumbing to exhaustion; when he tried to probe further, it was as if he was trying to see through a drifting fog.

'You'd better take her home. Do you live nearby?'

'Across the street.'

Simeon said: 'Make sure she gets a good sleep. Bring her in to see me tomorrow.'

When the mother had gone Simeon asked: 'Did that child mean what I thought she meant?'

Niall nodded. 'I'm afraid she did.'

Phelim was looking baffled: '*What* did she mean?'

Simeon said: 'The man with the funny lips was one of the killers.'

'But she said they were friends.' He looked from Niall to Simeon. 'Perhaps she was dreaming? Or suffering from delirium?'

Niall shook his head. 'I'm certain she wasn't.'

'But that's absurd. Why should Skorbo be friendly with one of his killers?'

Niall said: 'It could mean one of two things. Either that this man betrayed his comrades to Skorbo . . .'

Simeon finished the sentence: 'Or Skorbo was in league with the magician.'

'Oh, surely not – that doesn't make sense. If Skorbo was in league with them why did he drag two of them off to his larder? And why did they kill him?'

Niall shook his head. 'Perhaps they betrayed him. Perhaps he betrayed them. I don't know. But I'm certain she wasn't dreaming.'

There was a silence, while each of them was lost in his own thoughts. Finally Simeon shrugged.

'I agree. It doesn't make sense. But we have work to do.' He asked Phelim: 'How much serum is there left?'

Phelim held up the bottle against the light. 'About an inch.'

'Then we might have enough.'

For the next ten minutes he moved deliberately among the prostrate bodies, injecting each with a carefully measured quantity of the serum. A few woke up almost immediately; others took several minutes before they showed signs of returning consciousness. Some of these began to moan, as if in the grip of a nightmare. But most gave the characteristic shake of the head, and gazed around them in perplexity. Simeon grunted with satisfaction.

'Amazing stuff.'

Phelim asked: 'Why does it work so quickly?'

'I imagine it's because the spiders inject a precise amount of poison to paralyse the nervous system but not to kill. As soon as the balance is altered, the victim begins to recover.'

The last to be injected was the girl who had reacted so badly to the snake serum. Niall watched her with anxiety, and was relieved when her eyelids opened almost immediately. As her eyes met Niall's, her face broke into a warm and gentle smile, which was succeeded a moment later by a look of alarm and embarrassment. What had happened, he realized, was that she had recognized him from the depth of her dream consciousness as someone with whom she had experienced some form of intimacy; a moment later, she recognized him, and was plunged into confusion. He took her hand and helped her into a sitting position.

'What is your name?'

'Amaryllis.'

'Did you see the spider that attacked you?'

She shook her head. 'I remember nothing.'

'Where were you when you were attacked?'

'In the slave quarter.'

Niall and Simeon exchanged glances.

'Please tell me all you can remember.' When she still hesitated, he asked: 'What were you doing in the slave quarter?'

'I had been to see my old nurse.' In the days of slavery, all children had been reared in nurseries, with female slaves as wet nurses. The result was that children often regarded the nurse as their true mother.

'Then what happened?'

'It was a full moon, and we walked down to the new lake while Dinah's sister was cooking supper. Then we started to walk back . . .'

'Can you remember which way you walked?'

'Along the river bank. But we turned into a side street.'

'Which one?'

'I cannot recall. We were talking . . .'

'And what happened?'

'Dinah screamed, and something knocked me down . . .'

'Did you see or feel anything?'

'It all happened so quickly.' She began to cry. 'What happened to Dinah?'

Simeon patted her hand. 'We'll try to find her, don't worry.'

While they had been speaking, the room had gradually emptied as patients were led away to be reunited with relatives. Some were so weak that they had to be supported by nurses; many seemed dazed and distressed. Now, at a signal from Simeon, Amaryllis was also led away by the matron. Niall watched her go with regret. Because he had infused some of his vitality into her, he felt that she was taking a part of his identity with her. It was a sad, yet at the same time an oddly pleasant sensation.

Simeon said: 'It's strange that she was in the slave quarter. Do you think . . . ?'

'I'm afraid so. The hide-out was within fifty yards of the new lake. She may have been attacked in the same street.'

Simeon ran his fingers through his stubbly grey hair.

'This is insane. Why should Skorbo be in league with them? What would be the advantage to either side?'

Niall shook his head. 'I don't know.'

Phelim said: 'What I can't understand is how Skorbo could keep such a secret. Surely the other spiders would be able to read his mind?'

Niall saw he was suffering from a familiar misconception about telepathy.

'Not necessarily. It's not difficult to hide your thoughts, particularly if no one has any reason to suspect you. Skorbo was the captain of the guard, so none of his subordinates would dare to probe his mind. And his superiors – the Spider Lord and his council – wouldn't want to read his mind.'

'Why not?'

It was not easy to explain. 'Skorbo was a commoner, an ordinary soldier of no particular distinction. They simply wouldn't be interested in what went on in his mind. They'd find it slightly distasteful.'

Simeon had noticed the box wrapped in the slave tunic; Niall had left it on a chair.

'What's this?'

'I found it in the hide-out. It's a sort of seaweed. You remember the brown fragments on that girl's body . . .'

He broke off, and he and Simeon stared at one another with sudden dismay; the same thought had struck them both at the same time. Simeon smote his forehead.

'We've used up all the serum!'

'Are you sure. There was some in the bottle . . .'

But the bottle and the hypodermic syringe both proved to be empty. Simeon groaned:

'What an idiot I am!'

Niall turned the bottle upside down; there was not even a drop left.

Phelim said: Couldn't we make more?'

Simeon sighed. 'It looks as if we'll have to.'

Niall asked: 'How is it made?'

'Oh, that's straightforward enough. First of all you have to get hold of some spider venom. Then you dilute it and inject someone with tiny quantities until they've formed a resistance. When that happens, the blood serum becomes an antidote to spider venom.'

Phelim asked; 'Don't we have any in the dispensary?'

'No, for a simple reason. It's never been possible to get hold of spider venom. They obviously don't want anyone to develop an antidote.'

Niall said: 'I'm sure Dravig could arrange it. How long does it take to make serum?'

'Two weeks. Perhaps three.'

Phelim said: 'Does it really matter how long the girl remains unconscious?'

It was Simeon who answered. 'While she is unconscious she cannot be questioned. And she is now our only link with the magician.' He shook his head. 'How the devil did we *both* manage to forget the girl?'

The question was rhetorical; but as their eyes met, both realized they were thinking the same thing.

A moment later, Boyd came into the room. He looked startled to see that the tables were now empty.

'Hello! Where's everyone gone?'

Phelim said: 'We found the antidote to the poison.'

'Pity. I've got another idea.'

Simeon said quickly: 'What is it?'

'But it's no use now, is it?'

Phelim said: 'Tell us all the same.'

'One of these.' Boyd reached up, and tugged from around his head something that Niall had taken for a metal hair-band. It was of a pale gold colour.

Niall asked: 'What is it?'

'It's called a Gullstrand apparatus. It's supposed to help brain-damaged patients.'

Niall took it from him. It looked so much like a hair-band that he wondered whether Boyd was mistaken.

'It doesn't seem to have any controls.'

'It doesn't need any. It's made of two substances, a conductor and a non-conductor, and when the ends make contact with the skin, it fires random bursts of electric current into the brain. Why don't you try it?'

Niall slipped it on to his head, with the centre of the band across his forehead and the ends above his ears. He expected to feel some kind of electrical tingling sensation; in fact, he felt nothing.

'Are you sure it works?'

'It takes a minute or two.'

'Then what happens?'

'I got strange sort of flashes, then some rather weird sensations.' Something in Boyd's expression suggested that he was saying rather less than he meant.

They stood there, watching him in silence. Niall finally shook his head.

'Nothing's happening. Are you sure it's switched on?'

'It's on all the time. It works off permanent batteries.'

'Perhaps they're worn out.'

'Not likely.' Boyd spoke with confidence. 'They only use a few millivolts. They'll last forever.'

Niall slipped it off his head and held it out to Simeon.

'I don't think it's going to work.'

Simeon said: 'Keep it. It's yours.'

'Mine?'

'It was found in this city. You are the ruler of this city. Therefore everything in it belongs to you.'

'Thank you.' Niall replaced it on his head, this time using it as a circlet to hold the hair in place.

Boyd said: 'It worked for me. There must be something peculiar about your brain.'

He opened his eyes and stared around him in bewilderment. It took him a few moments to recognize where he was. He was lying in the empty hallway of the hospital, at the foot of the stairs. Outside, the avenue was almost deserted. A few yards away, down the corridor, he could hear the voice of the matron holding a conversation with one of the nurses. The last thing he remembered was a flash of light inside his head, followed by a sharp pain like an incipient headache.

He clambered hastily to his feet, glad that no one had noticed him lying there – the thought of fainting filled him with embarrassment. The circlet was lying on the floor; he picked it up and replaced it on his head. The moment he did so, he realized that this was what had been responsible for his loss of consciousness. His brain lurched, as if he had stepped on to the deck of a ship tossing in a storm, and he had to steady himself by grabbing the banister at the bottom of the stairway. He hastily snatched the circlet from his head, and dropped it into the wide pocket of his tunic. The moment he did so, the feeling of dizziness vanished, but a feeling of weakness remained.

He sat down on the bottom step and closed his eyes. It was best to relax and allow himself to become totally passive; any attempt to think brought a return of the weariness. But after a few minutes, his sensations returned to normal. When he stood up, he was relieved to find that there was no return of the nausea.

But as soon as he stepped out into the winter sunlight

he noticed the difference. It was as distinct as waking up from sleep. Everything around him seemed oddly clear, as if some kind of a veil had been withdrawn. The outline of everything he looked at was oddly sharp and bright. There was a similar heightening in his physical sensations. The wind against his face seemed somehow cooler and stronger, as if he had just stepped out of a hot bath. The sensation of his clothing against his body, normally unnoticed, was now almost painfully intrusive, as if a layer of skin had been removed. This new sense of clarity was at once delightful and uncomfortable; even the sunlight seemed too bright, so that he was forced to half-close his eyelids against it. In this state of wide-awakeness, his normal consciousness seemed like a form of sleep.

One thing was clear: that the Gullstrand apparatus caused peculiar changes in the brain. Boyd had said that it was used to help brain-damaged patients. He was tempted to return to the hospital, to see if the medical textbook contained any further information; but since his forehead was covered in perspiration, and he felt a strong desire to lie down, he decided against it.

Now, as he walked along the southern side of the square towards the palace, he realized that strange things were still happening inside his head. He was now experiencing a disturbingly strange sensation – as if everything had suddenly been magnified and then shrunk back to normal size. It felt rather as if some enormous object was rushing towards him at great speed, then receding again, or as if his brain was on a swing, swooping backwards and forwards. It was a vertiginous experience, and brought back some of the earlier feeling of nausea. But he comforted himself with the thought that, since it had been caused by the Gullstrand apparatus, which was now in his pocket, the effect should be only temporary.

Staring at the pavement helped. But this had the curious effect of making the pavement seem closer and somehow more real; although he had been staring at it for only a few seconds, he felt that he would remember it for the rest of his life. He made a kind of effort – like pushing it to arm's length – and this overpowering sense of reality disappeared, to be replaced by a curious sensation as if he was seeing the pavement through the long end of a telescope.

He had almost reached the palace when he heard the sound of footsteps running behind him. It was Boyd.

'You forgot this.' He held out the box containing the lakeweed.

'Oh, thank you.'

Boyd looked at him closely. 'Are you all right? You look a bit funny.'

'Yes. I'm all right. Just rather tired.'

Boyd looked down at the gold circlet, which was sticking out of the wide tunic pocket.

'It was that thing, wasn't it? It made me feel as if I'd had too many glasses of mead. But it soon wears off.'

'Do you know how it works?'

'Yes, I think so. But it would take a long time to explain.'

'Then why don't you come in? Or are they expecting you back?'

'Oh no. They're trying to analyse the blood on that hatchet. That'll take hours.' He looked up at the palace. 'Is this where you live?'

'Yes.'

'What a marvellous place. Does it have marble staircases?'

'Yes. Would you like to come and see it?'

Boyd said eagerly: 'I'll say!' The piece of slang was new to Niall, but he gathered that it signified assent.

As they approached the door, Boyd glanced nervously at the wolf spider who stood on guard; the spider betrayed no sign of being aware of their presence. When the door had closed behind them, Boyd asked in an undertone:

'Is that thing real?'

'Of course.' Niall looked at him in surprise.

'I thought it might be a statue. Doesn't it give you the creeps?'

Niall was surprised to find himself feeling defensive about the spiders. 'Human beings give spiders the creeps. We have to learn to get used to one another.'

Oblivious to the implied rebuke, Boyd was staring around the hallway. 'I say, what a place to live! It's like our town hall.' He ran over to the fireplace and peered up the chimney. 'Isn't it huge? Why doesn't the rain come down?'

'I don't know.'

Boyd opened the cellar door. 'What's this place?'

'The cellar.'

'Can I have a look?'

'It's dark down there.'

'There's a lamp here.' In a niche at the top of the stairs, there was an unlighted oil lamp, with a tinder box beside it. (Matches had been available since the end of slavery, but were still in short supply.) With an expertise born of long experience Boyd kindled the wick and replaced the chimney. Then, with Niall behind him, he went down into the cellar. Half a dozen smoked hams were hanging from the beams, and there were a few barrels of pickles, preserves and boxes of spices. Boyd said with disappointment:

'Not much here.'

'No. It was cleaned out six months ago.'

'What's in them?' Boyd pointed to the massive black jars that stood against the far wall.

'Nothing – they're empty.' As he spoke, Niall's heart

contracted with foreboding. The jar in which he had placed the two pendants was broken, so that one fragment was lying on the floor, together with the stone plug that had sealed the neck. Boyd caught the gold-coloured glint in the lamplight.

'Look, there's something in this one.' He started to bend forward.

Niall said sharply: 'Don't touch!'

Boyd straightened up obediently. Niall took the lamp from him, and knelt on one knee. The jar had been cracked into three pieces, as if struck with a sledgehammer. Two pieces remained upright; the third had fallen down.

His first thought was that the jar had been accidentally broken by a servant – perhaps someone had removed the stone plug, found it unexpectedly heavy, and dropped it back into the neck, splitting the jar. Then he realized that this was improbable. No one knew that he had put the pendants into the jar, so no one had any reason to look into it.

Niall studied the pendants, holding the lamp close to them, then reached out cautiously and touched them. They were completely inert. He picked them up and held them at arm's length.

Boyd said: 'There was one of those back in the hospital. What are they?'

'They are worn by the servants of the magician. Do you know about the magician?'

Boyd nodded. 'Uncle Simeon's been telling us.'

'Then you know they can be dangerous.'

As he was speaking, Niall was trying to untangle the chains of the pendants; it was impossible; they had been virtually knotted together. Yet he could clearly remember dropping them from the glass into the jar, and noticing that they were separate. It should have been impossible for them to become entangled. He finally gave a hard tug that snapped one of the chains, and was able to pull them apart. Boyd asked:

'Why are you doing that?'

'Because when they are separated they have less power.'

If he had been alone, Niall would have taken the pendants to the white tower. Instead, he dropped them separately into two stone jars, deliberately choosing the two that were furthest apart, and carefully resealing them with the stone plugs.

As they were returning up the stairs, Boyd asked:

'But who broke the jar?'

'The magician.'

Boyd gazed at him with astonishment. 'He's been here?'

'No. But the pendants are here, and that is enough. That is why they are so dangerous.'

Boyd was full of questions, but Niall answered them in a state of abstraction. He was still wondering about the broken jar, and about the effect of the two pendants. It probably meant that the magician was aware of everything that had happened in the palace in the past two days. Niall cursed himself for his carelessness, and vowed to take them to the white tower at the first opportunity.

His room was empty; Jarita, like many other women in the palace, was inclined to take a siesta in the afternoon. He laid the box containing the lakeweed on the table, and removed the metal circlet from his pocket and placed it beside it. Now he became aware of the pressure of some object against his thigh; it was the black figurine. Before Boyd could ask what it was, Niall said:

'Tell me about the Gullstrand apparatus.'

'Shall I go and fetch the textbook?'

'No. Just tell me what you can remember.'

Boyd wrinkled his brow.

'Well let's see . . . It's something about nerve pathways in the brain. They carry different impulses . . .' He stopped, drew a deep breath, and began again. 'They discovered that if someone has damage to some particular area of the brain – let's say he falls out of a tree and can't use his left hand – he'd often recover without any help – especially if he kept trying to use the hand. And that wasn't because the damaged area in the brain had healed up. It was because he'd developed new nerve pathways around the damaged area. I think that's correct, anyway.'

Niall nodded. 'It sounds right.'

'So this man Gullstrand thought they must be discovering the new pathways by trial and error. So he invented this thing to make it easier. It keeps on stimulating different nerve pathways at random. It's a bit like sending a lot of people off down dark lanes, carrying torches. Sooner or later, one finds a way.'

Niall nodded slowly. He was beginning to understand some of the strange sensations he had experienced when he left the hospital. New nerve pathways would explain the sensation of freshness and newness, as if seeing things for the first time. Yet he still failed to understand that other sensation: as if his brain was on a swing, swooping backwards and forwards, so that objects seemed to come closer, then recede. Even thinking about it seemed to revive it, bringing a momentary feeling of dizziness.

He asked Boyd:

'Can you describe how you felt when you tried it?'

'There was a strange sort of flash – as if somebody had hit me on the head. Then I felt sick. Then I began to get a strange sort of feeling as though everything was alive . . .'

'Alive?'

'That's right. And as if I was being watched. It began to get better after that – a sort of excited feeling.'

Niall picked up the circlet.

'I'm going to try it on this girl . . .'

'Can I come?'

'Of course.'

In the corridor he almost bumped into Dona, who was carrying an armful of children's clothes. When she saw Niall, she flushed with pleasure.

'Hello. I haven't seen you for a long time.'

'No. I've been very busy.' Her smile made him feel guilty. There was a time when he had intended to marry Dona. And although nothing had ever been said, he knew that she was aware of it. The duties of kingship had made him push the idea to the back of his mind. Yet he still experienced the same curious feeling of gladness every time he saw her, a glow of affection that made him want to take her in his arms.

Boyd was staring at her with obvious curiosity. He hastened to introduce them.

'This is Boyd, Simeon's nephew. This is my cousin Dona.'

They exchanged smiles, and Boyd made the odd little half-bow that was the standard formal greeting between males in the city of the bombardier beetles.

There was a moment of embarrassed silence, then Dona looked down at the circlet in Niall's hand.

'What's that?'

'Oh, it's a . . .' Niall would have preferred to leave it unexplained, but Boyd broke in eagerly:

'It's called a Gullstrand apparatus, and we're going to try it on this girl who's been bitten by a spider.'

'Which girl?' It was obvious that Dona knew nothing about it.

Niall said: 'Come and see.' He spoke reluctantly, feeling that Boyd had obliged him to issue the invitation.

For some reason, he experienced deep inner resistance to allowing his womenfolk to see the unconscious girl. But Dona immediately placed her pile of washing on the floor outside the door.

'Yes, I'd like to.'

The girl was lying there, exactly as Niall had left her that morning, with the blanket drawn up to her chin. The tangled bundle of web that Simeon had cut from her body still lay on the floor. Her breathing was scarcely perceptible. The face with its closed eyes looked as peaceful as a sleeping child.

Dona said: 'She's beautiful.'

For some odd reason, Niall felt embarrassed by the remark. Without further delay he took the gold circlet and slipped it on to her head, with the two ends behind her ears.

For a moment nothing happened. Then the girl's head jerked on the pillow and Niall knew that the flash of light had penetrated her sleeping brain. As they all watched intently, the girl's eyelids began to twitch. Boyd said:

'It's working.'

As he spoke, her eyes opened and she stared at Niall. Her hands moved convulsively under the blanket, as if she was trying to free herself. Then, with a suddenness that startled them all, she sat up, as if impelled by a spring. Her eyes stared direct into Niall's, and she seemed to be on the point of asking him who he was. Then the eyes seemed to change. She continued to look at Niall, but it was as if she had ceased to be aware of him, or as if she had become blind. A moment later she fell backward on to the pillow, and lay there as before, her face turned to the ceiling. The only difference was that her breathing had become faster. But after a few moments, even this subsided, and she seemed to relapse into deep unconsciousness. Niall pulled the blanket – which had fallen down – over her breasts; he noticed that Boyd blushed and looked away.

The circlet had become detached from her head, and now Niall picked it up from the pillow and readjusted it across her forehead. This time nothing happened. They waited for almost five minutes, but when it became plain that there was no change in the girl's condition, Niall sighed and turned away.

'Tell your uncle he'll have to make the serum after all.'

Boyd said: 'There's one thing I don't understand. If she woke up like that, why did she go back to sleep again?'

Dona said: 'Well, people *do* wake up and go back to sleep again.'

Boyd said lamely: 'Yes, but you see what I mean . . .'

In fact, Niall did see what he meant. He had watched a dozen people recover from spider venom. Once they were awake, they stayed awake.

He turned to Boyd.

'I'll ask Dravig if we can have some spider venom.'

As Niall locked the door once again behind them, Boyd said:

'Can I go and look at the view from the roof before I go?'

'Of course.' Niall turned to Dona. 'Would you mind showing him? Or are you busy?'

'No. The children are asleep. He can stay for tea if he likes.'

Boyd said politely: 'If you're sure I'm no trouble.' But Niall caught the expression in his eyes as he looked at Dona, and knew that he would be happy to stay all afternoon.

It was a relief to be alone again. He flung himself down on the cushions and closed his eyes. But this immediately brought a return of the giddy sensation –

the feeling that his brain was on a swing. He sat up and propped a cushion between his back and the wall. As he did so, his eyes fell on the box of lakeweed on the table, and curiosity overcame his tiredness. Kneeling on a cushion, he removed the mat from the box and laid it out on the tabletop. It felt cold and clammy to the touch. Yet when he placed the palms of his hands on it, there was something delightfully soothing about the slippery dampness – so much so that he bent forward and allowed his forehead to rest on the mat. It was as pleasantly relaxing as a soft pillow. There was undoubtedly something powerfully sensual in its damp coolness; but these feelings soon blended with a relaxed, floating sensation that brought images of massive dark forests whose trees overshadowed deep lakes. As this continued, he became aware that something was happening to his body. It was difficult to say precisely what this was, for it seemed to consist of a tingling feeling of anticipation. It was as if the contact between his flesh and the mat of lakeweed was only the beginning of the process, and he remained poised on the brink of the first stage.

After half a minute or so, he noticed something else: that there seemed to be no transmission of heat from his flesh to the weed; it remained as cool as when he first touched it. Even when he wrapped it around his hand, the coolness remained, exactly as if he had immersed the hand in cold water. But as his hand came into contact with the tabletop, he noticed something else that intrigued him: the wood was warm. It took a few moments for the implications to dawn on him, and as they did, he sat upright with excitement. The mat was conducting the heat from his body direct to the tabletop, while itself remaining cool. This meant that it was not – as the Steegmaster had suggested – a purely ritual object. It served some other purpose. And Niall already had a glimmering of what that purpose might be.

He folded the mat and replaced it in the box. Then he tiptoed into the corridor – afraid that his movements might bring Jarita out of her room – and quietly unlocked the room next door. Once inside, he locked the door behind him.

He removed the mat from its box, and draped it over the back of the chair. Then he pulled back the blanket from the girl's body and allowed it to drop on to the floor.

With its small breasts and round, firm belly, there was something oddly child-like and vulnerable about the naked body. Brown fragments of lakeweed still adhered to her thighs. He took the mat of lakeweed and carefully spread it over her body. A moment later, he realized that her breathing had become deeper, and that there were faint spots of colour in the pale cheeks. He watched intently, wondering if she was about to wake up; but after several minutes, she still showed no further sign of life.

He drew the chair up beside the bed, then sat down and placed both his hands on the mat. The lakeweed felt pleasantly cool under his palms. Yet when he closed his eyes, he had a sense that there was something wrong. There was a subtle sense of discord that was quite unlike the feeling he had experienced in his own room, a tension that made his heart beat irregularly. Then, suddenly, he understood. He had placed the mat upside down. In his own room, he had placed the side that contained the sucker-like fronds against the tabletop. He now turned it over, so the fronds were against her body. Then, once again, he rested both hands on the mat.

A few moments later he became aware of a tingling sensation in both hands. It spread to the wrists, then into the lower part of the forearms. There was an almost blissful feeling of relaxation, such as he often experienced when immersing his hands and wrists in warm water. It took him a few minutes to realize what was happening: that he was drawing vital energy from the girl.

Yet after only a few moments he became aware that the method he was now using – merely resting his hands on the lakeweed – was inadequate. To experience the full benefit of this overflowing energy, their bodies had to be in total contact.

Niall stripped off his tunic and dropped it on the floor; then he lowered himself slowly on to the girl, allowing his weight to rest on his elbows. He was six inches taller than she was, and he was concerned that he might be too heavy for her; in fact, when he was lying on top of her, his weight was so evenly distributed that it was obvious that, even if she had been awake, she would have experienced no discomfort.

Even though he had been half-expecting it, what happened next still came as a surprise. She began to breathe more deeply, and a glowing sensation rose upward from her body. It was exactly like turning on a tap; vital energy flowed from her, then through the mat and into his body. In some strange way, the mat was sucking vital energy from her body, and allowing it to flow into Niall. He tried pressing his lips against hers, but this actually impeded the flow, even when he moistened them with his tongue. Meanwhile, the girl breathed deeply and regularly, as if accustomed to this process of energy-transfusion; he could even sense that she was enjoying it, glad to be rid of some of the vital fluid that had accumulated in her body.

This process of drinking her energy was among the most unusual sensations Niall had ever experienced. In some ways it reminded him of the first time he had held Merlew in his arms – the same tingling sense of aliveness that had communicated itself from her body to his. But compared to what he was now experiencing, even embracing Merlew was a poor second best. This was far deeper and more complete than lovemaking; or rather, lovemaking was an incomplete version of this experience. When Merlew allowed him to kiss her and press his body against hers, she was retreating into a private world of pleasure, and he was merely an instrument of her pleasure. This girl was giving unselfishly, giving because he was a man, and he needed her vital energy; she gave as unselfishly and naturally as a cow gives milk. In Niall, the flow satisfied some deep masculine craving, a craving of which he had not even been consciously aware a few moments ago. It was like a cool drink when the throat is harsh and dry, and it sent waves of pleasure into remote corners of his being, as if his nerves were telegraph wires that stretched out into the remote regions of some unknown country.

He was reminded of one of the most striking experiences of his childhood: the day the rains fell on the desert at the foot of the plateau. Black clouds had been carried on the cool westerly breeze, and suddenly water was gushing from the sky as though some god had upturned an enormous bucket or diverted a waterfall. As the torrent flooded down a dried watercourse, the ground had burst open, and bullfrogs pushed their way out of the mud; dry pods exploded and within half an hour the ground was covered with a multicoloured carpet of flowers, white, red, yellow, blue, orange and mauve. Soon small pools were full of tadpoles and algae, and the croaking of frogs was louder than the beating of the rain. It was perhaps the greatest exhilaration Niall had experienced during his years of childhood. And now, as his being absorbed this girl's energy, he felt that his own being was bursting into flower, and that unsuspected areas of awareness were suddenly glowing into life.

At the end of five minutes, his body felt sated with pleasure; he was like a starving man who has eaten an enormous meal. When he stood up again, his naked body was glowing as if a thousand points of light were sparkling over the surface of the flesh. He dropped into the chair – an old-fashioned wooden armchair with a cushion attached to its seat – and allowed himself to relax with a deep sigh. His heart seemed to have slowed to half its normal speed.

Now, at least, he understood why the assassins had brought the girl with them. She was their source of energy, the renewer of their vitality. While his body had been in contact with hers, he had even been able to sense the presence of those other men who had preceded him. He experienced no sense of jealousy; it was her business to give energy – she was willing to give to anyone who could receive it from her.

And now, with a sudden flash of insight, he also understood why Veig had behaved so strangely in the girl's presence. Surely it must be because his brother had somehow sensed that she had the power to renew his depleted energies? This thought awakened a surge of hope and optimism. His own sense of glowing vitality convinced him that this girl could cure Veig's sickness – that it would be a simple matter for his brother to draw energy from her body until his own vital powers had been restored . . . This thought so excited Niall that he started to his feet and had taken a stride towards the door before remembering that he was naked. Then, as he started to pull on his tunic, he remembered the old man's warning about impatience – he had paid the price of ignoring it once already today.

The thought sobered him; he dropped the tunic on the floor and sat down again.

When he gazed at the sleeping girl, he felt a mixture of pity and gratitude. She carried within her the secret of life; yet men had seized her for their own purposes, and turned her into a kind of milch-cow. As she lay with closed eyes, she looked like a corpse; the spots of colour had vanished from her cheeks, and her breathing was hardly visible. When he probed her mind, it was like entering primeval darkness, without even a flicker of the unconscious life of dreams. Earlier in the day, when he had entered the mind of the girl in the hospital, he had been aware of her sleeping consciousness, like a faint glow on the horizon. In this girl's mind, there was merely emptiness, like eternal night.

He suddenly experienced a powerful desire to express his gratitude, to return to her a little of the brimming vitality that she had allowed him to absorb, and which had, in turn, raised his own vitality to a still higher level. The mat of lakeweed had half-slipped from her body, and it had the effect of making her seem somehow pathetic and abandoned, as if she had been thrown there from a passing cart. Niall leaned forward and removed it, then turned it over and replaced it on her body. Then he once again lay on top of her, resting his weight on his elbows. Yet his position made him feel uncomfortable; it seemed somehow oddly wrong. He slipped off her and lay beside her on the bed; then, placing one arm under her waist, and the other on her buttock, he lifted her until she was resting on top of him. She was surprisingly light, but the completely relaxed state of her body made it difficult to keep her in position; he had to reach down and straighten her legs, then readjust the mat between them, and hold her in position with his hands on both buttocks. Her face turned sideways, so that her cheek rested against his mouth.

Niall allowed himself to relax into a state of total receptivity, until his consciousness was like an empty vessel. He realized now why his first contact had produced a subtle sense of discord. He had been expecting to absorb energy from her, and this was opposed by the polarity of the mat. Moreover, he had been lying on top of her, and the mat was designed to conduct energy upward, against the force of gravity. Now all he had to do was to use the mat to absorb some of the energy that was now throbbing inside him; he did this by imagining that the energy was accumulating in the skin of his chest and thighs. At a certain point, he imagined that the energy was being absorbed from him by the cool and slippery lakeweed, and as this happened, he felt this process taking place. A moment later the skin of her face became warm as it rested against his lips.

The process of giving energy was, in an obvious sense, the opposite of the process of receiving it. Yet in another way, they were curiously similar. To begin with, their individual identities dissolved away, and united together like two raindrops. This union turned them, in effect, into lovers, as if they had mutually given themselves to one another. In some primitive sense, he had become her husband. Giving became an intense pleasure – so intense that, a few moments later, he experienced a compulsion to repeat the process, once again summoning energy into the skin of his chest and thighs, and then allowing it to pass into her through the lakeweed. He was aware as he did so that he was repeating some deep universal process that had existed since the beginning of time.

The third time he repeated the transmission, he became aware that she was responding. The pleasure of receiving vital energy was stirring her back into wakefulness. In the darkness of her consciousness, he could sense a glow like the rising dawn. A moment later, her breathing faltered, and he had to make an effort to control his own excitement and calm the beating of his heart. She stirred, as if in her sleep, and moved her head, so that her lips were now resting directly against his. He could feel the fluttering of her eyelids, and the lips parted.

A moment later he screamed aloud in pain as her teeth sank into his lower lip. In his state of total concentration, the shock was like an explosion inside his head. Even when he twisted sideways and she fell on to the bed, she continued to bite until he thought her teeth would meet through his flesh. A frantic push released him, and she fell off the bed and on to the floor. He scrambled off the bed, half-expecting her to attack him. But her position on the floor – face downward, with one leg twisted under the other – remained unchanged.

His first reaction was anger. The pain was agonizing, and tears were running down his cheeks and mingling with the blood that ran on to his chest. He seized her garment, which still lay on the floor, and pressed it to his lower lip. When the cloth had absorbed most of the blood, he cautiously prodded the torn flesh with the tip of one finger, at the same time probing from inside with his tongue. To his relief, his tongue and fingertip failed to meet through the flesh. But the lip itself was already swelling, as if from a violent blow.

He turned her over roughly with his foot. As she flopped on to her back, he observed that her eyes were now open. The mouth was also open, and a trickle of blood, mixed with saliva, ran down her face. The grey flesh reminded him of the corpse he had seen that morning in the hospital, and his heart suddenly contracted with fear. If she was dead, he had destroyed his last link with the magician. He dropped on his knees beside her, but his heart was pounding so violently that it was impossible to achieve the relaxation necessary to probe her mind. Instead, he seized her wrist and tried to take her pulse; when he failed to find it, he suddenly became convinced that she was dead, and experienced a cold sense of despair. He bent his head and placed his ear against her left breast. A moment later, as his own breathing became calmer, he was able to detect a faint pulse. The relief was so enormous that he closed his eyes, and expelled his breath in a long sigh.

He slid both hands underneath her, and lifted her on to the bed. A thin trickle of blood ran from the corner of her mouth, and although he knew it was his own blood, the sight disturbed him. He wiped it off with his handkerchief, then closed the staring eyes.

Now his alarm had subsided, he was able to probe her mind. As he expected, it was totally blank, without any hint of consciousness. He stared down at her, frowning with perplexity. His first assumption had been that she had awakened, recognized him as an alien presence, and instinctively attacked him. But in that case, she would still be awake – or at least, show some sign of reviving consciousness.

Was it conceivable that she was still being controlled by the magician? The thought stirred the hairs on the back of his neck. Then he dismissed the idea. Everything that had happened so far convinced him that the magician communicated with his servants through the pendants. And these were now safely confined within the magnetic field of the stone jars in the cellar.

Yet it was equally difficult to believe that this girl had regained consciousness, attacked him, then plunged back into this state of profound unconsciousness. As he stared down at the still face, still pressing the handkerchief against his swollen lip, he knew that it would be absurd to take further risks; the pendants must be taken to the white tower. He covered her with the blanket, folded the lakeweed and replaced it in its box, then left the room and locked the door behind him.

Although he could hear voices, and the sound of pans clattering in the kitchen, he met no one on his way downstairs; this was a relief, since he had no wish to explain his swollen lip. At the top of the cellar steps, he paused to light the oil lamp, then trod carefully down into the cool gloom.

The black stone jars were exactly as he had left them. He placed the lamp on the floor, and removed the plug from the neck of the nearest one – it had jammed in tight, and required some twisting to remove. He reached inside cautiously, but as his fingers made contact with the pendant, he realized that it was completely inert. This was the pendant whose chain he had snapped in his impatience to separate them; he dropped it into the pocket of his tunic, then moved the oil lamp close to the second jar.

This plug came out easily. He reached into the depths of the jar and found the chain – it was also inert. But as his hand emerged, the back brushed against the neck of the jar, and he detected a sharp edge. He picked up the lamp and held it over the jar. There was a crack, about an eighth of an inch wide at the top, running vertically down the jar. His first thought was that he had caused it himself when he sealed the jar with the heavy plug. But when he examined it in the lamplight, he could see that it ran all the way down the side of the jar. It seemed unlikely that he could have caused such a crack simply by dropping the plug into the neck. He held the lamp close to the other side of the jar. Here he could detect a hair-line crack that ran from the neck down to the base. But when he reached inside the neck, and tried to pull the two halves apart, it was impossible. This second crack was apparently only on the surface. Yet he remained puzzled and vaguely disturbed. It was possible, of course, that the crack had been in the jar all the time, and that he had simply failed to notice it. But he found this hard to believe. As he dropped the pendant into the other side of his tunic pocket – making sure there was the maximum distance between them – he was unable to suppress a shiver of apprehension.

It vanished as he stepped out into the pale afternoon sunlight. The sky was already blue with dusk; the north wind seemed to carry the scent of autumn. Men were returning home from work; a pregnant woman came past carrying two bags of shopping. It was the hour of the day that Niall loved best, the time for relaxation after work, when the world seemed full of a warm glow of happiness. It had been a long, and in some ways a frustrating day; but now he looked back on it, it seemed that luck had been with him.

Since there were so many people in the square, he decided not to approach the white tower from the south side, which faced the headquarters of the Spider Lord; this would be inviting attention and curiosity. Instead he crossed the square as if approaching the bridge that led to the slave quarter. On this side of the tower there was a wide open space consisting partly of grass and partly of hard pavement. Since this was usually deserted, it was easy to cross the grass with the certainty that the tower itself would conceal him from pedestrians on the other side of the square.

But even when he was halfway across the grass, he became aware of a feeling of inner discord. It was the same sensation that he had experienced earlier in the day, when he had approached the tower carrying the stone figurine. Now it was even stronger. Instead of feeling a kind of magnetic attraction as he approached the tower – not unlike the feeling a dowser experiences in the presence of underground water – there was a sense of repulsion that produced a sensation like walking into a strong wind. He knew that it would be pointless to try to enter its force-field; it was warning him to keep his distance. Therefore he removed both pendants from his pocket, and placed them on the blue-grey marble that surrounded the base of the tower. To his surprise, the feeling of repulsion remained, although less powerful than a moment ago. He stood there, bewildered, wondering what to do next. A moment later uncertainty changed to relief as the old man walked through the solid wall, stepping out of its milky surface like someone emerging from water. Niall waited for an explanation. Instead, the old man raised his right arm and pointed at the gold chains, which were lying a few feet away. Niall said:

'They are pendants, like the one . . .'

But before he could finish the sentence, a narrow beam of pale orange light emanated from the end of the old man's index finger and struck one of the pendants. This glowed into a bright golden colour, then melted and coagulated into a globule which seemed to simmer and sizzle on the marble. Then as the marble itself began to glow and become red hot, the golden ball became smaller and smaller, like a drop of water evaporating on a hot plate. As this happened, Niall observed that the other pendant was no longer lying where he had placed it; then he saw that it had moved close to the edge of the platform. For a moment he assumed that this was due to the force of the energy blast emanating from the old man's finger; then, with a shock, he realized that the gold chain was moving with an odd rolling motion, as if trying to escape. Before it could reach the edge, it had been caught in the orange beam, and had turned into a pool of liquid metal.

Seconds later, it was another golden ball, still rolling towards the edge of the platform. It became smaller and smaller, then disappeared, leaving the marble glowing with dull heat that Niall could feel from a distance of five yards.

Niall asked: 'Why was that necessary?'

'Have you ever heard of a booby trap?'

Niall said doubtfully: 'A kind of practical joke?'

'In this case, more than a joke. To have brought them into the tower would have been a disaster.'

'But I brought one in the other day.'

'That has also been destroyed.'

'But why did you let it in?'

'Because I did not know then what I have learned since.'

'What was that?'

'That these devices can be animated with some kind of living force.'

'How did you find out?'

'The device that you brought into the tower was able to neutralize the electric field in which I enclosed it.'

'What happened?'

'The alarm system gave warning of an intruder, and specified the electromagnetic enclosure. By then the device had once again become inert. I vaporized it immediately.'

'Did the alarm system give any indication of the nature of the intruder?'

'None – merely that it was a living presence.'

Niall said: 'It was the magician.'

The old man shrugged. 'If so, it is too late to do anything about it.'

Niall was concerned. 'Do you think he could have learned anything?'

'Unfortunately that is impossible to say. It was not

noticed until it tried to interfere with the circuits of the Steegmaster.'

'Great goddess!'

'These two devices would have been even more dangerous. When two are brought into contact, their power is greatly augmented.'

'I know.' Niall remembered the cracked stone jar. 'That's why I separated them.'

'But you were too impatient and left part of one chain entangled with the other.'

Niall coloured. 'But I didn't think the chains made any difference.'

'That is what you were intended to think. In fact, they are a part of the device.'

'I'm sorry.'

'That is unnecessary. Now we understand the danger, it is possible to anticipate it.'

Niall said: 'But do you understand how it works?'

'No. I said I understand the danger. But since I am designed for purely rational thinking, I am unable to understand the principles of magic.'

The words caused a prickling sensation in Niall's scalp. 'But are you sure it *is* magic?'

'The ability to make living forces manifest in dead matter must be defined as magic.'

'But is there nothing we can do about it?'

'At the moment I lack information to make a competent assessment. You must try to learn more.'

Niall asked in perplexity: 'But how?'

The old man shook his head. Niall waited for him to speak – then, as the silence lengthened, realized that he was not going to speak. His sense of rising frustration was cut short by a recognition that came as a shock: that the old man was not going to speak because he had nothing to say. Suddenly, for the first time,

Niall realized fully that the old man was a machine, and that it would be as pointless to feel impatient with him as to feel angry with a clock whose hands have ceased to move.

He turned without speaking, and walked in the direction of the headquarters of the Spider Lord. For the first time, he realized that he was alone.

Two brown wolf spiders stood on either side of the black doors; they recognized him and lowered themselves to the ground. Then, seeing that he wished to enter, one of them sent a telepathic message to the guard inside, and the doors swung open. The death spider who stood in the hall was squat and powerful, bearing a distinct resemblance to the late Captain Skorbo – most of the Spider Lord's personal guard came from the same distant province. Its crooked legs made it easy to prostrate itself, but also made the gesture seem somehow disrespectful.

'Is the Lord Dravig here?'

'No, sire. He has gone home. Do you wish me to send for him?'

'No thank you.' Niall was speaking slowly, realizing that this spider was unskilled in communicating with humans. 'I wish to speak to Asmak.'

The spider gazed back blankly; the name evidently meant nothing to him. Niall said:

'He is the commander of the aerial survey.' He accompanied the words with a mental image of a spider balloon.

'Please wait.'

The guard turned and ascended the marble staircase. He could have summoned any spider in the building by a telepathic message; but this would have been regarded as impolite, like a human being shouting for a servant.

Niall was alone in the hall, with its curiously stale air, and smell of ancient dust. He had never understood why the spiders made no attempt to keep their head-quarters clean. Now, suddenly, he realized that it must be some atavistic memory of days when all spiders lived in dusty corners. It meant that dust and cobwebs denoted comfort.

The guard had reappeared on the stairs. He was followed by another death spider, whose glossy black coat and small stature revealed that he had still not reached adulthood. This spider lowered itself to the ground with a grace that was totally unlike the crab-like awkwardness of the guard.

Niall asked: 'Are you Asmak?'

'No, sire, I am his son. I am known as Grel.'

He said 'known as' because, in the human sense of the word, few spiders had proper names; being telepathic, they had no need for names when addressing one another. Most spider names were adopted for the convenience of human intercourse.

'Please stand up.' Grel had remained in the position of homage, and Niall could sense his nervousness. 'The Lord Dravig advised me to speak to your father.'

'He is not here, sire.' The young spider straightened up; in the upright position, he was about the same height as Niall. The folded fangs seemed undeveloped, and the smooth black hair that covered the body looked as soft as the fur of a kitten. It seemed to Niall that the black eyes shone with intelligence, although he was aware that this might be merely the effect of the amount of light they reflected – compared to the eyes of an adult spider, they seemed to be covered with a thin layer of oil.

'Where is he?'

'At his workplace. Would you like me to take you to him?'

Niall started to refuse, then changed his mind. To

begin with, he wanted a chance to talk to the young spider.

'Is it far away?'

'No, very close.'

'Yes. Thank you. I would like to see him.'

The guard opened the double doors for them. But Niall could sense his deep disapproval. So could the young spider, and he followed Niall outside with a visible air of guilt. But as soon as the doors had closed, and they were outside on the pavement, this evaporated; he was obviously proud to be seen in public with the ruler of the spider city. He asked eagerly:

'Shall I summon your charioteers?'

'No thank you. If it is close, I would prefer to walk.'

The spider led the way to the side street that ran out of the south-west side of the square. The pavement was thronged with people, and Niall drew his cloak around him to avoid recognition. But at the end of two blocks, he felt so warm that he allowed it to fall open again.

'Grel.'

'Yes, sire?' The young spider stopped, and turned respectfully.

'Not so fast. My human legs are shorter than yours.'

Grel looked abashed. 'I'm sorry, sire.' He walked on with exaggerated slowness. But since his stride was about ten feet long, Niall still had to walk at a brisk pace to keep up.

They were walking in the direction of the old part of the city; this, until recently, had been the women's quarter, and had been forbidden to males. A high wall, whose enormous stone blocks required no cement, divided it from the eastern half of the city. Now its iron gates stood open and unguarded. Niall's history lessons had taught him that this wall dated from ancient times, although it had been rebuilt as a historic showpiece in the twenty-first century.

Now, instead of passing through the nearest gate, they turned south along the broad avenue, and walked parallel to the wall which divided it down the centre. It was obvious that this had once been the main thoroughfare of the city. The avenue was a steep incline, peaking in a hilltop surmounted by a tower. Niall had often wondered what lay on the far side.

'How old are you?'

'Five and a half, sire.'

'And are you a member of the Death Lord's personal guard?'

'No, sire. I am the junior assistant to the lady Sidonia.' Sidonia was the commander of the Spider Lord's guard.

'You speak English very well.' (What Niall meant was: 'You communicate in human language very well', but he knew that he would be understood.)

The young spider glowed with satisfaction. 'Thank you, sire. The lady Sidonia taught me herself.' Then, to Niall's astonishment, he loped across the avenue, and proceeded to climb the wall with the agility of an acrobat. Spiders, like flies, are able to climb vertical surfaces, but the sheer weight of the giant spiders meant that few of them attempted to practise this accomplishment. Grel's lightness and speed carried him to the top of the wall with the ease of a bird in flight. His objective, Niall realized, was a large bird that had perched on the far side of one of the gate towers that subdivided the wall. As if aware of its danger, the bird stretched its legs and raised its head, as if about to launch into flight. It was too late. The young spider took advantage of the sloping roof of the gate tower to conceal itself as it slid, like some boneless mollusc, over the parapet; then, as the bird saw the movement and prepared to fly, launched itself like a projectile, striking the bird as it rose into the air. Niall expected to see them both crash down on to the pavement below; in fact, they landed on the parapet, then fell backwards. There was a brief and pathetic squawk. A moment later, the spider reappeared on the edge of the roof and lowered itself to the ground on a length of silk, which it jerked free and reabsorbed into its body as it was crossing the street. Its jaws closed on the bird with a crunch that made Niall wince.

As if suddenly recalling Niall's presence, the young spider became apologetic.

'I beg your pardon, sire. Do you care for bird?'

'Not uncooked.' Niall found it impossible to smile. Now, suddenly, he understood why the guard had shown disapproval. Although he possessed the strength and speed of an adult, Grel was as impulsive as a child. And Niall knew enough about spiders to recognize that they attached enormous importance to self-control.

The young spider gripped the bird in its tarsal claws – he was able to balance comfortably on the other six legs – and tore out feathers with his jaws, scattering them by blowing them out of his mouth. The breeze carried them away down the street. Then he bit into the breast with the relish of a schoolboy sinking his teeth into an apple.

Niall asked: 'How far do we have to go?'

'Not very far.' Since the spider was communicating telepathically, he could speak with his mouth full. Looking up the wide, empty avenue, Niall experienced a twinge of dismay, recognizing suddenly that a spider's idea of a short distance was based upon the length of its stride, which was more than twice that of a human being.

At least Grel was now walking more slowly. And as

he strolled beside him, Niall allowed himself to relax and to examine his companion more closely. As he ate the bird, Grel had left his mind open, as if to apologize for not giving Niall his full attention. The result was interesting. Niall's response to the crunching jaws – and to the drops of blood that fell on to the pavement – was a certain repulsion. Yet he was also able to enter the young spider's mind, and share its pleasure in the tender flesh. For a spider, eating a bird which had only just been killed was an intensely interesting activity which demanded its full attention. To begin with, the flesh was still permeated with the flavour of life, which Niall perceived as a warm glow. Then there was the fascination of the bird's craw, which contained two small rodents – baby rats – and a large insect like a dragon fly. These were an additional bonus, a delightful fringe benefit. For the spider, the bird tasted like a succulent fruit, in the depths of which someone had concealed delicious sweetmeats. Niall actually began to find himself feeling hungry.

It was curiously pleasant to allow himself to relax into the spider's vital rhythms. It was brimming with a kind of cheerful wellbeing which is totally unlike the normal state of human consciousness. By comparison with spiders, Niall realized, human beings are hopelessly self-divided, even the simplest. Their minds have been trained to *scan* reality, looking for meaning, like a bird of prey looking down at a broad landscape, watching for any sign of movement that might betray a small animal. This, in turn, means that a part of human awareness is permanently passive, waiting for something to happen. Grel's consciousness was completely and magically different. He had no need of 'thought'. Consequently, he lived in a totally real universe in which everything was fascinating in its own right.

And this, Niall now realized, explained why the spiders had developed their tremendous will-power. When they wanted something, they wanted it with their whole being. If it was bad for them, their instincts told them so. 'Thinking' was unnecessary. So they used the secret powers of the mind – powers of which human beings are scarcely aware – as naturally as an athlete uses his strength and agility.

What excited Niall was that he now shared the secret. He realized, for example, that when they had set out on this walk he had been very tired. Now, although his legs were still aching, he was aware that he was not genuinely tired. It was an illusion caused by the fact that he *thought* he was tired. As he shared the mind-world of the young spider, he began to feel a glow of interest and purpose that made him aware that *he* was the one who decided whether he was tired or not. Even as this thought took shape in his mind, the ache in his legs disappeared, and was replaced by a tingling sense of energy.

Grel dropped the bird into the gutter. Niall was surprised; it still contained a great deal of tender meat. Then he realized that they were approaching the tower on the hilltop.

'Is your father here?'

'Yes. This is the headquarters of the aerial survey.'

The tower was built of black stone, and was therefore known among humans as the Black Tower; it had a sinister reputation among city dwellers as a prison, and even a torture chamber. Built as part of the wall, it was obviously intended as a vantage point to survey the whole city. Beyond the hilltop the wall – and the avenue – turned westward around the old part of the city. To the south, the flat winter landscape was touched by the rays of the setting sun; the sea, which lay on the horizon, was already in shadow. On the far side of the thirty-mile strip of ocean lay the deserts of North

Khaybad, the land where Niall was born, and where his father's ashes were now scattered on the wind.

Grel manipulated an iron ring and pushed open the massive door. They were met by the smell of cold and dust that seemed so typical of spider dwellings. There was also a trace of another smell, which released in Niall a curious flash of nostalgia. It was, in fact, a rather unpleasant smell, a combination of rotting vegetation and decaying meat. This was the smell of the porifids, the primitive organism that provided the gas used to inflate the spider balloons. It brought back to Niall the journey to the Delta that had culminated in his encounter with the empress plant, the extra-terrestrial creature that the spiders worshipped as the goddess Nuada.

They were in a circular chamber, whose low ceiling was supported by stone columns. A narrow flight of steps ran up to the next floor; as the door slammed, a man in the uniform of a worker came to the head of the stairs and peered at them through the gloom. Light streamed through the open door behind him.

'Who's there?'

Niall said: 'We have come to see the Lord Asmak.'

The man – obviously an overseer – said: 'No one is allowed in this place without the permission of the Spider Lord.'

He looked so combative that for a moment Niall felt disconcerted. Then Grel stepped out of the shadows.

'Please tell my father we are here.'

The overseer started with astonishment; then he shrugged and went back into the room, closing the door firmly behind him, and leaving them in almost total darkness. Niall, irritated by this display of bad manners, and by the implication that they had to wait there like unwelcome guests, mounted the stairs – Grel walked behind him as a matter of protocol – and groped for the latch of the door. The chamber beyond proved to be large and well lighted, with pressure lamps suspended from hooks on the wall. Most of the room was occupied by a huge circular work-table, which must have been fifteen feet in diameter, and whose top was occupied by a deflated spider balloon, whose blue-white silk glowed softly in the lamplight. The men who stood around the table were occupied in sewing together the edges of the balloon. On the far side of the room there was a large glass tank whose sides were as high as a man; in the depths of its slimy green water lay the porifids – short for *porifera mephitis* – whose smell permeated the room. It was, in fact, too faint to be unpleasant; porifids only produced their asphyxiating stench when plunged in total darkness – as in the interior of a spider balloon.

The men went on working with averted eyes, concentrating on their sewing. But as Grel closed the door, the nearest one shot them a sideways glance. His eyes widened, and he dropped the scissors he was holding. Niall realized with embarrassment that he had been recognized. He shook his head, and started to turn away, but he was too late to prevent the man from falling on to his knees. He said in a low voice:

'Please go on with your work.'

But this led the others to look up, and as soon as they recognized Niall, they also fell on to their knees. This was not – as with the spiders – a matter of reverence for the living representative of the great goddess, but merely the fact that these men had been trained to absolute obedience to the will of their superiors. In the days before freedom, the slightest failure to show proper respect could lead to brutal punishment. A habit formed over many generations could not be uprooted in a few months. Niall grimaced with embarrassment.

'Please get up.'

At that moment, the door on the far side of the room opened, and the overseer returned. He stared at the kneeling men with incredulity – as if suspecting some kind of joke – and his face reddened with anger. Then he also recognized the emissary of the goddess, and fell on to his knees. Niall cleared his throat.

'Is the Lord Asmak ready to see me?'

The man stammered: 'Forgive me, sire, I did not recognize you.'

'No need for apology. You did your duty.' He crossed the room and opened the door, which led to a further flight of stairs. The overseer seized his hand as he went past.

'You see, sire, this place is supposed to be secret . . .'

'Please say no more about it.' He disengaged his hand with some difficulty and mounted the stairs; Grel followed behind. Niall could sense his amusement.

The next door led into a room that was obviously a warehouse, piled high with folded spider balloons. The same was true of the next floor, and the next. The sixth floor was occupied by large tanks of porifids, and wooden containers of the white, worm-like grubs on which they were fed; these smelt considerably worse than the porifids.

At the head of the steps leading to the seventh floor stood a tall death spider, whose natural dignity and grace reminded Niall of Dravig. He stood back to allow Niall to enter, then lowered himself to the ground in homage. As they exchanged formal greetings, Niall realized that he had already met the commander of the aerial survey. Asmak had been present on the previous day, at the trial of Skorbo's former associates. They had not communicated directly; but since Niall had shared the consciousness of every spider in the room, he had become aware of their individual identities. Now he felt as if he was encountering an old friend.

The formalities over, the spider waited respectfully for Niall to speak first.

'The Lord Dravig advised me to come and see you.'

'I am honoured. In what way can I be of service?'

'As the commander of the aerial survey, you must be familiar with the lands to the north?'

'I have flown over them many times.'

'Dravig believes that Skorbo's killers came from these northlands.'

'That is possible. But it is also possible that they came from the south, east or west.'

'Where do *you* think they came from?'

The spider made a gesture whose human equivalent would have been shaking his head.

'Dravig asked me the same question. And I had to admit that I could not answer.'

'Dravig says there are legends of an underground city. Have you any idea where that might be?'

'None. If there is such a place, it is so well concealed that our patrols have never even suspected its existence.'

Niall remembered the underground city of Dira, and realized how difficult it would be for an aerial patrol to detect its existence.

'Do your patrols fly close to the ground?'

'Sometimes. But it can be dangerous, particularly in the mountains. That is how Skorbo crashed.'

'Skorbo crashed? Do you know *where*?'

'Yes.'

Niall felt a tingle of excitement.

'Could you take me there?'

'Of course.'

'How far is it?'

'Only a few hours – if the wind is blowing in the right direction.'

'Ah, yes.' Niall had forgotten the wind. It was, in fact, possible for a spider balloon to fly against the wind; the spider could use its will-power to create an opposing force, so the balloon chose a path between two vectors. Niall had experienced the effect, on his return journey from the Delta. But it was exhausting work, like rowing a boat against the current.

'But of course, it is unnecessary to wait for the wind to change.'

'Unnecessary?' Niall failed to understand him.

Asmak said: 'I am familiar with the area, and I can describe it to you.'

Niall said politely: 'Then please do so.'

'Would my lord care to follow me?' Asmak turned and led the way across the room. Puzzled and intrigued, Niall followed him up another flight of stairs. The door at the top led out on to a flat roof, which was surrounded by a crenellated parapet. The sky overhead had turned to a deep blue, and stars were visible on the eastern horizon. But in the west, the landscape was bathed in red sunlight. The wind that blew from the mountains carried a hint of snow.

Asmak led him to the edge of the roof that faced northward. The mountains were almost invisible in blue shadows; only the western slopes reflected the setting sun. Niall leaned against the parapet, placing his foot in the embrasure.

Asmak raised his tarsal claw and pointed towards the mountains – a gesture that spiders had learned from their human servants.

'All these lands that you can see are the domain of the Death Lord.' As he spoke, Niall experienced a curious sensation, as if his body had become as light as a feather, and was floating up into the air. It was so unexpected that he reached out in panic and gripped the parapet with both hands. Contact with the cold stone made him realize that he was still standing securely on the roof. Asmak said apologetically:

'I beg your pardon. I should have warned you . . .'

With a twinge of embarrassment, Niall realized that the illusion had been due to the spider's power of suggestion. As soon as he relaxed, he once again felt himself rising gently from the roof, and floating out above the rooftops. For a moment or so, his mind divided into two parts, one of which continued to be aware of his body. Then, fascinated by the panorama that was unfolding below him, he forgot his body, and became absorbed in the strange sensation of flying through space.

What was happening was that the spider was describing a typical reconnaissance flight, exactly as a human being might describe it in words. But since he was using images and sensations, Niall experienced what he was 'saying' as a series of visual impressions. Never before had he experienced such a clear sense of sharing the mind of another – not even at the trial of Skorbo's associates, when he had been privileged to enter the collective consciousness of the spiders. And it was, he now realized, as a consequence of that experience that he was now able to enter the mind of Asmak.

He could see the city – which was bathed in sunlight – as clearly as if he was in a spider balloon. Asmak's recall of detail was clearly extraordinary; he knew this terrain so well that his mind had photographed it with the accuracy of a camera – only a blurring effect towards the horizon revealed that this was merely a mental image. The mountains in the distance looked exactly as they looked from the roof of the palace. To the north-west of the city, across a range of low hills, Niall could see the city of the bombardier beetles, with its twisted red towers which were actually spiral cones made of beeswax. As they floated over the river that divided the city from east to west, Niall looked with curiosity towards the east – a region he never explored – and saw that the river lost itself in a region of low hills covered with woodland. Amongst these undulating treetops, he was intrigued to see a building like a half-derelict castle on a hilltop, and pointed towards it.

'What is that?'

'A ruin. This land is full of ruins.'

The words were factual, but for Niall they brought a wave of melancholy, an image of this land as it had been in the remote past, when men took it for granted that they were lords of the earth.

Now they were passing over the slave quarter, flying low enough to see the people who thronged the streets. What puzzled Niall was that all the slaves looked absolutely identical, as if they were all copies of the same person. Then the answer dawned on him: to a spider, all human beings looked alike.

Beyond the slave quarter lay an area of empty houses which had once been the middle-class residential area of the city. Slaves had no use for such houses, with their overgrown back gardens that might shelter dangerous predators, so this part of the city had been left to fall into ruin.

Soon they were passing over the northern edge of the city, where the main road turned north-west towards the city of the bombardier beetles. Another road, obviously in a poor state of repair, continued towards the mountains, then lost itself in an area of brown heather, which clothed the slopes of a low range of hills. On the far side of these lay more dense woodland, in which the trees were so close together that the ground was invisible. Among the treetops to the right, Niall glimpsed a sheet of water that reflected the blue of the sky.

'What is that?'

'An abandoned quarry.'

'Could we see it?'

As if changing direction in mid-air, the spider obedi-

ently veered to the east. A moment later they were
poised above a water-filled quarry that was at least a
mile wide – it reminded him of the disused marble
quarry that the bombardier beetles used for their explo-
sive exhibitions. As far as Niall could see, no flowing
streams fed this enormous stagnant lake. On its
northern edge, a vertical cliff face plunged into the dark
water. But the southern edge of the quarry shelved
more gently, and there was even a kind of beach. As
Niall looked down at this he saw something that made
his heart leap: a gently-heaving surface of brown lakeweed that covered the shallows to a distance of about
fifty yards from the shore. As far as he could see, it
was similar to the mat of lakeweed that he had found
in the abandoned hide-out. But when he tried to look
more closely, the image blurred, as he reached the limit
of the spider's perceptions.

He asked: 'Have you ever landed near the lake?'

'No. We have no reason to go there.'

Niall recalled that death spiders disliked water. It
even avoided floating above the dark surface, preferring
to skirt the edge of the quarry.

Now once again they were moving towards the
mountains. They were crossing a hollow land that
looked like a swamp: rivulets of brown water, brown
tussocks of coarse swamp grass, and areas of a bright
green vegetation that reminded Niall of the Delta. Then
came wooded foothills, whose twisted, olive-coloured
trees covered a landscape of rocky outcrops. Then came
the mountains, whose green lower slopes soon turned
into barren expanses of grey rock and scree which rose
steeply until they vanished into the mist. They passed
into a black raincloud, and Niall was aware of drops of
water blowing against his face, although when he raised
his hand to brush them away, he discovered that his
skin was dry.

The mist flew past them, then dissolved suddenly into dazzling sunlight. The scenery below them was breathtaking: deep valleys, some of them descending to the plains on either side, bare rocky slopes with knife-edged outcrops of rock, and streams of white rushing water that plunged down the mountain side and wound their way into sky-blue lakes that filled the hollows. As they floated above one of these lakes, Niall was able to see through its crystal-clear water into the brown mud in its depths.

On the lower slopes of the mountains there were patches of woodland and an occasional ruined building; one of them looked like an ancient monastery, with its bell tower still defying the elements, another like a shattered fortress. And on the coastal plain that lay between the foothills of two dome-like mountains there were even the remains of a town. Whenever such a place aroused his curiosity, the spider's mind obligingly enlarged the object, so that Niall was able to study it in detail. Now he found himself looking down on a desolation of roofless houses and rubble-filled streets that left no doubt that the town had been deserted for centuries. It had once been fortified, for it was surrounded by an embankment of earth, with lookout posts built of stone. A closer view of the town revealed smoke-blackened walls and charred roof beams. On the banks of the river that flowed through its centre lay the blackened remains of several boats. Nearby on the mud was an object that was unmistakably the rib-cage of a man. A few feet away lay a human skull.

'Does this place have a name?'

'Men call it Cibilla, after their moon goddess.'

'And who destroyed it?'

'I do not know. It happened in the days of the great war between spiders and humans, long before I was born.'

'But do you people keep no records?'

'Records? I do not understand the word.'

Now, at last, Niall was able to understand why the spiders were unable to offer any suggestions about the whereabouts of the kingdom of the magician. Unlike human beings, they seemed to have no legends and traditions that enshrined the knowledge of the past. It was also clear that, in this vast wilderness of rock and barren moorland, the entrance to an underground city would be virtually undetectable, even to a fleet of a million spider balloons. The underground city of Dira had remained undetected for many years, even though its goatherds and shepherds had risked discovery every day as they drove their flocks out to graze. And these misty hills, with their caves and rocky outcrops, offered far more protection than the glaring desert landscape on the shores of the great salt lake.

'Could we go higher?'

'Of course.'

A moment later, they were surveying the same land-scape from a height of at least ten thousand feet. Now he was able to see that the mountains stretched north-ward like a gigantic backbone, bending eventually to the north-east. To the left and right lay wide flat plains that stretched towards the sea; the eastern plain seemed to be a country of lakes and rivers, with hills to the north. From this height he was able to see that the backbone was broken in two places by wide transversal valleys, the nearest of which was about ten miles away.

Asmak pointed towards it.

'That is the limit of the domain of the Death Lord. We call it the Valley of the Dead.'

'Who chose that limit?'

'Why, the Death Lord himself.'

'Have you ever been beyond it?'

'A few miles only. More than that would serve no purpose.'

Niall could see his point; the mountains beyond the Valley of the Dead looked more bleak and forbidding than those that lay behind them to the south.

'Please take me to the boundary.'

With the speed of thought, they were hovering over a wide green valley, in the centre of which there was a long and narrow lake, from whose ends issued two rivers. The Valley of the Dead must have been carved by a glacier, for its sides were steep, towering up to a height of more than a thousand feet. But what immediately drew Niall's attention was the battlemented wall that ran across the flat plain to the north of the lake. Niall had never seen such a wall. Its colour was grey-green, like that of the landscape, and it ran from the sea coast to the west for as far as the eye could see on to the eastern plain. Its surface was smooth, unbroken by doors or other entrances. In response to Niall's curiosity, Asmak descended until they seemed to be standing on top of the wall, which was constructed of rough slabs of stone held together by some kind of cement. It was flat and about twenty feet wide, with a low parapet on either side. The southern side, Niall observed, sloped down at an angle to its base, while the northern side was a sheer drop of about eighty feet to the plain below. At regular intervals of a few hundred yards there were square towers that rose a dozen feet above the top of the wall. They were now standing within a few feet of one of these, and Niall could see that it was a kind of guardhouse, with a passageway running straight through it. Like the rest of the wall, the structure gave an impression of enormous strength.

'Who built the wall?'

'I do not know. They say it was there before the

coming of the spiders. Perhaps the men who built that place.'

Niall followed the spider's gaze, and for the first time noticed the buildings halfway up the great cliff. They were the same grey-blue colour as the rock, which is why Niall had not noticed them immediately. There were dozens – perhaps hundreds – of these buildings, carved out of the solid rock face. Niall experienced a cold sensation down his spine.

'Could that be the city of the magician?'

But the spider made a gesture of dissent.

'Impossible. It has always been deserted.'

Niall gazed on the valley for a long time. Even the lake was awe-inspiring. Its steep sides plunged down to water whose black surface suggested enormous depths. It looked as if the earth had split asunder in some volcanic convulsion, and then filled with water.

'And where is the place where Skorbo crashed?'

'Over there, in the Grey Mountains.' The spider pointed to the mountains to the north. At the same time, their perspective changed, so they were looking down on them from above. This part of the range was far more wild and precipitous than its southern reaches. Some of the peaks were like needles; others had the flat tops of volcanoes. It was a phantasmagoric landscape, quite unlike the mountain landscape in the desert of North Khaybad, where Niall had spent his childhood.

The place that Asmak was now indicating was a high plateau between two snow-covered peaks; it looked bare and inhospitable, covered with broken fragments of rock.

'Did he tell you how it happened?'

'Yes. He said that he was caught in a storm, and that the wind had made him lose control.'

Niall stared at the unsheltered landscape.

'What happened to the spider balloon?'

'It was torn against the rocks.'

That was easy to understand; some of the rock-shards had edges that looked like razors.

'But what did he do with the balloon?'

Asmak was evidently troubled by the question. On an open plateau like this, the material of a torn spider balloon should have been clearly visible, even from a height of a thousand feet.

'I cannot recall seeing it.'

As he spoke, Niall realized suddenly that this was not a real plateau that he was looking at, but merely the image of the plateau in the spider's mind. He laughed at his own forgetfulness.

'I'm sorry. That was stupid of me.'

But Asmak replied seriously: 'You are right. None of our patrols have reported seeing the remains of the balloon. But why should Skorbo lie about it?'

'Perhaps he wasn't lying. Perhaps someone removed the balloon so we wouldn't know exactly where he crashed.'

'The magician?'

'That seems possible.'

The spider instantly understood the implication. 'You believe that Skorbo was a traitor?'

'I believe Skorbo may have fallen into the hands of the magician. Did he ever explain what happened to him during the period after he crashed?'

'He said that he was injured, and took shelter until the storm passed. He *did* receive an injury to his right foreleg – I saw it.'

Niall stared at the strange landscape before him – at the massive wall that stretched as far as the eye could see in both directions, at the deserted city carved into the mountainside, and at the mist-covered mountains, with their snowy peaks, that vanished into the distance.

The city still seemed to him the likeliest entrance to the kingdom of the magician. The human beings who had carved these dwellings out of the solid rock could surely burrow into the earth beneath?

But the spider, who had read Niall's thoughts, made a gesture of dissent.

'Such a labour could not be completed in a thousand years.'

'Even for the men who built that wall?'

'A wall is a simple task. It requires only a sufficient number of slaves. But to tear out the heart of a mountain would be a labour of giants.'

His mind was able to convey the full extent of his objection: an image of giant spiders (for this is how Asmak envisaged giants) burrowing into the solid rock, while an army of slaves removed the debris, carrying it to some distant place where it would not betray its origin.

Niall stared at the lower slopes of the mountain to the west.

'Then where *could* it be? You know these mountains better than any other. Is there no place that could be the entrance to an underground kingdom?'

'I know of none.'

For a long time, Niall stared at the twisted, snow-covered landscape, as if trying to wrest its secret from it. Asmak waited respectfully, prepared to answer further questions; yet Niall could sense that he felt the quest was hopeless. Niall said finally:

'Thank you, commander.'

As he spoke, the spider released his grip on Niall's imagination, and he found himself once more standing on the roof of the tower.

It was so dark that for a moment Niall had the strange impression that he was in some chilly dungeon. Then he felt the wind against his face, and saw stars in the blackness overhead. It came as a shock to realize that night had fallen, and that his strange mental voyage had therefore taken more than an hour. As his mind readjusted to present reality, he realized that his arm, which was resting on the parapet, had become completely dead; when he allowed it to fall to his side, it began to prickle with pins and needles. Yet the rest of his body felt normal and comfortable, and even his face, which had been exposed to the wind, was pleasantly warm.

The spider noticed his perplexity, but was too polite to ask questions. Niall explained:

'The wind is cold, yet my body is warm.'

The spider's response – the equivalent of a puzzled stare – made Niall realize that he found the comment baffling. Then the solution dawned on him. The will-power of the spiders meant that they never experienced cold; when the temperature fell, they merely increased their circulation by an act of concentration. And since Niall had been sharing Asmak's consciousness, his own body had responded in the same way.

As his eyes adjusted to the darkness, Niall saw that Grel was still standing a few feet away, exactly as he had been standing an hour ago, when they had stepped out on the roof; again, he experienced wonderment at the apparently inexhaustible patience of spiders.

The night wind was already beginning to chill him.

He turned and led the way back down the stairs.

The room in which the men had been working was empty; they had returned to their homes. The spider balloon on which they had been working was neatly folded in the corner of the room. And since there were no chairs, Niall went and sat down on it. He asked Grel:

'Were you with us on the flight?'

For a moment the spider was puzzled; then he grasped Niall's meaning.

'Yes, sire.'

Now he thought about it, it was obvious. There had been no 'flight'; Asmak had merely told him a story, using his telepathic powers to make it seem real. And Grel had also 'listened' to the story, as any normal child would.

Niall asked: 'Have you ever been in a spider balloon?'

'Only once, when I was a child. My father took me on a flight over the mountains.' His mind conveyed an image of the mountains to the north.

'If you were searching for the kingdom of the magician, where would you look?'

He was aware that it was a difficult question, and was surprised when the spider answered without hesitation:

'At the root of the mountains.'

This was an intriguing idea. Niall had been thinking of an entrance through the crater of some extinct volcano, or perhaps beneath the city carved out of the mountainside. He asked:

'Why the root?'

Grel found this too difficult to explain; but his mind conveyed a picture of a river flowing into the heart of a mountain.

Niall turned to Asmak.

'Do you know of any such place?'

'No, sire. But then, I have never been beyond the

great wall. Shall I order our patrols to explore further north?'

Niall considered this, then shook his head.

'No. It might warn our enemy that we are looking for him.'

His thoughts returned to the great wall. Who had built it and why? Could it be a coincidence that it was so close to the place where Skorbo's balloon had crashed?

'Do you think that the Death Lord would know who built the wall?'

'No, sire.'

'But how can you be sure?'

Asmak's reply was conveyed in a single condensed thought, whose richness and complexity would have been inexpressible in human language. What Asmak embodied, in that burst of thought-energy, was an insight into the minds of spiders: their interest in all living creatures, and their total lack of interest in such inanimate objects as walls. He made no attempt to disguise the fact that the spiders' interest in living creatures was based on their preoccupation with food, and their desire to absorb vital energy. Also implied was the admission that spiders saw the absorption of life energy as their chief means of evolution. For human beings, food is merely a chemical substance that keeps them alive; for spiders, it is the source of life itself. All this, and far more, was conveyed directly into Niall's mind, and it made him aware of the absurd poverty of human language, and of the richness of communication possible between spiders.

'But are there none among you who preserve knowledge of the past?'

'Assuredly. But only of the past of our own race.'

'But perhaps the great wall *is* a part of your past.'

'How so, my lord?'

Niall found himself wishing that he had the skill to

convey his own thoughts in a single burst.

'The great wall must have been built by men. Do you agree?'

'Of course.'

'But *which* men? The human beings who lived on earth in the age before the coming of the spiders had no use for such a wall. They had flying machines that could carry them through the air like birds, and weapons that could demolish the strongest wall into dust.'

'But were human beings always so skilled in technology?'

'No. The men of the ancient past built many great walls. But those walls are now ruins. This wall looks as if it has been built more recently.'

The spider said with astonishment: 'The human mind is amazingly subtle.'

The remark made Niall aware once more of the curious limitations of the spider mind: that for all its shrewdness and sagacity, it lacked the power of logical induction.

'Who are these spiders who are versed in the history of your race?'

'The great ones of the past: Cheb the Mighty, Qisib the Wise, Greeb the Subtle, Kasib the Warrior . . .'

'But among the living?'

There was a pause, as if Asmak was searching for the right words. He said finally:

'Their knowledge lives on.'

'But how can I share this knowledge?'

'By entering its presence.'

Niall was baffled.

'But how?'

The question seemed to cause the spider some difficulty, as if he failed to grasp Niall's meaning.

'You wish to do this now, sire?'

Niall said hesitantly:

'If it is permitted.'

Asmak answered: 'You are the lord of this city. To you all things are permitted.'

'Then I would like to speak with these spiders who know the history of your race.'

Asmak made a semi-obeisance, symbolic of acquiescence. Then he turned towards the door, gesturing for Niall to follow.

As they descended the stairs to the hallway, Niall experienced misgivings. He had a suspicion that his simple enquiry had given rise to some misunderstanding, whose nature escaped him. Yet there was something about Asmak's manner that aroused intense curiosity. His perplexity increased when, instead of crossing the flagstones to the main door, Asmak turned to the right and descended a further flight of stairs. Niall found himself in total darkness, and had to place a hand on the wall to recover his bearings. A moment later, as the stairs made a right-angle turn, he tripped and stumbled; it was Grel who saved him from falling by hooking a foreleg around his waist. Asmak immediately recognized his difficulty, and extended assistance. The darkness seemed to vanish, to be replaced by a soft luminescence which enabled Niall to see the walls and the stairway. It took several moments for him to realize that he was still in complete darkness, and that the spider was simply conveying a kind of mental picture of their surroundings, exactly as on the 'flight' over the mountains.

Niall had expected to be led into some kind of cellar or underground vault; instead, he found himself turning more right-angle bends and descending further flights of stairs. When they finally reached level ground, Niall calculated that they must be as far below the roadway as the roof of the tower was above it.

The corridor in which he found himself was about six feet wide and seven feet high; its ceiling was curved, and, like the walls, was made of irregular stones set in cement. Asmak's height meant that he had to walk with his belly lowered, to avoid striking his head on the ceiling; from this, Niall deduced that the tunnel had not been built by spiders, or for them.

A dozen yards ahead, the corridor was blocked by a massive door, whose timbers were held together by wrought-iron bands. As they approached, there were sounds of bolts being withdrawn; then the door swung open, to reveal a brown wolf spider, who immediately prostrated himself at Asmak's feet. There was some kind of interchange – spiders were always punctilious in greeting one another – then the wolf spider withdrew into an alcove in the wall, leaving them room to pass. For a moment Niall felt sorry for him, standing guard for hour after hour in this cold darkness – until he recalled that all the spiders in this city were bound together in a kind of mutual awareness, and that therefore no spider was ever completely alone. It was the human beings who deserved pity.

The air was damp, and had a smell of mildew; it was also extremely cold, although Niall experienced no discomfort – his contact with the spider's mind ensured that his body remained pleasantly warm, as if he had been taking vigorous exercise on a winter's day.

It also ensured that, although the spider's body would normally have blocked his view along the tunnel, he was able to 'see' for a considerable distance beyond it. He was impressed by the fact that Asmak must have been familiar with literally every inch of their surroundings, for his mind reflected them as literally as if he had been able to see them. There were places where the walls had fallen into a state of disrepair, and slabs of stone lay on the ground. In another place, the ceiling had started to collapse, and had been supported by baulks of timber, including a beam that lay across the floor holding the uprights in place. Asmak skirted such obstacles without the slightest hesitation. At one point, the corridor was crossed by a lower tunnel with a downhill slope, and the ground there was covered with a slimy liquid with an unpleasant smell of stagnation; Asmak's warning of the slippery surface caused him to tread cautiously, and enabled him to avoid a fall.

So far, Niall had shared the spider's mental states in the sense of being an onlooker. His awareness of what was being communicated by Asmak was more direct than listening to a human voice, yet essentially of the same nature. But now, as he allowed himself to relax, he found that his own consciousness was beginning to blend with Asmak's, so that it was difficult to tell where his own began and Asmak's ended. It was an extraordinary sensation. To begin with, Asmak's consciousness was so much 'stronger' than his own that it made him acutely aware of the inadequacies of the human mind. He was reminded of the state he achieved when using the thought mirror, which amplified the will. But the thought mirror was tiring; it left him physically drained. Spider consciousness had a tremendous, unflagging power which somehow renewed itself through its own sheer enthusiasm and interest in the world. Yet although Niall found this marvellously exhilarating, he was not entirely happy about it. There was something crude and practical about this spider consciousness; it failed to satisfy some deep hunger for subtlety and complexity . . .

He was aroused from these reflections by the realization that they were no longer walking along a manmade tunnel. It had widened, and the walls on either side of him were made of a white rock-like material that might have been chalk or limestone. The ground underfoot was irregular, although there were many places where it had obviously been levelled with tools. A hundred yards further on, the tunnel widened again, and they were in a wide gallery whose roof was supported by irregular pillars of the white rock. It was obvious to Niall that this had been carved by water in some remote geological era. Shallow pools of water still covered the irregular floor; they waded through one that was ankle-deep, and the water was icy. Drops of water fell from the ceiling, and the sound was unusually loud in the stillness.

They had been walking for almost half an hour, and had probably covered a distance of more than two miles. Niall found himself wondering which direction they had taken; his question was 'overheard' by the spider, who immediately made him aware that they were walking due east. As far as Niall could calculate, that placed them somewhere beneath the 'industrial estate' to the east of the main square.

Ten minutes later, he became aware of another sound, like a distant rumble. As it grew louder, he realized that it was the sound of rushing water. And in spite of his sense of heightened vitality, he found it hard to suppress a rising nervous tension. This was not due to any lack of trust in Asmak's guidance, but merely to an instinctive fear of unknown perils. It cost a genuine effort to assure himself that Asmak would not allow any harm to befall him.

Moments later, the rushing sound filled the air like a tempest, and they came to a halt on the bank of a wide river. The black water was flowing very fast, but so smoothly that only a few ripples on its surface betrayed its speed. Niall was relieved to see that it was spanned by a metal bridge with a railing on either side; as they walked across this, the water flowed only a few inches below their feet. In the centre of the bridge – which was made of welded metal plates – the noise was deafening; Niall's impression was that the river plunged over a waterfall, perhaps another quarter of a mile downstream. Asmak, he noticed, was also nervous; like all death spiders, he had a natural dislike of water.

On the far side of the river, the nature of the terrain changed; the white rock was replaced by a dark, granite-like substance. They were no longer walking along a tunnel, but along some kind of cleft in the rock; Niall surmised that it had been caused by an earthquake or volcanic eruption, and again the thought made him irrationally nervous. The ground sloped towards the left, and it was necessary to walk carefully to avoid slipping. This 'road' twisted and turned between sheer rock faces. The sound of water was soon left behind them, and they were once again walking in a silence in which Niall's footsteps sounded eerily loud. (The spiders walked as softly as cats.)

He could now recognize in Asmak a sense of anticipation that told him that they were drawing close to their goal. He could easily have learned the nature of this goal by seeking access to a deeper level of Asmak's consciousness; but he sensed that the spider would regard such uncontrolled curiosity with a certain disapproval.

The rock faces on either side now came closer together, and finally joined overhead to form a pointed arch. The rocky path underfoot had obviously been levelled, but the sheer hardness of the rock had frustrated all efforts to make it smooth, and Niall had to tread carefully to avoid twisting his ankle. Grel and Asmak had no such problem; the number of their legs made it virtually impossible for them to stumble. But as the tunnel became narrower and lower, both had to bend their legs, so that their bellies were close to the ground. A point came where the walls were scarcely a yard apart, and Niall had to bend his head to avoid striking it on the roof. Asmak had to walk very slowly to squeeze his considerable bulk between the walls. Then, just as Niall was beginning to feel claustrophobic, the tunnel widened suddenly and came to an end.

He found himself standing in a large cave, whose roof was perhaps fifty feet above them. As far as he could see, there was no other way out; the cave was virtually a cul-de-sac. But he was aware of its size only because he was 'seeing' it through Asmak's mind; like the lair of the Death Lord, it was so full of cobwebs that even the most powerful light could not have pierced its depths. Cobwebs stretched like vast curtains from the walls to the floor; others, with strands like thick rope, stretched across the ceiling. But these were not the casually arranged cobwebs that formed a network above most of the streets of the spider city; Niall sensed immediately that they had been created by an artistic intelligence of a high order, and that their strange symmetry had some profound meaning for the spider mind. Unlike the dust-covered cobwebs in the headquarters of the Death Lord, these looked new and sticky; they even carried the faint, distinctive smell – not unlike some vegetable gum – of fresh cobwebs. This place, he realized, was a kind of spider cathedral, a place of worship, and the cobwebs were its woven tapestries, constantly renewed as an act of homage.

Slight sounds from overhead made him aware that spiders were lurking there. Although the cave was in total darkness, Asmak's familiarity with its geography, and his telepathic awareness of other spiders, created an illusion of a kind of grey twilight in which everything was clearly visible. He was able to sense that the spiders were all young – some even younger than Grel – and that there were about a dozen of them. Their youth was obvious because they were transmitting involuntary signals of excitement at the interruption of their lonely vigil; an older spider would have learned to restrain these signals. It was also clear to Niall that they were intensely curious about his own presence.

Asmak stood there silently for several minutes, waiting for this buzz of excitement to die down. Spiders always took their time in greeting one another – it was a point of honour as well as a natural instinct. During this time, Niall's mind was able to explore the recesses of the cave. Running up the far wall he could see a kind of ascending ramp, not unlike a flight of steps, which had obviously been carved out of the rock. This suggested that human beings sometimes made use of this cave – for spiders, in spite of their weight, would have no difficulty scaling its uneven walls. He was also able to perceive a number of deep recesses in the walls, all at floor level, although these appeared to be empty. Since these were all of the same size, and at regular intervals, it was clear that they had been carved by human workmen.

Niall was puzzled. He had been expecting to meet some older spider who might be able to answer his questions about the great wall. In fact, it was obvious that none of the spiders present had passed beyond the age which in human beings would be regarded as puberty.

Asmak finally spoke. The message he transmitted was a formal one of greeting; after a decent interval, it was answered by the young spiders speaking in unison. This proceeding had the effect of finally blocking off the signals of curiosity that were still being transmitted by the younger spiders.

Asmak's greeting, and the answer of the young spiders, had been an instantaneous telepathic signal, whose human equivalent would have been a bow or a handshake. Now Asmak deliberately spoke in human language – that is, in the type of signal that spiders used to communicate with human beings.

'The person I have brought with me is an honorary spider.' Asmak said 'person' rather than 'human being' because among spiders, 'human being' was a term of contempt – like 'pig' among humans. 'He is also the lord of our city.' This statement caused a buzz of astonishment among the young spiders, and Niall inferred from it that they knew nothing of what had taken place in the past six months. This in turn implied that these young spiders had been living in this cold darkness since the days of slavery. Were they being punished? Or perhaps trained for some kind of priesthood? The latter seemed perhaps the most likely.

Asmak resumed: 'He is also the chosen one of the great goddess, and therefore our master.'

For a few seconds there was total silence, unbroken by even a quiver of astonishment. Then Niall heard the rustling sound of soft, furry bodies descending on strands of web. A moment later he was surrounded by spiders who had lowered their stomachs to the ground in a gesture of homage. He stood there, feeling awkward and embarrassed, yet realizing that this was an essential part of spider ritual, and that he would be showing discourtesy if he allowed the slightest hint of his embarrassment to become apparent. As the moments lengthened, he realized that they were awaiting some gesture on his part. He therefore said aloud: 'Greetings', accompanying it with a courteous gesture of acknowledgement. The ritual reply – 'Greetings, lord' – came back like an echo; it was followed immediately by the rustling sound of spiders re-absorbing their strands of silk, and ascending once more into their webs. As this happened, Niall felt his body pierced by a pleasant glow, as warm and delicious as a spring breeze, and realized that the young spiders were transmitting a message of respect and affection. His sense of awkwardness vanished, and was replaced by an answering warmth and affection. It was as if some barrier inside him had broken down, and he could accept for the first time that he was truly an 'honorary spider'.

Asmak spoke again. 'Do any of you know the history of the great wall across the Valley of the Dead?'

Niall was astonished by the question. How could these young spiders know anything of the ancient history of their race? In fact, the silence that greeted the question seemed to indicate that they found it baffling. But after a long pause, a voice replied from above him in the darkness.

'I think it may have been built in the reign of Cheb the Mighty.'

Asmak said: 'Very well. Let us consult him. Are you his preserver?'

A voice from another part of the hall answered: 'No, lord, I am.'

'Good. Take us into his presence.'

Niall was baffled; his sensitivity to the aura of living creatures made him certain that this place contained none apart from themselves.

There was a soft rustle as a young spider descended to the ground. As it made the ritual obeisance before him, Niall realized that it was little more than a child – the equivalent of a human seven-year-old. It was so young that its poison fangs had not even begun to develop. It spoke to Niall haltingly, as one who was unused to human speech.

'Please follow me, sire.'

It led him towards one of the recesses that Niall had already observed. Asmak stood aside to allow Niall to pass, then followed behind. Grel, Niall observed, remained where he was. The young spider's mind took control of Niall's feet – a gesture of courtesy – steering him skilfully between thick strands of web that anchored overhead cobwebs to the floor. The recess itself was guarded by a curtain of webs that was virtually a miniature labyrinth. When they had steered their way between its overlapping sheets, Niall found himself standing in the entrance to a cave that extended back about twenty feet. To Niall's surprise, it seemed to be empty. Then, as they advanced towards its end, he realized that it turned a corner. Here the passage narrowed, and the ceiling became lower. Another turn brought them into a low-roofed chamber, not more than a dozen feet wide. Its walls were roughly carved, and glistened with moisture. Against the farther wall there was a low stone altar, on which some roughly spherical object was lying. A young spider was crouched in front of it, its legs bunched under its body. For a moment, Niall assumed that this was the spider who might answer his question; then, as it rose to its feet, he realized that it was a mere child.

They approached the centre of the chamber and halted. For a moment Niall found himself in complete darkness, as his guide abandoned telepathic contact; a moment later, the contact was renewed as Asmak entered the chamber. In that moment, Niall realized with a shock that the spherical object lying on the altar was the shrivelled remains of a dead spider. It was lying on a kind of cushion made of tangled spider web; its withered legs looked like broken stalks, while the leathery body was devoid of the usual hairs, and was cracked and shiny with age, like brittle leather.

Asmak said: 'You are in the presence of Cheb the Mighty.' He lowered himself to the ground and, after a moment of indecision, Niall did the same.

Niall was in a state of bewilderment; he found it incredible that the great Spider Lord should be so small. According to legend, Cheb was a hundred-eyed monster who could bite a man in half with his enormous chelicerae. In fact, he was hardly larger than a domestic cat; even with his legs fully extended, he could hardly have stood more than three feet high.

After a few moments Asmak straightened up again, and Niall did the same. He was fascinated by the sight of the Spider Lord. As a child, he had often shuddered when his grandfather, Jomar, told him stories about Cheb's cruelty and ferocity – on one occasion he was said to have ordered the piecemeal execution of a thousand human beings, who were injected with spider venom to paralyse them, and then eaten over the course of several days. On another occasion Cheb had personally decapitated a hundred prisoners with his pincers. It was obvious that this story, at least, was untrue; Cheb's infolded pincers looked scarcely more than two inches long.

Asmak said: 'Do you wish to speak direct to the Great One? Or do you wish me to speak on your behalf?'

Niall looked at him with amazement.

'But how . . .' He had to make an effort not to stammer. 'But surely the Great One is dead?'

'No, lord, he is not dead. Neither is he alive.'

Niall stared at the mummified shell on the altar.

'Not dead or alive? Surely that is impossible?'

In answer, Asmak conveyed another of those compressed bursts of information, which presented itself to

Niall's mind as a kind of pictograph. Its content was so astonishing that Niall had to allow it to unfold slowly in order to absorb it. Asmak, it seemed, was being strictly accurate in saying that the Lord Cheb was neither alive nor dead. It was true that his body had been dead for many centuries; so had much of his brain. But the parts of the brain that stored information had been kept alive, so that Cheb's memory remained available to his own race, a kind of library preserved in the mummified shell of the body. Keeping his memory cells alive was a task assigned to young spiders; they prevented him from dying simply by feeding him with their own vital power. This was the explanation of the curious glow of warmth that Niall had experienced in the presence of the young spiders – a glow whose nature combined respect and love. It was with this same living force that the spiders prevented Cheb's brain from dying.

Now, as Niall watched, the young spider reached into the brain of the Mighty Cheb, and poured forth a current of living energy. For the first time in his life, Niall understood a vital truth concerning the nature of love. He had always made the natural assumption that it was a mutually-shared emotion. Now he recognized it as a vital force which existed in its own right, and which could be conveyed directly from one being to another in the form of a flow of life-energy.

What he found difficult to accept was that the shrivelled corpse was in some sense alive. Niall's own telepathic sensitivity, amplified by the power of Asmak's mind, was unable to detect the slightest sign of life; the Lord Cheb might have been a piece of dead wood. The living current that flowed from the young spider was simply being absorbed, like water flowing into dry sand. What astonished Niall was that a spider who was obviously no more than a child was able to sustain such

323

a stream of energy. Then, as he became more attuned to what was happening, he realized that the young spider was not alone in his efforts; he was a channel for the vital force of all the spiders gathered together in the cave. His task was to canalize and direct it, like a gardener directing the stream from a hosepipe.

As Niall watched, the mummified body seemed to glow and expand; moments later, the stream of energy was literally rebounding, filling the narrow space of the cave with an unutterably joyous sense of spring-like vitality – a sensation that reminded him of the shimmering energy he had experienced among the plants and bushes near Skorbo's warehouse. Moments later, Niall realized that the Mighty Cheb was becoming aware of his surroundings. He almost expected to see him stir and stretch his legs, and the thought caused a momentary shock of alarm – for the shrivelled shell was obviously too frail to move without falling apart. It was a relief to realize, a moment later, that the body remained as dead as it had been five minutes ago. Only the mind was alive, and was contemplating its surroundings with curiosity, like someone who has awakened from a deep sleep.

Almost immediately, he became aware of Niall's presence.

'Who is this?'

Asmak answered: 'He is the chosen emissary of the great goddess.'

The Lord Cheb surveyed Niall with a kind of cold curiosity, which reminded Niall of his first meeting with the present Death Lord.

'Is this true?'

Six months ago, that question would have filled Niall with nervous misgivings. But in that time, he had become accustomed to the respect and obedience of the spiders. Now he replied indifferently:

'They tell me so.'

'You seem little more than a child.'

This seemed to require no reply, so Niall merely stood silently.

What had happened in this brief exchange was complex and yet strangely simple. Cheb had known human beings only as enemies or as slaves; therefore he had never met anyone like Niall, who faced him without reverence or fear, and who seemed indifferent to whether he was believed or not. Moreover, Niall faced him as an equal, possibly a superior. Until Cheb addressed him, Niall had seen him through the eyes of Asmak and the other spiders, and shared their sense of reverence. But the moment Cheb spoke, Niall entered his consciousness. It was like looking another man in the eyes, and immediately assessing his character. Cheb's character was that of a ruler whose major traits are strength and cunning – the cunning of one who has achieved power and intends to keep it. Compared to Asmak or Dravig, his mind lacked subtlety; he certainly lacked their intelligence. Yet he emanated a sense of potency; even his 'voice' was masculine and dominant. Niall could understand why he was known as Cheb the Mighty. In his coarse way, he was the most powerful spider Niall had ever met.

It was plain that Cheb found this human alien puzzling. He was aware of Niall's intelligence, and accorded it a reluctant admiration. Yet he was also aware of Niall's immaturity and inexperience – that if they had been face to face in the days when Cheb was alive, Niall would have been easy to outmanoeuvre. Therefore the admiration was tinged with a patronizing disrespect. This shocked Asmak; and Cheb, in turn, was amused by Asmak's dismay. There was a sense, therefore, in which Niall and Cheb the Mighty met as equals, while the others were mere onlookers.

Cheb asked: 'Why have you come here?'

'To ask you a question.'

'Very well. Ask it.'

'I want to know who built the great wall across the Valley of the Dead.'

'I do not know. It was after my time.'

This was a disappointment; and Niall could sense that Asmak was also disappointed.

Cheb asked: 'Is that all?'

'No. I have one more question.'

'Ask it.'

'Is it true that you were the first spider to understand the secrets of the human soul?'

There was a silence, then Cheb asked:

'Who told you that story?'

'My grandfather.' And since it was obvious that Cheb was waiting for further information, Niall went on: 'He told me that a prince called Hallat had fallen in love with a maiden named Turool. But she was in love with a poor chieftain named Basat. The prince tried to kidnap her from Basat's camp, but a dog betrayed his presence by barking, and he was driven away. So – according to my grandfather – Hallat came to you, and offered to betray the secrets of the human soul in exchange for Turool. He taught you how to read the minds of human beings, and in exchange, your warriors descended on the camp of Basat, and captured it in a surprise attack by night. Prince Hallat executed Basat by striking off his head. But Turool became insane with grief, and sacrificed her life by attacking a spider, who killed her.'

As he was speaking, Niall was aware that Cheb was listening with total attention. And so, he realized a moment later, were Asmak and the young spider. Since it was obvious that they wanted him to go on, and since Niall had heard the story so often that he knew it by heart, he continued:

'At this time, according to my grandfather, the spiders were already living in this city, and were curious to learn the secret of the white tower. You offered to make him the king of all men on earth if he would help you to penetrate the secret of the tower. Hallat agreed, and had many prisoners tortured to force them to reveal what they knew. Finally, an old woman agreed to tell him the answer to the riddle if he would spare her husband's life. She told him that the secret of the tower was a "mind lock" – the mind of man must interact with the walls of the tower, which would then dissolve away like smoke. This could be done with the aid of a magic rod. The old woman's husband possessed such a rod, for it was a symbol of his power as a chief. Hallat took it from him, and went to the tower the next day at dawn – for the old woman told him that the rays of the rising sun would fall on a secret door at the foot of the tower. But when Hallat tried to approach the tower with the magic rod, some force threw him to the ground. He tried again, and the same thing happened. The third time, he stretched out both arms and shouted: "I command you to open!" But when he tried to touch it with the magic rod, there was a flash like lightning, and Hallat was burned to a piece of black charcoal.'

At this point Niall paused, having decided to tactfully omit the last lines of the story. But Cheb was obviously aware that there was more to come, and his manner made it clear that he was still waiting. Niall suppressed his embarrassment and went on:

'When you heard what had happened, you had all the prisoners executed, including the old chief and his wife. And the mystery of the white tower remained unsolved.'

This time, Niall's manner made it clear that the story had come to an end. Yet the spiders remained silent for a long time. Finally, Cheb made a gesture that was amazingly like a human being shaking his head. Then he said:

'You speak with the tongue of a *sheevad*.'

'A *sheevad*?' It was the first time Niall had heard the expression.

Asmak explained: 'A *sheevad* is one who speaks words of wisdom, like the Lord Dravig.'

Niall was flattered but puzzled; as far as he could see, there was nothing particularly wise about his story. Then something about the attitude of the young spider brought a glimmer of understanding. It had been listening with the absorption of a child listening to a fairy tale. Niall was suddenly struck by the realization that the art of storytelling must be totally new to the spiders. When they 'spoke' to one another, they did so in images which transmitted their meaning instantaneously. This meant, in turn, that there could be no 'suspense'; the whole story, with its beginning and end, was transmitted in a single flash of information. When Cheb spoke of wisdom, he meant something more like 'mind control', the ability to unfold an ordered sequence of images. It was startling to realize that human language, for all its inbuilt limitations, struck the spiders as in some respects superior to their own method of communication.

Since Cheb was apparently absorbed in his own reflections, Niall cleared his throat and asked:

'Is the story true?'

'True?' The Spider Lord seemed taken aback by the question.

'Did Prince Hallat really exist?'

'A human being called Hallat certainly existed. But he was not a prince. He was a slave – my slave.'

'And did he teach you to understand the human soul?'

'No. But he taught me to understand human language.'

'And how did that come about?'

In asking such questions, Niall did not attempt to formulate them in words. For example, in asking if Hallat existed, he merely transmitted an image of Hallat with a general sense of interrogation. To ask how this came about, it was merely necessary to transmit a kind of question mark. Compared to spoken words, the method was pleasingly economical.

Unfortunately, Cheb's answer, couched in the same mode, was equally economical; it came as a bewildering explosion of information that outran Niall's powers of understanding, and left him feeling breathless. Cheb perceived his bewilderment, and in the spider mode – which he obviously preferred to human language – transmitted the message:

'I am sorry. Let me try again.'

His second attempt was less precipitate. The first image was of a bare, bleak landscape covered in snow, the next of spiders crouching in caves or ruined houses to escape the icy wind. These images were accompanied by a kind of background information – like the background of a picture – to which Niall could either pay attention, or merely absorb as a part of the general effect.

Translated into human language, Cheb was saying, in effect:

'When I was born, the world was suffering from a great ice age. Millions of my people died before they had reached adulthood. The snow fell day and night, and the wind changed continually so that shelter was almost impossible to find. The sky was always dark, and for a period of many years, no one saw the sun.'

All this made it clear that Cheb was speaking of the

period immediately after the earth had been brushed by the tail of the comet Opik. Niall had learned of 'the great winter' during his history lessons in the white tower. In the twenty-second century of the modern era, the earth had been threatened with destruction by a radioactive comet, and most of the human race had left in giant space transports, to undertake the nine-year voyage – at half the speed of light – to a planet in the star system Alpha Centauri. The settlers christened this planet New Earth.

In fact, the head of the comet missed the earth by more than a million miles. But material from its tail fell into the earth's atmosphere, destroying nine-tenths of all animal life. And its gravitational field caused a perturbation in the moon's orbit, which in turn caused a violent outbreak of volcanic activity on earth. The atmosphere turned into a kind of fog which formed an impenetrable barrier against the sunlight. The planet entered a new ice age, which continued until the dust particles slowly fell back to earth. Two centuries after the disaster, the ice fields began to retreat, as other climatic factors transformed the surface from a refrigerator into a hothouse.

The comet which had brought destruction also brought a new form of life. It originated on the planet Alpha-Lyrae 3, the third in the solar system of the blue star called Vega, in the constellation Lyra, twenty-seven light years away. On this planet, the force of gravity was so immense – a hundred times greater than that of earth – that a man on its surface would have weighed ten tons and been unable to lift his eyelids. Under these conditions, the only intelligent life form to develop consisted of giant globular creatures, which on earth would have been called vegetables.

A hundred and fifty million years ago, a fragment from an exploding galaxy passed through the Vega system, causing a catastrophic upheaval on Alpha-Lyrae 3, and tearing loose a segment almost as large as the earth. This material was dragged through space in the wake of the star-fragment until, many millions of years later, it came into near-collision with the comet Opik – whose head was fifty thousand miles in diameter – and was captured in its tail. This is how the seeds of the vegetable life form of the planet Alpha-Lyrae 3 came to land on earth.

Some fell in deserts or polar regions and perished. Only five succeeded in germinating, and one of these was in the tropical region of the Great Delta. Because earth's gravity was so much lower than that of their own planet, their molecular processes were accelerated, and they became immense – the plant in the Great Delta, half-buried in the earth, looked like a small mountain.

These giant plants possessed highly developed powers of telepathy; on their own planet, evolution was a communal effort. On earth, their evolution soon came to a halt because a mere five superbeings could not build up sufficient thought-pressure. There was only one solution: for the plants to create more superbeings by accelerating the evolution of other species. The plants became giant transmitters of vital energy, causing it to flow through the earth itself. All creatures who could receive the vibrations began to evolve at an accelerated rate. Unfortunately, most animals on earth – including man – had already evolved too far to be able to receive these vibrations. Insects, on the other hand, seemed highly receptive to these waves of pure vitality, and many species quickly developed into giants. But certain types of spider were the most receptive of all; this is how they quickly replaced man as the most dominant species on earth. Aware that they owed their life to the energy transmitted by the giant plant of the Delta

– men called it the empress plant – they worshipped it as the great goddess. It was because Niall had spoken with the goddess face to face that the spiders now revered him as a kind of god.

The Mighty Cheb must have been among the earliest of the giant spiders; this is why he was so much smaller than his modern descendants.

Now Niall asked the question that had always puzzled him, even as a child.

'But why did the spiders become the enemies of men, instead of their friends and allies?'

Cheb answered: 'It was not our choice. During the great winter, many of our people were forced to share habitations with men. When they found us, they killed us. We would have been glad to live in peace. But long before I was born, men and spiders had been bitter enemies.'

And now, transmitting his images more slowly, Cheb told a story of murder and cruelty that made Niall feel slightly sick. During Cheb's lifetime, the spiders were already increasing in size and intelligence at an astonishing rate. Oddly enough, many human beings regarded them with respect, believing that it was unlucky to kill a spider unnecessarily. But the steady increase in size was noted with alarm. With the exception of a few rare species – such as the black widow – few spiders secreted a venom that could kill human beings, and the venom of the large and hairy tarantula – the species to which Cheb belonged – was too weak to kill even a cat or dog. It was unfortunate, therefore, that during the great winter, the bite of a hairy tarantula was responsible for the death of a sick child, and that the child's brother, a youth named Ivar, thereafter killed every spider he came upon. In due course, Ivar became a great leader, known among his own people as Ivar the Strong, but to others as Ivar the Cruel. It was Ivar who conquered most of his neighbours in the country of the two rivers, and who seized its largest city and massacred its inhabitants. This city he renamed Korsh – meaning stronghold – and he and his descendants built its great walls and towers with slave labour.

The land to the far north of Korsh was a mountainous region, full of deep valleys, and it was in these valleys that the hairy spiders had established their own kingdom. They lived on birds and small animals and reptiles. Their nearest human neighbours had allowed them to live in peace. But when Ivar conquered these neighbours, he learned of the existence of the 'Valley of the Spiders', and decided that the hairy tarantulas had to be exterminated. The entrance to the valley was blocked by webs; these were destroyed by fire. Ivar had discovered an underground source of a black, tarry substance which burned fiercely and gave off a poisonous smoke. The spiders, confident that they were safe in the depths of their caves, made no attempt to resist the invaders; they learned too late that the black smoke could suffocate them. As spiders tried to flee from the depths of the caves, men waiting above the entrance covered them with the black tar, while others drove them towards bushes that had been set on fire. The spiders, blinded and half-poisoned by the smoke, were easy prey; by evening, the valley was piled high with their burnt bodies. Because they were telepathic, the pain and misery of the dying spread panic and madness among the living. Spiders in other valleys retreated to the north, into a land still in the grip of winter, and thousands died there. And because of the massacre of the spiders, Ivar became known as Ivar the Strong.

So great were Cheb's powers of description that Niall could smell the charred flesh and the choking odour of burning tar; he witnessed the spectacle of mothers, with their young clinging to their back, battered to a pulp with wooden clubs, or deliberately burned alive by men who ignited their tar-sprayed bodies with blazing straw. Now, at last, he understood why the death spiders regarded man as the most evil and depraved creature on earth.

Ivar's cruelty led to his downfall. The spiders were already evolving at an accelerated rate; now their misery and hatred concentrated the powers of the will. Within a few generations, they had developed a poison strong enough to kill the largest man or horse, and a will-power capable of paralysing a man in his tracks, and preventing him from moving until he had been injected with venom. This was how the spiders became the deadliest creatures on the planet – out of a desperate need to prevent their extermination by human beings. Ivar, of course, knew nothing of this – he had been too busy conquering the lands to the east. So when he learned – from shepherds and herdsmen – that the spiders had returned to their valleys, he prepared for another massacre. The webs that blocked the entrance to the valley were burned, and wood soaked in tar was piled outside the caves. Ivar himself, on a mighty black horse, prepared to give the order to ignite the bonfires. His men, holding their blazing torches, awaited the signal. But the signal never came. As Ivar began to raise his arm, a look of surprise and alarm crossed his face, and he seemed to be struck dumb. And the men who were holding the torches also found that they were unable to move; even the strongest could only twitch their limbs and roll their eyes. Then the spiders swarmed out of the caves, while others blocked the entrance to the valley. Fleeing men – for many were still able to move – were overwhelmed by spiders that climbed their backs and sank fangs into their necks. No fires were lit that day. Instead, more than a thousand paralysed men were dragged into caves, and their clothes stripped from them by the powerful chelicerae of the male spiders. Then the children drank their warm juices, while the adults gorged on their living flesh. Ivar the Cruel lasted for three days; his eyelids were eaten away so that his eyes remained open until the hour of his death. It was said that he remained fully conscious until a few minutes before he died.

So great was Niall's state of empathy with the Spider Lord that he experienced no horror at this recital – rather a feeling of satisfaction that the humans had received the punishment they deserved.

He asked: 'And were you alive at the time of these events?'

'No. I was born a thousand moons later.' (It took Niall a few moments to work out that this was approximately eighty years.) 'That was in the reign of the king called Vaken the Terrible. His warriors hunted and killed our people in order to obtain their poison, which they used to preserve animals in winter.'

Niall interrupted: 'But if your people had developed the power of the mind, surely they had nothing to fear from human beings?'

'Unfortunately, that is not so. My people are peace-loving and unsuspicious. All they wanted was to be allowed to live without fear. This is why we moved away from the valley of the massacre – even after our triumph over Ivar the Cruel – and went to live in the valleys of the north. But human beings were full of desire for revenge, and they often took us by surprise. The grandson of Ivar the Cruel started an avalanche that buried alive thousands of our most courageous warriors. We retreated to a ruined city between the mountains and the sea, hoping to find safety. But on the night of the strong winds, Skapta the Cunning started a fire which swept through the city with the speed of a storm cloud, and again thousands of my people were burnt to death.

'After that came Vaken the Terrible, and he never ceased to persecute us until my people were driven to find refuge on the mountainous side of the great river. I was born in these cold lands which are far to the north. I can remember the year of the icy winds, when many of our people froze to death. When my father failed to return from hunting, I went out to look for him. I found him buried in snow, still standing guard over the carcase of a stag, which had frozen into a block of ice. And since my father was our ruler, and I was his strongest son, I became Death Ruler in his place.

'It was I who decided that we should leave the lands of the north wind and return to the south, even if it meant being killed by human hunters. I was the first of our kind to decide that we had to make war if we were to survive. That is why I became known as Cheb the Mighty. I led my people back to the city that had been burnt by Skapta the Cunning, and for many years we lived amongst its ruins, undetected by human beings. I taught my people to be vigilant – to keep guard so that we could no longer be surprised by enemies. If herdsmen came close to our city, we hid ourselves until they went away. If they came too close, and discovered our presence, we captured and killed them.

'Now my chief adviser was a counsellor called Qisib, who was entrusted with the task of demolishing the dangerous parts of the city. And it was he who realized that our human captives could perform these tasks more efficiently than my people. They were physically stronger than we were, yet their minds were feeble by comparison. So instead of killing our captives, we began to use them as slaves. Among these was a boy called Hallat, who was as strong as an ox. One day, when he was demolishing a building, his guard was killed by a falling beam. He had the opportunity to escape, yet he preferred to remain. That is why I began to trust him, and to treat him with kindness. And it was through Hallat that I began to understand the ways of men.'

Niall asked: 'And who was Princess Turool?'

'I do not know. Hallat was allowed to take his pick of female prisoners. But I never knew their names.'

'And is it true that he was killed by lightning when he tried to enter the white tower?'

'No. Hallat was never in this city, for in those days it was still occupied by human beings. But it was through my counsellor Qisib that the city finally fell into our hands. One of Hallat's wives died in childbirth, and the child was given to one of Qisib's daughters. Instead of eating him, she decided to keep him as a pet. And when the child was old enough to walk, some other human children were sent to play with him. Instead of welcoming them, the child rushed at them and tried to bite them. And Qisib, who happened to be in the room, realized that the child did not regard himself as a human being. Because he had been brought up among our people, he regarded himself as a spider.

'It was now that Qisib displayed the wisdom for which he was famous. He ordered that all human children should be taken away from their mothers when they were newly born, and brought up by our women. Until the child was old enough to walk, it was not allowed to see another human being. Only then was it taught human language by our slaves. In this way, Qisib created a class of humans who regarded their own kind with contempt, and preferred the company of our people.

'When they were old enough, these humans were sent out among the shepherds of the wilderness to act as spies. They always told the same story – that their parents had been captured by spiders, that they had been brought up as slaves, and had seized the first opportunity to escape. They were welcomed everywhere as heroes. When they came to the city of Korsh, the son of Vaken the Terrible, known as Vaken the Fair, commanded a feast in their honour. Some of them even married maidens from the city. Yet they remained faithful to their task. And those who became shepherds and goatherds were able to bring us information about the defences of the city.

'Finally the night came when a million of my people surrounded the city of Korsh. There was no need to launch a surprise attack, for we merely had to paralyse the minds of all its inhabitants. When this was done, the city was ours. The next morning, Vaken the Fair was brought before me, bound hand and foot with spider web, and I made him pledge his loyalty and swear to be my slave for the rest of his days. When that was done, my own subjects proclaimed me the first Death Lord. And from that day forth, my people were masters of all the lands between the two rivers.'

As he ended his story, the Death Lord lapsed once more into human language, which – compared to telepathy – seemed cold and expressionless. This was a gesture of politeness, a recognition that Niall's loyalties might be divided; yet nothing could disguise the note of triumph and excitement in Cheb's voice as he described his greatest victory. And although Niall was aware that this victory marked the beginning of human slavery, he still found it impossible not to thrill with sympathy. The spiders had been a subject people; yet in one day, they had displaced man as the lords of the earth. It was surely one of the most momentous days in the history of the planet.

Cheb was studying Niall's reactions with interest –

unlike the other spiders, he felt no inhibitions about probing Niall's mind. Now he asked with a kind of rough humour:

'Well, human, did we not deserve our victory?'

'Yes, lord, you deserved to live in peace. But there can be no true peace while there is slavery.'

The Spider Lord responded with a sound like a grunt.

'Perhaps. But while I was alive, there was no alternative.'

Niall asked curiously:

'Are you not still alive?'

'In your sense, no.' The Death Lord suddenly sounded weary. 'My brain is kept alive by the strength of these children.' He sent an impulse of affection towards the young spider, who responded with a movement of gratitude, like a dog being stroked. 'But now this one is becoming tired, and I must not exhaust him further.'

Niall made a formal obeisance.

'I thank you for your courtesy and patience.'

'The pleasure was mine. Before I go, do you have anything further to ask me?'

Niall was reminded of why he had been brought to this sacred place.

'Only one thing, lord. Have you ever heard of a race of humans who live underground, and whose leader is a great magician?'

'No. But wait . . .' The Death Lord paused to reflect. Then he sighed wearily. 'No, I can no longer remember. Speak to my adviser. He knows everything. Now it is time for me to return. Goodbye and safe voyage.'

A moment later, Cheb was gone. He vanished so quickly that Niall was taken by surprise. His mind, still in contact with the mummified brain, found itself suddenly surrounded by emptiness. The sensation was like waking from a deep sleep. It seemed incredible that this long-dead shell had ever contained a living presence.

For several minutes, no one spoke – spiders were never in a hurry to break silence. Finally Asmak said:

'The Great One was in a good humour today.'

His voice sounded oddly hesitant, and it made Niall aware of the momentousness of what had just taken place. Cheb was a legendary being, almost a god; yet he had spoken to Niall as to an equal. Asmak was hesitant because he was overwhelmed by what he had just witnessed: a dialogue between the Mighty Cheb and the emissary of the goddess.

Niall asked: 'What did he mean by "Speak to my adviser"?'

'The Mighty One was referring to Qisib the Wise.'

'And is it possible for me to speak to Qisib the Wise?'

It seemed to Niall that Asmak was troubled by this question; for a moment, he even wondered whether the request would be refused. Then, without replying, Asmak turned and led the way out of the sacred chamber. Their original guide followed behind. The young spider remained where he was, obviously in a daze of total exhaustion.

Now they were back in the sacred cave, Niall became aware of a strange tension in the atmosphere; it was as if all the spiders were holding their breath. It was when he allowed his mind to blend with that of Grel that he understood the reason. Like Asmak, these young servants of the mighty dead felt that they had been privileged to witness an encounter that would be preserved in legend. Niall himself was feeling oddly relaxed and alive, a feeling that seemed to be a presage of some interesting experience or discovery.

As they stood in the centre of the floor, three young spiders descended softly from above, and advanced towards them. Niall was surprised to observe that these were brown wolf spiders – they were physically bulkier and more powerful than death spiders. Since wolf spiders were generally treated as servants – and seemed to accept themselves in this role – Niall was surprised to see them in this sacred place. He was even more surprised when the three spiders ignored Asmak, and seemed to consult amongst themselves. It seemed clear that they possessed some kind of authority or responsibility. Finally, the largest of the three – he was almost full-grown – turned to Asmak and made a mental gesture of acquiescence. He then led the way across the cave, followed by his two companions. Asmak gestured for Niall to precede him. This time, Grel brought up the rear.

Niall expected to be led to another cave whose entrance was concealed by layers of spider web. He was surprised when the spiders halted at the foot of sheer rock face, then proceeded to climb upwards. At close quarters, he saw that the rough surface of the rock afforded many hand- and footholds. With only a moment's hesitation, he gripped a small projection a foot above his head, placed his right foot on an inch-wide ledge near the ground, and hauled himself up. A moment later he was relieved to feel himself supported by Asmak's will-force, which prevented him from falling backwards while he groped for further holds.

When he was about six feet from the ground, he realized that the three wolf spiders had vanished. The mystery was explained a few minutes later when – gasping from the exertion – he found himself looking into a small circular hole in the rock face. It was scarcely more than two feet high, and he was forced to scramble into it head-first. As he did so, he lost telepathic contact with Asmak, and for a moment experienced a queasy sensation as he found himself in total darkness, in a passageway so low and narrow that it induced a feeling of claustrophobia. A moment later, contact was again resumed, bringing an illusion of sight; but his ability to 'see' his surroundings brought no comfort. The 'hole' was man-made – its sides were covered with the marks of tools – but was so narrow that it would have been totally impossible to turn. Moreover, it sloped downward, increasing the sense of claustrophobia by making him feel that retreat was impossible. A dozen or so yards ahead, the rear of the young wolf spider was disappearing around a corner. In this narrow space, the acrid and distinctive smell of spiders was very strong.

If Asmak observed his alarm, he was too tactful to show it. When he had squeezed his own large bulk through the entrance, the passageway was effectively blocked, and Niall felt as if he was immured in a kind of rocky coffin. For a brief moment Niall struggled with panic that made him feel suffocated; then he forced himself to crawl on down the passageway, keeping his head low to avoid the roof.

A bend in the passage proved difficult to negotiate; it had been made for spiders rather than human beings. For a distance of perhaps ten feet it became even more narrow, so that the walls pressed upon his shoulders, and he had to push himself forward with his toes. Then, to his intense relief, it widened, and he found himself in a small chamber, pressed against the hairy bodies of the wolf spiders, with their oddly distinctive smell. It seemed impossible that there could be room for anyone else; but as Asmak pushed his way into the chamber, Niall had to squeeze against the wall, wedged tightly by the armoured, crab-like legs of one wolf spider and the upper portion of the soft abdomen of another.

Unlike the tomb of Cheb the Mighty, this tiny chamber, scarcely five feet in diameter and less than six feet high, contained no altar, nor any other repository for the body of a dead spider; it seemed to be empty. Then, on the opposite wall, Niall noticed the patch of newly-spun cobweb, little more than six inches in diameter, and realized that it must conceal some kind of hole in the rock.

In this narrow space, the heat of the spiders' bodies was oppressive, and their distinctive odour even more so. Yet in the presence of these young spiders, Niall made a decisive effort to overcome his feelings of oppression and alarm; as the representative of the goddess, he felt that it would be shameful to display weakness.

Now Asmak's attention centred upon the cobweb-covered hole in the opposite wall, and Niall became aware that it was no more than a small hollow, scarcely six inches deep, and that its backward-sloping floor was covered with a cushiony mass of cobweb. In the centre of this lay all that remained of Qisib the Wise, the spider who, according to legend, was the first to learn how human beings could be enslaved.

Niall had ceased to feel surprise; instead, he merely observed that Qisib was far smaller than his master Cheb. By comparison, Cheb was a giant. The body of Qisib was the size of a small bird, and most of the legs upon which it rested had broken away, so that they looked like withered segments of dry stick. The cephalic region and the thorax were complete, but the abdomen, which should have been the largest portion of its body, was so shrivelled that it was almost non-existent.

And now, for the first time, he understood why it had been necessary for three wolf spiders to accompany them. Qisib the Wise was in such a state of dissolution that he was scarcely more than a few mummified fragments. It was hardly surprising that Asmak had been troubled by Niall's request to speak to him – it seemed inconceivable that even the vital force of three healthy young wolf spiders could restore this dehydrated shell to some semblance of life and intelligence.

The moment the three wolf spiders began to concentrate their attention on the fragments of the corpse, Niall's sense of claustrophobia vanished; he was so totally absorbed in what was happening that his present situation was unimportant. This time, he allowed himself to become identified with the unified awareness of the spiders; like them, he entered into the shell of Qisib the Wise, and drifted into a kind of grey emptiness as his mind groped for a foothold in the world of non-existence. What amazed him was that the wolf spiders seemed in no way discouraged by this emptiness; their vitality poured into it like water pouring over some bottomless waterfall. For a moment he was gripped by a feeling of loneliness that was close to panic, as his own mind threatened to dissolve into the void. Then he became aware that the greyness was no longer a featureless nothing; some kind of life was erupting to the surface, like an expanding pattern of ripples. It was like a monster rising from the bottom of the sea. The sense of erupting energy was due to its attempt to awaken itself from non-existence. For a moment, it seemed doubtful that the energy of the spiders would suffice, and that they themselves would be dragged down into non-existence. Then, like a sleeper opening his eyelids, the consciousness of Qisib the Wise began to take its bearings, and to struggle for a foothold in the world of the living. Oddly enough, it seemed intensely reluctant to do this, as if to be alive was an unutterable burden.

The difference between Qisib and Cheb was immediately apparent. Cheb had treated his excursion to the world of the living as a kind of holiday; for Qisib it was a wearisome duty that he would have been glad to escape. Like a sleeper roused from a heavy slumber, he was anxious to sink back into oblivion. And at this point, Niall realized why wolf spiders had been chosen rather than death spiders. They were less intelligent than death spiders, but their minds possessed the kind of brute force to prevent Qisib from escaping back into the greyness.

What happened next took Niall by surprise. It was exactly as if one of the young spiders had seized Qisib in its powerful front legs and dragged him across the threshold of the living world. What happened, in fact, was that the spider transferred Qisib's consciousness into his own brain, then retreated into a kind of trance, leaving Qisib in possession. The dead spider had ceased to be a disembodied mind, and became part of a living entity, supported by its life system. For a moment, he remained passive, as if still unwilling to make any kind of effort. Then he turned his attention to Asmak, and asked wearily:

'What is it this time, guardian of the dead?'

The voice, unlike that of the Lord Cheb, was thin and without resonance. Niall had observed before that the 'voices' of spiders were as distinctive as those of humans, even though the communication was from mind to mind. They were clearly an expression of the spider's whole personality.

Asmak said: 'This youth is the emissary of the great goddess. He wants to ask you a question.'

Qisib surveyed Niall without interest.

'Let him ask it.'

The voice was bored and flat.

Niall said: 'I want to ask, lord, whether you know who built the great wall across the Valley of the Dead.'

'Yes. I did.'

'You!' Niall was aware that Asmak and Grel (who was standing behind him in the corridor) shared his astonishment.

'That is so. I don't mean on my own, of course.' Qisib sounded slightly defensive. 'I mean I supervised the work.'

'And that was after the time of Cheb the Mighty?'

'Yes, that's right. It was in the reign of his son Kasib the Warrior. Although, in fact, I suppose the whole thing started in the time of Cheb.'

Qisib spoke slowly, as if he was ruminating on his words. His voice had none of the vigour of Cheb's voice, nor any of his natural authority, and the reedy intonation made him sound very old. Yet there was something oddly likeable about Qisib the Wise, as if he combined modesty with a sense of humour. It was easy to understand why he had been chosen by the two great Spider Lords as their chief counsellor.

Niall asked: 'But *why* was the wall built?'

'To keep out those human creatures from the north.' The image Qisib used for 'human creatures' was vaguely insulting, as if referring to some particularly disgusting insects.

Niall made an effort to repress his excitement.

'Who were they?'

'I don't know. We never found out.'

He realized that it was going to be difficult getting specific information out of Qisib. It was not that the great counsellor was trying to be difficult, or was unwilling to tell what he knew. It was simply that Niall was questioning him in human language, and Qisib – who had obviously had little mental intercourse with humans – found it confusing, like a man trying to understand a foreign tongue.

Niall drew a deep breath, and reflected on how to phrase his next question.

'The mighty Lord Cheb has described to me how you conquered this city. He said that he then became master of all the lands between the two rivers. Yet now you tell me that he failed to conquer the humans from the north.' Niall paused, but Qisib made no reply; it was obvious that he failed to understand what Niall was asking. Niall tried to clarify:

'What land did these people come from?'

'I don't know. We never found out.'

'But didn't you want to find out?'

'Not in the beginning. We weren't interested in the mountains to the north of the Valley of the Dead. They weren't of any use to us, and the coastal plain was too narrow.'

And now, at last, Qisib's mind was beginning to convey geographical images, first of the Valley of the Dead, with its black volcanic lake, then of the bleak and precipitous mountains to the north, with their strange, needle-like spires. Niall also observed that these northern mountains were heavily coated with snow; it was clear that, in the time of Qisib the Wise, the land was only just emerging from the grip of the great ice age.

Niall was struck by the clarity of the mental image; it seemed even sharper and more real than his recent view of the same mountains through the mind of Asmak. It seemed incredible that memory – even the memory of a spider – could store any scene in such photographic detail.

Now their minds were in close contact, it suddenly became easier to communicate. When Qisib realized that Niall was interested in the mental image of the northern mountains, he sustained and enlarged it, so Niall could study it in more detail. Niall immediately became aware that the lake in the centre of the valley had been far larger at the end of the great ice age, and the rivers that flowed from it were more turbulent. The mountain streams that fed the lake were like cascades of white foam; they had filled it to the brim, so that the steep sides which Niall had noticed earlier were now hidden below the black surface.

Niall asked the question that he had been meaning to raise ever since his first sight of this valley.

'Why is it called the Valley of the Dead?'

'Because so many of our people died here on the night of the great storm.'

'How did this come about?'

For answer, Qisib conjured up a vision of torrential rain, followed by an image of rushing water that seemed to explode across the valley, sweeping away thousands of spiders who had taken shelter under the southern flank of the mountain. It lasted only a second – Qisib obviously had no desire to prolong it – but it left Niall feeling shaken and breathless. He could see that it had the same effect on the other spiders.

'But what were so many spiders doing in this valley?'

'They were preparing to march north, to seek out the enemy.'

'But you told me your people were not interested in the lands to the north.'

'That is true. But we had to defend ourselves from attack.'

And now Qisib's mind created an image of a coastal city with white houses and tree-lined terraces, and buildings that Niall recognized as old churches. There was something oddly familiar about the surrounding plain, and the two dome-like mountains that enclosed it. With a stir of excitement, Niall recognized the town of Cibilla, that he had seen an hour ago. It had then been a desolation of rubble-filled streets and smoke-blackened houses; yet the mountains in the background left no doubt that this was the same place.

Then, in a series of unambiguous images, Qisib told the story of the catastrophe in the Valley of the Dead.

The coastal town of Cibilla had been the one in which Cheb had taken refuge on his return from the northern wastes. More than a century earlier, it had been burnt by Skapta the Cunning. Men had never returned there, for the ruins were full of disgusting slimy creatures. (Niall knew that when a spider dies, its body turns into a lower form of life called a squid fungus – an octopus-like invertebrate that was fairly harmless to adults, but which loved to suffocate and consume sleeping children.) The spiders were unafraid of these creatures, for they could be controlled by will-force. So Cheb and his people had lived for many years in the ruined town, unsuspected by Vaken the Terrible, or by his son Vaken the Fair. When wandering shepherds came too close, they were captured and held as slaves. And this is how Qisib came to understand that he held the key to the conquest of the human race. Human babies were taken from their parents and brought up as spiders. And it was this new breed of spider-servants who enabled the Mighty Cheb to conquer Vaken the Fair, and to become lord of the spider city.

Within forty moons, all the human strongholds had been conquered, and Cheb was the undisputed master of the world. The conquest was not an easy one. In spite of their highly-developed will-force, few individual spiders were a match for individual men. Compared to the spiders of that time, men were giants. And when a fully-armed soldier, maddened with drink, charged into battle, he could kill a dozen spiders before their united will-force paralysed his sword arm. Even the poison of the spiders was useless against a warrior in protective clothing. And since, at this time, men vastly outnumbered the spiders, the war was long and bloody, and after one major defeat, Cheb even considered returning to the lands of the north. But with the aid of the great goddess, he finally prevailed, and his kingdom extended from the deserts of Khaybad to the Grey Mountains in the north.

And when Cheb was in his hundred-and-twentieth year, and his legs were no longer strong enough to support the weight of his body, he retreated to the sacred cave beneath his capital city, and there made his entry into the land of the unliving. His son Kasib the Warrior, who had conducted Cheb's last campaign against the men of the southern desert, became Death Lord in his place.

During the last years of his reign, the coastal town that men called Cibilla was used by Cheb and his ministers as a summer retreat – for now the great ice age was over, the weather was becoming increasingly hot. It had been rebuilt by slaves under the command of Cheb's faithful human servants, and the spiders and their servants often shared the same buildings, with the spiders living in the upper storeys. The cool sea breezes were welcome in the heat of midsummer. But as Cheb grew old, he began to dream of his childhood in the cold lands of the north. He sent an expedition there, and learned that the ice had now retreated, and that the marshes were full of birds and other wild game. And in the year after the death of Cheb, his son Kasib sent some of his human servants, under the command of Madig, grandson of Hallat, to select a site for a new city.

But Madig failed to return, and a search-party of spiders and human warriors could find no trace of him. He had vanished somewhere in the mountains to the north-east. But Kasib refused to believe that a dozen men could disappear without trace, even in the dangerous wastes of Kend, and he sent a second search-party, headed by the famous tracker Tubin. Tubin soon picked up their tracks, and they led him to Madig's last camp site. And a dozen miles from the camp site, he found a single clue – a dagger whose handle had been pushed into the damp earth, so that the blade pointed towards the Grey Mountains in the west. Madig's wife identified it as her husband's dagger, and said that he always kept it strapped to the inside of his leg, above the left ankle.

Tubin concluded that Madig's party had been attacked in the middle of the night, and overpowered without a struggle. Then they had been taken away towards the west. They must have halted briefly – perhaps to eat breakfast – so that Madig had an opportunity to draw the dagger from its sheath above his ankle, and leave it pointing in the direction of their march. He had driven the handle into the earth, to make sure that whoever found it would know it had been placed there deliberately, and not dropped by accident.

Yet all Tubin's skill could find no further trace of the

party. Throughout that day and the next they marched towards the Grey Mountains, without discovering even the remains of an encampment. And in the barren foothills of the Grey Mountains, they decided to abandon the search and return home.

Kasib concluded that Madig had been attacked by wandering nomads, perhaps fugitive survivors from one of the armies he had conquered. But although spider balloons searched the wastes of Kend and every habitable valley in the Grey Mountains, they found no sign of human habitation.

Before that summer came to an end, a guard on the walls of Cibilla sighted a lone man, dressed in a grey cloak, stumbling across the plain towards the town. Before the stranger could pass through the gate, he collapsed in a swoon, and lay face downward like a corpse. He was carried to a nearby house and placed in a bed. It was only when the captain of the guard went to look at the stranger that he recognized him as Madig. The face was so pale and emaciated that he looked like a living death's head.

Yet when he regained consciousness, Madig refused to tell his story, declaring that this was for the ear of the Death Lord alone. By this time, Kasib the Warrior had returned to his capital, and as soon as he was strong enough, Madig was sent to the spider city under escort. There he was taken immediately into the presence of the Death Lord. But what passed between them remained a secret, for Qisib and all his fellow counsellors were sent from the room. Qisib was allowed to return when the meeting was over, and he observed that Madig seemed weary and heartsick, while the Death Lord looked grim and thoughtful.

By the end of that day, Madig had sickened with a fever, so that he was unable to stand upright. He was lodged in a room at the top of the Death Lord's palace, and even his father – also called Hallat – was forbidden to see him. Finally, when Hallat heard that Madig was close to death, he cast himself to the ground before the Death Lord and begged to be allowed to take leave of his son. The Death Lord granted his request, and allowed him to sit by Madig's death bed. No one learned what passed between them; but a week after Madig's death, his father followed him to the grave. Qisib was with him when he died – for Hallat, like his own father, was a friend rather than a servant – and saw that the loss of his son had deprived him of the will to live. The last words he spoke to Qisib were: 'My son has been condemned to death.'

When the Death Lord next returned to Cibilla in the hot season, he found the town in a state of panic. In the course of a year, thirty more of his human servants had disappeared. Some had been shepherds who had been tending their flocks in the foothills. But others had been taken at night from the city itself; one man had even been kidnapped from his home while his wife and two sons were asleep. The guard had been doubled, and slaves began to build an embankment of earth around the town. And still men continued to disappear without trace. What caused so much disquiet was that no one had even caught a glimpse of the kidnappers.

It was Qisib who suggested that perhaps the enemy was entering the town from the sea. The Death Lord immediately ordered guards to patrol the shore line. Yet on that very night, two of the guards disappeared – one from the embankment, one from the seashore. When the Death Lord learnt of this latest outrage, he sent a hundred spider balloons to scour the surrounding country, as far as the Grey Mountains. But it was Tubin the Tracker, working alone, who found the body of one of the guards, buried in a shallow grave within a mile of the town. Both arms had been cut off at the elbow, and both legs removed at the knees. This was the only body that was ever found.

Now the Death Lord fell into a rage, and swore revenge. (This, Niall realized, was a considerable admission; unlike men, spiders were ashamed of strong emotion; it was a point of honour never to admit to it.) He called together all his counsellors – of whom Qisib was the oldest and most respected – and announced that he would search out the enemy and destroy him. Overawed by his wrath – as well as sharing his anger – most of them agreed that the enemy must be punished at all cost. Only Qisib, and an old general named Amalek, advised caution. Qisib felt that an enemy who was so skilled in concealment was more dangerous than the Death Lord realized. But Kasib was so angry that their advice was ignored.

And since everyone agreed that the enemy must be hiding in the Grey Mountains, and since it had always been Kasib's intention to lay claim to all the northern lands, Amalek was ordered to assemble an army of thousands of spiders and human warriors. These were gathered on the plain of Cibilla, then marched north to the Valley of the Great Lake. The human warriors marched along the coastal plain, while wolf spiders scaled the mountains and searched every valley. (Niall could imagine the tireless wolf spiders clambering up and down mountains as if they were hillocks.) Four days later, the army regrouped on the shores of the Great Lake, and prepared to begin the invasion of the northern mountains. The human soldiers, under Amalek, would march up the western coastal strip; the wolf spiders would once again scour the mountains and valleys; the death spiders, under Kasib the Warrior, would march eastward to the river valley that gave access to the wastes of Kend.

On the day before the armies of Kasib prepared to

march northward, the weather was stifling and humid, without a breath of wind. But in the late afternoon, the sun disappeared behind a great black cloud, and a cold wind sprang up from the south-east. By early evening the wind had turned into a gale, and the rain was so heavy that it beat the canvas tents of the foot soldiers to the ground. Kasib gave the order for the army to take shelter under the southern flank of the mountains, where a great cliff offered some refuge from the wind. Kasib himself, together with his counsellors and commanders, crossed the river on a pontoon bridge built by his engineers, and struggled to the north side of the valley – the wind was now so strong that they had to cling together to avoid being blown away – and took shelter in the mysterious city carved into the face of the cliff. There, from inside a deserted palace, they saw the pontoon bridge swept away by the torrent. The Death Lord was unconcerned, convinced that the storm would soon blow itself out. But by midnight, the gale was stronger than ever. In the early hours of the morning, they heard the sound that Qisib had feared – for the sixth sense told him that they were on the brink of disaster: the thunder of waters as the lake burst its bank. Qisib had already shut his mind to the misery being endured by the spiders exposed to the storm, but now he was overwhelmed by their anguish as the torrent struck them and smashed them against the rocky wall of the mountain. Within a minute, all had been destroyed; the force of the water swept the valley clean, leaving behind not a single trace of the mighty army that had been encamped there.

By dawn the next day, the rain and the wind had ceased, but the whole valley had turned into a brown river that ran towards the sea. The Death Lord and his retainers were forced to spend another day and night in the deserted city before the waters had subsided enough to permit their escape. The sun now blazed down on a deserted wilderness of mud.

The Death Lord was in a dangerous situation, and he knew it. Unlike human beings, spiders possess little imagination, and are therefore disinclined to exaggerate their problems by brooding on them. Yet it was clear to Kasib that he had lost most of his army, and that if his human subjects should hear about this and decide to revolt, the spiders would be annihilated. But then, since there were no survivors, there was no one who might carry the story back to the ears of men. This is why Kasib the Warrior decided to return to the spider city claiming a great victory in the north, and keeping silent about the disaster. For months afterwards the bodies of men and spiders were cast up along the coast on the incoming tide; but these bodies were instantly burned by squads of slaves, to prevent knowledge of the disaster from becoming known among men.

The strategem worked. Men never learned of what had happened in the Valley of the Dead, and the Death Lord continued to reign as if he had a million warriors at his command.

But the unknown enemy from the north continued to make incursions into the realm of the Spider Lord, killing shepherds, kidnapping guards, even destroying a death spider with their arrows. No one ever saw them – they seemed to possess the gift of invisibility. This is why, on the advice of his counsellor Qisib the Wise, the Death Lord decided to build a great wall across the Valley of the Dead, a wall that was too high even for humans to scale. It took half a century to build and cost the lives of twenty thousand slaves. (In the time of Qisib's successor Greeb, it led to a slave revolt that ended in the death of thousands of spiders and their human servants.) Before it was half-completed, Qisib had passed into the realm of the unliving. But from the moment the building began, the incursions ceased, and the Death Lord and his descendants were able to live in peace.

The voice of Qisib became silent. Every spider present was deeply moved by his narrative. The images of destruction were so vivid that it was as if they had all been present when the lake burst its banks and destroyed so many lives within seconds. None would ever forget the image of the valley on the morning after the catastrophe, a waste of brown-black mud and pools of standing water. (Qisib's mind had conveyed it exactly as he had seen it, and again Niall was amazed at the photographic accuracy of detail in the spider imagination.) Suddenly aware once more of his surroundings, Niall realized that the tiny chamber had become intolerably hot and stuffy. Yet this seemed unimportant compared to the significance of the story he had just heard.

He made a bow of acknowledgement and thanks, constrained only by the fact that he had almost no room to move.

'I thank you, my lord. I wish I could persuade you to preserve these stories in writing.'

Qisib was obviously puzzled.

'You mean the use of marks that signify speech?'

'Yes.'

'What purpose would that serve? We already communicate without the need for speech.'

'Of course. But because you communicate with your minds, you have kept no records. No spider in this city knows the history of how the great wall came to be built, or how the armies of Kasib the Warrior were destroyed in the Valley of the Dead. Do these things deserve to be forgotten?'

'But they are not forgotten. They are in my brain. That is why they keep me alive.'

'And do you want to be kept alive?'

'No.' A world of sadness was compressed into the syllable. 'I would prefer to be allowed to remain in the land of the unliving.'

Niall was unable to restrain his curiosity.

'What is it like to be dead?'

'Unfortunately, I cannot remember. As soon as I enter this world, I lose all memory of that other realm, like a dreamer who wakes from sleep. But I know, from my reluctance to enter this world, that the one I have left must be very beautiful.'

'But would you not like to be allowed to remain there?'

'No, for I have promised to remain alive, so that my memories shall never be lost.'

'But if your memories were preserved in writing, you would be absolved of your promise.'

'That is impossible.' Qisib spoke with conviction.

'It is true that writing could not capture the richness of your memories. But it could duplicate all the essential facts.' Sensing Qisib's objection, he went on quickly: 'Listen to me. There was a time when human beings did not possess writing. But they possessed speech, and minstrels and storytellers memorized accounts of great deeds, and kept them alive for generation after generation. Then writing was invented, and it became possible to keep records. From that time on, man was able to know his own history. Now all the known history of the human race is contained in the records of the white tower.'

Qisib was impressed. 'That must take many words.'

'Yes. Every page contains many words. And every book contains many pages. And every library contains many books.' Niall accompanied these words with images that made his meaning clear.

Qisib seemed appalled.

'That would be a labour of eternity.'

Niall, unaccustomed to expressing ideas, felt over-whelmed with frustration.

'You do not understand. You spiders dislike the idea because you think it sounds boring. You live in the present moment, and find it so interesting that you have no concern for the past. That is a kind of laziness.' In terms of spider etiquette, Niall was being appallingly rude; but he was so concerned with what he had to say that this seemed unimportant. 'Human beings are also lazy, but there have always been a few among them who were not lazy. It was these men who kept the records of history, and made maps of the stars in the sky, and studied the laws of geometry – all activities that most human beings consider boring. That is how men came to build great cities and to conquer the earth – by doing things that you consider boring. It is only by doing things that they consider boring that men cease to be slaves and learn to become masters.' As he spoke, he was despairingly conscious that his words were inadequate, and that no spider could understand what he was trying to say. It was only when he was finished that he realized that all the spiders in the room were listening to him with almost breathless attention; only then did it dawn upon him that, because he spoke with such passionate sincerity, they regarded his words as a message from the goddess herself.

In the silence that followed, Niall was aware that they were absorbing what he had said, and reflecting on its meaning. Finally Qisib said:

'It would not be easy to transcribe my memories in human language.'

'No. But it would be easier than you think. In the white tower there are machines that can read the mind. They could store the contents of your memory so that they would never be lost.'

'The Death Lord would never grant his permission.'

'That is unnecessary. *I* am the lord of this city.' It embarrassed Niall to make this assertion, but he felt there was no alternative. 'It is I who decide these things.'

Qisib turned an astonished gaze on Asmak.

'Is this true?'

'Yes, lord. He is the emissary of the goddess and therefore the ruler of this city.'

'And his will can overrule that of the Spider Lord?'

'Yes, lord.'

Qisib mastered his astonishment; not to have done so would have been considered unmannerly. He addressed Niall with the formal respect due to one in authority.

'Forgive me, sire. I did not realize who you were.'

Niall replied with a mental gesture signifying that it was unimportant.

But Qisib was still troubled.

'My vow to remain alive was made under solemn oath . . .'

Niall interrupted:

'By the authority vested in me by the goddess, I have the power to absolve you of that vow.'

Qisib considered this in silence. When he spoke again, it was obvious that he had come to a decision.

'Then you also have the power to absolve me of my promise about what passed between Madig and Kasib the Warrior.'

Niall asked with surprise:

'You learned the secret, then?'

'The Death Lord finally spoke of it on the night of the great storm, as we waited for the dawn in the Valley of the Dead. He was deeply troubled by the disaster, and needed someone to whom he could unburden his soul. Since I was the only one to share the secret, I was sworn to silence. But there are no secrets that may not be revealed to the emissary of the goddess.'

Niall's heart began to beat faster. But he restrained his eagerness and remained silent – to show that he had no desire to force Qisib to speak against his will.

The account that followed was couched in the language of images and sensations. Since Qisib himself had not been present during the events he described, it lacked the pictorial clarity of his earlier narrative; yet Niall was fascinated to observe how even this twice-told tale – recounted by Madig to the Death Lord, then by the Death Lord to Qisib – still possessed the authenticity of direct experience.

Qisib described how, sleeping in a sheltered valley in the waste of Kend, Madig and his companions had been attacked in the hour before dawn, and overwhelmed before they could defend themselves. They never saw the faces of the attackers, for they were blindfolded, and warned that if they made any attempt to remove them, they would be instantly killed. On the second day their captors carried out the threat and cut the throat of a man called Rolf the Wheelwright, because they said he was trying to peep underneath his blindfold.

For six days they marched across rough and uneven country, and picked their way across marshes that had a stench of decay. Their captors spoke very little, even amongst themselves. At the end of the sixth day, they halted at dusk in a grassy valley; in the distance Madig could hear a roaring noise like a waterfall or a river in full spate. The sound was a long way off, but Madig's hearing was exceptionally keen. The prisoners were then given a sweet-tasting drink, and soon after this, Madig began to feel sleepy. But he had guessed that the drink was a drug, and struggled hard to resist its effects. So he was still awake when their captors were joined by a band of men who came from the direction of the rushing torrent. This was the last thing Madig remembered before he was finally overcome by sleep.

When Madig woke up, he was on a kind of stretcher, and was being carried downhill. The sound of the rushing water was now very close. Soon after this, he saw daylight under the blindfold, and knew that it must be dawn. A few hours later their captors gave them a meal, then more of the sweet drink, which sent them to sleep again. But this time Madig succeeded in spilling half his drink down his chest, so he was able to remember something of the next part of the journey. They embarked on a boat and crossed a lake or a wide river. Then they were placed in chariots drawn by animals, and they travelled throughout the rest of the day. At evening, they were given another meal, and more of the sweet drink. Again Madig tried to spill it; but this time his captors noticed what he was doing, and he was given a brutal beating that left him bruised all over. He was not sorry when, after being forced to drink a large goblet of the sweet liquid, he lost consciousness again.

He awoke to find himself on a hard bed in a damp prison cell, with almost no light. The blindfold had been removed; but when he tried to question his jailer, he was warned that he would be killed if he opened his mouth again. Since he knew that these men would not hesitate to carry out their threats, he took care from then on to behave like a mute.

For many days he saw no one but the surly and taciturn man who brought him food. But one day, a girl came into his prison cell, followed by a man carrying a bucket of hot water. The man ordered him to undress, then the girl washed him from head to foot, and trimmed and combed his hair and beard. Madig guessed from these preparations that he was about to be taken before some important dignitary – probably the ruler himself.

After being washed, he was ordered to dress. Then he was blindfolded again, and led through echoing stone corridors and out of the jail. And although he could see nothing but a crack of daylight under the blindfold, he could tell that he was being escorted through the streets of a fairly large town or city, for the road underfoot was hard and smooth. He was also aware that there were other people in these streets, for he could hear their footsteps. Yet the strange thing was that it was all so silent that, although he strained his ears, he could hear no sound of voices. His companions also remained silent, and Madig was afraid to open his mouth.

Now they mounted a flight of steps, and he heard the creaking of a massive door, and the sound of it closing behind them. They crossed a stone-flagged floor, and he knew from the echo of his footsteps that they were in a large hallway; after that they passed through another great door, and into a chamber whose atmosphere was as cold as ice. Madig sensed that his companions had left him and that he was now in the presence of the ruler of this city. And although Madig was famous for his bravery, he now found himself over-come by a strange feeling of dread, as if in the presence of a dangerous predator, so that it was hard to control the trembling of his limbs. Then a soft voice spoke from a place that seemed to be in front of him and above his head – Madig guessed that the ruler of this city was seated on a throne at the top of a flight of steps.

'I want you to carry a message to the ruler of the spiders.' The voice had a whispering, throaty sound, as if there was something wrong with the vocal chords. 'Are you listening?'

'Yes, lord.'

'I want you to tell your master that these lands belong to me, and that I shall destroy anyone who invades them. Repeat that.'

'I am to tell my master . . .'

'Lower your voice. I am not deaf.'

'No, lord.' Madig was disconcerted; he had seemed to himself to be speaking in his normal voice. Now he lowered it to little more than a whisper. 'I am to tell my master that these lands belong to you, and that you will destroy anyone who invades them.'

'Good. You may also tell him that I am a magician, and that I can render this city invisible, so that it would serve no purpose to try to find it. Do you understand?'

'Yes, lord. I am sure my master . . .'

'Now go!'

'Yes, lord.' But as he turned to go, the hoarse voice said: 'Wait.' Madig heard the soft swish of garments descending towards him, but no sound of footsteps.

'You will also tell your master that I shall hold your companions as hostages, and that unless his answer is satisfactory, they will all die.'

'Yes, lord.' Madig's heart sank, for he already knew that Kasib the Warrior would be enraged by the threat, and that therefore his companions were already doomed. Yet at least he would be free to avenge them . . .

But, as if reading his thoughts, the unseen man continued:

'You will also die. My arm is long and I do not release my grip.'

Madig's hand was taken in a hand that was cold and strangely rough – it reminded him of the hand of a leper, covered with scales of decaying skin. As the fingers closed, Madig screamed with pain; the grip was so powerful that he felt it could have crushed the bones of his hand into powder.

Now the unseen man brought his mouth close to Madig's ear.

'One more thing.' And as he spoke, Madig realized, with a shock of horror, that although the mouth was within an inch of his ear, he could feel no breath. 'Tell your master that if he ignores my warning, his people will suffer a catastrophe that will make the massacres of Ivar the Cruel seem insignificant.' He released Madig's hand.

'Yes, lord.'

'You have one month – thirty days. If you return here with a satisfactory answer before that time, you and your companions will be spared. If not, you will all die.'

As the cold hand released his, Madig's senses felt as if they were being sucked from him. When he opened his eyes again, the blindfold had been removed, and he was back in his prison cell. He noticed that his right hand was covered with blood, and that his arm felt cold and numb. Later that evening, after supper, he fell into an exhausted slumber. When he woke up, he was again being carried on a stretcher, this time up an irregular slope, and was again blindfolded. In the distance he could hear the roaring of a river. The glimmer of light that penetrated the bottom of the blindfold was fitful, and he guessed that his captors were carrying torches, and that they were again travelling by night.

For the next six days he was made to march over rough and difficult terrain, and was always so exhausted by the end of the day that he slept heavily until aroused the next morning. He noticed that his companions spoke only in the briefest of monosyllables, but that for most of time, they were silent.

One morning, Madig was awakened by the sun on his face. It seemed to him that he had been allowed to sleep much longer than usual. He lay there, listening for some indication that his captors were preparing a meal, but the silence finally convinced him that he was alone. He pushed up the blindfold, and saw that he was lying in a wide valley which he recognized – it would later become known as the Valley of the Dead. The sun was high in the sky, and his companions were nowhere to be seen. But they had left a cloth containing food and drink, and this convinced him that he was free. It took him two days to make his way back to Cibilla.

By now, the numbness in his arm had crept into his shoulder, and he was suffering from a permanent fever. Madig calculated that he had twenty days still to live. This is why he refused the help of doctors, and insisted on being taken to the city of the Death Lord. There he was conducted immediately into the presence of Kasib the Warrior, where he delivered the message from the unknown enemy. The Death Lord listened silently, and when Madig had finished, questioned him closely about his period in captivity – how many days' march lay between the wastes of Kend and the stronghold of the enemy, and how far he had marched before being freed. From these questions, Madig knew that the Death Lord was contemplating an attack on the realm of the enemy, and that he himself was doomed to die. He felt no resentment, for he knew that it was impossible that the Death Lord should submit to the threats and insults of a mere human being.

Physicians attempted to cure Madig as he lay on his sick bed; but none could discover what was wrong with him. The sensation of paralysis had reached his chest, then began to pass downward towards his feet. The fever made him delirious, and he talked endlessly of the companions he had left in the hands of the enemy. And, exactly as the enemy foretold, he died on the thirtieth day.

Hundreds of spider balloons scoured the Grey Mountains from the wastes of Kend to the Lake of Silence, but found no trace of any city, or even so much as a shepherd's hut. By that time the first snows of the winter had begun to fall, and Kasib the Warrior knew that his revenge would have to be delayed until the following summer. And it was precisely one year later that the armies of the Death Lord were destroyed in the Valley of the Dead, the threat of the unknown enemy was fulfilled.

Qisib concluded:

'This was the story told to me by Kasib the Warrior, as we waited for daylight in the Valley of the Dead. He wanted me to reassure him that the disaster was not his fault. But for once, I was unable to offer my lord any comfort.' He fell into reflective silence, and Niall was also silent, understanding that, even after death, Qisib could still experience grief. Qisib asked finally: 'Well, chosen of the goddess, are your questions answered?'

'All but one, my lord.'

'Ask it.'

'What do you think was the ultimate purpose of this unknown enemy from the north?'

Qisib reflected for a long time. It was evident that this was a question he had never considered.

'To express his hatred and envy of our people. What else could it be?'

Niall shook his head; the answer seemed too simple. Qisib observed that he was troubled.

'What is your own explanation?'

'I do not have one. Yet my reason tells me that there must be one.'

There was a long silence, which was finally broken by Qisib.

'You must teach my people to use the powers of reason. We do not think enough.' He added after a pause: 'And now it is too late.'

'Not too late, my lord.'

'Too late for me, at any rate. For now I must return to the kingdom of the dead. Before I go, have you anything further to ask me?'

Niall considered this. 'No, lord.'

'Then I have one more thing to say to you. The land of the unliving is timeless, and the past is as the future. When I saw you, I knew that you would be making a dangerous journey, and that you would come close to despair. When that happens, remember that an unbroken spirit is unconquerable.'

'But . . .'

Even as Niall began to speak, he realized that Qisib had already gone. He had vanished with the abruptness of a bursting bubble, leaving all Niall's questions suspended in mid-air. It was only when Niall observed that the three wolf spiders were lying on the floor, their legs bunched underneath them in attitudes of total exhaustion that he understood how much living energy had been sucked from their bodies, and why Qisib – like Cheb – had vanished so abruptly. He also observed that the room had become strangely cold, and that the damp walls were now covered with a thin layer of frost and ice.

After a silence Asmak asked: 'Shall we return, my lord?'

'Should we not wait until these three have recovered?'

'That would take a long time – perhaps two days.'

'Then lead the way.'

Asmak turned, and vanished into the cleft in the rock. Niall followed, and realized with surprise that his claustrophobia had vanished, and that he was leaving this strange place with regret.

The moment he found himself back on the solid floor, he became aware that something strange was happening. Asmak was standing silently, as if reluctant to move, and the atmosphere seemed to be permeated with a peculiar, tingling quality, as if the air was full of tiny bubbles which burst as they came into contact with the skin. It was like the spray from some cataract of sheer vital energy, or like the ringing of a million tiny bells. Niall had experienced the sensation before, in the city of the bombardier beetles. He knew it was associated with the life-giving energies of the empress plant – the plant that the spiders knew as Nuada, goddess of the Great Delta. Every day at dawn, the plant transmitted waves of pure vitality – the same vitality that had caused the abnormal development of the spiders and other insect life.

But what was now happening was that the young spiders were absorbing these energies, and then, by a process of mutual interaction, combining them together, and then releasing them into the atmosphere of the sacred cave. It was as if each individual spider allowed himself to become filled to the brim with a vital fluid, and then emptied this fluid into some communal storage vessel. The storage vessel was the cave itself. In this way, they were able to conserve the living energy that was necessary to maintain the memory cells of long-dead spiders like Cheb the Mighty and Kasib the Warrior, and to prevent their spirits from taking up permanent residence in the land of the unliving.

Asmak himself was caught in this torrential flow of energy, reduced to immobility and ecstasy by its tremendous vibrations, which seemed to shake the cave like the notes of some mighty organ. Niall could also sense this energy, but on a far lower level; its vibrational rate was too low to affect humans, except in a state of deep relaxation; so that although he was able to sense its power, he was unable to respond to it. Yet he recognized that Asmak himself was too old to respond with the same total involvement as the young spiders; the development of his powers of control had alienated him from the voice of the goddess. Now Niall understood why young spiders had been chosen as the guardians of the mighty dead; they alone could respond with undivided intensity. Niall envied them.

Now the energies slowly subsided, until they were like a sound receding into the distance. When it vanished, there was a strange silence, like the silence after a heavy storm, when the only sound is the intermittent fall of a raindrop. Niall was leaning back against the wall of the cave, so blissfully relaxed that he had no desire to move. It would have been pleasant to lie on the hard floor and fall asleep. Yet he was also aware that a part of his being remained detached, craving some higher fulfilment than this dreamlike sense of emotional plenitude.

It was Asmak who was the first to stir. As his mind re-established contact, Niall realized suddenly that he had been standing in darkness; the intensity of the experience had made sight superfluous. Now once more he could 'see' the sacred cave, and sense the presence of the young spiders hidden among its overhanging webs. With an effort, he forced himself to stand upright, and to return to the world of normal consciousness.

Asmak also freed himself from the spell of the goddess; his enormous will-power enabled him to do this without effort.

'Shall we return, my lord?' Like Dravig, he had sensed that Niall preferred to dispense with formality. When Niall made a gesture of assent, he turned and led the way across the floor of the cave.

Niall had expected to be taken back to the low doorway through which they had entered; instead, Asmak led Niall in the opposite direction, along the wall towards the far end of the cave. They had to circumnavigate veils of cobweb that concealed entrances to the tombs of spider lords and counsellors since the days of Cheb the Mighty. The cave extended further than Niall had suspected; what he had supposed to be its far wall was pierced by a low arch, on the other side of which were irregular pinnacles of some sedimentary rock, which rose like immense stalagmites towards an invisible ceiling. Beyond these, the floor sloped, and they had to wade ankle deep through freezing water, which seemed to be flowing from a hole at the base of the wall. The moisture, Niall recognized, was essential if the corpses of the dead spiders were not to crumble into dust.

They were now advancing towards a vertical rock face, in which Niall could perceive no obvious exits. He was within a few feet of it before he recognized that a sloping ramp or ledge ran upwards in a roughly diagonal line.

Asmak halted.

'Would you prefer to go first?'

'No. You go first.'

As soon as they began to mount, he regretted his decision. The ledge was scarcely a foot wide, and its surface was rough and irregular. If his foot slipped, he would be hurtling downward before Asmak could save him. But it was too late to change his mind. Spiders attached a great deal of importance to face-saving, and if he reversed his decision, Asmak would be more embarrassed than he was. So he stepped on to the ledge, and cautiously followed Asmak into the darkness.

Spiders, he soon realized, had no fear of heights; it made no difference to them whether they were ten feet off the ground or a thousand. For a spider whose leg span was normally eight feet, bunching them together on to a narrow ledge should have been uncomfortable; but even in this awkward position, Asmak moved swiftly and unerringly. Niall, on the other hand, felt increasing alarm as his feet stumbled on the irregular surface. Within a few minutes they were hundreds of feet above the floor of the cave, and the ramp ahead of them seemed to stretch endlessly into the darkness. The rock face was rough, but afforded no hand-holds. Niall had never liked heights; they filled him with an instinctive dread over which his mind had little control. Now his alarm made his legs feel weak; this was even more terrifying than wriggling into a narrow tunnel in the rock. He pressed his back to the wall, and walked with a sideways motion, glad that Asmak was looking straight ahead.

Five minutes later the ledge became narrower still, and it struck him that his alarm was endangering his life more than the difficulties of the ascent; thought of the immense drop below flooded his bloodstream with adrenalin, making him feel weak and light-headed. At this point he recalled the thought mirror which he had left behind in his room, and experienced a despairing feeling of regret that he had forgotten to take it. But the thought brought a momentary sense of concentration which was like sudden relief from nausea. He wrinkled his forehead and clenched his fists, trying to recapture the feeling of control induced by the thought mirror. At the same time, he told himself that nothing could be more stupid than terminating his career through weakness and loss of nerve.

Then, in a flash, he saw the answer. What he recognized, with sudden total certainty, was that he was not here by chance. What had led him into his present situation was some kind of destiny – the same destiny that had brought him to the spider city, and enabled him to free his fellow humans from their slavery. If he fell now, it would be because he was destined to fall. And that, he saw, was an absurdity. Whatever he was destined for, it was not to die by accident.

The sense of panic evaporated, and was replaced by an almost dreamlike feeling of confidence and certainty. Suddenly, it seemed to him that he understood Qisib's last words – that an unbroken spirit is unconquerable. It was exactly as if a fence had been erected between himself and the abyss. It now seemed to him that the ledge was wide enough for two persons. He ceased to press his back against the wall, and once more began to walk forward in the normal manner.

Asmak said: 'We are almost there. If you will excuse me, I will guide your footsteps until the worst part is over.'

At this point, the rock face bulged outwards, and a series of foot- and hand-holds had been cut into it. But the slope of the bulge meant that these were narrow and inadequate; as Niall climbed up after Asmak, he became aware that the slightest movement towards the left would cause him to lose his grip. Asmak's guidance was necessary because the holds were at irregular intervals, and it was sometimes necessary to place both feet in the same narrow step to reach the next hand-hold. Towards the top of the bulge, their movement ceased to be diagonal, and became almost horizontal. But at least Niall felt that he was in Asmak's hands, and that the spider had no intention of allowing him to fall.

A moment later, they had surmounted the bulge, and Niall's feet were once again firmly planted on the narrow ledge. It struck him as amusing that he should feel as relieved as if they were back on solid ground.

A hundred yards further on, the ledge suddenly widened. The rock above bulged outward, so that it was necessary to crouch to avoid banging his head, but this was a minor inconvenience. A few yards further, he became aware that there was a rock face on his left as well as his right, and that they had entered a narrow tunnel that smelt of mould. There was another smell which he recognized with relief – that of damp earth. The air also became noticeably warmer. Now the roof of the tunnel was supported by wooden props, and the ground underfoot had been cut into a series of steps, also reinforced with wooden boards. Moments later, his eyes were dazzled by an explosion of light that made him close them tightly; he stumbled on a step and fell to his knees.

Asmak said: 'I am sorry, lord. I should have warned you.' The light vanished; when Niall cautiously opened his eyes, they were in a green twilight. Then Asmak again moved aside the curtain of vegetation, and the tunnel entrance was illuminated by the light of the rising sun.

He had to crawl out on his hands and knees – the entrance, which was in a steeply-sloping bank, was hidden by bushes that grew close to the ground, and concealed by a large moss-covered stone. The warm air was full of an odour that resembled new-mown hay, mingled with the scent of honeysuckle and gorse. Even before he pushed his way out into the daylight, Niall knew where he was; the sight of the banks of rich vegetation, with their red and yellow flowers, only confirmed it. He was standing at a spot within a hundred yards of the warehouse that Skorbo had used as a larder, and the air was full of the tingling vitality that was like a fine spray of water.

Now, suddenly, Niall understood why the flowers here bloomed in midwinter. It was because this spot stood directly above the sacred cave, and its earth was permeated by the tremendous energies that were stored there. The life-force of the goddess created a kind of permanent springtide. This was also the reason that Skorbo had chosen the site for his larder: its energies kept his paralysed victims alive.

It came as something of a surprise to find that it was already dawn – although Niall should have realized it when the young spiders were absorbing and storing the life-force of the empress plant. The total darkness of the sacred cave had prevented him from making the connection. Now he realized with astonishment that he had spent the whole night underground. The time had passed so quickly that it seemed no more than two hours.

Asmak said: 'Shall I summon a chariot to take you back to your palace?'

'No. It's such a lovely morning that I think I'll walk. But first I'd like to rest for a moment.'

'Of course.'

A patch of rich green lawn between the flowering shrubs looked very inviting; the thick, springy grass reminded Niall of the Great Delta. He lay down with his head against the root of a tree, and closed his eyes. The sun seemed to caress the skin of his cheeks and forehead. Buoyed up on a feeling of peace that was like a rising wave, he was carried into sleep.

He was aroused by a vague feeling of discomfort; the sun had moved around a few degrees, leaving him in shadow, and a cool breeze had sprung up from the east. A glance at the sky told him that he had been asleep for at least two hours.

As he sat up, he realized that the spider standing a few feet away was not Asmak, but his son Grel. The glossy black hairs on the young spider's body shone like ebony in the morning sunlight.

'Where is your father?'

'He apologizes for having to leave. He has to be at work.'

Niall yawned and rubbed his eyes. His stomach rumbled; he had never felt so hungry in his life.

'Thank you for waiting.'

'Thanks are unnecessary. It would be unlawful to leave you unguarded.'

'I did not intend to fall asleep – only to close my eyes. Are you not tired?'

'No. The sacred cave always makes me feel more awake.'

'You have been before then?'

'Seven times. But never before have I stood in the presence of Cheb the Mighty, or his counsellor Qisib.'

As Niall received these words – transmitted directly, without the encumbrance of language – he was able to see into the young spider's mind, and to recognize that the experiences of the past few hours had made a profound difference. The Grel of the previous evening had been little more than a thoughtless child; this Grel was almost an adult.

They were walking past Skorbo's larder, and Niall paused to look in through the open door. The warehouse was completely empty; not even a single strand of web now dangled from the beams that supported the ceiling. Only a red stain on the concrete floor – the blood of the bull spider – remained as a reminder of what had happened so recently.

The air was soft and warm, and heavy with the scent

of flowers; he realized that the wind was blowing from the south. As they walked back along the sandstone-coloured road, which looked as if it had been built only yesterday, past glowing banks of flowers, Niall became aware that his companion was bursting with a desire to ask him a question, but was forbidden by spider proto-col to address a superior without being spoken to first. In an older spider, this desire would have been unde-tectable; but Grel had not yet learned the art of self-concealment. Niall asked:

'What is it you want to know?'

If Grel had been a human child, he would have blushed. But the intensity of his curiosity overcame his embarrassment.

'Now you know the history of the enemy, do you intend to seek him out?'

Niall shook his head.

'What purpose would that serve?'

'But the Lord Qisib said you would be making a perilous journey.'

This was a point Niall had already considered.

'That is true. But I have already made a perilous journey – out of the sacred cave.'

But Grel was still unsatisfied.

'The Lord Cheb also wished you a safe voyage.'

Niall had noticed that, but assumed that it was simply a form of polite leave-taking. He said firmly:

'It is not my intention to seek out this magician. That would be foolish and very dangerous. It is obvious that he wants to be left alone.'

'Then why does he not leave *us* alone?'

Because Grel was so young and so obviously curious, Niall felt an impulse to take him into his confidence.

'I believe the enemy has been sending out spies since the days of Cheb the Mighty. He wants to know what is happening in the spider city. But when Skorbo captured two of his spies, and carried them off to his larder, he decided that Skorbo had to die.'

Grel asked: 'But why? What good could it do?'

This was a point that Niall himself had puzzled about during the past two days. If his spies were captured, surely it would be better for the enemy to send more spies, rather than alerting the spiders to his presence? Was it stupidity or miscalculation? Niall found that hard to believe.

'One reason could be that Skorbo himself was a spy.'

'What!' Grel was so staggered that the exclamation was a shriek of protest. 'Skorbo a spy? How is that possible?'

His amazement made Niall feel guilty; he had simply failed to see the implications of what he had just said. For a spider, nothing could be more shocking, more horrifying, than the thought of the treachery of one of their own kind. Human beings are accustomed to being unable to see into one another's minds – even those we love best. But all spiders experience a sense of mutual interaction that is inconceivable to human beings. So the thought of treachery was far worse than the shock a man might feel if he discovered that the wife he adored had been unfaithful, or was planning to murder him. Grel was shaken to his depths.

Niall said gently: 'There is evidence that Skorbo fell into the hands of the enemy, and was enrolled as a spy.'

'But how could he be so wicked?' Grel was almost in tears. 'How could he betray his fellow creatures?'

'I do not know. But the magician can be very persuasive.'

Grel dissented passionately. 'No. Skorbo could only be overcome by a will stronger than his own.'

'Perhaps the magician's will *was* stronger than Skorbo's.'

'I cannot believe that.'

Asmak would have been horrified to hear his son contradicting the emissary of the goddess; but Niall was flattered at this evidence of the young spider's trust.

'Then what do you believe?'

'Perhaps that Skorbo was tortured into submission. It is evident that the enemy is a man of extreme cruelty.'

'He is cunning, certainly. But why do you say he is cruel?'

Grel seemed puzzled by Niall's question.

'Does a benevolent ruler cut out the tongues of his subjects?'

'Who told you that?'

'Why, the lord Qisib himself.'

The mental image of Qisib was followed immediately by an image of Madig being washed and combed in his prison cell. And now Niall could see that, as the girl was trimming his beard, Madig caught a glimpse inside her mouth, and saw that she had no tongue.

Suddenly he understood why they had been speaking at cross-purposes. Qisib had told his story in a series of images. At the time, Niall has felt pleased with himself because he understood so well. Now he realized that his understanding had been crude and imperfect, like someone trying to understand a foreign language. Qisib's 'conversation' had been full of details that Niall had simply failed to notice. Madig's glimpse into the girl's mouth had been only one of these. And as Grel re-created the image of Madig's cell, Niall became aware of many others. He could now sense the atmosphere of suspicion, mistrust and anxiety that reigned in the city of the enemy, and the fear and misery that it created. And as Madig was led, blindfolded, through the streets of the city, Niall realized that the silence was the silence of dread.

He also understood many other things: how, when

the magician had told Madig that his companions would die if he failed to bring back a satisfactory answer, he meant that they would die slowly and painfully. Now it was clear that, from the beginning of the interview, the magician had set out to instil a feeling of terror and of danger, so that Madig would convey this to the Spider Lord.

Grel added with satisfaction: 'But he made one mistake. He failed to understand that no Spider Lord would give way to threats.'

Niall was about to reply when he was struck by the import of Grel's words. The insight that followed was accompanied by an odd sense of breathlessness, and a tingling of the hairs of the scalp.

'Perhaps it was not a mistake. Perhaps the enemy intended to anger the Spider Lord.'

'But why?'

Niall was suddenly astonished that it had taken him so long to grasp anything so obvious.

'Why do you think the attacks ceased as soon as the Lord Qisib began building the wall?'

Grel said hesitantly:

'Perhaps because it was too well guarded.'

'So was the town of Cibilla, yet they attacked it.'

'Then what do you believe was the reason?'

'Could it have been because they *wanted* the wall to be built?'

Grel was obviously puzzled by Niall's line of reasoning.

'But the wall was built to keep them out.'

'But it also served the purpose of keeping your people in.'

It took several moments for Grel to grasp the point. When he did so, he gazed at Niall with an air of almost reverential astonishment.

'Truly, you have more discernment than Qisib the

Wise.' Then his mind was beset by doubts: 'Yet how can we be certain of something that happened so long ago?'

'We cannot be certain. But consider what the Lord Qisib told us. First: that Cheb the Mighty sent an expedition to the lands of the north, and learned that the ice had retreated, and that the marshes were full of birds and other wild game. Then Kasib the Warrior sent Madig to select a site for the new city. Was it by chance, do you think, that Madig's party was waylaid and carried into captivity? Or was it because the magician was keeping watch for any sign that the Death Lord was extending his territory, and was determined to prevent him from establishing a new capital in the northlands?'

'But the northlands were the home of Cheb the Mighty. Why should he not return home?'

'Because the ice had retreated. The Death Lord himself told me that when he was born, the world was suffering from a great ice age when the snow fell day and night, and the sky was always dark. In such an age, there would be no temptation to explore. But when the ice melted, the northern lands ceased to be cold and forbidding. And if Kasib the Warrior had established a capital in the wastes of Kend, would he have been contented to rest there? Would he not have turned his attention to the Grey Mountains in the west, with their wide valleys?'

Grel listened with a mixture of astonishment and incredulity. Niall continued:

'The Lord Qisib also told us that when Tubin went in search of Madig, he found only his dagger, which was pointing towards the Grey Mountains. Were his captors so stupid that they failed to notice a dagger driven into the ground? Is it not more probable that they themselves set the dagger there?'

Grel was troubled. 'But why should the enemy tell us where he could be found?'

'As a warning and a message. He was telling the Death Lord: the Grey Mountains are my territory – keep away. But the Death Lord sent hundreds of spider balloons to search the Grey Mountains and the wastes of Kend, making it clear that he regarded them as *his* territory.'

'Then what purpose was served by harassing the city of Cibilla?'

'He knew that this would enrage the Death Lord into launching an attack.'

As Grel grasped the implications of these words, he reacted with shock.

'You are saying that the Death Lord and his army marched into a trap?'

'That would explain many things.'

Grel seemed stunned.

'But how could the enemy cause the great storm?'

'I do not know. But I know that all magicians believe they can control the weather.'

As if in answer to this remark, a low roll of thunder echoed across the city. Niall had been so absorbed in the conversation that he had not even noticed the dark clouds that had drifted across the sun. Now he realized they were close to the main square, and the clouds were reflected in the milky surface of the white tower as if in a mirror. A few moments later, the first light drops of rain spotted the pavement; within seconds, it had turned into a heavy downpour. All over the square, humans and spiders ran for shelter as the hammering of rain turned the pavement into a white mist. When the rain began, they had been within a few yards of the palace; yet by the time they stood under its portico, both were drenched. Waterdrops ran like pearls from

Grel's shiny black coat; some of them also gathered on his many-faceted eyes, so that he was forced to shake his head.

A few minutes later, the downpour had ceased. But the sudden change in the weather had made Niall reflective. It had made him recall the snow that had fallen only three days ago, and how quickly it had vanished. 'All magicians believe they can control the weather . . .' Now his own words were like an echo whose meaning eluded him. Could there be any significance in the fact that Skorbo's death had been accompanied by a fall of snow?

His train of thought was disturbed by the opening of the door. It was Dona, dressed in a cloak with a waterproof hood. Her gaze was so abstracted that for a moment she failed to recognize Niall. When she did, her face brightened.

'Where have you been? We've been looking for you all night.'

'I'm sorry . . .' As he looked into her eyes, he experienced a sudden sense of foreboding. 'Is anything wrong?'

'It's Veig . . .'

His heart turned to lead. 'Is he . . .'

'He has been unconscious since last night.'

As Niall started to follow her inside, he remembered Grel.

'Please come inside and wait. I have to go to my brother.'

He followed her along a corridor and across the courtyard, to the older part of the building; Veig occupied two large rooms on the ground floor.

At first sight, Veig seemed to be dead. He was lying on his back, and the black-bearded face looked pale and thin. His mother was sitting on the side of the bed, with her hand on Veig's forehead; she looked exhausted. Simeon was seated on a chair on the far side of the bed.

Niall went to the bedside, and touched his brother's cheek. He was relieved to find that it was warm. But when he probed Veig's mind, he realized that he was close to death. The fever had disappeared, but so had the determination to live. All conflicts had disappeared; in their place there was a flat calm that was like an endless plane of greyness.

Siris said: 'He was asking for you.'

'I'm sorry.' Her face was as bloodless as Veig's. He felt an overwhelming rush of affection, a desire to take her in his arms and comfort her. 'Why don't you go and rest? I'll sit with Veig.'

'No, I'd rather stay.' He knew she meant that she would never forgive herself if Veig died in her absence.

Once again Niall probed his brother's mind. It was like trying to plunge into a sea of nothingness. This greyness was somehow cold and repellent, resisting all efforts to see beyond it. Even to contemplate it had a numbing effect on his senses. What puzzled Niall was that a sleeping mind should be a mysterious whirlpool of forces, not a closed door. And even as he was about to abandon the effort, he seemed to sense Veig's presence behind the closed door. Then the greyness returned, as uniform as a blanket of snow.

Simeon stood up. 'I'll come back later.' Siris nodded without even raising her head.

Niall followed Simeon from the room.

'Have you any idea of what's wrong?'

'Only that it's not a poison. It's some kind of bacterium.'

'How do you know?'

'It was visible on the microscope slide – it looks like hundreds of black rods.'

'And it came from the blade of the axe?'

'Of course. You saw me take a scraping. But there's something very odd about these black rods. Most bacteria can't survive apart from a living body. But when I dissolved the scrapings in salt solution, it was immediately swarming with bacteria, like a pond full of tadpoles.' He pulled a face. 'And now Veig's bloodstream is full of tadpoles.'

'And do you think they came from Skorbo's blood?'

'It's possible. I just don't know.'

They emerged into the hallway; it was empty except for Grel, who was standing in the centre of the marble floor, with the total immobility that was so characteristic of spiders.

Niall said: 'I am sorry to keep you waiting. My brother is ill.'

Grel said drily: 'That does not surprise me.'

Niall looked at him in astonishment.

'Why do you say that?'

'Because this place is full of evil.'

'Evil!'

'Can you not feel it?'

Niall allowed his mind to blend with that of the young spider. The first thing he noticed was Grel's state of nervous tension, as if he was watching the approach of an enemy. Then, with startling suddenness, he himself was aware of the cause of the tension. It was so obvious that he was surprised that he had failed to notice it earlier. It was the now-familiar sensation that he was in the presence of some dangerous entity. He had experienced this same sense of danger in the presence of the force-field of the pendants. Yet this vibration was subtly different: at once more powerful and less obtrusive.

Niall turned to Simeon.

'Do you know if any strangers have been admitted while I have been away?'

'Not as far as I know. I've been here most of the night.'

As soon as Niall's mind lost contact with that of the spider, the sense of danger receded. Yet because he had been alerted to its presence, he remained aware of it as a disturbing vibration, like something glimpsed out of the corner of the eye.

He asked Grel: 'Is there someone here – some enemy?' He spoke aloud, so that Simeon could understand.

'There is some evil presence. We should summon my father, and have this building surrounded by guards.'

Simeon asked: 'What did he say?'

'He said we should summon the soldiers.'

Simeon looked around at the silent hall; the only sound was the clatter of cooking utensils from the kitchen.

'I think he's imagining things. No one could get past the guard.'

'No, he's speaking the truth. I can sense it too.' He asked Grel: 'Where do you think this enemy is hiding?'

Grel extended his pedipalps like feelers.

'He is upstairs somewhere.'

Niall experienced a cold sensation. He knew that his sisters would now be eating breakfast in the nursery, and that since Dona was in Veig's room, they would probably be alone. As Niall started up the stairs, Simeon said:

'Let me call the guard.'

Niall shook his head. 'If it's a man that shouldn't be necessary.' Even a spider as young as Grel could paralyse a man into immobility.

He paused on the first landing, and tried to soothe his senses into total immobility; but there was too much adrenalin in his bloodstream, and it was impossible. Instead, he stood and waited for Grel to join him. With his pedipalps still extended the spider turned right, and continued on up the second flight of stairs. As he did so, Niall experienced a sudden flash of intuitive certainty: where else would an enemy wait for him but in his own room? And when Grel paused in front of the door of Niall's chamber, and stayed there in a state of uncertainty – the spider claw was not designed to handle doorknobs – Niall tiptoed past him and stood with his ear pressed against the cold wood. There was not the slightest sound from inside. Very slowly and deliberately, he turned the knob and pushed open the door.

His chamber looked so normal that for a moment he was inclined to wonder if they were making some absurd mistake. But the tension in Grel's attitude – he looked like a snake poised to strike – made it clear that he could still sense danger. Since this room was empty, then it must lie either in the bedroom or in Jarita's scullery. The bedroom door was standing slightly ajar; Niall gave it a violent push so that it flew open. A glance inside told him that there was no one there – from this position he could even see under the bed.

As he hesitated, debating whether to investigate the scullery, or to summon the guard, Grel advanced past him and into the bedroom. He crossed the floor in a single stride, and, to Niall's surprise, halted in front of the table at the side of the bed. This contained only an oil lamp, a glass of water, and a neatly folded tunic that had been placed there by Jarita. Yet it was at this tunic that Grel seemed to be directing his attention.

Niall went and stood beside him. 'What is it?' He reached out cautiously, and twitched aside the tunic; all that it covered was the black figurine that he had found in the hide-out of the assassins.

In his relief, he allowed his mind to relax; as soon as he did so, he realized that Grel was not mistaken. This squat black figure, with its frog-like face and bulging eyes, was the source of the force-field that was filling the room with its curious vibration of menace. Moreover, as Niall removed the cloth, the entity seemed to become aware of their presence. In that moment, Niall was gripped by an acute sense of danger. His reaction was instinctive and instantaneous; he struck out and knocked the figurine on to the floor. As his hand touched it, he was convulsed by a feeling of nausea that was like an unutterably foul stench; it was so powerful that it seemed to distort his senses. As he looked round the room for some weapon, his eyes fell on the axe that was standing in the corner beside the wardrobe. It had been there since Simeon had taken scrapings from its blade, and its head was wrapped in a piece of sacking. Fighting off a desire to vomit, Niall tore off the sacking and raised the axe above his head; positioning himself carefully, he brought down the back of the blade with all his strength. It struck the figurine squarely, and the force of the blow almost split the floorboards beneath it. A moment later, he was engulfed by a wave of malevolence that burst over him like a flood of slimy water, the sheer rage of a being who could not believe that someone had dared to attack him.

Incredibly, the figurine was undamaged, although it was lying on its side. Again Niall raised the axe, this time turning the blade-side downward. The cutting edge struck the figurine a jarring blow, breaking it into two pieces. One half flew across the room to strike the wall; the other disappeared under the bed. In that moment the malevolent presence vanished as abruptly as a light that is extinguished. The stench also vanished – so completely that it seemed incredible that it had left no trace behind.

Simeon said: 'What in the name of the goddess was that?' His voice sounded breathless.

He bent and picked up the piece of stone that had

come to rest near his foot. It was the head of the figurine, and it had been severed in such a way that half the
back was still attached to it. Niall dropped on to his
hands and knees, and recovered the other half of the
figurine from under the bed.

Simeon took it, and studied it closely.

'This isn't just a toad. It's some kind of god.'

'How do you know?'

Simeon pointed to the tiny humanoid feet, which
now struck Niall as oddly repellent.

'Because it's half man . . . look.' He placed the two
halves of the figure together. The moment he did so,
the threatening presence seemed to darken the air like
a cloud, filling the room with its stench. Before Niall
could shout a warning, Simeon had given a cry of disgust and dropped the figurine. The presence instantly
vanished.

Niall asked: 'What happened?'

'I'm not sure. It seemed to come alive.' He grimaced
and spat. 'It was like touching a slug.'

Niall cautiously picked up the upper half of the
figure. But when he closed his eyes and withdrew into
the still centre of his mind, he could no longer detect
any kind of force-field. It was simply an ordinary piece
of green stone, probably jadeite or nephrite, and the
surface where it had been split glittered like fluorspar.

Jarita appeared in the doorway. She looked startled
to find Grel in the room. But Niall could see from her
expression that she had no idea that anything unusual
had taken place.

She said: 'Your guest is awake, my lord.'

'My guest?' He had no idea what she was talking
about.

'The guest in the room next door.' She made a gesture
in which Niall detected an element of disdain.

He was startled. 'How do you know?'

'I heard her trying the door.'

Niall snatched the key from his dressing table and hurried out into the corridor. As he unlocked the door, he experienced a curious mixture of anticipation and dread. But when he tried to open it, the door met some resistance. He forced it open a few inches, then saw the nature of the obstruction. The girl was resting against it in a kneeling posture, with her forehead against the wood. Her position suggested that she had been standing close to the door when she collapsed.

Niall pushed his way into the room, followed by Simeon. The movement of the door caused the girl to collapse sideways; as her cheek struck the floor, her mouth fell open. Simeon knelt beside her and took her wrist. Niall knew what he was going to say before he said it.

'She's dead.'

Jarita, who was standing in the doorway, said: 'She was alive half a minute ago.'

Niall said: 'I know.'

He turned and pushed his way past Jarita.

Simeon called: 'Where are you going?'

'To my brother.'

Fear compressed his heart as he hurried down the stairs and along the corridor that led to the courtyard. The thought of the dead girl filled him with baffled rage. What had happened was suddenly obvious. When he had split the figurine, the presence had vanished and the girl had recovered consciousness. But a few seconds later, Simeon had reunited the halves, and the presence had taken the opportunity to silence her. There was no point in feeling angry with Simeon; if he was to blame for reuniting the halves of the figurine, then Niall was also to blame for allowing it to happen.

The thought that now filled him with dread was that his brother might also have fallen victim to the force that had killed the girl. As he crossed the courtyard, he told himself that if his brother was dead, he would devote the rest of his life to destroying the magician.

What he saw as he entered the room made him feel as if his body had turned to stone. His mother was embracing Veig, her cheek pressed against his. Dona, who was standing by the bed, was crying. Then, as he hesitated, crushed and appalled, Veig's hand moved to caress his mother's hair. At the same moment, Dona turned towards him, and he saw that she was smiling. He sighed in an explosion of relief. A moment later, Veig was looking up at him with a puzzled expression, as if failing to recognize him. Then he smiled.

'Hello, brother.' The large hairy hand made a vague gesture of greeting, then fell back on to the counterpane.

Niall, suddenly ashamed of his panic, could not trust himself to speak.

Dona said: 'He's all right now.' Something in her voice made Niall aware that her feelings were also deeper than she was willing to show.

Niall asked: 'When did he wake up?'

'A few minutes ago.'

Siris asked: 'Has the doctor gone?'

'No.' It was Simeon who replied as he entered the room. Grel hesitated behind him in the doorway. Simeon placed a hand on Veig's forehead, and took his wrist between his finger and thumb. 'That's remarkable. His temperature's back to normal.'

Siris said: 'It's your medicine.'

'Not entirely.' His eyes met Niall's.

Dona asked: 'Is he going to be all right now?'

'Oh, I think so. The poison seems to have worked its way out of his system.' He asked Veig: 'How do you feel?'

'Better. Much better.'

'Give him some broth. He should be up and about in a few days.'

Dona flung an arm impulsively round his neck and kissed him on the cheek. Simeon was obviously pleased.

'Don't thank me. Thank him.' He gestured towards Grel. 'He found out what was causing it.'

Dona stared at Grel with wide eyes. 'What was causing it?'

Niall was anxious to avoid explanations.

'I'll go and tell the cook to bring soup.'

As they crossed the courtyard Grel said:

'He is wrong. Your brother is still sick.'

'How do you know?'

'His bloodstream is full of life-suckers.' The image that accompanied the words was of leeches.

Simeon caught up with them.

'Do you understand what's going on?'

'I think so. The stone frog was more dangerous than I thought.'

'I realize that.' He added sombrely: 'I also realize it was my fault that the girl died.'

'No, mine. The Steegmaster warned me it was alive. I thought it had been neutralized.'

Simeon shrugged. 'Nothing can bring her back now. But I'd like to know what it was trying to do to your brother. Why didn't it kill him too?'

Niall shook his head. 'Perhaps because you dropped the halves before it had time.' He asked Grel: 'What do you think?'

Grel hesitated before speaking. 'I think, lord, that your brother will die anyway.'

Niall was shocked. 'But why? He seems to be getting better.'

It obviously cost Grel an effort to speak his mind.

'He has been poisoned by the enemy. Just as Madig was poisoned. I am afraid that nothing can save him.'

'Madig poisoned? But how?'

'Did you not see?' In the sequence of images that followed, Grel somehow caused Niall to identify with Madig, as if seeing through his eyes. He was standing in the cold hall of the magician, listening to the soft swish of garments decending towards him, then to the voice that said:

'You will also tell your master that I shall hold your companions as hostages, and that unless his answer is satisfactory, they will also die.'

Niall's hand was taken in a hand that was cold and rough. And although he was anticipating what was to happen next, he found it difficult not to scream aloud as the powerful grip threatened to crush his bones. But this time he observed something that he had failed to notice when listening to Qisib the Wise: that something sharp – like a needle – had pierced his palm close to the base of the index finger. He guessed that the magician was wearing a ring with a spike on it.

The voice came close to his ear. 'One more thing. Tell your master that if he ignores my warning, his people will suffer a catastrophe that will make the massacres of Ivar the Cruel seem insignificant.' The hand released his. 'You have one month – thirty days.'

Simeon was watching his face closely, aware that something strange was happening.

Niall repeated: 'Thirty days.'

'What?'

'Thirty days. And it happened two days ago. My brother has another twenty-eight days to live.'

Simeon said brusquely: 'What are you talking about? He's already on the mend.'

Niall shook his head.

'No. Madig died after thirty days. This magician has the power to kill from a distance. That is why he said: My arm is long and I do not release my grip.'

He thought of his mother, and of his sisters and of

Dona, and for a moment felt vulnerable and helpless. It seemed unfair that he should have to deal with problems that were so completely beyond his normal experience. At that moment he saw the little kitchen maid descending the stairs with a tray in her hands. It jogged his memory.

'Nyra, please take some soup to my brother.'

Her face broke into a smile of delight, reminding him that, like Dona, she had a certain personal interest in his brother.

'Yes, lord.'

As she halted to curtsy, his moment of weakness passed. She had somehow reminded him that, as master of this city, he could not afford weakness. He waited for the kitchen door to close behind her, then said:

'I must seek out this magician.'

Simeon shot an astonished glance from under his bushy eyebrows.

'With an army?'

'No. There is no time to take an army. I must travel alone.'

'That would be dangerous and foolhardy.'

'I agree. But I must find out what he wants.'

'You know what he wants. He is a totally ruthless man who would not hesitate to kill you.'

'I know that. But I still don't know what he wants. And there is only one way I can find out.' He turned to Grel, smiling. 'So you see, you were right after all. I am going on a long journey.'

'It was not I but the Lord Qisib who foretold it. He is never wrong.'

'I believe you. And now I wish I had asked him one more question.'

'What question, lord?'

'Whether I shall also make the return journey.'

# The World at the End of Time
## Frederik Pohl

The most accomplished work yet by one of the genuinely great names of science fiction.

Wan-To is the oldest, most powerful intelligence in the universe. But even Wan-To can experience loneliness, so he creates companions. Such offspring, however, can turn dangerous. When this happens he simply destroys the stars in which they may be hiding . . .

The colonists of the New Mayflower, recently landed on Newmanhome, know nothing of Wan-To. Until the planet's stars begin to shift and the climate starts to cool down, causing a desperate struggle to survive before the colony has even had a chance to develop.

ISBN 0 586 212755 2

# Hot Head
## Simon Ings

'Hot Head is white-hot. Ings is incandescent. Watch this guy, he could just make the rest of us redundant.'

Colin Greenland, author of *Take Back Plenty*

Malise has a problem. She's come down well to Earth after spending too many years in deadly space combat. Her muscles have wasted away, her past is a confused torture of events she'd like to forget, and her brain is wired up to data-fat – addictive military hardware strictly illegal on Earth. She came back for a rest. But there can be no rest for the only woman who can save the world.

Years ago artificial intelligence probes were sent into the solar system to mine planets inaccessible to Man. The operation was highly successful – until the AIs stopped communicating and started breeding. Now a mass of highly intelligent machinery hundreds of miles wide is heading for Earth. It's indestructible and it wants more metal. And no one knows how to stop it.

Locked away in Malise's head is a blueprint for survival which she doesn't know is there. And when she meets Snow, who offers her the chance to escape into the dreamy, virtual world of cyberspace with the help of a revolutionary new data-fat, she doesn't *want* to know.

But sometimes there is no choice . . .

'A fast, intense sf novel. A thriller with an edge, combining a convincing vision of a near-future world of fragmentation and chaos with an ably-evoked eternal internal reality. A startling and impressive debut.'

Kim Newman

ISBN 0 586 21496 8

Grafton

# Raft
## Stephen Baxter

'This debut novel polishes its ideas with such realistic brilliance you
can see a whole civilization in it.'                                    *The Times*

Imagine a universe where the force of gravity is one billion times
stronger than on Earth. Where humans have detectable gravity
fields. Where stars are only a mile across and burn out within a year
of their formation.

Five hundred years after a spaceship accidentally crossed into this
universe the crew's descendants are struggling desperately to
survive. Society is divided into two mutually dependent groups –
the Miners, excavating the iron core of a dead star, and the scientists
who live on the Raft, made from the ramshackle wreckage of the
ship. Raw materials are exchanged for food – this way their
precarious survival is maintained. But for how long?

Rees is a young boy Miner whose natural curiosity leads him to
stowaway on a trade vessel to the Raft. Once there he is luckily taken
on as an apprentice scientist. What he learns is devastating – their
world is dying and nobody seems sure how to stop it.

Rarely has a first novel been so brilliantly conceived. Comparable to
the best of Greg Bear or Larry Niven, *Raft* is unique, wondrous,
utterly strange and peopled with believable characters.

'*Raft* is fast paced, strong on suspense, efficiently written, and has
moral weight, but it is in the creation of a genuinely strange and
believable new universe that Baxter excels . . . rigorous, vigorous sf
at its enjoyable best.'                                    Lisa Tuttle, *Time Out*

ISBN  0 586 21091 1

# Nemesis
## Louise Cooper

Nemesis begins an epic and compelling series by
the author of the bestselling Time Master Trilogy

She brought seven demons into the world. Now she must
destroy them. Her name is Indigo.

The Tower of Regrets: ancient, forbidding, forbidden.
Princess Anghara had no place there, had no business
tampering with its secrets.

But she did.

Now the demons are loose and her world stands cursed, prey
to the wrath of the Earth Goddess. Only Anghara can atone
for her crimes, and save her people. But Anghara has a curse
of her own.

She is known only as Indigo, destined to roam the world,
exiled, friendless and immortal, seeking and confronting the
very force of destruction she has released.

And Nemesis awaits her . . .

'A powerful epic.'
*Locus*

Other Indigo titles:
2. *Inferno*      6. *Avatar*
3. *Infanta*      7. *Revenant*
4. *Nocturne*      8. *Aisling*
5. *Troika*

ISBN 0 586 21333 3

# The Master of Whitestorm
## Janny Wurts

An epic tale of courage, magic and adventure, and a hero who will live in the reader's memory for years to come

Everyone knew there was no escape from the slave galleys of the Murghai: but Korendir, a man whose past was shrouded in mystery, recognized no impossibilities in life.

After leading a desperate and successful revolt, he frees the prisoners and sets out on a series of remarkable quests: battling the sorceress Anthei to lift the curse on the blighted land of Torresdyr; challenging the elemental Cyondide to win the lost hoard of the dragon Sharkash; travelling to far Northengard to save its people from a plague of poisonous wereleopards.

Always Korendir's goal was treasure: but never for its own sake. His ultimate aim was to build a fortress at Whitestorm, impregnable against all comers, be they mortal or supernatural, to protect himself, its Master, from the dark secret of his ancestry . . .

'Pace and fire . . . Janny Wurts writes with astonishing energy.'
Stephen Donaldson

'Janny Wurts is a gifted creator of wonder.'
Raymond E. Feist

ISBN 0 586 21068 7